THE SUMMER HOLIDAY

BOOKS BY S.E. LYNES

THE SUMMER HOLIDAY

S. E. LYNES

bookouture

Published by Bookouture in 2023

An imprint of Storyfire Ltd.
Carmelite House
50 Victoria Embankment
London EC4Y 0DZ

www.bookouture.com

ISBN: 978-1-83790-301-6
eBook ISBN: 978-1-83790-300-9

For Ruth Tross, with love and deep appreciation

PROLOGUE

A woman in white staggers into the road. She is raging. She is drunk. She has been running for over half an hour. Black eye make-up streams down her face. Her feet are raw, blistered. It is dark, darker than she thought it would be, and there is no one around. Perhaps she shouldn't have stormed off. Perhaps she should have stayed nearer town.

But no, she had to get away – away from them.

She stumbles, rights herself. Swearing, she takes off her sandals. Zigzags on barefoot, knuckling away black tears: the damn wonky pavements, the stupid invisible holes. She will walk down the middle of this pathetic potholed street. She will walk on broken glass if she has to. Who cares? Who cares if you're barefoot? Who cares if you're walking down the middle of the street? Who cares about where you are versus where you're supposed to be? She can *dance* down the middle of this road if she wants to. Wave her arms over her head, shout obscenities at the top of her lungs. She can throw herself under a bus if she wants to, flip two fat Vs to the world as the black tyres flatten her. Or off the top of a building, shout one last *to hell with you, to hell with both of you* before the tarmac smacks the life from her. Yes, why not?

No one cares. No one cares about anyone.

Her sandals dangle one from each hand: long, skinny straps, wedges swinging like wooden blocks, like doorstops. She is properly crying now, snotty wails of fury and frustration, alcohol and resentment. Her stomach burns, her chest, her throat. The injustice is so pure, so distilled, it burns through her, ice-cold as vodka. Her fists tighten, her nails dig into the palms of her hands. What a bloody doormat she has been. How rotten they are, both of them. They are evil. They are psychopaths. Who does that to another person? She's an idiot, an absolute idiot. Why didn't she see it? Why didn't she? She is blind, stupid. She is so bloody stupid. She will kill them. She will kill them for what they've done to her.

She does not see the car. Does not even hear it come around the corner. All she sees is the slow yellowing of the moonless night, the bleaching of the road ahead. Unnerved, she turns. Finds headlights flaring in the dark.

'Too bright,' she whispers, shielding her face with her hand.

CHAPTER 1

KATE

'Jeff?' Kate calls up the polished oak staircase. 'Jeff, are you coming?'

She waits, senses rather than hears him shift, his footsteps padding across their bedroom two floors up.

'Kate?'

She can tell from the squashed sound of her name that he's leaning over the banister. If she stood in a certain spot and glanced up, she would see him looking down on her, but she doesn't move.

'Are you coming?' In the hall mirror, she checks her appearance, grimaces, pulls her baseball cap low until it almost meets her shades.

'I've just got to finish something,' Jeff says. He has descended one floor, is standing now at the top of the first staircase. He is wearing his Lycra running shorts, his tanned, muscular legs all she can see, his white sports socks like the paws of a bulldog. 'You go on ahead,' the legs say. 'It won't take long. I'll see you at Bar Melitón in... shall we say an hour?'

'Really? But it's the first day of our holiday.' Kate hears and hates the whining tone in her voice. 'We only got here last night.'

'It's just a quick thing. I'll see you at the bar.'

She sighs heavily, hating this noise just as much as her tone of voice, hating him too, a bit. She has been so looking forward to this holiday, their first as just the two of them for seventeen years.

'OK,' she says, making an effort now to sound cheerful; it is, after all, just a loose end he has to tie up – understandable at his high career level. 'I'll text you when I get there. Just... try not to be too long, OK? Please?' She knows better than to push it any further; he'll get angry if she does, and it's so important to kick the holiday off on the right foot.

Besides which, his socks have disappeared, can be heard softly climbing back to the second floor. It'll be fine. He said he won't be long. Her husband might be as immovable as Gibraltar, as intransigent as a brick wall, but he is a hard-working guy, and she is proud of him for that.

Smiling, she leaves the villa and heads down to the seafront, intent on a quick swim. She is already regretting her disgruntlement. She needs to react better, be less moany, less... What's that thing she read about online recently? Co-dependent, that's it. Not having Lou here with them was always going to be tricky, but it will be so *great* to reconnect, remember why they married in the first place. With two luxurious long weeks ahead of them, they can hang out like they used to; fall in love all over again!

At nine, the smattering of tourists on the main beach is still sparse. Self-conscious at the prospect of unveiling the white glare of her skin, she reminds herself of what Jeff would say: *Don't be silly. You're fifty-three, no one's looking at you anyway.*

Steeling herself, she removes her cotton shorts and her ancient Gap vest top, and throws them down next to her rucksack, towel and FitFlops. Toes squidging the already warm sand, she approaches the sea with trepidation. Everyone, *everyone* else is tanned. Tans make you look better, they do, no matter what they say about the dangers of skin cancer. It is her hard luck that strong sun does nothing other than turn her into the classic British lobster mocked by Europeans – a raw, unpleasant pinkish-red that then peels to white. Kate spends most of her holidays in the shade. It is Jeff who loves the sun.

So. Here they are.

The sea is... Oh my, it is *glorious*. She closes her eyes, abandons herself to the cool caress of the water, her weightlessness in its gently undulating shallows. Lies back, floating, staring through her shades at the vast blue. Look at that, she thinks. Not a cloud!

The sun is getting warm. Not wanting to burn, she wades out, scuttles up the beach. Platja Gran is not her favourite. She doesn't like the black sand, prefers to go further along, to where it is paler, the beaches shingled, less crowded. She dries her hair and puts the baseball cap back on. Jeff says she looks like a soccer mom in it – he's always joking around like that – but it keeps the sun off her face, and it is comfortable.

Five to ten and already too hot! She dresses quickly, relieved to be at least partially covered, and not only because of the sun's growing intensity. Checks her phone: no text from Jeff. No real surprise there; the first morning away, she and Lou are often on their own while he finishes his bits and pieces, the two of them relishing their first Spanish breakfast together, ordering different pastries, Lou a hot chocolate or a mocha, Kate a café con leche. By now, they would be tearing and sharing and chatting about everything and nothing like girlfriends.

A pain tightens in her heart. It is, she realises, the physical ache of missing her daughter. The depth, the acuteness of this pain astonishes her.

Heading to bar, she texts Jeff. *Are you on the way? Xx*

In the generous shade of the Bar Melitón terrace, she orders

a café con leche and, after a moment's guilt-induced delibera-
tion, a croissant she knows from experience will be the size of a
duvet. A croissant of comfort, she thinks. A croissant of consolation. A compensatory croissant. She smiles to herself.

The waiter nods with the kind of brusque continental effi-
ciency that manages not to be rude and disappears into the bar.

Still no reply from Jeff. He must have got tied up. But that's
OK. This way, he will be freer to join her later, or tomorrow.
There's no rush. They have two whole weeks.

In the plaza, bronzed tourists wander back and forth across
the seafront. Vespas buzz like their namesake wasps, edge
through holidaymakers. Towels drape over bare shoulders;
sliders slap the tarmac; arms crook around inflatable crocodiles,
elephants, unicorns.

Three tables away, a woman in a huge floppy straw hat and
dark sunglasses is sitting with her family: two lanky teenage
sons and one *very* dishy husband. The husband is wearing a
straw panama and police shades, a mustard-coloured linen shirt;
the woman a white kaftan-style dress with rainbow embroidery
around the neckline, a low V against the even copper tone of
her skin. It looks a bit like a dress Kate saw in Zara a week ago
but didn't dare buy, though she doubts this dress is from a chain.
And Kate definitely would never have dared wear it without a
bra, as this woman has, her small, firm breasts pushing
discreetly against the thin fabric. The woman's huge sunglasses
and hat obscure her face, but the line of her jaw nudges at
Kate's memory, some seed of recognition catching in her chest.
A famous person, perhaps. You see them sometimes in
Cadaqués. An actress? A singer?

Dishy Husband is chatting to their boys, throwing out his
hands, grinning. Actually, now that Kate looks closer, the boys
are identical. Twins then. The woman appears distracted, even
bored. After a moment, she lifts off her hat, removes her huge
black sunglasses.

Kate gasps.

'Oh my God,' she whispers, instinctively covering her face with her hand. 'Oh my God.'

Keeping her head low, she continues to watch. The woman is dabbing at her face with a tissue, combing her hair with her fingertips. She shakes her head, glances about her as if she knows she is being admired by someone, somewhere. The movement is so utterly familiar that Kate's throat blocks. Those thick, dark lashes, so unlike Kate's own near-invisible white spokes, and those eyes: maple syrup flecked with black molasses, with gold leaf and bitter chocolate, irises like the tiger's eye rings Kate and her school friends used to obsess over in the eighties. Eyes that melt something inside you.

She feels tears prick.

'For God's sake,' she whispers, blinks to get rid of them, a vague and confused feeling of panic rising.

The woman returns the hat to her head, slides the shades up the bridge of that small, straight nose – and yes, after all these years, the diamond stud is still twinkling above her right nostril.

'Coco Moss.' The name is barely a breath on Kate's lips. 'Coco bloody Moss.'

Still composing herself, she leans forward, narrows her eyes. Thank God for shades. Thank *God*. She can really stare. Yes, it is her. Definitely. Kate's heart beats fat in her chest; her skin tingles.

So.

Coco Moss has blonde hair now, does she?

It wouldn't still be pink though, would it? Didn't stay pink even then. The roots are dark, the type of style that draws attention to its own artifice as if to say, *Yeah, so what?* Not balayage like they have back in Surrey, no. It's more street than that, the blonde more bleached, edgy, far cooler. Coco Moss would never pay two hundred quid for a fake grown-out sun-kissed effect. Coco Moss wouldn't get involved in that kind of nonsense, the kind in which Kate finds herself up to her elbows – her armpits actually. Coco would simply dye it herself then forget it and it would look effortlessly fabulous at whatever stage of grow-out it was. And, of course, a hundred women would want their hair exactly the same, maybe even be sad enough to take a photo of her without her knowing to take to the hairdresser and say: *Here, make me look like this.*

Like *her.*

Kate considers the camera on her iPhone.

No. For pity's sake, no.

The waiter slides her order onto the table, glides away. But Kate barely notices. A memory swims before her: Coco, aged eighteen, in ripped tights, fringed suede jacket and that iconic pink shaggy hair. A rock star. An icon.

Lots of people have pink hair these days, Kate thinks, tearing a thin strip of fluffy croissant and lifting it to her mouth. But thirty years ago, Coco was the only one. Coco was a two-dimensional image: unknowable, someone to be gazed at from afar. When people started copying her pink hair, she dyed it electric blue. When they dyed it blue, she went canary yellow, then shaved it off completely like Sinead O'Connor. When it grew back a bit, she dyed it orange like Annie Lennox in the 'Sweet Dreams' video. She looked amazing, like she was on fire. The others, the wannabes, looked like demented matches.

Kate suppresses a laugh. Coco was always ahead, never got it wrong. No one could touch her. And now here she is on holiday with her family in the same Spanish town as Kate, drinking coffee at the same bar.

There is a strange levelling to it, as if here, her former fame counts for nothing.

Excitement stirs. Kate cannot *wait* to tell Jeff! She will gather every detail and regale him when she gets back. Who knows, he might even stop checking his emails for five minutes.

Coco Moss. My God, it must be, what, thirty years? Longer?

Coco's sunglasses are Gucci; Kate can tell from the tiny gold *G* on the arm, suddenly glad beyond measure that she's wearing her Tom Fords, a twenty-fifth-anniversary gift from Jeff. Not that it matters. It's not as if Coco would recognise her anyway, and let's face it, huge sunglasses don't exactly mean she has her finger on the pulse, do they?

She tears another strip of croissant, too self-conscious now to pick up the whole thing and bite it. Actually, she too has some Guccis somewhere. Jeff bought them for her after he completed on a big deal he'd negotiated – she hadn't seen him for months, not even at weekends. What a shame she didn't bring them with her, although they're not this year's, so maybe not. She also has an old pair of Chanels that she bought herself with the profit from her first serious commission – a five-tier wedding cake that was, if she says so herself, one of the most beautiful she's ever done. Those Chanels might even pass for vintage, now she thinks about it. She wonders how many pairs of shades Coco—

Oh my God, she just looked over. But it's OK. Her gaze didn't settle on the scruffy middle-aged woman in the crappy vest and stupid baseball hat. Thank God. What was she thinking, coming out like this, in an outfit she wouldn't be caught *dead* in back home?

Kate fumbles in her rucksack, pretends to drop her key, a pantomime entirely for herself alone, but when she bends to the floor, she can't see what kind of footwear Coco is wearing because her white dress is too long. Damn. She might have gone for the plastic Birkenstocks everyone's wearing this year – at least in Surrey – or maybe she's a faithful Havaianas flip-flop girl. Kate has both with her, so if she sees Coco walking about, she'll know which to wear.

Dishy Husband, by now christened DH in Kate's mind, is

really very good-looking. The whole family look like they've stepped out of the pages of a magazine: golden, long-limbed, loose – an old-school-wealthy way of being that Kate knows in the very cells of her being she will never achieve. It's a millionaire look that now, in her mature years, she understands comes from a thousand smaller expenses, a thousand pieces of *knowledge*, which add together to create a larger whole, one that doesn't scream money, doesn't even whisper it, just nods it, almost imperceptibly, to those in the know.

Except Coco and her family have something else too. They have what the French call *je ne sais quoi*, and *that* is something Kate has never been able to pin down in words.

DH is rolling a cigarette. He sits back, lights it with a silver Zippo, blows out smoke in a long grey flute. The lighter clinks shut. His arm falls, hangs beside his wicker chair, the roll-up drooping from his fingers like he could give up any time if he wanted to. He looks a little younger than Coco, though it is hard to tell with the sunglasses and the hat.

Kate tries to tune out the background noise so she can hear what they're saying, but only the rhythm of their speech reaches her, the rise and fall of the words. Coco's husband sounds terse, a bit monosyllabic, like Jeff is with Kate sometimes. Kate wonders if they're being tetchy with one another like she and Jeff have been lately, whether DH too has a lot of pressure from work.

DH pinches a thread of tobacco from his tongue and flicks it to the ground, appears not to want to look at his wife.

There's definitely something going on.

DH has stopped speaking altogether now. His mouth is pressed into a line. The teenagers – both in red bucket hats and red vests of the shiny, perforated American basketball type, 15 in large white numbers on both their backs – are eating ice cream. At 10 a.m.! There is no way Jeff would let her or Lou eat ice cream at 10 a.m. Kate wonders if the 15 refers to their age.

What a shame Lou isn't here, she thinks. OK, so they're a little younger, but she could've had some teenage company for a change, maybe even a holiday romance, if they're mature for their age. No, maybe not. But if Coco and her family come here every year as she and Jeff do, then the age difference will soon be negligible. Oh my God, if they became lifelong friends and Lou fell in love with one of Coco's boys, they could get married and then she and Coco would be thrown together to talk wedding arrangements, heads pressed close over the menu choices, Kate pulling out her trump card: *Hey, I'll do the cake!*

Kate, she thinks. *What is wrong with you?*

'I'm gonna head back up,' she hears DH say, pushing his chair back a little. 'I need to practise.'

Practise what? Kate wonders. Tennis? T'ai chi? Handstands?

He stands up, takes a credit card from the back pocket of his lovely navy shorts. After a moment's hesitation, he throws the card down on the table with what looks a lot like disdain. Even in the way he holds himself – something tight in the set of his shoulders – he looks pissed off. Perhaps they aren't just tetchy; perhaps they've had an actual fight.

Kate fights a vague feeling of glee. Bad patches happen to everyone. Even Coco Moss.

But DH has turned to his kids now and is smiling with such obvious love it makes her heart melt. Pointing to one of the boys, he says, 'Hey. You've got ice cream on your T-shirt, you slob.' But his tone is good-humoured.

When the kid looks down, DH draws up his finger so it brushes the kid on the nose.

'Every time,' he says, chuckling with a warmth that makes fresh tears prick in Kate's eyes.

What the hell? That's the second time in a few minutes. Not that it matters. Coco and her family haven't noticed her at all.

DH and the boys are laughing in a way that makes Kate think this is a common joke between them. She laughs too, hoping that maybe DH will look up and they can share a 'Kids, eh?' kind of smile and that this will enable them to fall into conversation.

But he doesn't. Of course he doesn't. There is no way he or Coco would ever notice her.

Thank God actually, because she is not dressed right *at all*.

And if she's to introduce herself to Coco Moss on this holiday, she needs to look her absolute best.

CHAPTER 2

Dishy Husband is walking away from the café, his gait languorous, as if the pavement is made of sponge. He walks like a European: head and torso slightly back, not tipped forward in a half-run like a maths lecturer late for a class like so many English men – or stomping along like a games teacher like so many English women. Europeans never race; they'd rather arrive late. Actually, this place doesn't attract many British tourists. Perhaps Coco and her family are like Kate and Jeff: they prefer to escape their fellow countrymen when they go abroad.

Yikes, she sounds like such a snob, even in her head. But she didn't study modern languages to speak English on her hols, did she?

Why is she justifying herself?

A blush heats her face. Coco is why. And yet Coco wouldn't justify herself to anyone. No, Coco Moss would confess all her most shameful thoughts out loud, quite brazenly – joyfully even. She would never apologise for herself, never pretend to like something she didn't or behave like someone she was not...

Coco is alone with her boys now. All three of them are hooked over their iPhones. Who is Coco texting? Not her husband presumably; he's only just left. Perhaps she's catching up on emails from her high-flying job or posting something arty on social media. What does she do? She did English at uni, so she's probably a journalist for the *Guardian* or the *Independent*. A columnist. A television presenter. No. Kate would know if she were; she would have tuned in every week.

Once again Coco glances around her as if to spot an admirer. A flare of panic blooms in Kate's chest. Even though Coco won't, absolutely will not, recognise her, suddenly it becomes imperative that she does not. There is no way Kate can be caught looking like this. She calls the waiter over and pays quickly. She will dash to the other end of town. She will head for the little boutiques, go straight to the one that sells straw hats. She will throw this bloody awful baseball cap in the bin.

Inside the store, Kate finds a wide-brimmed straw hat that is similar to Coco's but not exactly the same. In the next shop along, some strappy cream espadrille-style sandals catch her eye. They have a straw wedge heel and long laces to tie up the leg. She tries them on – a bit uncomfortable, but they do give her some height. Coco is a couple of inches taller, if Kate remembers rightly.

In the same shop, she finds to her great joy a cheesecloth kaftan-type dress almost identical to Coco's but in baby pink. Coco must have bought hers here! The only one large enough to hang loosely is a little too long but will be OK with the wedges.

At the till, she sees a large straw bag and adds it to the dress and the sandals. She didn't see Coco's bag but is pretty sure it must be a bit like this one. She gives the shop assistant her ruck-sack to dispose of, throws her beach towel, sunscreen and Kindle into the new straw bag and steps out onto the square.

'Goodbye, Frumpelstiltskin,' she mutters to herself. 'Hello, boho beach babe.'

Really, she thinks. There is no need to sacrifice style for comfort.

The sun is hot now – too hot. Usually Kate is back at the villa before eleven, but her shopping trip has delayed her. She takes the hill slowly, mind full of memories, of Coco Moss and her friends. What's that old saying? *Men want to sleep with her; women want to be her.* Something like that. But the thing is, you couldn't *be* Coco Moss. No one could. That's what all those sad-sucker students didn't realise back then. You couldn't become Coco Moss simply by dying your hair pink or ripping your tights or buying some Doc Martens and scuffing them against a wall over and over to make them look worn-in.

Kate should know.

But at least I never dyed my hair, she thinks, climbing the last few steps, short of breath now and sweating absolute fountains. Even then, maybe especially then, she knew that a boring suburban girl like Kate Hanson couldn't possibly go for that kind of hip, thrown-together look. You have to really rock a look like that, and if there's a rock in this scenario, she's under it.

She giggles, pleased with her little joke, and digs out her keys. Jeff is the same, she thinks. Always was. Neither of them ever rocked anything, least of all the boat. Sticking to their lanes was what brought them together during those first shaky months at Leeds. All these years later, it's what keeps them together – always did, always will. Jeff was her number one and she was his. *We belong together*, they would say in their first loved-up months.

The feeling has faded over the years of course – it's only natural. But it is still lovely to be his first choice. Hopefully their first holiday alone together since Lou was born will remind him of that.

CHAPTER 3

'Jeff?' Slamming the front door behind her, Kate throws her husband's name at the mouth of the stairs. 'Jeff? Je-eff! The most unbelievable thing has just happened! You will *never* guess who I've just seen!'

Hearing no reply, she half runs across the glossy marble floor to the open-plan living space. 'Jeff? Love? Honestly, you're going to *freak*!'

In the sleek, gargantuan room, she stops. On the far side of the caramel leather corner sofa is a Jeff's-backside-shaped indentation. A John Grisham thriller lies open and face down next to an empty cappuccino cup on the retro smoked-glass coffee table. The abstract painting above the hearth is little more than a burnt brown splash on pure white, and in that moment it looks to Kate like the coffee has not been drunk at all but instead thrown across the canvas in a fit of uncontrollable rage.

On the mottled granite-topped breakfast bar, half a rustic baguette sits in a pool of golden crumbs, its fluffy white innards exposed where it has been torn apart, crisping as it goes slowly, silently stale. Next to it, yoke-yellow butter melts in a foil wrap;

a shining petrol-blue fly settles on the lip of a freshly opened jar of strawberry jam.

'Jeff?' she cries out, one last time.

She throws down her keys and wanders back into the hallway. The villa is silent and still. Too silent, too still. Empty, in fact.

Inside her, disappointment sinks like a stone. She grabs her phone from her new straw beach bag and texts him.

Hey. I'm back at the villa. Where r u?

He must have gone down into town a different way. There are so many little lanes; they must have missed each other. Maybe he arrived at the bar just after she left. Hopefully not. Hopefully he didn't bump into Coco Moss. Coco Moss is *her* surprise; Kate feels really quite possessive of it.

She throws her bag onto one of the Philippe Starck stools, pulls off her hat and wipes her wet forehead with the back of her hand. That hat is quite heavy actually, and she is sweating like a marathon runner in a desert. Walking up the hill in the midday sun was a stupid idea. She shouldn't even have been *out* in the midday sun, even in her new hat, let alone hiking up the steep slate lanes in this blistering heat. Cadaqués is one beautiful workout for the legs, however. She always feels so much fitter after their fortnights here, always returns home determined to exercise more, drink more water, less alcohol, only to find herself back to long days running the business and the home, longer evenings waiting for Jeff to finish work or return from the gym; poor posture, caffeine fixes, a cheeky evening glass of rosé.

She tidies Jeff's breakfast mess and spoons out the top bit of the jam where the fly might have put its horrid little feet. Do flies have feet? she wonders, before putting the shopping she's picked up in the fridge: sparkling mineral water for Jeff, some dusky coral-pink Rioja for her, Manchego cheese, bright queen olives, a strung loop of chorizo, two wildly frizzy lettuces and four fat tomatoes of the type you can never find in the UK, not even in Whole Foods.

She pours herself a glass of water, peruses the cupboards while she gulps it down, searching for inspiration. They're reasonably well stocked with jars and cans built up over the last few years: salt, pepper, spices, extra-virgin olive oil. They can have a lazy, picky lunch on the patio by the pool, take a day to get over the flight. She can flick through the juicy-looking *Hola!* she bought from Donna at Quiosco Morana on her way home. Jeff will criticise her of course – some offhand comment about brain rot disguised as a joke – but she can tell him she's actually brushing up on her Spanish, so there!

Out on the terrace, she pulls off her shorts and sees to her horror that they are dark with the imprint of her swimming costume, that her vest top too has two large transparent circles from her damp breasts. Really, though, thank God she didn't introduce herself earlier. She shivers. Thank *God*.

A second later, as blancmange from a plate, Kate slides into the pool. Comes up gasping with the frisson of fresh water on hot, salty skin. Her shoulders are tightening already with sunburn from the brief walk into town and back, even though she stuck to the shade. Jeff's right. She needs to make sure she's factor 50'd up to the eyeballs at all times. Besides, at her age, a tan is not the instant beauty treatment it once was; some of the women she knows back in Surrey are really quite leathery. And anyway, she is far too old to be pining for everything she isn't; she needs to embrace what she actually *is*. That loose cotton kaftan she bought alongside the straw hat is so perfect. Boho is the go-to, age-appropriate-yet-chic-yet-also-comfortable look *du jour*; she's amazed she didn't think of it sooner.

She pulls herself halfway out of the pool, fingers pale starfish on the red stone tiles. She's hoping for a deft, athletic exit, but the strength goes from her wrists, and she ends up flopping on her front and dragging her legs out after her, one after the other like dead seals.

Panting a little with the exertion, she rolls onto her side and performs the world's most inelegant manoeuvre to finally raise herself to standing. Thank God this villa isn't overlooked; it was one of the reasons they bought it. From now on, she'll use the pool steps to get in and out of the water, like a woman in her early fifties should. Really, she must strive to be more elegant.

She returns to the kitchen, trying not to notice the loose fold of her white, dimpled belly, part of her that steadfastly refuses to budge, no matter how many sessions she puts in with the personal trainer Jeff got her for Christmas. On the terracotta floor, her feet leave amorphous watery prints. A minute later, they have evaporated, as if she were never there at all.

There is still no reply from Jeff. She claps her hands together, sighs. Checks her phone again. Sighs. Sits down. Stands up. Checks her phone. Decides to call Lou for a chat, just a quick chat, literally just a hello and goodbye.

Lou picks up instantly.

'Hey, lovely girl,' Kate says, keeping her voice bright.

'Mum? Is everything OK?'

'Of course! Just checking in. You got there OK? Everything all right? Are you having a good time?'

'Yeah, yeah, yeah, everything's great. We're just heading out actually. Natasha's taking us on a hike to this amazing lake in the mountains, so—'

'Off you go then!' Kate gives a light trill of a laugh. 'Have a great day, kid!'

'Thanks, Mum! Love you!'

'Love you too, honey!'

She rings off, a dull throb of melancholy in her chest. Surely it was only last week that she and Lou were building sandcastles on that beach in Cornwall? How is it even possible that this same beautiful girl is old enough to go off with her friends and not be here, chatting, helping fix lunch while Jeff goes jet-skiing or paddleboarding or whatever? Without her, the space feels like emptiness, the peace more like silence.

Kate climbs the stairs to the first floor, where the second lounge, spare bedroom and guest bathroom are, before continuing up to the master bedroom with its en suite and another terrace. Here, she stops a moment to take in the view from the balcony, the roofs descending like raked theatre seating, the twinkling sea, bodies reduced to ants on the beach. Beyond, the dark line of the land undulates towards Sa Conca, Cala Nans. The Costa Brava: the Wild Coast.

I am lucky, she thinks. *I must try to remember that.*

From her dressing table, she grabs her journal and fountain pen and heads back downstairs, taking care to grip the banister. These wooden stairs give her the willies, frankly. One trip and you'd have no chance – split head, broken neck, ambulance.

Out on the patio, settled on the sunlounger in the shade of a huge umbrella, she opens her journal.

The most unbelievable thing has just happened! she writes, a secret smile pushing at her mouth. *I'm SO desperate to tell Jeff but he's nowhere to be found! The look on his face will be solid gold!*

'You're joking,' he'll say. 'Coco Moss, here in Cadaqués?'

'Yes!' I'll say. 'Can you believe it? And on the first day of our holiday!'

I can't get my head around it. He's going to FREAK!!!!

She needs to stop with the exclamation marks. Jeff says they're naff, but then again, it's her diary and she'll cry if she wants to, shout if she wants to, scream if she wants to. Besides, she needs them, because right now she's about eighty per cent exclamation marks.

Coco Moss, she continues. *Of all the places, of all the people...*

She writes her account of this morning's excitement before

setting her journal to one side and making her way back to the kitchen area. Finally there's a text from Jeff, hallelujah.

Went snorkelling. Back for lunch.

How great it must be, she thinks with a pinch of resentment, to be able to simply text *Back for lunch*, without any thought as to how said lunch might materialise. There's a strong chance Jeff has forgotten how food even comes to be in the house, let alone how it transforms into actual meals. He is convinced he's the only one who works while on holiday – laptop always open, iPhone always in his pocket, primed like Superman to tear back his shirt and swoop to the rescue of Riddell-Coombes and Co. A stranger to the out-of-office reply, he is indispensable, according to... well, Jeff. No one, no one else, can possibly do what he does, doesn't she see? She doesn't understand. She doesn't get it. Leave him alone.

What *Jeff* doesn't understand is that for Kate, holidays *also* involve work. Kate is queen of the unseen; the chores that are only noticed when they are not done, the ones that bleed from their day-to-day life back in Surrey into their holidays, wherever they go: washing, shopping, cooking. Rosalita cleans, yes, but no matter how much money they have now compared to when they started out, short of bringing a full-time maid with them, these chores still fall to Kate for no other reason than her being female, as far as she can see.

What would happen if she didn't do any of it? she thinks now. She would simply brief Vincent at work and that would be it! No booking Fiona, the dog sitter, no helping Lou off on her holiday with all that entails, no suitcase packing for herself *and* Jeff, no flight booking, no food shopping, no cooking, no clearing up. She could look up blankly from her novel – or better, her accounts – and say, *Huh? No lunch? Sorry, I thought you'd done the shopping.*

Still, she thinks, looking about her with creeping guilt at the polished floors, the custom-made kitchen with its state-of-the-art boiling-water tap and American fridge with ice-maker, the creamy sun trembling on the pool, she doesn't have it too bad.

Besides, there's no way she'd skip lunch.

She grabs a handful of crisps and pours a second glass of water. Back on the sunlounger, she picks up her pen. The past has come rushing in, memories teeming so fast she can barely hold them in her mind, let alone commit them to paper.

Coco and her lot were always pretending to live like common people, she writes, *as the song goes – second-hand clothes, the scuzziest pubs, roll-ups thin as cocktail sticks while somehow having enough money for endless rounds of drinks. Coco got away with it because she was funny – that was the difference. Outrageous, acerbic in a way that made you giggle when you knew you shouldn't. Not that she ever spoke to me directly. But I overheard whenever I happened to sit near them in the Old Bar. You couldn't help but overhear, because they spoke so loudly. It wasn't as if I was earwigging or anything.*

She lays down her pen a moment, a memory of herself crystallising – alone in her room, trying to learn how to roll a cigarette. She had stopped at the off-licence on the way back to halls and bought a packet of Golden Virginia tobacco (she had noticed this was the brand Coco smoked) and a green envelope of Rizla papers. She was determined to get to the point where she could roll one in public – casually, as if she'd been doing it for years.

Now, here, middle-aged Kate laughs at her younger self. How sad she was, really. How little grip she had on who she was as a person, that tentative, near-mute girl. Besides, rolling those cigarettes was impossible! Trying to make a roach from the Rizla card was a kind of stressful and not at all artistic form of micro-origami, and then the so-called roll-ups themselves were either so tight they choked and went out immediately or as loose as loo-roll tubes, the thin, folded card dropping out of the bottom, the tobacco falling like damp wool all over her lap.

When she finally did manage to get one stuck down enough to light, it went up like a bonfire and nearly took her fringe with it. Thank God she'd been alone.

But things are different now. They are adults, with lives lived and nothing to prove. She doesn't need to pretend to be anything she's not, not any more.

An epiphany lands – hard, like a vision of God to a fasting nun (well, she is *really* peckish). There is one big advantage to Coco Moss never having noticed her at uni, and it is this: if Coco couldn't even remember her back when they saw one another daily, there is *no way* she'll remember her now. And that means that Kate can *completely* reinvent not only her present self but her past self too. She knows what kind of people Coco Moss likes because she remembers that crowd so very vividly – cool, knowing, confident. Rich. People don't change, not in Kate's experience, not deep down. And hasn't she *almost* become that kind of person, at least on the surface? Her Sheffield accent has softened over decades spent in Surrey; her tastes have evolved, no matter what Jeff says. If Coco cannot remember that rather dull brown-haired student with the thick glasses and the bitten nails, she will never know that grown-up Kate hasn't always been like this: a woman of style, *savoir faire,* a woman who wears a kaftan. And of course, owning a villa with views and a pool can't hurt, can it?

Yes. Yes, yes, yes.

There's a chance, a real chance, that cool girl Coco Moss and mousy little Kate Hanson can finally, *finally*, be friends.

CHAPTER 4

Kate's stomach rumbles. This morning's croissant feels like she ate it a week ago. She wonders whether to wait or to go ahead and have lunch without Jeff.

Her Baume & Mercier watch, another anniversary gift from Jeff, tells her it's getting on for 2 p.m. She knows holiday lunches are supposed to be more leisurely, but her stomach is starting to sound like a lawnmower.

She gets up and moves into the cool interior of the villa. Where the hell is Jeff? If Kate had a pound for every time he said he'd be back by a certain time, only for that time to roll on by like a ball of tumbleweed through an empty cowboy town, she'd have enough funding to make a movie where the main character says *OK, honey, but don't be late!* to her workaholic corporate lawyer husband – for example – then the scene would cut to four hours later and the protagonist would be sitting in her soft-lit hand-made kitchen eating beef tagine directly from the casserole dish, since once again she is alone, having believed him for the trillionth time. A life spent waiting. A life of broken promises. The movie would star Carey Mulligan, because she has similar colouring and probably can't take the sun either, and it would be called *Kate Barrett: A Life on Hold*.

Actually, maybe that wouldn't be a very exciting movie.

Kate makes her way upstairs, sits at her dressing table and reads over what she has written. Breath held, she pauses for a moment, compelled to make sure no one is looking over her shoulder. The heat of a blush climbs her neck, her cheeks. What she's confessing to here is embarrassing. If anyone were ever to read this, she would have to live in a basement for the rest of her life. But it's the dark truth and she cannot control it. There's something about Coco Moss – always was – that turns her slightly psychotic.

Quarter past two. Jeff is MIA. He is AWOL. She will wait ten more minutes. He's bound to be back by then. If only Lou were here. But Lou is having the time of her life at a friend's parents' ski chalet, an idea that made Kate laugh loudly when Lou first told her – not at the idea of a summer walking holiday, more at the thought of herself at Lou's age being able even to conceive of doing something so glamorous, so expensive; herself at seventeen knowing someone who owned a ski chalet rather than, say, a static caravan in Grimsby.

The villa door slams shut. At last! Kate closes her journal and slides it into the drawer. Not that there's any need to keep it hidden; she could leave it wide open and Jeff would not read one line.

In the three-way mirror, she studies herself. She is not ageing as well as Coco, has put on two stone since her student days. Many of her friends back home have had eye tucks, Botox, filler. These things frighten her; she has no idea how she views them any more, what the twenty-something feminist version of herself would say to the fifty-something version if she were to have some 'work' done. But isn't that the point? That she *was* twenty-something then? She had not had a child, had not suffered two miscarriages, had not had to cope with life's

murkier shades of grey let alone the flesh's long creep towards
earth. It was easier to be a feminist then, wasn't it, when she had
things all worked out?

OK, so she never had things all worked out.

She can hear Jeff downstairs, whistling; the sucking sound
of the fridge door. A moment later, the distinctive hiss of the
sparkling mineral water. He will have expected the fridge to be
full, his breakfast mess tidied away. And indeed, the fridge is a
cornucopia of savoury treats; of his baguette and fly-trampled
jam, no trace. There are no surprises for him, not any more. We
don't see what has long been in front of us, Kate supposes, only
things we are not expecting.

Her back straightens. An amazing idea has sparked in her.
She waits. The idea is bound to wane. In a moment she will see
that it's rubbish.

But the idea stays.

If anything, it grows brighter by the second.

What if she showed Jeff something he was not expecting?

What if she gave her husband the surprise of his life?

'For Christ's sake,' she hears him say, pictures him pressing
his hands on the back of the sofa in their Surrey home. It was
last week; she hadn't wanted to go to a boring dinner with his
even more boring, not to mention halitosis-afflicted, boss. 'You
need to *evolve*, Kate. Go with it, yes? You're so limited; for
Christ's sake, you even tried to stop me buying the share in the
yacht! It was only a quarter-share! Most people with a half-
decent job can afford that if they set their minds to it.'

Humph. And he thinks *she* doesn't have a grip on reality.

She applies a little Estée Lauder balm to her fraying lips.
Well, she thinks, angling her face this way and that, covering
her neck with the flat of her hand. *I might just knock the wind
out of your starched white sails yet, Jeffrey Barrett. What if I
could get the girl we always thought was so out of our reach to*

come here – to our home? You would see that actually I have evolved. You would see... you would see...

You would see me very differently indeed.

There is no way this can fail to impress. The two of them are not the shaky suburban children they once were. They are successful, cultured. And though their fortune has not been passed down through the generations, bestowed at birth like a kind of freedom pass for life, money is money. It opens doors, wherever it comes from.

Pulse beating in her temples, Kate scrambles for her journal. To the last written page, she presses the inky nib.

I will find Coco Moss, she writes. *Somehow I will persuade her to come to the villa! Jeff will be amazed!!!*

'Kate?' Jeff's voice floats up the staircase.

She stuffs the journal back into the dressing-table drawer.

'Coming,' she calls down.

She sprays on perfume, applies a little waterproof mascara and more lip balm. A fresh pair of bikini bottoms; she decides to leave the top off – why not? Over her head she pulls her new kaftan. The embroidery is lovely – a geometric floral design in orange, fuchsia, red and yellow – and there are two rope-like attachments at the neck: the same colours, all intertwined, with tassels on the ends. Her breasts aren't as pert as Coco's unfortunately; they are bigger, and gravity favours the smaller breast. But the dress is loose, and it should be OK, maybe even as far as a bit sexy. She slides her feet into the white plastic Birkenstocks she picked up at Heathrow and puts on her rather stiff straw hat.

The stairs she takes slowly, carefully. The hat obscures her vision, and the hem of the kaftan almost trips her up. She grabs a bunch of it with her free hand and pulls it up, is relieved to get to the bottom without falling. As she crosses the open-plan area to the terrace, she affects a slower walk, tries to throw her hips forward, keep her head high. It feels unnatural, a little ridiculous, but she supposes these things take practice.

Jeff is on the sunlounger. She tries not to notice that he has not unfolded one for himself but has instead taken hers.

'Hi.' She tenses with hope, wonders what he'll make of her new hat and dress, whether he'll notice she is braless, what he might do about that, maybe later. There are advantages to Lou not being around after all.

He looks up, asks: 'What's for lunch?'

CHAPTER 5

Jeff has gone for a siesta. She wonders why she even thought he might suggest they go upstairs together. It's been years since he's looked at her in that particular way, asked if she's feeling sleepy, also in that particular way, and today is no exception.

Towards four, suspecting that he is either asleep or furtively caressing the keys of his laptop, she leaves a scribbled note on the bar – *Gone for a walk! Xx* – before heading out of the villa. She will say she didn't want to disturb him; she has her phone if he needs her. Not that he will.

But for once, she doesn't mind heading out alone. It isn't that she doesn't want him with her, not exactly, but he would only get in the way of her mission, namely to accidentally bump into Coco Moss. He would tease her for it, maybe even accuse her of stalking, which is not what this is, not at all. This is going to be the best surprise ever!

Halfway down the hill, she becomes aware of the hem of her kaftan catching on the toe of her sandals. Gah – the dress is too long for flats. She knew this. She *knew* it.

Bunching up a handful of fabric in one hand, she continues. Another few steps and sweat begins to pool beneath her breasts.

The lack of bikini top was a mistake. Why, *why* did she think she could get away without it?

She knows why – Coco Moss is why – and the flash of self-knowledge makes her cheeks burn.

Momentarily she considers climbing back up the steep rise to the villa to pick up a belt and put on a bikini top, but she is almost at sea level now, the sugary vanilla smell of chocolate con churros reaching her on the hot breeze.

Pulling the fabric away from her breasts with her free hand, she shifts the straw bag forward so that it disguises her wardrobe malfunction before gathering up a new handful of material and proceeding along the pathway that runs alongside the town beach. Leaving Bar Casino on her right, she follows the curving contours of the coast. Leisure boats bob on the aquamarine water, which winks with stars of sunlight. Bronzed bodies of every possible size and shape pack the beach, brown and glazed as sausages.

Through the slowly diminishing edges of the town, Kate continues to the beach she likes on the far side. From here, she can make out their villa up on the hill. She imagines her hard-working husband struggling to put away his job and take his much-needed holiday, poor thing. She pulls out her phone to text him but decides against it. Better to let him tie up any loose ends; that way they can focus on one another, really have a holiday at last. A second honeymoon even.

More sunbathers lie glossily on the shoreline. Kids in flippers and snorkels cruise along the flat surface of the sea. Teens play beach tennis – *pop, pop, pop*. Their beauty makes her catch her breath; their youth. Further back, cross-legged under umbrellas, families play cards, eat breadsticks, laugh, and again her heart contracts with longing for her daughter. Seen through the eyes of these people, she is no longer a mother. If they see her at all, they will see a middle-aged woman, possibly a divorcee or a widow, out for a stroll in her large-brimmed hat and casual-yet-chic kaftan.

But she is not out for a stroll. She is on a pilgrimage fraught with small discomforts and, she must admit, private agonies. The only reason she has come this far in this intolerable heat is because she is searching for *her*.

But *she* is nowhere to be seen.

There is one more beach to try.

Perspiration is pouring down her belly now. The kaftan has stuck to her back, and this new hat is heavy compared to the baseball cap – she has to push it down low to stop it from slipping forward. Her hair is glued to her head. More rivulets trickle down the sides of her face. She could stop, go home; she's bound to bump into Coco again before the fortnight is through.

But she doesn't stop, of course she doesn't, pulled despite herself by some unfathomable tractor beam to exhaust every possibility, to find her *today*.

The path to the last beach is quite treacherous, especially in the too-long smock. Her sandals slip against the slick soles of her feet. The smooth, flat rocks slant towards the sea, as if deliberately trying to tip her headlong towards the dark rocks beneath. She cannot fall in; she could really hurt herself – or worse, look foolish.

Deciding that actually, mild embarrassment is a shade more tolerable than the greater humiliation of hospitalisation, she grabs handfuls of her kaftan and shoves the spare fabric up into the legs of her bikini pants to make a kind of half-arsed crinoline. This should in theory keep it from falling over her feet and tripping her up.

Awkwardly and very, very slowly, she pin-steps over the rocks, half slithers down the last one, lands a little harder than she intended on the soft sand. She rights herself, looks about. No one noticed her inelegant arrival – a strong advantage of middle age's invisibility cloak. There are about twenty people here, rewarded for their bravery in crossing the rocks with a more spacious, secluded place to soak up the rays.

Hands on hips, panting with exertion, Kate scans the prone bodies.

'Bugger,' she mutters.

After all that effort, Coco is not here either.

Two hours later, with no word from Jeff, she makes her way back to the town. She feels heavy, sticky and, of course, hideously hot. The rocks, the bricks, the tarmac radiate stored sunshine in thick, warm waves. From a roadside vendor she buys a red ice lolly, which she eats in bites, back pressed to the wall, in a sliver of shade. The ice refreshes her; the sugary burst restores her a little. On the beaches, the crowds have thinned; the café terraces by contrast bubble with tourists eating ice creams, sipping iced tea and coffee, brightly coloured cold drinks. Waiters slide bills onto tabletops, wait with hurried indifference for euros to be handed over, credit cards and phones to be touched to hand-held machines.

Kate is about to return home when...

Oh my *God*. Yes. Sitting outside Blau Bar. It's *her*. Definitely. Same hat, same shades, though she's changed into a sheer burnt-orange shirt dress, the spindly knot of a string bikini top at the back of her neck. She's wearing old blue flip-flops with worn, soft-looking soles. All that guesswork about what she might have on her feet, but of course, Coco Moss doesn't need logos; she is queen of the kind of thrown-together scruffiness that drips zero-fucks-given-here wealth. What she also is is alone.

Kate's heart races. She dabs at her face with her towel, wishes she could somehow lower her body temperature through some meditative mind trick. Keeping to the shade, she stands perfectly still, trying not to stare, her gaze glancing, moving on, returning to Coco.

On her table is an empty espresso cup. If Kate is to act, it has to be now, but she cannot, cannot *possibly* greet Coco Moss bathed in a shining film of sweat.

Filling her lungs with air, she strides over to the bar. In the dark interior, tucked away at the back, there is one loo. It's small, not particularly fragrant, the sink tiny and a little scummy.

Door locked, she pulls the kaftan over her head and hangs it on the flimsy hook. Then she bends to the tap and lets cold water soak her hair until her scalp almost hurts before splashing her face again and again, hand-shovelling the water over her neck, under her breasts and armpits.

Straightening up, she throws up her arms and lets herself air-dry, almost weeping with relief.

Someone bangs on the door; a burst of Catalan.

'*Momentito.*'

Kate's not even sure if that's Spanish for 'just a moment'. Her brain is wizened, perforated. So much has drained away through its many tiny holes.

She pulls the dress back over her head, pushes her hair back with more water. Good. OK. She looks like she's been for a swim. She replaces her hat and shades and emerges. Taking no notice of the short, stony-faced woman waiting outside, she heads back to the terrace.

The waiter is standing next to Coco's table with feigned disinterest as she pays with her phone. Kate has only seconds now. Coco is returning her phone to a cotton tote bag, pulling the bag over her shoulder. It is now or never. She steps forward. She is inches away. Centimetres. Coco stands up. Kate takes a step back, affects surprise.

'Oh,' she says breathily. 'Are you leaving?'

'Yes.' A perfunctory smile.

'Sorry! Didn't mean to jump in.' Kate's laughter is a tinkling bell. She lowers her sunglasses. Frowns, as if concentrating. And makes the leap.

'Coco? Sorry, are you... Is your name Coco Moss?'

Coco peers at her. Her brow creases. 'Yes?'

Kate shakes her head with as much well-I-never astonishment as she can muster. 'Oh my God! I *thought* I recognised you! I was at Leeds? Leeds Uni? You won't remember me, but we were in the same year?'

'OK.' The delivery is wary. Kate is already regretting having gabbled at her.

Coco pulls her tote further onto her shoulder, as if to leave.

'I'm Kate,' Kate says hurriedly, deciding in that second that she will not mention Jeff. That way, if she pulls this off, the surprise will work both ways. 'I was Kate Hanson then,' she adds. 'I was in Roundhay Halls in first year. I think you were too? Cedar House.'

'Cedar House,' Coco repeats. 'I was in Cedar.'

'That's what I'm saying – '86 to '87? Oh my God, this is surreal! You haven't changed at all! Well, apart from the pink hair!'

At this, Coco's mouth opens slightly. After all these years, her skin is still amazing. Just... amazing. 'You were in Cedar?'

'I was indeed! With Drew and Mia and those guys. I mean, I didn't hang out with them or anything, but we played table tennis a few times.' This is a small white lie; there is no way that group would ever, *ever* have asked her to play table tennis with them.

'You were there in '86?' Coco's voice is as low and as posh as Kate remembers, the 't' of eighty almost a 'd'. A slight raise of eyebrows, an inscrutable pursing of lips. She is thawing, slowly, though this not-recognising is depressingly familiar, this appraisal, this *Are you a person I should know?*

'Yeah,' Kate says, nodding. 'With Mia and Drew and I think there was a girl called Bunny?'

'Cool.' Coco takes a step away from the table. The appraisal is complete. The verdict is *no*.

Panic flares in Kate's chest.

'As I said,' she rushes on, 'you probably wouldn't remember me. I was quite shy back then. I'm here with my husband actually. Our daughter's off on her own holiday this year – first time it's been just the two of us in seventeen years!' She laughs, for no reason, no reason whatsoever.

'We have a place here, so we're here a lot.' The outright brag on her own tongue is so astonishing she almost gasps in shock at herself. It is panic that has made her do this, a desperate need to reverse the verdict, for once in her life to get a *yes*.

'We love it here,' she adds, in freefall now. 'I did Spanish at uni, so, y'know... *hablo español*, well, only *un poco* now, not Catalan unfortunately, which would've been handier.'

Oh, good grief. Stop, Kate. Stop talking.

'You have your own place here?' A doubtful smile plays on Coco's mouth, a mouth that shows no sign of puckering despite her years, jaw as firm as a fighter pilot's. The smile widens a fraction. The verdict hovers.

'Didn't you read English?' Kate tries. Even the word *read* is a lie – no one from her background would say *read*; they would say 'Didn't you *do* English?' How quickly we betray ourselves, she thinks. But also, in the same moment, doesn't care. Where has authenticity ever got her, really? She wouldn't have a single friend in Surrey if she'd relied on authenticity, for God's sake.

'English,' Coco is saying. 'I did, yeah.'

'Mia did English too, didn't she?' Kate screws up her eyes, as if struggling to remember.

But still Coco looks unsure. Damn her! Surely, surely to *God*, there's a way through this... this *wall*. She can't just dismiss Kate like she did back then, not now that they're grown-ups, not now that Kate's thrown in a villa, for crying out loud.

'Kate,' she says, her brow furrowing. 'Hanson, did you say?'

Kate nods – too many times, too quickly. 'You won't remember me.' This is the third time she's said this. *Stop, Kate. Please. Stop.* 'Sorry to have barged in like that. It's just so nice to see someone from Leeds, you know?'

'Whereabouts is your place?'

Mild curiosity: a small victory.

Kate gestures vaguely towards the other side of town. 'It's back that way, overlooking the bay. It's called Vista Hermosa actually; that means "beautiful view". We just fell in love with it, you know? And it comes in handy when we want to trade for a week's skiing.'

She feels herself blush. She disgusts herself. What a fraud. She doesn't even ski; Jeff goes with the professional contacts he calls friends. But at uni, the in-crowd always went skiing. They went skiing the way Kate's family went camping: moderate excitement, all the gear. And so she has mentioned skiing in the way a quiz-show contestant, feeling their advantage slipping, blurts an answer, any answer, in a last-ditch attempt to win the prize money.

But Coco has not walked away. Not yet.

'Listen.' Kate's heart thumps. 'Can I get you another coffee or something? A drink? Only if you've time.'

It could be her imagination, but Coco's expression seems warmer now. She checks her phone, then looks up and, to Kate's wild, suppressed joy, says: 'Sure.'

CHAPTER 6

'Yes, we have a pool. A great pool actually.' Through a black paper straw, Kate is sucking at a gin and tonic so strong she'll have to check her chest later for hairs. Coco – drinking a small glass of lager – appears fascinated. It's like she's seeing Kate for the first time.

'And you're only here four weeks of the year?' she asks. 'Do you rent it out?'

'We have a letting agent, but we're not too worried about that side of things. Besides which, I'm sure my daughter and her friends will be using it a lot over the next few years. Where are you staying?'

'Oh, a friend let me have his place because I'm seriously broke right now. and he wasn't using it. He's...' She frowns. 'I think he's on safari or something, God knows. He only comes here off-season.'

'Safari.' Kate is careful to keep the exclamation mark out of her voice. 'Cool.'

The air stills. The moment of silence extends. Kate cannot think of a single thing to say. She can't ask about Coco's family because she's claimed that this is the first time she's seen her. Heat climbs her neck. *Think, Kate. Think.*

But Coco saves her. 'I like your dress. I have one a bit like it actually.'

Kate presses the flat of her hand to her chest. 'Really? I picked it up this morning. Just saw it and thought, yep, you'll do. I love the little boutiques here, don't you?'

Coco is sipping her beer. She nods. 'Yeah, they're cool.'

'So,' Kate tries, 'are you here on your own, or...'

'With my boys actually. I should get back really, although Troy'll be taking good care of them, I'm sure. He's taken them off snorkelling somewhere.'

Troy. Epic. Kate banks the name, files it under *Husband, Dishy.*

'Have you been to the Dalí house over in Port Lligat? It's amazing.' Kate feels herself going ever redder. She's done rich; is now moving on to *hey, I'm also cultured as hell.* She is pathetic; if anyone saw into her thoughts, she'd have to kill herself.

But Coco is smiling, properly smiling, and then she says something that makes Kate's heart hammer.

'You know, now that I'm looking at you more closely, you *do* look familiar. I'm sorry, it's totally my fault – I was probably drunk when we met. God knows, it's all a bit of a blur to be honest.'

'Oh, don't worry about it,' Kate gushes. 'We were all pretty wrecked back then.' She thinks of Jeff, who was such a lush in those days but who now watches her when she pours herself a glass of wine.

Coco is looking at her phone. She picks up her glass and drains it. 'I'd better get back.'

'Cool, yeah, me too. His lordship will be wondering where I am!'

Sweat pricks at Kate's hairline, lies wet on her belly. She

pulls at the kaftan to try and create some air flow. Coco is shifting in her seat, preparing for take-off.

'I'll get these,' Kate says, signalling for the waiter. 'So, you're... you're here for the fortnight?'

'We're here all month actually.' Coco stands up, hooks her thumb beneath the straps of her tote bag. Her nails are natural, unpainted, unbitten. 'Troy's taken a month out to write. He's recording an album in September.'

Kate feels the round, dry bulge of her eyes. Coco's husband is a musician. Of course he is. Because that's the coolest thing he could be. 'Wow. That's amazing. Is he pop, or...'

'Modern classical. Philip Glass, Max Richter? That kind of vibe.'

'Ah, sure.' Kate nods, not a clue, not the tiniest, weeniest Scooby-Doo. 'Is he on Spotify? What's his surname?'

'Vignetti. His father's Italian. Not that we ever see him.'

'Gosh,' Kate says, but it feels too intrusive to ask what caused them to be estranged, so instead she says: 'Do you go by Vignetti?'

Coco shakes her head. 'God, no. I'd never give up my name for anyone.' She gives a brief laugh.

Kate is still wondering if this is a dig at her own decision to take Jeff's name, before remembering she never gave it, when Coco throws up a hand in goodbye. Oh no. Should she jump up and kiss her on both cheeks, or shake her hand or what?

No. Do nothing. Stay still.

'Thanks for the beer,' Coco says.

'Just... th-thinking,' Kate stammers. 'Why don't you guys come over for a drink or something tomorrow night? The boys can go in the pool while we catch up. A quick aperitif, a drink before dinner?' *Oh, well done, Kate. Because Coco won't know what an aperitif is, will she?* 'What do you think?'

Behind her shades, Coco's eyes are hidden. But after a

moment that feels almost unbearably long, she pushes her bottom lip up against the top and gives a slow nod.

'Sure.' She holds out her hand. 'If you give me your phone, I'll put my number in, then just text me the deets, yeah?'

Kate's throat almost blocks. As she watches Coco's slim, tanned thumbs with their perfect half-moon nails typing into her phone, she tries not to think about the sweat now running so fast down her torso she fears it will start dripping on the ground. She holds her breath.

'Nice phone,' Coco says, handing it back to her. 'See you tomorrow.'

And like that, she turns and wanders away down the road, her soft flip-flops slapping the tarmac. She doesn't look back. But that's OK. It's OK because the verdict is in – and this time it is a *yes*.

CHAPTER 7

They are in Es Baluard, their favourite fish restaurant, at the far end of Platja Gran. To Kate's delight, the owner, Eduarda, has greeted her and Jeff like long-lost friends, asking after them, asking after Lou, informing them that the lobster today is *fenomenal* and insisting on sending them a complimentary bowl of olives to nibble on while they study the menu. They have duly ordered the lobster to share, a couple of starters to keep them going, and Jeff has poured the usual mineral water for himself, a glass of rosé for her – without comment. Kate decides this is a good sign. Perhaps they can finally manage to talk to each other, really talk, without Lou to act as a buffer, now that they are far from their increasingly stultifying home life, and what better way to enliven the conversation than...

'So, I have a surprise,' she says and smiles.

'Oh yes?' Jeff's tone borders on interested – he is looking right at her.

She raises her eyebrows, takes a long swig of the crisp, ice-cold wine. She is stalling. Enjoying herself.

'Tomorrow evening,' she begins, but has to pause once more because the waiter has brought the oysters for her, calamari for

Jeff. She squeezes lemon onto the first oyster and tips it down her throat. It took her several attempts to be able to even eat oysters; she is determined to get as far as liking them one day, though privately she wishes she'd ordered the boquerones, the exquisite deep-fried anchovies she loves.

'Tomorrow evening,' Jeff prompts. He is still looking directly at her, his phone nowhere in sight.

'Yes, sorry. Tomorrow evening, we... will be having visitors.'

He frowns, but it is an amused frown, she thinks.

'To stay?'

'God, no! Just for drinks!'

'Who?'

'Someone you know... but haven't seen for *ages*.' She giggles, blocks her nose in the way she does when diving underwater and swallows down another glob of cold, salty flesh. Two down, one more to go.

'Who?' Jeff runs his knife through a calamari ring with one clean slice. 'Look at that,' he says, smiling down at his plate. 'Everything is so fresh here; the food is better than London, and at half the price. This lot would set you back twenty quid in Soho.' He forks the half ring into his mouth and closes his eyes momentarily in appreciation – Kate is not sure whether of the taste or the price.

She takes another long slug of wine, feels herself glow in the warmth of Jeff's full attention. Well, three quarters of his attention, which seems a fair split with the squid.

'If I tell you,' she says, imbuing her voice with as much flirtatious mystery as she can manage, 'it won't be a surprise, will it?'

'Give me a clue?'

She shakes her head, grinning now. 'No. No clues. You'll never guess. They're coming at seven, just for drinks.'

'They? Is it work people? Is it Toby and Nikita? Mike and Tina? James and Patrick? Simon? Is it Simon and Bev?'

She smirks, shakes her head, enjoys the sensation of the tips of her freshly washed hair brushing softly against her slightly sunburnt shoulders. Her upper arms are hidden in a thin silk pashmina bought for this purpose – blue to match her blue-and-white Massimo Dutti dress. 'I guarantee that no matter how many times you guess, you won't get it. You won't get it in a million years.'

He smiles, a genuine smile of pleasure, like the ones he used to give her back then, when they were young – dressed in baggy Levis and bobbly jumpers, holes in their socks, not a care. It is impossible to match that student boy with the man he is now, so polished and European in his linen shirt and carefully tended shadow of stubble, his Apple Watch, his Prada shades pushed back into his shining, thick, barely greying black hair. His career has been stratospheric, whereas hers has been, at best, patchy. Sometimes she thinks, what's the point? No matter how well her business does, it brings in a fraction of what he earns. It's like taking a sandwich to a banquet. But it's not about the money, she reminds herself. It's about being her own person: herself.

The strange vowels and consonants of Catalan drift in the air. On the walls, posters and graffiti claim independence for the region.

Eduarda appears, collects their plates and tells them, '*No pasará mucho tiempo por la langosta.*'

'*No hay prisa,*' Kate replies and smiles, before leaning towards Jeff, who hates to be out of any kind of loop. 'She said the lobster won't be long. I said there's no rush.'

Jeff nods. 'Are they colleagues?' he asks. 'Can you at least tell me that? Or someone from the golf club?' He does not get as far as university friends. Doesn't even mention Lizzie or Ben.

'No. And... no.'

'Someone from the past?' This is warm, at least.

'Maybe, maybe not.'

'I'll get it out of you,' he says, picking up the bottle from its bucket of ice and pouring her another large glass. 'By the time you're at the end of that, you won't be able to help yourself.'

She tries not to read a subtext of judgement. Whatever his intention, he is wrong. She will not tell him. And she doesn't. Even after they have called in at Bar Casino on the way home and she orders a brandy that looks more like a glass of black tea, even when they get home and are lying in bed in the hazy, warm dark. The evening has been almost perfect. The urge to tell him about Coco is strong. But the surprise is too good, too sweet.

Running her fingertips up his chest, she turns to kiss him but sees he has fallen asleep. No matter. Tomorrow will be so exciting.

She cannot wait to see his face when Coco Moss walks through the door.

CHAPTER 8

It is a little after six. She has spent all afternoon preparing for
the evening while somehow achieving practically nothing. The
truth is, there was little to do. Rosalita has given the place its
daily clean, and the wine merchants have delivered a mixed
case of wine, a box of San Miguel and six bottles of sparking
mineral water – quite how the delivery guy gets it all up the hill
on the back of a moped without being catapulted into the
nearest vineyard is beyond her, but he does, that's the important
thing, and she did enough of those kind of jobs growing up to
always give him a big tip. Really, all Kate's had to do is buy some
snacks and clear up after Jeff, who is the husband equivalent of
Hansel and Gretel. Actually, though, Jeff won't be leaving any
more crumb/coffee-cup/apple-core trails today since he has
gone sea-fishing with Felix, a local friend he made last year. For
once, he asked her to come along, but she said no, worried she
wouldn't have time to make everything right for Coco and her
family.

Where is he? She told him their guests would be here at
seven. She opens the text thread, winces at the one-sided row of
messages, closes it. She'll leave it a few more minutes. Jeff

doesn't like it when she nags, and she doesn't want to spoil what has turned out to be a surprisingly promising start to their holiday.

Butterflies stirring, she analyses the villa with fresh eyes. Wishes desperately that she'd told Coco they were renting. If they were renting, she wouldn't have to be responsible for the taste. As it is, the moment Coco comes in, she'll somehow know that Kate is still, after all these years, *not right* – that's if she was telling the truth when she said she was beginning to remember her. You can't begin to remember – you either remember or you don't.

It occurs to Kate only now that Coco was being polite, that she is coming here tonight because she is curious to see the villa, that she is only curious because Kate said she owned it, and that in an hour's time, she will arrive and will regret coming the moment she walks through the door.

Kate opens the freezer, stares at the vodka nestled amid the ice cubes, the frozen croquetas and the petits pois. She closes the freezer, makes herself take three deep breaths. *Calm down, Kate. Calm down.* She pours a half glass of rosé and takes a sip, staring again at the gargantuan room, thinking of her huge, immaculate detached home in Surrey with its acre of land. When she and Jeff first bought that place, she asked him if they could pay someone to come in and choose everything: the furnishings, the crockery, the paint colours, the ornaments, the art.

'There are companies who do that,' she said. 'Interior design experts who know about this stuff, you know?'

'Don't be so wet,' Jeff told her. 'Just buy some magazines and work it out. Take the credit card and get yourself to Liberty. They make the taste for you; it's what you pay for. How far wrong can you go, really?'

Very far, she had thought. Somewhere north of very far. The Outer Hebrides. Norway. Now, she wishes this same mythical consultant she was not allowed to hire could pop in and take a quick look and tell her that what she has chosen is all right. But suddenly the plain stone-coloured walls she saw in *Elle Decor* seem out of date, the art on the wall as naff as a *Live, Laugh, Love* poster, the scatter cushions as advertised in *House Beautiful* just... wrong.

It serves her right. It totally serves her right. She should never have boasted the way she did. She should never have invited Coco Moss here. Her family, she means. Them.

It is 6.20 and still no sign of Jeff.

Kate showers and changes. Changes again. She's looking for something that will give her a waist. Another change; she remembers she hasn't had a waist since 2006 and so chooses a straight up and down loose COS sundress that is no worse than the others, she supposes. After several attempts at adding a belt, she decides to leave it loose: at home, casual, is the look she is going for. In a dress that cost over a hundred pounds in the sale.

'No big deal,' she whispers, pouting, to her reflection. 'Literally just threw this on last min, hon.'

Considering the hairdryer momentarily, she decides it will give her a hot flash, so she ties her damp hair back in a ponytail and applies a little tinted moisturiser, mascara and a nude lipstick. She meets her own gaze in the mirror, thinks: silk purses, sow's ears. Thinks: it'll have to do.

At 6.45, Jeff is still not here. Kate pours herself a glass of Rioja Rosado to take the edge off. By 6.50, almost bald with stress, she is on to her second glass. She has resisted and resisted, not wanting to be a shrew, but now she can resist no more. She texts Jeff.

Where are you????

She hopes the four question marks will provide a subtext even he can pick up.

But a buzz comes from upstairs.

Jeff's phone.

'*What?*' she whispers. Jeff never, ever goes anywhere without his iPhone, at least not when he's with her.

She is about to throw her glass against the wall just to hear it smash when Jeff stumbles through the door in his old shorts, scruffy T-shirt and deck shoes, dragging a kitbag behind him.

'Hey,' he says. The smell of fresh sweat, of the sea, of stinky fishing kit fills the hallway.

'Where the hell have you been?' she almost shrieks. 'They'll be here in seven minutes!'

'Chill,' he says. Moves past her, takes the stairs two at a time, calls over his shoulder. 'I'll just grab a quick shower. Can you stick my rods and stuff in the garage?'

She stares at the fishing bag and rods. She doesn't need a degree in feminism to see that there's no reason, no reason on this earth, that justifies her being expected to go anywhere near them. But if she doesn't move them, Coco and her family will arrive to a home that reeks of this fishing kit. It is a no-win situation she has already lost. And so, trying her best to hold the bag and rods at arm's length, she opens the connecting door to the garage, dumps them in and closes the door.

Nerves beginning to get the better of her now, she checks her appearance in the hall mirror, straightens her dress. Her upper arms are dimpled, fleshy. Her silk pashmina will cover them. Actually, where is her pashmina?

In the kitchen, she pours another half-glass of Rioja and drinks it down before reapplying her lipstick in the downstairs loo. She is turning the scented Jo Malone sticks upside down in the diffuser to refresh the aroma in the hallway when the door-bell rings.

'Christ,' she whimpers, hand flying to her chest. She wishes, oh how she wishes, she hadn't invited Coco and her family, that she could turn back time and pretend she had never seen her. She wants, suddenly, to go upstairs and hide in the wardrobe.

'Jeff,' she calls up the stairs, his name edged with fear. 'Are you coming down?'

'There in a sec.'

She hates him. Truly, she hates him.

Taking a deep breath, she opens the front door.

'Hi-iii,' she says, infusing her voice with brightness, setting her mouth into a smile wide enough to welcome Coco's family into her Catalonian home. But seeing only Coco, dressed in the same burnt-orange shirt dress and flip-flops as yesterday, she tries to keep her features from falling.

'It's just me,' Coco says from behind the black screen of her sunglasses. Kate tries not to notice, not to care, that she is empty-handed. 'Is that OK? The boys were on their Xboxes and Troy was working. Honestly, this is my sad life.' She laughs.

'Don't worry at all,' Kate coos, fighting the dual disappointments of DH's no-show and the fact that Coco has made zero effort. Her hair looks really quite grubby. Has she even showered? 'I guess Troy might find the old Leeds Uni chat a bit boring anyway.'

'Not at all. It's just evenings he practises, you know, and—'

'Come in, come in. Let me get you a drink!'

Blood racing with adrenaline, Kate strides ahead into the open-plan living area, aware of Coco behind her, of her husband still upstairs. What the *hell* is he doing?

'Wow,' Coco says. 'Oh my God, wow. Seriously. This place is *incredible*. It's stunning. Is that the pool? Of course it is. Oh my God. It's huge. And you've got two parasols and a whole sun deck, oh my God, I love the whole chill-out zone on the far side. And it's so shaded here. God, it's gorgeous. Wow.'

Under the onslaught of Coco's gushing praise, Kate feels herself blush. 'Well, I can't really take the sun, so we...' She trails off, unsure what she was intending to say.

Coco is leaning against the frame of the concertinaed doors, still surveying the terrace beyond, the celestial blue pool a living

Hockney in the bright evening light. The expression of mild wonder on her face goes a little way to soothing Kate's anxiety. She clearly loves the villa; everything will be fine.

'Kate,' Coco says, as if to wake her up, turning now to face her with an expression of real warmth. 'Truly. It's stunning.'

'We're very lucky.' She feels her blush deepen, creep down her neck. But it is pleasurable, this feeling of being admired, and in such an uncomplicated, generous way. Her parents come to her mind: their flat refusal to have a holiday here. *Oh, I don't think so, not really our scene.* This without them even knowing the villa is owned, not rented. But it's OK, Coco is loaded. Kate has nothing to apologise for.

'What can I get you?' she asks brightly. 'Rosé? White? G and T?'

'Do you have, like, a San Miguel or something?'

'Sure.' Of course. Women like Coco can drink beer. They don't bloat like mortals.

Kate opens a bottle and passes it to Coco, who refuses a glass – again, of course. Kate pours herself another glass of wine and gestures for Coco to take a stool at the breakfast bar. 'Jeff's been out sea-fishing,' she says. 'He'll be down in a sec.'

'You have a boat? What, like a yacht?' Coco's eyes glitter. She is still glancing about her, as if to take in every detail of her surroundings.

'No, just a friend's boat, although technically we *do* own part of a yacht.' Kate's face flushes hot. What is it about Coco that brings out this braggy monster in her? 'B-But no,' she stutters, 'Jeff knows this guy, Felix, who takes him—'

Kate stops. Coco's mouth has dropped open, her eyes wide as plates. She is staring over Kate's shoulder, her face frozen in what looks like utter horror.

Heart beating hard with a kind of terror, Kate makes herself turn to see whatever it is Coco has seen. But there is no monster, no wild-eyed axe murderer, only Jeff, dressed in his pale pink Ralph Lauren polo shirt and charcoal linen shorts, standing in the rectangle of the doorway.

Kate is about to say hi, but his expression silences her. His mouth gapes, his eyes are round, all colour has drained from his face. Shock. Unmistakably. Horror, even.

Just like Coco.

CHAPTER 9

Kate tries to find her voice. Fails. Another moment passes – and it is only a moment – before her husband's eyebrows rise in something more like surprise, his lips curling up in a strange open-mouthed grimace.

'Jeff?' His name is a question on Kate's lips. In confusion, she throws out her hand, but her eyes do not move from his face. 'Do you remember—'

'Coco?' The name leaves him in a stuttering cough. He is frowning now, his head bent slightly forward, peering at Coco as if to figure out whether it is truly her.

He straightens up, shakes his head, eyes still screwed up a little. For reasons Kate cannot identify, it feels like he is acting, like he's been acting for the last couple of seconds but that what came before was very real. 'Coco Moss, isn't it?'

'Told you you'd never guess!' Kate's voice is a grating half-screech. Heart still thudding, she shifts her gaze back to Coco, who, like Jeff, appears to be recovering her composure. Another second passes before Kate realises no one is speaking.

'Coco,' she manages, 'this is Jeff, my other half. He was at Leeds too. Do you... do you remember him at all?'

Of course she does; it is obvious.

But Coco is shaking her head, her brow furrowed, her mouth pressed tightly closed. It is as if she is being shown a photofit of someone wanted by the police, someone she recognises but does not want to admit to knowing.

'I'm so sorry,' she says, her hand flat to her chest. 'I thought you were someone else there for a second.' She blows a breath of air up to her hairline. 'Sorry,' she says again and gives a suppressed gasp of relief. 'Phew. That gave me quite a turn. My ex wasn't exactly very... nice. That's who I thought you were. My ex-boyfriend from... oh, from a few years ago.'

'So you *don't* remember him?' Kate asks, flailing. The air is fraught, the particles frozen.

Coco shakes her head, the stress lines in her face fading. 'Sorry, I don't, I'm afraid.' She looks directly at Jeff with a neutral flattening of her mouth. 'It's nice to meet you anyway.' Almost grinning now, she thrusts out her hand to shake, a gesture so un-Coco-like it feels as wrong as an impromptu cartwheel in the middle of the open-plan living space.

But Jeff is still staring at her, eyes black, arms fixed by his sides as if he can't figure out how to move. Turned to stone by Medusa, Kate thinks. Petrified.

'Jeff?' She hears the nerves in her own brief laugh. 'Darling, are you OK?'

Her husband glances briefly at her with something like accusation, then at Coco, then back at Kate. His hand rises slowly, as if separate from the rest of him. He shivers then appears to come back to himself, to the room.

'Kate said it was a surprise.' He takes Coco's hand, shakes it. 'But I wasn't expecting... I mean, I would never've guessed... I'm quite shocked actually. I was expecting someone from work, or maybe my brother, Simon, and his wife, or... But yes, I'm Jeff – Jeff Barrett.' He laughs. 'Sorry. Yes, er, we never really met at Leeds, did we? But you were pretty famous. Coco

Moss, coolest girl in the year. Nearest thing we had to a living pop star!'

Kate feels herself blush, tries to communicate to Jeff with a quick flare of her eyes to shut up. He is giving too much away, underlining the disparity she wants so much to deny.

'Don't be ridiculous,' Coco says, a brief, derisive chuckle escaping. 'I saw a photo of myself the other day and realised I had actual candy floss on my head for about three months. No wonder I shaved it off.' Another laugh, more relaxed now, nostalgic. 'We were all trying so hard back then.'

'Oh my God, weren't we?' Kate laughs, too loudly, sensing that she is battling to try and bring the atmosphere back to normal, that it shows. That this is what they are all doing, for different reasons, but that none of them can possibly admit to it.

The air crackles. The look of horror moments ago on both Jeff and Coco's faces is still hanging in invisible molecules all around. Kate wonders if they feel it too. They must. She could perhaps write off her husband's expression as genuine surprise. He would never have imagined in a million years that Coco Moss would be the surprise guest. But Coco's momentary loss of composure was totally at odds with her claim not to recognise Jeff at all. When she said she thought he was an ex-boyfriend, she sounded as if she was stumbling her way blindly towards an invented excuse. Yes, Kate is almost sure that was a lie.

They know one another. It is obvious. But do they know one another from uni, or from somewhere else? From thirty years ago... or from more recently?

And wherever and whenever they know each other from – and this is bigger, much bigger – *why lie?*

Her face heats with the very specific humiliation of being trapped by etiquette. She desperately wants to ask them both what the hell is going on but finds she cannot. She is stuck fast in a comedy of errors of her own making: a horribly strange drinks party for three. If she were an authentic human being, if she had one shred of courage, she would ask Coco to leave before squaring up to Jeff. But she can't. It's like the fishing kit in the hall: a no-win predicament. Except she, not Jeff, is the author of it. It is she who wanted Coco's friendship, she who wanted her husband's attention. And so she organised something that would bring her these things. The vanity of it is so clear now it pains her. She told herself she wanted to surprise them both, but even if that were true, it was not out of a desire to delight them but out of her own need to be seen, liked, loved.

But it has not played out as she imagined.

The roar of fizzing water filling a tumbler brings her to her senses. Jeff is pouring San Pellegrino, his jaw clenched so hard the bone makes an angular bulge in his cheek.

'Shall we take our drinks outside?' Kate manages.

Hopefully the change of scene will give her time to get herself together, calm the blood pulsing at her temples. Hopefully, the air will clear once they sit down at the new heinously expensive sofa and coffee table set, where Kate has arranged terracotta tapas bowls with crisps, nuts and pimiento-stuffed olives.

'Sure,' Coco says. 'After you.'

Outside, the sun is still hot, but Kate feels too flustered, too rushed to fetch her hat. Neither Jeff nor Coco has said a word. They have taken their seats as if at a funeral. Coco is placing her beer on the coffee table with more care than is necessary. Jeff has put on his sunglasses. He is still holding his glass, fingertips white around his nails.

'So,' Kate tries, a vaguely hysterical swelling in her chest, 'how's your... did you say it was your friend's villa?'

Coco shrugs. 'It's fine. Not a patch on this place though.'

'Oh, I'm sure that's not true.' Kate tries not to gulp her wine.

'And it's further out,' Coco adds, ignoring her. 'It's actually on the main road at the back of town. And there's no pool.' She plucks a single crisp from the bowl but doesn't eat it, instead using it to gesture. 'Anyway, mustn't complain. Drew's a dear for letting me have it.'

'Is that Drew Richman? From uni?' Kate trills. 'Oh my God! So are you guys still in touch?' *Duh, no they're not, Kate. That's why she's staying in his villa.*

But Coco doesn't appear to notice the stupidity of the question.

'I don't see much of him,' she says, almost wearily. 'But we WhatsApp a lot. He's so minted now, you wouldn't believe.'

'What does he do these days?' Despite everything, Kate is grateful to Coco for speaking.

'City.' Coco eats the crisp, swigs her beer. 'House in Islington, kids at Westminster, suits from Savile Row. The whole deal.'

'Jeff gets his suits from Savile Row, don't you, darling?' No sooner have the words left her lips than Kate feels her face redden.

Jeff offers a tight smile. 'I don't think it's a competition, Kate.' His tone, the use of her name, is scathing. She fights the urge to burst into tears.

Coco slots another crisp into her mouth. The crunch, when it comes, is audible. 'Well,' she says, 'let's face it, Drew was never going to be skint, was he?'

Kate remembers this drawling irony, the kind that hovers between affection and damning disdain. She overheard a lot of it back in the day, often when its subject was not present. She remembers the strong flirtatious energy between Coco and Drew, the kind that sexually confident girls have with their male friends, the kind that makes those male friends cling on, ever hopeful that friendship might cross over into something more. She wants to ask Coco if she and Drew ever had a thing but doesn't of course; wonders instead what it would feel like to have that Pied Piper effect on the opposite sex. But then even if

Kate possessed that particular flute, she would have no idea what tune to play.

'So you kept in touch with Drew,' Jeff says, clearing his throat. Even if he is merely repeating what Coco has just said, it is a relief to hear him say something vaguely conversational.

'Yeah. And Bunny, Mia and a few others.' Coco has apparently completely recovered from the horrified shock of a few minutes ago, enough to grab a handful of peanuts and drop them from bunched fingers into her wide-open mouth.

Jeff's face is blank, his eyes hidden behind his wraparound Oakleys.

'So easy to keep in touch now,' Kate tries, addressing her words to Coco. 'Compared to then, I mean. I mean, no one had a mobile then, did they? When I was in Spain for my year abroad, we didn't even have a phone in the flat. I used to have to call Jeff from the phone box at the end of my street, didn't I, darling?'

She looks up, just in time to see Jeff's head twitch – as if he'd been staring at Coco and had not wanted to be caught. The thought gives rise to a hot, confused feeling inside Kate. But it isn't Jeff's fault, not really. It's the effect Coco Moss always had – still has evidently – on everyone. Nothing has changed. Nothing ever does. Kate feels herself sink. She has not changed either.

'So, did you two go out at uni?' Coco asks, waggling her finger between Kate and Jeff.

Kate grins, on safer ground finally. 'We went out *all through* uni. We met in Cedar House in first year. We knew Lizzie Evans and Ben Shaw – not sure if you remember them?' Coco shakes her head, no. 'Doesn't matter. We moved in with them in second year, then Jeff stayed with Ben and Lizzie in final year. You guys got a smaller place, didn't you? Elizabeth Road, was it?'

'Street.' Jeff sips his water but says nothing more.

Confused, Kate reaches for an olive and pops it in her mouth. Is there some taboo here, something to do with Lizzie and Ben?

Mirroring Jeff, Coco sips her beer. She is drinking at a glacial pace, has hardly drunk any of it. Kate's glass is pretty much empty, but she's too embarrassed to go and get a refill, doesn't want to look like she has a drinking problem, which she does not, no, absolutely not. No way. She chews the olive, arrives at the stone, wishes she hadn't picked the olive, has no idea how to get the stone out, how she usually does this in polite company, oh God, oh God... She'll leave it in. Swallow it if necessary.

'We're still in touch with Lizzie and Ben,' she offers, flailing, olive stone tucked up in her gum. It is a half-lie – they are not still in touch with Ben, because Jeff hasn't made the effort. 'In fact, Lizzie's still my best friend. She has four kids now – four girls! – and she's an absolute super-mum, though she'd never admit it.' She makes herself stop. Coco doesn't even know Lizzie, for God's sake.

'So how come you didn't live with Jeff in your final year?' Coco asks, the question a complete non-sequitur. 'Were you still going out together or did you split up for a bit?'

'It wasn't my final year, only my third, because my course was four years. I was in Spain while you guys were doing your finals. Actually, I was in France in the final term of second year, then Spain in my third year. That would've been, what? October '88 that I went to Rioja?' She looks at Jeff for confirmation, but he just shrugs.

Another silence threatens. Kate makes herself continue. 'I missed Jeff's graduation actually, because I stayed on in Spain for the summer. Got a bar job.' She leans over to Coco confidentially. 'Jeff was being *quite* the grumpy-pants, to be honest. He didn't even come over to see me at New Year, which he'd promised to do – said he had too much work on.'

'We're not all humanities students,' Jeff says, his tone cold.

'Ouch,' Coco says.

'Because law is a serious degree.' Kate mock-frowns. 'Whereas modern languages is for flibbertigibbets.'

She and Coco share a giggle.

'That's not what I meant,' Jeff says flatly. 'I just didn't have time to spend the entire Christmas holiday in Spain during my final year, that's all.'

'It was hardly the entire holiday.' Kate attempts a humorous tone but hears the tension in her voice even so. She turns towards Coco. 'It was only going to be three or four nights. I didn't book a flight to come home at Christmas because he told me he was coming to me, and then he didn't come, the bar steward.' There. She has called Jeff a bastard – well, almost. If he's going to try and humiliate her, well, frankly she'll humiliate him back.

'Naughty Jeff,' Coco drawls, teasing.

'Right?' Emboldened, Kate warms to her theme. 'Then, when he graduated, he insisted on paying off his overdraft *immediately*, like some kind of martyr. We had a massive row about it.'

Though the memory is hazy, what remains clear is that Jeff was being a bit of an arse back then, behaviour that, in her darker moments, Kate thinks might have stuck.

'Actually, that was part of why I stayed on in Rioja. He was being no fun at all.'

'Oh, forgive me for working over the summer to save for my conversion!' This time, Jeff's tone is lighter, ironic, possibly even playful. Perhaps he's realised he's coming across badly, something he wouldn't want to do in front of a woman he does not know, least of all Coco Moss.

'So did you go into law?' Coco asks. 'I mean, you said you did law. Was it criminal law?'

'Corporate,' Jeff answers, rather abruptly.

'He had a job offer,' Kate jumps in, embarrassed. 'On completion, you know? So he moved to Manchester Uni while I did my finals. He was working all the hours, literally twenty-four-seven, which turned out to be a sign of things to come.' She sits back, finishes her wine. Fuck you, Jeff, she thinks.

But Jeff is looking directly at Coco, his head angled towards her. 'Kate doesn't understand the meaning of deadlines, or targets, or the constant threat of redundancy. She has her little cake business, don't you, dear? And if that goes bust, she's absolutely fine, because this *martyr* pays for our lifestyle.'

Kate glares at him. What is he doing? He is being hateful, just hateful.

But instead of freezing with embarrassment at this burst of public bickering, Coco simply scoffs. 'That's a little harsh, don't you think? I'm guessing Kate brought up your daughter – you know, looked after her when she was sick and went to all her piano recitals and school plays while you were busy meeting your targets like a *legend*.' Her tone is laced with sarcasm. Kate wants to kiss her on the forehead. Viva la... er, sisterhood.

Jeff forces out a brief breath of a laugh. 'She certainly did.' He raises his glass. 'You're right. I'm a lucky man.' It isn't clear whether he is being sincere.

'I never stopped work,' Kate says, without knowing why. 'Not once Lou started primary school. I always had some part-time job or other, always kept busy, you know?'

'So,' Coco says through a mouthful of crisps, leaning forward to address her question to Kate, 'we must have all left by the time you got back to Leeds?'

Kate nods, grateful. 'Yep. You'd all gone to pastures new! You, Drew, Mia, all those guys.' The in-crowd, she doesn't add. The Untouchables. The *Unapproachables*.

She glances at Jeff, who is sitting bolt upright, his arms folded across his chest. What is going on with him? Really?

'Do you remember that little cinema?' Coco asks. 'It was

right in the middle of Leeds 6. Tiny place. The guy who ran it had these really strong glasses.'

'Hyde Park Picture House,' Jeff says and – hallelujah – grins.

Coco points at him and laughs. 'Well done! God, I can barely remember a thing. I think I must've destroyed so many brain cells. All that cheap cider and... Oh God, what was that terrible wine we used to drink? It was, like, thirty per cent proof or something ridiculous. You'd see homeless people drinking it.'

'Thunderbird.' Kate almost cries the word.

Coco points to her now, laughing. 'That's the one. Actual turps – you could've stripped paint with it. We were fucking feral, weren't we?'

In her upper-class accent, the bad language sounds classy somehow. Kate remembers that about her as something like fragile hope expands in her chest. Coco and Jeff are reminiscing about the places they all used to go as students, the crazy dance nights at the Union.

'Theo's kebabs!' Coco presses her palms to the sides of her forehead.

'Oh my God, Theo's,' Jeff says, almost laughing. 'And that chilli sauce – rank. It's a wonder we don't all have mad cow disease.'

'Well, we might,' Coco jokes, that dark humour of hers surfacing. 'Maybe it wasn't beef at all. Maybe it was dog... Alsatian or Labrador mince.'

'I quite liked those kebabs,' Kate says, and to her wild relief, they both laugh – properly laugh, like they actually find her funny. Still a little disoriented, she tries to join in but swallows the olive stone, feels it in her throat.

'Oh, totally,' Coco is saying as Kate dislodges the olive stone with the rest of her wine. 'I mean, after six pints of piss-weak lager from the Old Bar, those doners were so delicious I didn't care if they *were* dog meat, frankly.'

Fragile hope becomes a flickering flame of triumph. Coco has almost finished her lager, enough for Kate to suggest another. She rises, offers and to her near-hysterical delight, Coco says *yeah, sure,* and pushes the bottle to her lips to drain it.

Kate tries not to run to the kitchen. Quite why she wants to run she doesn't know – an unnamed, uneasy feeling, like she should get back quickly. Is it excitement, the desire to not miss one word now that they're all getting along? Or is it, she thinks as she opens the fridge, because she doesn't want to leave the two of them alone together? What was wrong with Jeff just now, being so rude like that? And what exactly passed between him and Coco when he came downstairs? Why did Coco claim not to remember him when she clearly did? And why, in both their faces, did Kate read, fleetingly but unmistakably, utter horror?

There is no way to get a straight answer right now; it would be social suicide. The best way to do this is to make sure the evening is a success. But whatever happens, the moment Coco Moss leaves this villa, Kate will confront Jeff and ask him what the hell is going on.

CHAPTER 10

An hour and a half later, the front door closes behind Coco Moss. One hand still on the catch, Kate rounds on Jeff.

'What the hell was that?'

He blinks, frowns. He has pushed his sunglasses up onto his head, the effect a rather foolish footballer's Alice band. 'What do you mean, what the hell was that?'

She opens her mouth to reply, but he has already turned away from her, is already heading back into the living space, forcing her to follow him like a nagging wife in a cartoon. His espadrilles slap on the hard stone floor. The sound makes her want to scream.

'Jeff,' she says, her voice low and trembling. 'I'm trying to talk to you.'

He stops, pulls open the fridge: *suck*.

'What are we eating?' he asks. 'I'm starving.'

She slams her hand on the bar. 'Don't! Do *not* ask me what we're eating!' Her palm stings; embarrassment hovers; whether or not she is right to be angry shimmers like a mirage. But no. No. She is right, she *is*. 'What was going on between you and Coco? When you first came in?'

He closes the fridge door and faces her, his eyebrows low, his eyes cynical. 'What do you mean, what was going on?'

'Oh my God, are you going to continually repeat my questions back to me and prefix them with *what do you mean?* Just so I know.'

'What? Calm down. What could possibly have been going on? She was only here a couple of hours.'

Kate swallows the scream. Breathes deeply, in and out, but it feels self-conscious, doesn't do the trick at all.

'When you first came down the stairs and stood there.' She points to the door for emphasis, hates herself for indulging him like this – he knows perfectly well what she means. 'You were standing right there and you looked... horrified. Like you'd seen something horrible, a ghost. And she... she looked the same but then she kind of changed her expression and pretended she thought you were someone else. And don't say she didn't. I was there, Jeff. I saw.'

He shakes his head. 'I don't know what you saw, but I was shocked, that's all. If I was thinking anything at all, I was thinking, what the hell is Coco sodding Moss doing in my living room? I didn't even know her at uni, and what little I did know of her, I didn't like. You know that! We were never friends, and neither were you. Of course I was shocked to see her. If I looked horrified, it's maybe because I couldn't believe you'd invite that woman here without asking me. You don't know her. *We* don't know her. What were you trying to do? What were you *thinking*? No wonder I looked horrified; it was embarrassing... really awkward. I was furious. OK? There. Happy?'

Kate clasps her head, digs her fingertips into her scalp as if to hold on to the reason she can feel slipping away. Without changing the subject, Jeff has somehow changed the subject.

'When Coco saw you,' she says slowly, oh so slowly, 'her eyes went all wide and her mouth dropped open and she looked like she'd seen... like she'd seen a monster. Come on! You were there!'

Jeff throws out his hands. 'I don't know! I can't speak for Coco bloody Moss! Maybe she was as embarrassed as I was. Maybe you should ask her, since you're such good friends. I mean, it's not shocking so much as... as a bit sad, if you want my honest opinion. You always were obsessed with her, weren't you? Back at Leeds?'

'What? You can't say that! You were obsessed with her too, every bit as much as me.'

'Well, I wasn't the one hanging around the Old Bar like the Little Match Girl, *oh hi, Coco, it's me, Kate.* You were always so crushed when she had no idea who you were and yet you kept on trying to get her attention like... like an abused spaniel or something. You never got that she was out of your league, did you? At least I understood that. At least I *knew* I was a nobody.'

'What? What are you saying? That Coco Moss is *better* than me? Than *us*?'

'Don't be obtuse. It's just life, the way it is. No one says it out loud, but it is. You and me, we didn't talk the right way, we didn't have the right clothes, we didn't even *stand* like them. I'm perfectly comfortable with that; it's you who isn't. We were the comp kids! We ate Findus Crispy Pancakes growing up, and played kerby, and we only had one pair of trainers. So what? We didn't exactly have it tough, did we? And at least I didn't run out and buy a burgundy cardigan and change my name to Binky or Tobes like some people did. And neither did you. So for God's sake don't start now.' He sighs, as if spent, knuckles pressing against the granite worktop. 'Right. Are we going out to eat or what? I'm starving.'

Stunned, Kate closes her eyes. How casually he has delivered his annihilation; how casually he can segue into thinking about his stomach. And sure enough, when she opens her eyes, he is dropping a long pink tongue of jamón ibérico into his open mouth just like Coco did with the peanuts. She hates him. She hates him she hates him she hates him.

She hates him because she can't pretend to be anything she's not in front of him. She hates him because every word he has said is true. This, this is why she didn't tackle him when Coco went to use the loo earlier. She knew the conversation would escalate into a full-blown row. Instead she asked only about his fishing trip, as if it were of utmost interest to her, asked him if he'd had word from Lou at all. He had sent her a photo on WhatsApp, he told her, of the octopus they'd caught, once he'd made it back to the villa, and Kate felt pathetically pleased that he'd made this small effort with his own daughter. She didn't tackle him about Coco – she knew this even at the time – because she wanted Coco to return to find them chatting amicably, like two people who were happy together, happy and in love after all these years.

'I'm sorry,' she says quietly now – an apology laced with sarcasm – pouring the last of the wine into her glass. 'But *you're* the one who joined the golf club. *You're* the one who bought a share in a *yacht* even though you have no clue how to sail. *You're* the one who criticises me for not enjoying your dry corporate dinners with the foie gras, wah wah wah. It's not me who's putting on airs, *mate*. If you want the truth, I wish we could go back to the way we were.' Her voice is breaking into jagged pieces. 'God, I wish we could go back, you have no idea. We were so happy before all... this.' She gestures around her. 'Now, we're so... so bloated with... stuff. We have far too much, and it doesn't feel... it doesn't feel real. Don't you miss living on a shoestring? Picnics on the beach when Lou was little? Do you even remember that?'

To her dismay, her eyes have filled with tears; she feels something close to longing. 'I wish we could go back – I really do. Not to that, not exactly, but to something... something simpler. Something real.'

'Really? You want to go back? What, to having to work to pay off your overdraft while that lot miraculously found themselves travelling to Argentina for the summer? To worrying about the half a lager you bought while they left their credit card behind the bar – at nineteen fucking years old? To having to interview for countless jobs only to start at the absolute bottom because Daddy couldn't pull in any contacts? Because from where I'm standing' – it is his turn to gesture: to her dress, her shoes, the villa, as she knew he would – 'you don't look like you're suffering too much. You don't *look* like someone who'd rather be staying in a mosquito-infested campsite praying the car makes it home. For Christ's sake, there are people out there who can't afford to heat their houses! Grow up, Kate.'

Tears fall. Whatever grip she had, she has lost. What was her point? Did she even have one? How did this horrible argument start? She sniffs, grabs a piece of kitchen roll to wipe her eyes.

'Look,' Jeff says, more softly now, 'you've had a few drinks. You're emotional. If I'm being defensive, it's because I hate it when you run down the life I've... *we've* worked so hard for. I was just shocked, that's all. Earlier. I genuinely would never have imagined Coco Moss walking through the door. If it was awkward, it's because, as I said, we don't know her. We never did. We were never friends with her. We were never meant to *be* friends with her. And that probably hasn't changed.'

'You always say I need to evolve,' Kate manages, sniffing again. 'An inverted snob, you call me. And we used to talk about her all the time. Her and her friends. I thought you'd be pleased.'

'I know,' he says, stepping towards her, taking hold of her shoulders. 'But she was a pop star, nothing but a pop star you tear out of *Smash Hits* and put on your bedroom wall. Idols are for teenagers. And I've grown up.'

'Are you saying I haven't?'

He sighs. 'I'm saying I'm older now. I'm not so desperate to prove myself or to be a part of social groups that I don't fit into. I joined the golf club because it's good for me professionally and I wanted something to keep me fit as I got older. Matthew, who I play with, he used to sell fruit and veg in the East End. Bill is a building contractor. It's really quite down to earth.' He sighs. 'Look, I just don't want you abasing yourself for some scraps of attention from the likes of Coco Moss.'

His voice is so even; it is at odds with what he's saying. Abasing herself? Scraps of attention?

'I'm not *abasing myself*,' she says, matching his calm. 'I just thought it'd be nice to make friends, that's all. Have someone to talk to for a change now that Lou isn't with us on holiday any more. You're never... even on holiday, when we're supposed to be together, you're always... you're never... you're never *here*. Coco's husband's a musician and he has to practise in the evenings so she's pretty lonely too, she said that, and I just thought maybe we could hang out, you know? That's all. Have a coffee. Just for some company. To not be alone.'

He shakes his head sadly. 'Kate. Listen to yourself. Think. She only came to the villa because you told her we owned it.'

'How do you know? How could you possibly know that?'

'Because she told me when you went to get the drinks. Not in so many words, but she asked when we'd bought it. You must have told her within seconds of meeting her. What were you hoping to achieve?'

Kate's cheeks burn. Once again, he has seen through her. It is so humiliating. She thought the argument was over, but now she can feel the panicky rise of a second wave. 'Nothing,' she says. 'I just—'

'You hoped she'd be impressed? Hoped she'd want to be your friend now you've come up in the world?' He shakes his head. His tone is conciliatory, his words a violent slap. 'You're right, I'll admit. She will. But it won't be for *you*. It's not about you – or me, so don't take it personally. Coco and that crowd don't give a toss about anyone. All they care about is how much money you have. The only reason she came here is because... Well, I bet she changed her tune the moment you mentioned the words villa and pool, didn't she?'

Kate shakes her head. 'She was friendly *before* that. I don't understand why you're... It's like you're saying I've got nothing to offer apart from money – no personality, no sense of humour, nothing.' But even as she says it, part of her thinks: *Jeff is right. He always is. His knowledge of me is a prison from which I cannot escape.*

'I'm just trying to make sure you see her for what she is, that's all. An opportunist at best, a sponging socialite at worst. I'm not trying to be cruel. It's actually because I'd hate for you to get hurt. She isn't paying for her villa, is she?'

'You don't know that. What's that got to do with anything anyway?'

He throws up his arms in exasperation. 'It's just typical of these people! They're loaded and yet they go round staying in each other's luxury holiday homes. It's galling, frankly. Not as if they need a free holiday, is it?'

'We invite friends to stay here! Krish and his wife came for New Year last year!'

'That's not quite the same. And I bet she doesn't work for a living; probably on some trust fund.'

'She didn't say what she did.' Her voice is fading. She feels suddenly too tired for this conversation. She has lost, comprehensively, as she always does.

Jeff takes her hands in his. The gesture is tender. 'Exactly. Trust me, people like Coco Moss eat people like us for breakfast. She'll chew you up and spit you out. You know this. I just don't understand why you put her on such a pedestal or why you would want to insinuate yourself into her affections when we both know you'll end up a nervous wreck.'

'I'm not a wreck!' Her voice betrays her. She sounds shrill, shaky. She sounds tipsy and yes, full of anxiety. 'It's you who's made me a wreck, not her.'

But again, as she says the words, she knows they are not true. That she's been lying for some minutes now, perhaps for this whole argument. Because the truth is, Coco does make her feel like she has to change everything about herself just to be good enough.

And yet... And yet she'd do anything, anything to be her friend.

CHAPTER 11

JEFF

Upstairs in the en suite, Jeff strips and throws himself under the shower, gasping at the shock of the cold water on his flaming skin. Coco Moss. Coco fucking Moss. Jesus. Jesus Christ.

He pushes his hands to the tiled wall, lets the water cascade down his back. It is almost unbearable, but he makes himself stand in the icy stream until his head starts to ache, his arms go numb. And then more, more again, whimpering and swearing at the near pain of it, at his own simmering panic. He is shivering. His teeth are chattering. Christ Almighty, he is almost crying. Coco Moss. Here. In his house. My God.

He turns off the water. Stands feet planted wide in the walk-in frosted glass cubicle, letting himself air-dry. He is shaking violently with cold, with fear. He has left Kate downstairs. She is still upset but he had to get away from her scrutinising glare, her questions, the slam of her hand on the breakfast bar. Because she might have had a drink, but she knows. She knows something is off because she knows him. For Christ's sake, she's known him since they were eighteen. The only reason he's been able to hide anything, anything at all from her until now is because *until now* he has always had time to get his story straight and move on. Move on, always move on – to work: the relentlessness of it, the sheer time it takes out of every single day. To the gym: pushing his body to its limit to white-out his mind. As long as he's working or exercising, there is, there has been, no time to think about his choices. Anything outside work or sport or the jocular and mildly competitive banter of the golf course he has lived through as if in a dream: at a distance, ears plugged, eyes half closed.

Until now.

'Does she know?' Coco came straight out with it the moment Kate went stumbling off for the drinks. Typical Kate, already a few ahead, thinking no one had noticed.

'Of course not,' he replied, skin heating. 'I'm not a complete idiot.'

'Does *anyone* know?' Coco's eyes were hidden behind black lenses, but he could still see them in his mind's eye: swirling chocolate, flecks of honeycomb, eyelashes to make a grown man weep.

'No! Of course not. Why, have *you* told anyone?'

'Don't be ridiculous.' Coco's lips closed tight then, the subject dropped like a rock into a pool, the two of them sitting in the silence that followed, watching the circles shrink. Coco still every bit as irresistible as thirty years ago, of course she was. She was always going to be.

She looked about her then, her gaze resting, continuing, resting while he tried not to stare at her mouth. 'Nice place. Ve-ery nice. I have to say, I didn't have you pegged for greatness.'

'Thanks a lot.'

'Don't be offended. I didn't know you, remember? I don't know you.'

'No,' he replied. 'No, you didn't. Don't. And I don't know you. Sounds like you landed on your feet though.' *But I do know you*, he wanted to say. *I know you in every cell of my being.*

She looked bored. 'And you own this place. Wow.'

'I need to see you,' he said then, failing to curb the urgency in his voice. 'Alone, I mean. We need to... talk.'

She turned to face him. 'We've talked. What else is there to say?'

'Please.' It was all he could do not to grab her wrist and pull her to him.

'My number's in your wife's phone.' She shrugged. 'Or maybe I should suggest a cosy WhatsApp group?'

At the sound of Kate's footsteps, they fell silent. If Kate picked up on the two of them springing away from their conversation as if they'd touched their hands to a hotplate, she didn't show it. Jeff thanked God for his sunglasses, for Coco's steely calm. He had forgotten that calm. Had almost forgotten her. Almost. At least he'd tried to, putting her into a mental box and closing the lid, sitting on the lid if he had to, nailing it shut with refusal, with work, with... whatever it took. But still she leaked out – in dreams, in fantasies of that other life he might have led: the one with her in it.

Desperate for her to leave, he feared he might give himself away, blurt it all out, fall on his knees and say, *Kate, oh Kate, I need to tell you something.* But Kate was babbling away, handing out drinks, telling Coco to help herself to... Actually, he has no idea what his wife was saying because he was on that warm dusk patio in body only, his mind back there in his seedy student house that night, just as he is now, again, even as he's standing wet and wretched in the obscene marble bathroom of his second home, his gym-muscled naked body reflected by mirrors that cost a month's wages for some people, for his own parents actually, and for Kate's, for everyone he has ever been close to, oh God, he is back in that stinking room, can smell the mould creeping blackish green down from the ceiling, making Stilton of the damp walls. He and Ben and Lizzie.

They thought it was funny, the squalor. Joked about it all the time. Because they were *playing* at being poor. They *knew*

this was temporary. No central heating was hilarious –
chilblains, ha ha ha! The fungus growing out of the wall in the
basement kitchen was a right laugh – they could make mush-
room risotto with it, if only they could afford Parmesan!

What arseholes they were. And there was no bigger arse-
hole than him.

He reaches for the towel and wraps it around his waist. His
curated reflection is almost unbearable. He has no right to have
aged this well. The gold card at the gym, the triathlons, two
London Marathons, snorkelling, canoeing and, in the last two
years, paddleboarding – so great for the core! His honed
physique is as obscene as this two-grand mirror, as the sunken
Roman bath, as the gleaming German taps.

Ben and Lizzie are waiting for him in that mould-streaked
room. They won't, will never, leave. He can see them as if they
were here in front of him. Holograms. Himself a hologram too,
one he wants to shout at and say, 'Don't. Do not go out tonight.'
But he can't because he is here, locked in a never-ending present
conditioned by a never-ending past.

Lizzie and Ben are drinking cheap cider from a two-litre
bottle in the cramped space. The huge poster of the Cure he
bought from WHSmith hangs on the wall over the defunct fire-
place; a brown incense stick fumes on a chipped white saucer.
They are full of it, full of themselves. They are getting ready for
Lizzie's friend's fancy dress party. It smells so damn musty, the
spores competing with the smoking sandalwood, the decades-
old carpet, the singed dust from the plug-in heater. They should
open a window. But the night is too cold. Halloween in Leeds.
Bloody freezing. It was so cold that night. Enough to catch your
death.

CHAPTER 12

Jeff wakes at 5.30. Although *wakes* is perhaps not the right term for what is essentially giving up on the idea of sleep, peeling his eyes from the ceiling and thinking, *Sod this, I may as well be up doing something.*

Slowly he walks into the bathroom. Lizzie and Ben have been with him all night, are with him now as he pees, as he washes his hands, examines his bloodshot eyeballs in the mirror. In his memory, Lizzie is, will forever be, dressed as she was that night, the night that will not stop playing itself out over and over and over.

Lizzie is a cat, a cat of sorts anyway: black leggings baggy at the knee, misshapen black polo neck, ears cut from a cereal packet, painted black and attached to a plastic hairband; whiskers and nose drawn on with eyeliner, more eyeliner in thick black licks across her lids. She's always such a sport when it comes to fancy dress. By contrast, Ben sits sulking in jeans and an old Siouxsie and the Banshees T-shirt, his costume in an off-white heap behind him on Jeff's bed: a sheet with eye holes cut out.

'I hate fancy dress,' he says – Jeff can hear him, the exact way he says it, can see the rounded set of his shoulders, the bad-tempered swig from a tea-stained Liverpool FC mug. 'Since when was Halloween a thing in England anyway?'

Jeff has on the tuxedo he bought from Parker's Apparel Second Hand Clothes for the Cedar House freshers' ball in first year, a white formal shirt, a bow tie, a pair of black Gola trainers with a hole in the left toe. He is sitting on his desk chair, Lizzie cross-legged on the floor in front of him, telling him to keep still while she paints his nails with a dark burgundy varnish she tells him is called Black Cherry. The costume was all her idea. She has already whited out his face with powder and applied black kohl to the rims of his eyes, which made him sneeze. He is not allowed to look in a mirror until she has finished. No danger there. He doesn't have one in his room. Ben has already made the joke about vampires not being able to see their reflections or something, he can't really remember exactly, maybe it's that the mirror will kill him, and of course, there is no Google.

'You look amazing,' Lizzie says, screwing the top back on the varnish, looking up at him and grinning. 'I hardly recognise you.'

Ben nods, his bottom lip pushing up against the top. 'You'll defo pull in that, mate.'

Lizzie throws the bottle of nail varnish at him. 'Oi. Jeff's a married man.'

Ben shrugs, eyebrows rising, mock-belligerent. 'Er, he's not? And he's also a *young* man. Doesn't have to take a vow of chastity quite yet, does he? If you can't be wild at twenty, when can you?'

Lizzie laughs, throwing back her head before fixing Ben with a withering stare. 'Like you'd know, I suppose.'

Ben raises his hands. 'I'm just saying. If you don't try stuff now, then when?'

'Then never,' Lizzie says. 'Sorry to disappoint you.'

'Look at him! He's so obviously into the whole kinky ambiguous thing, that's all I'm saying.'

'I am in the room, you know,' says Jeff, enjoying the attention.

Ben's encouragement to cheat on Kate is a thin veil over his true feelings. Jeff wishes he would get a boyfriend, but he is, as Lizzie would say in her thick Yorkshire accent, *all gob and no trousers*. Which in the kinder language of hindsight might be termed *afraid*.

'You look... edgy,' Lizzie is saying. 'Cool. Yeah. Maybe Ben's right. A bit... fluid.'

Jeff wiggles his eyebrows. 'I can't take this any more. I'm going to have a look.'

He leaves them and goes to the bathroom, where there is a not-quite-full-length mirror, the only mirror in the house. If you stand on a chair, you can see the bottom half of yourself; you just can't see all of yourself at the same moment.

'Bloody hell,' he says to his reflection – the top half of it.

The contrast of the whiteness of his face with the deep blackness of his slicked-back hair is so stark, the eyeliner making his eyes huge rich pools of brown, lending them a kind of intensity, almost danger. He steps back so that he can see a little more of himself. Despite the standard student binge-drinking, he is still slim from playing rugby for the firsts, the punishing training sessions, the super-competitive matches. The suit is still as loose as it was when he bought it; it falls off him in a way that makes him look thinner than he is. The nail varnish is the final touch. He looks like the kind of guy who would give anything a try, the kind who would smoke a joint with Coco Moss and her friends, the kind of guy who would've arrived late to supper at the halls canteen in first year, complaining that he'd just woken up, that he was *so wasted last night*. Yes, he looks cool. He thinks. Cool-ish.

He brings one varnished hand up, lets it rest flat against his chest.

'My name is Vlad,' he says, in a Slavic accent with a hint of Warrington. 'I have crossed many centuries to meet you.'

Lizzie appears at the bathroom door, leans on the frame, cocks her head. She too looks edgier than usual. And then he finds the word he has not dared to use even to himself. Sexy. She looks sexy. They both do. He doesn't fancy Lizzie, but he can see, objectively, that she looks hot. Poor Ben; he is the only one of them who is desperate to find love, the one who least wants to look silly, and yet he's the only one who *will* look silly, not to mention invisible – under a sheet, for God's sake. Maybe that's the paradox of fancy dress: the less effort you make, the more ridiculous you look.

'Told you,' Lizzie says. 'Who is this mysterious, sexually ambiguous time-travelling dude?'

'I'm not going to pull,' he says, without really knowing why, since that is not what Lizzie said at all.

'I know!' She hits him on the shoulder. 'I'm your chaperone anyway. One false move...'

Behind her on the landing looms the world's crappest ghost. Even under his sheet, with only his blue eyes visible, Ben looks pissed off.

'You look like an oversized shuttlecock,' Jeff says.

'I wish I *had* an oversized shuttlecock,' Ben deadpans. 'Are we going then? Get this over with?'

Jeff takes one last look at Dracula, a feline Lizzie behind him, her eyes narrow. 'Hey,' he says without turning. 'Where's your camera? We should get a photo.'

They drive to Woodhouse. As they turn into the road and park up, the thump and chatter of the party reaches them. An orange glow emanates from the windows of the house, a huddle of people outside, smoke rising off them like steam. Jeff parks a little way up, far enough that they can observe without being noticed.

'Oh my God, it's heaving,' says Lizzie. 'Cindy knows literally everyone.'

'I can't believe I came as a ghost,' Ben grumbles. 'I feel like such a dick.'

They get out of the car. Flimsy red-and-white stripy carrier bags clink with booze. Ben stands on the pavement. From the drape of the sheet, it is clear his arms are stuck to his sides with embarrassment. 'You could've told me Coco Moss and all her lot were going.'

'Coco Moss is going?' Jeff says. 'When did she say that?'

'Literally half an hour ago,' Ben says miserably. 'Lizzie told me in the house, when you were in the bathroom admiring yourself. I wish you'd told me before. I can't go in like this. Look!' The sheet moves – a ghostly gesture towards the crowd outside the house, all of whom look like they're dressed in black – a couple of witch's hats, a neon skeleton, three prongs of a devil's fork: silly, yes, fancy dress, yes, but *sexy*.

'Oh, for pity's sake,' Lizzie says, rolling her eyes. 'You could literally moan for Great Britain, d'you know that? What difference does it make who's there? They're just people, that lot, no better than anyone else. Look, take the sheet off. Take it off!'

The smell of sweet smoke reaches them on the cold air. The dull rolling thump of a bassline.

Lizzie sighs, gesturing at Ben. 'Ben! Come on. Quick.' She adjusts her camera strap so that the camera rests on her back.

Ben does as he's told, the sheet sliding off him, ruffling a squashed blonde shelf of hair back into its usual mess of curls. Lizzie rootles in the make-up bag she has dug out from underneath the passenger seat. She brought it, she tells them, for last-minute touching-up. The innuendo elicits a giggle from all three of them and the tension dies.

'We'll just have to...' She produces a pair of nail scissors.

Christ, it's cold. Leeds is much colder than Warrington, Jeff is sure of it.

'What're you doing?' Ben asks, still standing like a petulant child.

'I'm going to rip your T-shirt, then I'm going to just... I dunno. Improvise. With make-up.'

'No you're not!' He takes a step back.

'Ben.' Lizzie holds the scissors up to his face like a flick knife. 'It's bloody freezing out here. I've done all the costumes, all the make-up, and now I want to go to the party, OK? It's nearly half ten and everyone is already off their face, and I too wish to be off my face. Do you want to look cool or do you want to look like a ten-year-old who can't join in on musical chairs?'

Ben sulks while Lizzie cuts into his T-shirt. Jeff watches, though most of him is focused on what has just been said. Coco Moss is here. Could be here anyway. Lizzie's friend must have some connection to her. And here he is, looking right for once – it has taken a fancy dress party for this to happen. As Dracula, he looks cool in a way he doesn't normally, and yes: sexy – for him, for someone like him. But that's the point. He doesn't look like someone like him. He doesn't look like him at all.

He hears a rip, a cry of outrage from Ben. Another rip, the two of them giggling and swearing now, Ben shouting *Oi!* as Lizzie puts both hands inside one of the tears and pulls it apart.

'That's it,' she says. 'Get that manly chest out.'

Jeff considers his hands, his dark-blood nails. Black Cherry. He licks his lips, tastes the greasy film of cosmetics. In a last flash of inspiration, Lizzie painted his mouth black before they got in the car. He checks his appearance in the wing mirror and stares into his own dangerous kohl-rimmed eyes. Coco Moss is somewhere in that house. He is young. He is not married. Now is the time to try things. To experiment. Dressed like this, he can make a mistake.

He can make one beautiful mistake, can't he?

CHAPTER 13

Jeff creeps downstairs. Kate is snoring on the sofa, still in last night's dress. The sound is thick; it makes him think of mucus. The air smells of stale wine. On the coffee table, an empty bottle stands beside a glass with a smear of grease at the lip.

He looks down on his wife. She is lying face up, arms straight at her sides, palms up, her legs apart – a pose of surrender. Her mouth is open, a white line of dried drool snaking from the corner. Her chin melts into a neck that is ringed like an elephant's leg. Her upper arms are patchy and reddish where the sun has infiltrated the high-factor suncream she never quite puts on properly. At her crown, an almost imperceptible grey-white line drives through the blonde and brown of her expensively highlighted hair – her natural colour edging in like a stain she tries to scrub away, only for it to creep back. All in all, an unattractive sight, yet one from which he can't seem to tear himself. Like a road accident, he thinks. Or a couple having a whispered fight in a restaurant.

But he does. Tear himself away that is. Gathers up the detritus of Kate's pity party for one. She will have felt misunderstood, confused. But he can't help that. The cost of her understanding is too high. Hopefully her fury will have burnt itself out or, failing that, the hangover will be so bad she won't be able to think of anything else. As for him, he will simply have to grit his teeth and get through this fortnight. Go through the motions until all thoughts of Coco Moss and the way the two of them looked at one another in shock and recognition, the resulting avalanche of memories he had thought buried forever, fall from his mind.

The past must be kept where he left it. The past is like that white line of hair. It is edging in. He needs to stand guard and make sure that stain doesn't creep any further into his life. He needs to see Coco and make sure she's fully on board. He has worked too hard, too fucking hard, for what happened that night to take away everything he has now.

A sweet espresso, and two seconds later he is out on the lane, The Prodigy pounding in his headphones. He runs down towards the shops and bars, away from the main coastal road, the Carretera de Cadaqués, which wraps itself around the town like a vine, climbing out to the treacherous curves and sheer drops of the Cap de Creus. Every time they drive up from Barcelona airport, Kate exclaims how frightening it is.

'Oh my God,' she will say, or, 'I can't look,' or, 'Tell you what, one false move and we'd be right over that edge. There'd be no coming back from that, would there?'

He runs past the beaches, takes the super-steep road that cuts up to the left after Sa Conca bay, sweat pouring off him now. Panting heavily, down to pin-steps, but he will not stop, he will not. Stop equals surrender, and it's all downhill from there.

Finally, the road levels. He sucks in lungfuls of air. Indian fig trees, parched and spiky, sponge moisture from deep underground. He runs, more comfortable on the flat. The rhythm and the music have begun, finally, to calm him.

Another long bend, another. Finally, below, his favourite cove, Sa Cebolla, shimmers into view, its impossibly turquoise water a jewel against the yellow rocks. He rounds the bay, runs all the way up to the lighthouse, Far de Cala Nans, where he allows himself to stop, hands on hips, chest rising and falling, looking across the ocean, back to where he has come from: the white crust of the town, the place he fell in love with that first time he came with Kate and Lou, when Lou was still a little girl. He had run here, to this spot, and stared at that view and thought, *I can still do this. If we buy something here, it will soften things somehow. I can still make this life something to enjoy. To bear at least. I must. There are comforts. Money has eased the pain.*

If I can have moments like this, he thought then as he thinks now, *I can survive.*

That was why he bought the villa. Not an investment, not property, nothing so solid as that. All he really wanted was to capture that moment in solid form so that there might be others like it, so he could get a regular fix to carry him through.

It was his compensation for not being allowed to live his life, the life he should have lived, with *her*.

CHAPTER 14

KATE

An urgent pressing on her bladder. Heat comes at her next: the fan-oven blast of Spanish summer air. Then the sandpaper where her tongue should be. Kate opens her sticky eyes, finds herself on the sofa, still in her dress. On the coffee table is a packet of paracetamol and a glass of water. She didn't put them there.

Jeff then. Silently. Judgementally.

She throws her legs over the side of the couch. Bare feet touch cool tile. Gingerly she lifts herself upright. Her head pounds. There is no way, no *way* she can stand up.

She drains the glass in one, feels water run through her as through the dry, cracked soil of a house plant. A moment. Two. *Steady yourself, girl.*

Slowly she raises her torso from the cushions, pushes her legs almost straight. Another moment, for balance, hands pressed to the scorched air, before she is fully upright.

As if in chains, she shuffles towards the kitchen area. On the bar are two empty wine bottles. Coco drank beer, Jeff water. How awful it is when you don't share; there's really no getting around the fact that she must have drunk all of it. Only then does she remember opening the second bottle – wrestling with the corkscrew, swearing at it after Jeff went to bed – a perfunctory, angry, lonely sozzling. Being tiddly was not enough, nowhere near enough.

Jeff is not here. She knows this without looking for him, without calling his name. His coffee cup stands next to the empty bottles. No crumbs, no cereal fossilising on the side of a bowl. He will have gone out for his daily run and swim. Perhaps he left the coffee cup next to the wine bottles as a kind of rebuke. It is so hard to live with a teetotaller sometimes, with someone so morally upright who works so hard, who provides so much, who keeps fit, who never falls out with anyone and who is always, always right. At least if he drank, he would relax, wouldn't he? Maybe even mess up occasionally, fall off his high horse. He would laugh more, exercise less, let himself *go*.

She remembers bringing him two bottles of wine when she came back from her time abroad: one white and one rosé. She was excited for him to try them, had only ever tried red Rioja before she lived there, didn't realise it came in other colours. But he shook his head, no.

'I don't drink,' he said.

And that really was all he said, as if she were meeting him for the first time, not, as was the case, being reunited with him after many months apart. Not *I don't drink any more*. Not *Actually, I've given up alcohol*. Not *I'm so sorry, I should have told you*. Just *I don't drink*.

'What do you mean, you don't drink?' She laughed. Yes, that's right, she thought he was joking. 'Of course you do! You love drinking!'

But he shook his head. 'I have to focus on my career now. This conversion will be tough, and then there's the internship. Corporate law is cut-throat, and I'll be a small fish in a very big pond. I'm just not prepared to let anything stop me becoming a bigger fish. A shark even.'

She stared at him, waiting for him to point at her and say, *Ha ha, fooled you*. But he didn't.

'A shark?' she said, mocking him openly now, but only because she was beginning to panic. 'So let me get this straight. In this whole workplace-as-aquarium scenario, you're working your way up from a minnow to, what, a trout? What's next, a piranha? Or maybe a really big tuna?' She was still half laughing, still incredulous.

But Jeff didn't laugh. He didn't even smile. Looking at his expression, she felt like she was taking the piss out of his dying relative or something. She stopped laughing.

'You can mock me if you want,' he said. 'But it's what I need to do, and I'd appreciate your support.'

He was deadly serious, she realised. The reliable strait-laced boy she had fallen in love with was... well, more reliable than she'd thought. As for his laces, they were steam-pressed. Ruler-sharp.

'OK.' She lowered the bottles, which until now she had, incredibly, still been holding up like the gifts they were supposed to have been. 'Of course. Yeah. Of course. Sorry.'

Sighing, she picks up last night's empties and drops them into the recycling bin. The sight of Jeff's empty plastic bottle of San Pellegrino is another silent shake of the head.

That was it, she thinks. *I don't drink.* Not a drop has passed his lips since then. A brief phase of evangelical sermons on the evils of pouring ethanol down your throat, which soon passed, thank God. But that was Jeff: once he'd made his mind up, he ploughed forward like... well, like a plough – it's far too hot and she's far too hung-over for metaphors. She needs iced water and two of those paracetamol. She needs to get her swimming costume on and go and throw herself in the cool blue Mediterranean.

Back on the sofa with the water and a heavily sugared luke-warm espresso, the scatter cushion tips her sideways. On inspection, she finds her journal half hidden beneath it. She has no memory of bringing it downstairs. None whatsoever. Finds the thought of herself climbing and descending those unforgiving slats of solid wood while inebriated quite unsettling.

She pops the painkillers, downs half her coffee and flicks through the notebook.

Coco would never go for balayage, she reads. *... so effortlessly cool... so beautiful I actually had tears in my eyes.*

'Oh God,' she whispers, blushing, skim-reading.

Imagine if Lou fell in love with one of Coco's boys...

On and on it goes.

'Oh. Oh no, no, no.'

She sounds like a schoolgirl and a maiden aunt all at once. It's a good job she'll never be famous; this diary would be embarrassing even if it were published posthumously.

The last two pages are nothing but scrawl. She can barely read her own handwriting, but the names Jeff and Coco are just distinguishable in the crazy, looping frenzy. *What the hell*, she deciphers in one bit; *something going on* in another; over on the next page, *look that passed between them*; further down, simply: *what?* More, increasingly erratic, on the same theme – an uncomfortable reminder of herself drunk, obsessing.

But she's not drunk now, and she's still wondering what that look was.

Because it was something.

And something else, coalescing from the fog of her brain. When she came out from fetching the fresh drinks, Jeff and Coco had kind of sprung apart, as if they'd been gossiping or talking about her or... something. Last night, she didn't even get round to challenging Jeff about that, was too far out at sea, drowning in his ability to argue better than her, to win.

But winning an argument is not the same as being right, is it?

Throwing the journal to one side, she makes herself get up again.

She needs to find her phone. She needs to message Lizzie.

CHAPTER 15

Lizzie, hey!

Kate tries to nutshell everything that has happened since she saw Coco Moss outside Bar Melitón, but the WhatsApp that follows is as long as a till receipt, then two till receipts. After the how-are-yous, she has to recount the first sighting of Coco, the 'chance' encounter, the 'casual' invitation to the villa. She does not admit to how overawed she felt, nor how she went and bought the same dress and trailed around town in the blistering heat, nor indeed to her feelings of somehow having bribed this woman to socialise with them.

Some things you can't even tell your best friend.

Besides, this is merely the prologue. Finally, on to the second message now, she feels there is enough preamble to ask the question.

So I'm just wondering, did Jeff ever have some sort of fling with Coco Moss while I was in Spain? Did you see or hear anything? Or do you know if he knew her at all? Sorry. My mind's going off in all sorts of directions. I'm convinced they're hiding something. Maybe it's the heat, but I'm going a bit mad over here!

Pressing send, she feels a pang of nostalgia for her friend, who has been such a rock these thirty-odd years. It was Lizzie who encouraged her to start her own business. Bored at home and with Jeff keen for her to stick with her part-time secretarial job at Lou's primary until she reached secondary-school age, Kate had been making birthday cakes for Lou's friends for years. She always refused payment, wouldn't even accept enough to cover the ingredients – it was not, is not, a world in which anyone worries about the cost of living.

Oh, just buy me a coffee! she'd say, voice high, in the secret hope that this would allow her into the coffee-drinking clique, which, as it turned out, once she was in it, was not for her. It didn't matter; the cakes were still a way to fill the time, be creative, involve her daughter in something fun, at least more fun than sitting on the floor playing with Barbies.

Lou's circle grew up, grew out of that kind of birthday party. Kate baked cakes for a few of the siblings, but not as often. Payment became a bottle of wine, which she couldn't share with Jeff. Jeff was spending more and more time at the office, at the gym, at the golf course, and when Lou started secondary school, it was Lizzie who pointed out that even if Kate didn't need the money, as a highly educated woman she needed more than a glorified hobby.

And she was right. An advert in the local glossy magazine, an interview in the local paper courtesy of one of the journalist mums, and the orders trickled in. At first Kate made the cakes herself, but soon she had to employ a professional – who was quicker and, frankly, better. The cakes looked more polished, less home-made. More word-of-mouth clients got in touch. In such a wealthy area, people were prepared to pay more than Kate would ever have thought. She hired premises, branched out into party catering, hired Vincent as a manager and slowly receded into a more directorial role: marketing, creating media content, a catalogue and a coherent price list. She was good at it, a good businesswoman, good at all the customer-facing stuff, the phone calls, the reassurances. Her clients were happy – delighted actually – and the company got, still has in fact, a lot of repeat business.

Birthdays, weddings, leaving dos, new babies... so many important moments to mark in this life. Such a shame Jeff has not been there for so many of them.

Lizzie is typing.

Kate waits.

Hi!

That's all. But Lizzie is still typing. She does this – flurries of short individual messages. This is because she is never sure of finishing what she wants to say without one of the kids needing something from her. Sometimes the whole thread stops for hours at a time, reprised later when the crisis – and by crisis, she means one of them needing a drink or a snack or their bum wiped – is over.

The second message lands.

No, Jeff did NOT have a fling with Coco Moss!!! No way!

Kate's outbreath is a receding tide, clawing at pebbles on the shore. Lizzie is still typing. The third message appears with a soft *ting*.

He was probably just shocked, that's all. I mean, that's like inviting Claudia Schiffer or something. Don't start overthinking. You know what you're like. How is he now?

He's out, Kate replies. *We had a bit of a fight last night. I drank too much and now I feel like 10 lb of shite in a 5 lb bag. Deep shame.*

Lizzie posts a laughing emoji, followed by, *You're on holiday, you're allowed a glass of wine. Just get to the beach and forget about it. Jeff will have. You know what he's like.*

OK, Kate replies. *Thanks, doll. Xxx*

She throws her phone onto the coffee table and sighs. Jeff will have forgotten about it. Will he? *You know what he's like.*

Does she? She did. When they were first together, she did. Then when she got back from Spain, she took the change in him, his reasons for it, at face value. Why wouldn't she have done? They were always so open with one another. His conversion course was intense, then once she finished uni and went to join him in Manchester, the internship was even worse. She never saw him. His time was not his own. The hours were killing him. She tried to reason with him, but he insisted it was only going to be like this at the start, until he proved himself; that he'd soon move to something less life-suctioning.

So she waited for another year. Two. Five. She was twenty-seven. They got married. She wanted kids sooner rather than later. He said best to wait. He didn't have time. They left it, then, when he finally relented, she miscarried, miscarried again. Meanwhile she had taken a job at a small independent wine company, liaising with French and Spanish vintners, travelling a little, expanding and deepening her love of wine. A love that, in her darker moments, she fears has become lust.

Where are you? she texts Jeff with, she realises, no expectation of a reply, and steels herself to face the day alone.

Fifteen minutes later, in her new kaftan, worn with a fine leather belt and a swimming costume underneath – lesson learnt – she is putting on her new straw hat and heading out of the door. As she turns the key to double-lock it, her phone pings.

Lizzie.

Just remembered. Coco was at a Halloween party we went to in our final year. I think Jeff might have spoken to her then. We were all pretty wasted. Don't overthink. Xx

CHAPTER 16

JEFF

It is after 7 a.m. when he returns to the town. The main beach, Platja Gran, is still empty. He pulls his running vest over his head, unlaces and pulls off his trainers, puts his phone inside one of them, stuffs his socks in afterwards. There is no one about. Even the bar isn't open yet.

In his running shorts, he jogs over the black sand and into the sea, barely breaking stride before diving into the cool salt water. He closes his eyes against the sting, finds Coco in the blackness. Coco. Whose number he took from his wife's phone and texted last night before he went to sleep. She is a dream, a siren, calling him silently. Last night he convinced Kate – thinks he convinced her – that Coco meant nothing to him, that he disliked her even. But even now, years later, he cannot convince himself. There is no view, no moment, no amount of money that has the power to erase Coco Moss or what happened that night. That cold Halloween night.

By the time Lizzie has stopped fussing with Ben's impromptu zombie costume, Jeff is getting cold and impatient. The prospect of seeing Coco has begun to gnaw at him, a sensation he knows he has to ignore if he wants to even get through the door of that house.

The front garden – such as it is: three metal bins stuffed with plastic bags, some scrubby grass and a broken washing machine – is filled with a twenty-legged beast, thick smoke rising from its ten heads. Shadows in the windows, the throb of dance music. The party looks like it got going a while ago, all inhibitions long diluted by cheap booze and roll-ups spiced with crumbled hash. Inside it is hot and sticky, the sour smell of bodies sweating in poorly dried clothes, of old food, cigarettes, damp. In the living room, skeletons, wizards and monsters are dancing to 'She Sells Sanctuary' by The Cult, singing the chorus at the top of their voices.

Jeff scans the room, Lizzie and Ben all but forgotten. Where is Coco? Is she still here or has she already gone? Gone probably. That would be typical. The moment it becomes too popular, too full of plebs like him, she would move on to something better.

'Here.' Lizzie is pressing a chipped mug into his hand and pouring white wine into it.

'I'm driving,' he shouts into her ear.

'Thought you were going to leave the car.'

'I suppose. What is it?'

'Chardonnay. Warm. Classy.'

'Excellent.' He gulps the wine, smooth as paint stripper. He takes another gulp, another. Dutch courage. He'll just have one, enough to ease him in, then let it wear off so he can drive home. He has an essay to do tomorrow, due on Wednesday.

'You're playing catch-up,' Ben says, looking more than a little like Martin thingummyjig from Depeche Mode now that Lizzie has applied eyeliner to him too.

'Smile.' Lizzie points the camera at Jeff.

The white flash makes stars in his eyes.

'I'm going to explore,' she says and moves deeper into the house. With the camera round her neck, she looks like an investigative reporter, albeit one who has come to work dressed as a cat.

From the far side of the lounge, through a door that appears to lead onto a small side patio, emerges the familiar towering form of Andrew Richman. Head and shoulders above everyone else, he pushes his long fingers through his slick floppy hair, his eyelids hooded, his gaze glancing, reptilian. Jeff knows this look; has seen it flash past him many times on the rugby pitch. A large plastic joke bolt runs through Drew's long neck; a crude line of stitches has been drawn on the top right-hand corner of his wide forehead. A nod to fancy dress, but nothing that would ruin his superior-being good looks.

'Drew,' Jeff says, raising a hand in greeting. 'Hey. How's it—'

Drew pushes past, unseeing, unflinching; Jeff feels a blush rise hot and quick up his face.

'Awkward.' Ben is still at his elbow, clinging on like a limpet.

'Do you think they recognise us?' Jeff asks him. 'You know, secretly, but they just pretend they don't?'

Ben shrugs. 'There's a guy in my electrodynamics module never recognises me. When I say hello, he literally looks through me. I wouldn't mind, but he sits next to me every week.'

The door to the patio opens again. A pointy hat edges into the room. Ben is talking to Jeff about the next track, giving him the full history of the band. They're from Iceland. The lead singer is fit but nuts. Pretending to listen, Jeff tunes out, eyes fixed on the hat, which has halted at the far side. For some reason, he has the strong feeling it's her – Coco.

After a moment, a gap between the heads reveals a girl about her height. But the wrong hair, wrong face, wrong stance, wrong everything.

'I'm going to grab more drinks,' Ben says. 'Do you want anything?'

'Beer. Please no more wine. I dumped my carrier bag in the kitchen – there's some cans in there.'

'Coming up.'

Eyes still trained on the bodies moving in the hot, smoky room, Jeff senses Ben go. Dead or Alive is playing now. Most people are spinning round and round. Like a record, in fact.

And then she *is* there, impossible to miss, impossible to mistake for anyone else, so much so he wonders how he could ever have considered the earlier witch to be her. She's talking to Mia, who is dressed as a cat, though not in the way Lizzie is. Mia is wearing a black basque, stockings and stiletto heels. Her ears are made of furry fabric. Funny, Jeff thinks, how even in fancy dress, these guys are still cooler, sexier. But the thought passes quickly, edged out by Coco, who looks simply incredible. She has dyed half her hair white, the other half black. She is wearing thick black eye make-up, a black top covered in chains and zips, a leather miniskirt, ripped fishnet tights and Doc Marten boots. She turns to gesture at her friend, revealing Dalmatian tails hanging from her back pockets.

A punk Cruella de Vil then. Genius. That's what he could say, couldn't he? By way of introduction? *Punk Cruella de Vil, right? That's a brilliant idea.* But no. She would freeze him with a look that said she'd heard that line fifty times tonight.

But he will think of something. He must. In his costume, he is unrecognisable after all. He is different, and this difference will give him courage. He must talk to her tonight. If not tonight, then when? When will he ever get the chance again? One more beer. One more beer and he will make his move.

Jeff breaks the surface of the water, pushes it from his eyes, feels it run from his chest, the beat of the sun on his skin. He strides out and across the beach, feeling the power in his thighs, pushing back his hair with the flat of his hand. The cafés are opening up; a delivery van is dropping off fresh fruit and vegetables to the crêperie, a huge crate of oranges for the juicer. His Fitbit tells him it's 7.40, that he has run fifteen thousand steps and that he has covered just over ten kilometres. He sits down on the sand, pulls his phone from his trainer, stares at the text, the text he sent Coco last night, the text that is as yet unanswered.

We need to talk. J x

CHAPTER 17

COCO

Well, well, well. Well, well, well, well, well.

Jeff Barrett. Here, in Cadaqués, who'd have thought it? Honestly, I'm still reeling, and not just because of the almighty stunt your wife pulled last night. I nearly died when you walked into the kitchen. That is, once I'd recognised you in your new incarnation as a suave and sophisticated man of the world. You meanwhile looked like you actually *had* died, despite having aged about two years in thirty, you jammy bastard. The colour completely drained from your face, and you became so still, so very still, you looked fit for wheeling off to Madame Tussauds. I resisted the urge to get the hell out of there, pulled myself together. Thank God you weren't far behind. Cool in a crisis, both of us, aren't we, my darling?

We know that about one another at least.

What I can't fathom is why Kate didn't tell me who her husband was yesterday and ask me if I knew him. Perhaps the thought of us knowing one another was just so far-fetched, so utterly outside the realms of possibility, she didn't think it worth mentioning.

But we know different, don't we? If only she knew. If only

you did, come to think of it. Yes, even you, Jeff, have no idea what you did to me.

I find I'm deeply curious to know what she said after I left. I guess I'm hoping she laid into you, gave you a tongue-lashing to make your hair curl. It was what you deserved after all. I tried to sneak around the back so I could listen through the patio doors, but the side gate was like a fortress, so I went on my merry way, already talking to you in my head.

What the hell is going on?

Is that what the lovely Kate said? I bet that was the gist. All through the drinks, I could see she was itching to confront you – well, both of us. But humans are such polite creatures; God knows I've built most of my life on that premise. We don't cause a scene if we can help it, do we? Look at me. I didn't, all those years ago. And if she was harbouring a big old hand grenade of a question, she would have been terrified of the emotional shrapnel the answer might rain down. Few people can ask something like that outright. Most have to build up to it.

More than anything, I think, no one wishes to appear foolish. If Kate had dared to ask what had passed between us in that moment and we had come up with something plausible or simply said, *sorry, we have no idea what you mean*, then where would she have been? My feeling is you've made enough of a fool of her already over the years, though I could be wrong. God knows you made a fool of me. But honestly, I could barely stand to watch how invested she was in the evening going well while you sulked in the corner making cutting remarks like a petulant teenager.

Was that designed to throw her off the scent? I'm not sure it worked, there being a thin line between love and hate and all that. But bless her. Bless lovely Kate! At heart, she is a true Brit, a real *I'm sorry, my toe seems to be under your boot* kind of gal. We think this stoicism *in extremis* is the preserve of the aristocracy, but even those of modest descent can have a leg hanging off and they still think it better to stem the bleeding with one hand, pour the drinks with the other and make small talk until the guest has left before they call an ambulance.

I quite admire her actually. The way she clung on. Dear, dear Kate.

We were all clinging on, I think. I know I was.

I must admit to having gained a small insight into your lives during my little visit. I like to know who I'm dealing with, especially when there's history. So when I popped to the loo, I went upstairs. I was desperately curious for a through-the-keyhole-style gander. That amazing master bedroom with the balcony overlooking the bay, my God, Jeff! I could so see myself clasping those wrought-iron railings as if on the prow of the *Titanic*, silk robe billowing in the light breeze, you behind me, circling my waist. We would look divine, I thought, staring wistfully at the sun setting over the bay.

As it was, I was more interested in finding out a little more about you both. You'd already showed me so much more than you realised. What is it about couples that makes them think their relationship isn't as plain as glass? A stranger like me can literally wander in and, after two seconds, know things you don't even know about yourselves.

Then there are the more private things: you fold your boxers and put them neatly under your pillow; her long flowery nightdress hangs on the back of the en-suite door, so I'm guessing she's shy, perhaps keeps it there so as not to scuttle naked across the bedroom. What else? Electric toothbrushes naturally. Whitening toothpaste. Floss. Expensive eau de toilette for him and her. She reads from a Kindle, you a paperback – John Grisham; I'm guessing you don't care to access worlds beyond your own. And all this I gleaned *before* I found Kate's journal. Heavens, now there's a book that makes for sad reading. Gratifyingly, it is as I suspected: she still has the most almighty crush on me. Really, it is heart-wrenching. Do you know she actually went as far as imagining your daughter marrying one of my boys?

But back to you, darling. You. You were always handsome, but now you're quite the revelation with your lovely new haircut and that sexy curated stubble. And the clothes. Can't remember you being such a fine dresser back then, my love, but then I wouldn't, would I? You weren't exactly in normal attire when we met, were you, and boy, am I kicking myself now. If only I'd thought ahead all those years ago. If only I'd seen through the disguise to the *potential*. If only you hadn't ruined me. As it was, I married a rich shitball, divorced him when the twins were eleven, and life has been pretty hand-to-mouth ever since.

I suppose I'm lucky; the settlement was extremely generous. But after I'd swelled up to twice my normal size carrying his twins, not to mention the fourteen hours in labour, it was only right he should pay over the odds. Not like he was going to bring them up, was it? I'm simply not cut out for an average life, never have been. It's the creative temperament, you see. And now, of course, Troy is very successful, so while money isn't exactly pouring down on us, there's enough of a shower to keep the roses watered, as it were.

But that night, that long-ago night, I saw you as nothing more than a pretty consolation trinket on a very shitty evening, when all the time you were an investment piece. I should have used what happened between us not as a disaster but a down-payment, a bond. Shares in you were so cheap back then. I could have bought the whole company. When I think of the life I could have lived...

Still, all is not lost. From what I've seen this evening, your marriage is... how shall I put this... dead in the water. The way you speak to her! You don't love her, do you? And she... she loves you, I think, but all that passive aggression! The classic preserve of the angry disempowered. And she is one angry, disempowered lady.

I might be wrong. First impressions and all that. But I'm usually pretty accurate.

On the way home last night, I really noticed how steep the lanes are here. Drew's villa is ten minutes' walk further up, and it doesn't even have a pool. Frankly, I'm flabbergasted to learn that I live in a world where Jeff Barrett has a better second home than Drew Richman.

But seriously, Jeff, I would never in a million years put you with a woman like Kate – maybe then, but not now. The thing is, you see, I *did* know her back then. Not that I knew her name until yesterday. But I had no idea that night that you two were an item, and now I know why – she was on her year abroad! And you, you naughty boy – while the Kat's away, eh?

Did you know your missus used to hang around the Old Bar pretending to read Lorca with her Diet Coke and her home-made sandwiches, eavesdropping on us? From time to time, she'd look up, hoping to catch a smile, waiting for crumbs from our table. She even used to chip in sometimes – if someone said something loud or made a joke – completely uninvited. It was so embarrassing, so transparent. We'd smile weakly at her and try not to make eye contact until she gave up and sank her face back into her book, cheeks blushing that deep, rashy pink she goes when she's hot or embarrassed. I wonder if she told you any of it, how she perceived what she was doing back then. When I get to know you better, I'll ask you. Because that's what's going to happen, I've decided: I'm going to be getting to know both of you *a lot* better. Given what I saw tonight, I don't think it'll take much to shove a wedge into that gaping crack in your marriage. To coin sexist drivers everywhere, *you could get a bus through that, love.* After what you did to me, it's only fair. You owe me.

Time to give you a call, I think.

CHAPTER 18

JEFF

Jeff looks up at the wide ocean, tries to enjoy the cool water drying on his skin, tries to focus on this small physical sensation and not let himself think of her, of his text, of the fact that she must have read it, read it and not responded. Maybe she didn't see it last night. Maybe she's still asleep. Maybe...

His phone is buzzing in his hand. Kate, he thinks. Awoken from her stupor. He organises his face into a smile so that it might translate in his voice. It is not her fault. None of this is her fault, and he can't afford to forget it.

But it isn't Kate. It's Coco.

His throat blocks. He swipes. In wonder, he places the phone to his ear.

'Coco?'

'Where are you?' Her voice is low, husky, as if she has just woken up.

'I'm on the main beach. I just went for a—'

'Are you alone?'

'Yes.'

'Don't move. I'll be there in ten.'

In his chest, what feels like a ball of hot gas flares. Coco

Moss has just called him. Thirty years too late, but she has called him, and now the memory of her is entwined with the reality and it is rolling towards him, gathering a momentum he is not sure he can withstand.

Shit.

Breath quickening, he considers his running vest. It will stink. It might. He takes it to the sea and rinses it, wrings out the excess seawater, slaps it across his shoulder. Tells himself it's too wet to put on but knows that this is not the reason, that really what he wants is for Coco to see his physique, to see it and feel desire. That he can get away with meeting her half undressed like this is because it is possible to stand on a beach with his chest exposed and not look like an exhibitionist or like he's trying to impress someone in the most pathetic way. Context is everything. Yes, he thinks, it is possible to be this much of a prick and know you are all at the same time. He feels at a strange distance from himself, yet intensely inside himself at the same time. His heart knocks, his skin tingles.

Here he is then, inside and outside himself. It is the same sense he had when he spoke to Coco that night, when he told himself he wanted only to talk to her, that he wasn't doing anything wrong, knowing all the time that he was lying to no one but himself. Because what he wanted was much more than conversation; he had already made love to her countless times in his mind, sometimes while he was with Kate. He had pushed down the shame of that, resolved never to do it again, only to relapse. But it was more again, more than love or the making of it, the thinking about the making of it; he feared, genuinely, that even having her in that way wouldn't be enough, that he wanted Coco Moss to a degree that was fathomless, insatiable and utterly terrifying. What he wanted was to somehow *ingest* her, until she occupied his every cell, ran in his veins, pumped his heart with her beautiful bloodied hands.

He felt grubby then. He feels grubby now. He is waiting for

a woman whose effect on him is beyond his control. He knows that this is what he is doing, and that he could leave, and that he will not. He has chosen to wait here and meet her to discuss what they have already discussed: they haven't told anyone what happened that night; they have no intention of telling anyone. There is nothing left to say. There is no reason to meet.

And yet Coco Moss is on her way to him. And his feet are rooted in the black sand.

'Jeff.'

And like that, there she is. Her blonde hair is hidden by a large straw hat, her slim frame draped in a soft cotton dress, transparent enough for him to see that she is only wearing bikini bottoms. He suppresses a gasp. He just wants to talk to her, he tells himself, almost believing it. That's all. Clarify their position. He is still telling himself this as the word *Hi* leaves his mouth in a choked whisper.

Coco steps down onto the beach, glances left and right, fixes her blank insectile lenses on him. 'Where's Kate?'

She is lying too, he thinks. She knows Kate is not here.

'Still asleep.'

'Are you sure?' There. The merest acknowledgement that what they are doing is not innocent.

'She drank another bottle after you left. Passed out on the sofa.'

'Does she suspect anything?'

'She did, but I just said it was a shock to see you, that was all. I made out I was embarrassed she'd invited you when we didn't know you.'

'I don't know you. I don't know either of you.'

'I... I know that. I—'

'But you've changed. You've changed *a lot*.'

He breathes deeply, purposefully, making his chest expand,

his shoulders square, his waist thin. 'How so?' Is it possible he is smiling? That this flirtatious tone has come from his lips?

'You were such a skinny thing, but... not any more.' Her eyes travel the length of his torso, back to his face. Even behind her shades, her gaze is direct – he can feel the heat of it.

'I always played a lot of rugby,' he says. He grins. 'Student budget didn't run to supplements, I'm afraid, though I do seem to remember eating a lot of porridge from that scoop-and-weigh shop in the Merrion Centre.'

Even though it was his intention to make her laugh, he is still surprised when she does. He imagined she'd come here to tell him to stay the hell away from her and her family. But that's not what seems to be happening.

'I lived on Marlboro Lights and coffee, I think.' She laughs again and shakes her head. The laughter fades into a melancholy smile, the urgency of her phone call apparently forgotten.

'We were kids,' she adds quietly. 'Just kids.'

'We were.' He wonders if that was the preamble, if she will dare voice what they were to one another, what seeing each other again means. He waits.

'So, you and Kate,' she says instead, reaching forward and touching his fingers. 'Are you as horribly unhappy as you look?'

His eyes prick with shock. Recovering himself, he lets his fingertips slide over hers, manoeuvres them until he is holding her hand. With one clean dart she has pierced him, and he feels himself deflate with a kind of relief.

'You have no idea,' he says.

CHAPTER 19

KATE

It is only seconds since Lizzie messaged; Kate has just locked
the villa, literally just this second, phone held in the crook of
her neck, but now the phone rings out and Lizzie doesn't pick
up. Shit. For crying out loud. Kate could really have done with
talking to her. What did she mean, Jeff might have spoken to
Coco at that party? Spoken how? And why isn't Lizzie more
sure? How can she just drop a bomb like that then not be there?

Calm down, Kate. It was a student party, years ago. Lizzie
won't have been stuck to his side all night, monitoring his every
move, but she would know if something major had happened.
Even if she didn't see anything, she would have heard.

Kate messages – *Let me know when's a good time to call.
Really want to chat to you about that party* – and returns her
phone to her bag.

There is no sign of Jeff at the beach or in any of the cafés
near the plaza. It is after eleven. He could, she supposes, be
anywhere.

At Bar Melitón, she orders a cortado and a croissant and
takes a seat on the terrace in the shade of a large parasol. She
can see most of the main square from here. If Jeff were to jog

past, she would spot him immediately. It must be a long run this morning, else he's gone snorkelling or paddleboarding already.

The town is busy, heaving. Because of her intolerance to the heat, she has suggested to Jeff that they start coming here out of season. Now that Lou will be finishing school earlier in the summer, they are not confined to July and August as they once were. But Jeff always says he prefers it to be busy. He likes the hustle and bustle, and for it to be blisteringly hot. She suspects he likes to parade his body. He is one step short of patting his flat stomach and asking strangers to guess his age.

She is waiting for the coffee when she sees Coco walking from the direction of Platja del Ros to the left of town. She is about to wave, but to her absolute astonishment, Coco waves first. She. Waves. First. It is a wave of recognition, of affection even. Kate has not had to remind Coco who she is – which in that moment she realises is what she feared having to do.

With a flush of something like panic, she remembers Lizzie's text. Coco Moss was at a Halloween party in final year and Jeff was there too. They might have spoken. That's all Kate knows. Without talking to Lizzie, she can't know if Jeff actually did speak to Coco, and if he did, what could possibly have happened to make the two of them react as they did to the sight of one another. Jeff never even mentioned the party, which is odd, isn't it? Unless it was no big deal. Knowing Jeff, he probably left after an hour to do some assignment or other; whenever she spoke to him from Spain, he always said he wasn't going out much, that there was too much work. OK, so their phone contact was limited, but they did speak at least once a week.

The thought that he and Coco might have got together presses in, has been niggling at her since before she even messaged Lizzie, but now Coco is coming towards her and smiling quite openly. She wouldn't smile like that if she had history with Jeff, would she? No one is that brazen, surely.

'Kate! Hey!' Coco looks for once out of breath, flushed, a little sweaty even.

'Coco! Good to see you.' Kate is about to invite her to join her, but Coco is already sitting down.

'I might grab a coffee actually,' she says.

The waiter arrives with Kate's breakfast. Kate is outrageously glad of it – she's still feeling more than a little green around the gills – but now that Coco is here, she won't be able to inhale it quite so greedily. And she certainly won't be able to order a second croissant.

Coco orders a café con leche and a cinnamon roll in pretty passable Castilian.

'Do you speak Spanish?' Kate asks.

'I've been here enough times to manage the basics.'

'Your accent is really good.'

She gives a funny little bow. 'I suppose I was always a good mimic. At boarding school, it was my superpower. You need a superpower at boarding school.'

'How come?'

'To disarm the bullies, darling. I could impersonate most of the teachers to perfection. Make the bitches laugh into not terrorising me.'

Kate nods. 'I guess it was the same at my comprehensive. You either went big or kept your head down. I... I kept my head down. As did Jeff.'

The whole time she is speaking, she is aware of herself gauging Coco's reactions, assessing them for strangeness. But Coco is as natural as if they were just two new friends, happy and a little excited to see one another.

The waiter slides Coco's coffee and roll onto the table with a brusque nod. A second later, he is gone.

'So, hey, thanks so much for last night,' Coco says, her posh voice a slow drawl. 'Your villa is absolutely amazing. I love the way you've done it too.'

'Really? Aw, thanks.'

'You have a great eye.'

She can't mean it, Kate thinks. No way. But sod it. It feels so good to hear it from Coco Moss that she doesn't care if she means it or not. Nor, suddenly, does she care if Jeff did talk to her, flirt with her even, all those years ago. Well, she does, but not enough to get up and walk away. It was thirty sodding years ago, it obviously didn't go anywhere and they were kids. Kids!

'Where are the boys?' she asks.

Coco waves her hand. 'Oh, they've gone to a distant cove with their snorkels. They literally left at, like, 7 a.m. I couldn't be arsed, to be honest. I'm just going to chill and read my book.'

'Good idea.' Kate sips her coffee, tears off a chunk of croissant and puts it in her mouth. It is warm, fluffy, delicious. She wonders if she should invite Coco to hang out at her pool. They could have a cheeky G and T, giggle over the *Hola!* magazine.

Coco picks at her cinnamon roll, inserts a pinch of it into her mouth. For some reason, Kate has the impression she is studying her from behind her sunglasses. Her cup rises, tips, clanks back into the saucer. She unravels a glistening strip of sticky pastry. She doesn't look like she ever eats pastries. If she does, she's probably one of those people who can leave half on the plate.

'Can I ask you a question?' she says.

This has always struck Kate as the oddest thing to say. What is anyone supposed to answer? *No, you can't?*

'Sure,' she says simply, though her stomach has begun to churn.

'Are you and Jeff OK? I mean, it's none of my business, but I couldn't help noticing he doesn't... I mean, things seemed a little tense last night. Sorry if I'm overstepping, but you'd gone to all that trouble and... I don't know... he seemed a little off with you, that's all. Well, quite rude actually.'

It takes Kate a few seconds to realise her mouth is hanging

open. She closes it. Tears off some more croissant, puts it in her mouth, chews it slowly, delaying. What to reply? What on earth to reply? Coco has taken a sharp knife and inserted the point right into the heart of her life.

'He arrived about two seconds before you got there, that's all,' she manages. 'He's always doing that, leaving it until the last second. I was a bit cross.'

'Of course you were.' Coco shakes her head. 'That's fucking outrageous. No wonder you were pissed off.'

'I wasn't pissed off, just—'

'Well, I would've been. God, men are such pigs, aren't they? And I'm guessing you'd tidied up and lit those lovely little scented candles, and I bet you're the one who organised the booze and the snacks and everything.'

'Well, yes, but—'

'But what? Absolutely outrageous, darling. I'd have been livid.'

'H-He works hard,' Kate stammers. 'It's his holiday.'

'And it isn't your holiday too?'

Coco leans over and takes Kate's hand in hers. A pulse of electricity runs up Kate's arm. The heat of a blush climbs her neck, her face. It feels so wonderful to be touched – kindly, affectionately. At all. For one horrible moment, she fears she might burst into tears.

'I was the one who'd asked you to come,' she says, her voice shaky. 'I guess it was down to me.'

'Bollocks. Marriage is a team effort. You were doing something that was important to you. He should've shown some solidarity, a bit of support.'

Coco traces her fingertips up and down the inside of Kate's forearm. The gesture is far too intimate. Panic rises in Kate's chest, but she finds she cannot remove her arm. She doesn't want to appear uptight. But there's something else too. She doesn't want Coco to take her hand away. It is... She doesn't know what it is, only that her eyes have pricked with tears.

Coco stops, holds Kate's hand now in both of hers.

'You can talk to me, you know,' she says softly. 'I've been there. Boy, have I been there.'

No one, *no one* has spoken to Kate this way for a very long time. Not even Lizzie. Lizzie doesn't need to say anything like this – that they can share secrets is an unspoken understanding: trust, love, the safe space of long decades spent having each other's backs. So why hasn't Kate shared anything with her, anything real or painful, at least lately? For years, in fact? Where has that pain gone, that reality; where has she put it? And why, since she entered Jeff's world of golf clubs and ski chalets and drinks parties where no one *ever* drinks too much, no one ever dances, no one ever confides, hasn't she found a friend to really talk to?

'Thank you.' It is all she dares say. She is not at all confident that she won't start sobbing if she says anything more.

'I know we've only just met,' Coco goes on, 'but I think I know a fellow lonely soul when I see one.'

'Lonely? What do you mean?'

She rolls her hand, shakes her head. 'Troy is always, *always* practising, and the twins have all the conversational skills of a sports pro, i.e., zero, and women... well, women can be so buttoned up, don't you think? I've always got on so much better with men.'

'It's because they're jealous,' Kate blurts. 'The women, I mean.'

'I can't think why.'

Coco throws herself back in her chair. The contact is broken. The warm air cools on Kate's wrist.

'You're not serious?' she says, with a kind of alarm. 'You're... you're so cool. Literally every girl at uni wanted to be you, and all the guys fancied you. You can't not know that!' She laughs, is almost scoffing. 'That won't have changed. I bet the women you meet are consumed with jealousy. Or afraid maybe.'

'Afraid? Oh my God, why would anyone be afraid of me?' Coco laughs, as if the idea were amusing.

'You're a bit terrifying, you know. I almost didn't come up to you the other day. I had to pretend I'd bumped into you by mistake, but really I'd seen you hours before.'

'What?' Her hand flies to her chest. 'Oh my God, that's so sweet! You should have just come over. I'm not scary *at all*.'

She leans forward, takes Kate's hand in hers once again. Kate wills herself not to sweat, feels perspiration coursing down the sides of her body, her hair stuck to her head under the too large, too heavy hat she has bought because Coco Moss has one similar. She is pathetic. Worse than pathetic. But Coco is holding her hand. For some reason utterly mysterious to Kate, Coco Moss appears to want to be friends.

'I'm glad I did,' she says quietly and smiles.

'Me too. But you've got to stick up for yourself with that husband of yours, OK? Promise me. I think you've let him get away with far too much.' Coco sighs, cocks her head as if thinking. 'I know! Why don't you and I go on a girly night out together tonight? There's a couple of bars open late, and no one minds if you smoke; it's so freeing. I know a place that does wicked cocktails for practically nothing. We can score some illicit tobacco from the kiosk. What do you say?'

Kate feels herself falling. The whole scenario is unreal. Coco Moss has asked her out for a drink, just the two of them, like best buddies – a friend date!

'Oh my God, yes,' she hears herself say, too keenly, far too keenly, but what the hell. 'Yes, let's do that.'

Coco raises her coffee cup in a toast. 'Sod lousy men who don't pay us any attention!'

Kate laughs, raises hers to match. 'Yes! Sod lousy men!'

CHAPTER 20

JEFF

Jeff gets back to the villa and takes the stairs at a run, two at a time. He is under the shower a moment later, trembling with a kind of fear, scrubbing himself with foaming shower gel, fingers frantic over his ribs, his thighs, his shins. Even now, almost an hour later, he cannot believe what has just happened.

Coco Moss kissed him – kissed him deeply on the mouth and caressed the back of his neck – and there was no room, no room whatsoever for misinterpretation. He can still feel her nails on his skin, her lips on his, her tongue, oh God. What he has done is terrible. He is a bastard, an absolute bastard, but oh, he couldn't help it. He *knows* that he knew exactly what he was agreeing to when she held out her hand and said, *Let's walk*. It was just like before. She is everything he has tried to push from his mind. But he has not been able to forget her. Not work, not the gym, not the villa in this white idyll of a town have been enough. How ironic that it should be here, of all places, that he has lost himself to her once again. Because lost is what he is. Utterly, hopelessly lost.

'Let's walk.'

And he followed her like a dog. They headed left, along the

coastal road past Platja del Ros, the town dwindling behind them, up past the small harbour of tourist boats, the beach with the cool, shady bar that does good burgers. The backs of their hands touched, sent his blood beating through him.

He went after her over the rocks, silent, focused, to the quiet bay the name of which he can't remember. Watched the drape of her dress over her slim waist, the angles of her shoulder blades, their sloping rise to her neck. At every step he wondered if she was thinking the same as him: that they needed somewhere private, that the reason they were not speaking was because they were both fixed on finding a place with no one in it, that they were doing this because they were heading inexorably towards that kiss.

'I've wanted to do that since I saw you last night,' she said afterwards, fingers still in his hair.

He rested his hands on the perfect curve of her hip. The sheer fabric moved as easily as silk over her smooth skin. It took the most incredible restraint not to push her down to the sand and pull up her dress and cover the length of her with his mouth.

He pressed his forehead to hers, to protect himself. 'What now?'

'We have to be careful.'

'Yes. Kate can't know. She can't. It's not fair on her. She's done nothing wrong – she doesn't deserve this.'

She nodded in understanding. 'It's out of my control. I'm in love with you, Jeff.'

'Since yesterday?'

She shook her head. 'Since before.'

'Oh God, really?' A kind of terror struck him, the burning sense of something having gone very wrong. 'I had no idea. You... It... I had no idea it was the same for you. I can't believe it. But... you said we could never see each other again.'

'It was... complicated. You know it was.'

'I know. I know that. But still... Oh my God.'

All that time without her when he could have been with her. If only he'd known. But she didn't get in touch and neither did he; the years passed, became decades. Oh God.

Now, in the shower, he recalls that night again – again and again. There is no way to make it stop: that night in all its details. That night, that night, that fucking night.

A beer, another beer, another. The idea of driving home is a non-starter now. He'll have one more, then, if he still hasn't spoken to her, he'll give up and go, get to bed before one with only his self-loathing for company. He'll set the alarm for ten, get straight up, write the essay. He can do it under exam conditions, just make himself do it. It's not impossible. One more beer, that's all.

His cans have been stolen. It was stupid of him to leave them in the kitchen. He finds a bottle on the side – Beck's. Rinses it under the tap. He searches for the bottle opener. The table is a crowd of empties, mugs, cigarette butts floating in unspeakable dregs, torn fag packets, tortilla chips that turn out to be soaking wet with God only knows what. He grimaces. He is not drunk enough for wet tortilla chips, nowhere near dr—

'Why haven't I seen you before?'

He looks up to see who is speaking. Coco Moss is standing on the opposite side of the table, with that black-and-white pelt of hair, eyes dark and round as a Day of the Dead doll. Lolling from one hand is a bottle opener. Is she talking to him? Surely not.

She gestures with her free hand. 'Here.'

It takes him a short age to figure out that she means for him to pass her the bottle, not that she is passing him the opener.

'Oh,' he says. 'Sorry. Yeah. Cheers.'

She takes the bottle from him and opens it. The soft *pfst* is lost in Madonna's 'Holiday'. Behind Coco's two-tone head, people are dancing – wild movements and expressions just in case no one realises they're being ironic. She takes a swig of his beer and hands it back to him.

'I'm so wasted,' she says, but her eyes are clear and meet his with a directness that is disconcerting.

'Me too.'

Was that a declaration of intent, even then? A kind of contract? We are both wasted; we are giving ourselves permission for whatever might follow while taking no responsibility.

He wants to move towards her but cannot remember how to walk. Lizzie has gone... somewhere. Ben – anyone's guess. Dancing probably. Jeff wonders how long he's been on his own.

Coco has moved around the table – closer, closer, close. The ugliness of her hair makes her face even more beautiful somehow. His mind drifts towards an analogy but comes up with nothing. Maybe he should say something like *hey, your harsh haircut makes your beauty even more powerful,* no, *gives your beauty more...* no, *your hair,* no, shit, it's impossible. Men like him don't try to be original or bold. They're too grateful simply to find themselves in the conversation.

'Seriously,' she says, her vowels and consonants lush as a period drama on the BBC. 'Why haven't I seen you before? Are you in first year?'

'Final year. Law.' Instant regret. He has admitted to thinking about his future. He doubts Coco Moss thinks about her future.

But she doesn't scoff or roll her eyes, says only, 'Oh, that would explain it. But I must have seen you on campus. In the Union? Actually no, I can't have.' She pushes his shoulder – lightly but firmly – until he is facing her. She looks deeply into his eyes. 'I would have remembered.'

He laughs, a breathy, pathetic, nervous sound. 'How come you're on your own?'

She shrugs, her expression mildly appalled. 'Oh, Drew's girlfriend just had some fucking hissy fit on me and stormed out. She's such a drama queen.'

'Oh dear.' He makes a face, to show her he sympathises.

'Mia's gone after her, but I can't be bothered with it, to be honest. So frickin' dramatic.'

'Where's Drew?'

Another shrug. 'Probably snorting something in the loo. God knows.'

He waits for her to continue, perhaps elaborate on the argument, which sounds stressful, but she says nothing more.

'I like your hair.' He cannot think of a single other thing to say. 'Are you going to keep it like that? The black and white, I mean. It looks kind of cool. Like a yin and yang sort of thing.'

She grins and rubs the palm of her hand over the baby spikes. He imagines what that would feel like, for those soft bristles to brush against the palm of his hand. He would never dare.

He looks away, embarrassed, catches a glimpse of himself in the dark pane of the kitchen window. A shock: not himself but a vampire. He has forgotten he's in costume. He is unrecognisable; he remembers it now. Different. He is a guy who wears nail varnish and eyeliner. He is ancient, bloodthirsty, possibly aristocratic. Black Cherry fingernails. Count Dracula. Here to haunt the night hours and put his teeth to the long white necks of beautiful women.

'Can I do that?' He nods to her hand, still resting on her hair. 'I want to feel it.' He wonders if these are the most daring words he has ever uttered.

Again she grins, as if he's said something that has pleased her. 'Sure.'

Leaning towards him, she reaches for his wrist and guides his hand. He runs his palm over the warm, sweat-damp fuzz, back, back again to where, eyes closed, he can picture the gentle slope of her shoulders, the line that meets her slim nape, the perfect rounds of her ears flat against her lovely, lovely head.

The music stops. Suddenly aware of himself, of them both, he lifts his hand. His heart is beating fast. After a long few seconds, another song begins: a slow one.

'Uh-oh,' he says. 'Cheesy.'

But she pulls him by the hand and says, 'Let's dance.'

He steps out of the shower. Slowly the steam clears from the mirror, revealing his reflection: unclothed, no disguise. Thirty years ago and yesterday all at once, he was someone else, briefly. And now it is today, and he has kissed someone who is not his wife and agreed to go to her villa tomorrow morning where they can be alone. He will wait for her text. He will tell Kate he's going swimming or— Oh God, he will think of something, or actually he probably won't have to tell her anything because she is never awake when he leaves for his morning run. He will simply leave the villa and walk up to Coco. She will be waiting for him. She will fold him in her arms, and they will finish what they started on the quiet beach.

Two weeks, that's all. If Kate doesn't find out, she won't be hurt. It's only a fortnight. Twelve days really. Little more than a week. After that, he can go back to the before. He will find the strength to face his life and give Kate everything, everything she wants. If he can just have this one thing, this one exquisite fix, this one beautiful mistake.

CHAPTER 21

COCO

Thank God I told you to wait half an hour before you followed me from the beach. Oh, Jeff! We have to be so careful. Even so, my heart still plummeted to my belly when I saw Kate at the café on her own like a little lost soul. And she *is* lost – an abandoned kitten. Do you know she almost cried when I touched her? Seriously, I thought she was going to break down in tears. It made me feel so sad for her. You left her a long time ago, I think. We are not so different, your wife and I. Both of us disappointed in love, in life; both messed up by you, despite outward appearances to the contrary.

I know how to hide it better is all.

I joined her at the café, tried not to notice how pathetically delighted she was to see me sitting down at her table. Before you object, Jeff, you might want to consider what else I could have done. The best option when hiding something is to act as if you have nothing at all to hide. The very worst thing you can do is act differently. If you convince yourself you've done nothing underhand, it's possible, I've found, to believe you have not. It takes practice, but you can hold the belief firmly inside you until it becomes a kind of alternative truth. And if Kate was harbouring any suspicions about us, she didn't show it. I think I was pretty convincing. I usually am. As for having moments ago all but seduced her husband on the other beach and pretty much professed my undying love, that was easy to hide. It is as you said, Jeff: we don't know one another. We never did. And yet we are bonded together forever. I know you feel it too.

I must admit I am still wondering what I'm going to do. The way I see it, we *all* want something. Of the three of us, Kate almost has the upper hand in that it's harder to tell what it is she actually wants. Perhaps because she doesn't know it herself. Perhaps.

We chatted easily enough. Which was just as well because it meant she didn't notice you sneaking back to the villa via the lane behind Quiosco Morana. Last night I noticed that you never touched her. Not one brush of your hand over her shoulder, no affectionate pinch on her waist, no smile, no eye contact, nothing. No wonder she teared up when I took her hand in mine. All I did was stroke her arm and she just... melted. If her love life is as dry as a desert, as I suspect it is, then I was an oasis. She drank me in, Jeff.

You are both so easy. You are rich pickings. It was obvious from the moment I came to the villa – well, from the moment I'd got over the shock of seeing you, that is. And when she confessed – oh my God, so sweetly, like a little girl! – to being apprehensive about approaching me the other afternoon, my heart squeezed for her. It's as if she's stuck in a form of arrested development. I mean, I get that she had a girl crush on me at uni. She's not alone; a lot of girls did – but to admit it openly? Wow, I thought. Just wow. Talk about handing over the power.

I'm afraid you didn't come up smelling of roses. It was only right for me to point out your shortcomings. It will be less painful for her in the long run, won't it? I'm hoping she won't even need to find out about us to discover her own inner goddess and kick you into touch.

You're right about her, my darling.

She deserves better.

CHAPTER 22

KATE

By some miracle, Jeff is back at the villa, reading his John Grisham by the pool. He looks so fresh, as if he's just this second showered. How can anyone look so fresh in this stifling heat?

She throws her straw hat on the sofa and pushes back her hair. Heads out to the patio.

'Hey,' she says warily.

He looks up. 'Hey,' he says.

No mention of last night's fight, no mention of bringing her water and painkillers while she slept. The sight of him reminds her she must nudge Lizzie, find out what if anything went on at that party. Perhaps Coco will tell her tonight.

She steps outside. The sun on the pool is almost blinding, even in her sunglasses. Jeff smells of sun lotion. He is drinking San Pellegrino on ice with a slice of lemon, looking every inch the sophisticated success story on holiday. He could be in *Hola!*, except for the lizard sunbathing brazenly on the ground by his sunlounger, ruining the otherwise perfect picture. The lizard could be airbrushed out, she supposes. Everything can be airbrushed out.

'You OK?' he asks.

'Yeah,' she says. 'I bumped into Coco actually, and we had a quick coffee. We arranged to go out for a drink later, just the two of us. You don't mind, do you?'

His novel twitches; his brow furrows. It takes a couple of seconds for him to reply. 'With Coco? You're going for a drink with Coco?' He closes his novel, his expression perplexed.

'Is that so outlandish? Just a couple of drinks, maybe get a bite to eat, I imagine.'

He frowns. 'But... so... would I just hang out here? On my own?'

'Erm...' His question floors her momentarily. She hasn't thought for one second about what he might do. He's always doing stuff without her; she spends most of her life alone.

'I suppose,' she says. 'Is that a problem?'

His bottom lip pushes up. 'I just didn't think you'd particularly enjoyed last night, that's all. You were incredibly stressed.'

'But I told you why that was, and you told me there was nothing to be stressed about.' She pauses before adding, 'Anyway, I thought it would be nice to go for a girly drink. Not like I do much of that at home, is it?'

'But you don't even know her.'

'Well, no, but how does anyone get to know anyone? They go out for a drink, have a chat. That's how it works.'

'There's no need to be sarcastic.'

'Really? I kind of think there is.' Her voice trembles. Her chest tightens, heats. But Coco's words come to her: *You've got to stick up for yourself with that husband of yours, OK?* She pulls herself tall. 'Are you telling me I *can't* go? A bit psycho, don't you think?'

'Telling you you can't... What are you talking about?'

'You. Browbeating me with this *but what about me?* routine. Are you trying to shame me into not going? When do I ever do that to you?' She half laughs, nerves still racing through her, still making her voice unsteady.

'I'm only pointing out that you don't know her, that's all.'

'Well, that's not how it feels. I mean, you're completely absent at all hours, but you don't want me to organise something that might fill those hours.'

'But I'm not working tonight. I don't work when we're away. Not in the evenings.'

'So... what? I'm supposed to wait around until you become available? And if I have plans, I should drop them in service to your entertainment, is that it? And here's me thinking I was a person.' Her heart is beating hard. She can almost hear Coco backing her up, cheering her on.

'Oh, for God's sake.' He throws down his book, brings his legs over the side of the sunlounger, hands in fists at his hips. 'I thought you'd understood about people like her. We talked about this last night, didn't we? She's only interested in the money. She didn't look twice at you at uni, you know that. You used to follow her around like an acolyte.'

'I did not follow her around! I lived on the same corridor as her, that's all. I saw her and her friends sometimes in the Old Bar. If I said hello, it was only because it would have been weird not to.'

'Yes, but you were always so upset when she didn't say hello back. She didn't know who the hell you were! For Christ's sake, can't you remember how upset you used to get? You must have told her your name a hundred times, but it didn't register because she *didn't care*. You're not one of her kind. She doesn't care now either. She's just bored and lonely and...'

'I know how she feels,' Kate mutters, but Jeff presses on, as if he hasn't heard.

'... she'll probably get you to pay for all the drinks. You do know she's not paying for her villa, don't you?'

'You've already said that.' She draws herself up; her chest expands. 'You're being really... really... controlling actually.'

'Controlling?' His laugh is full of disbelief, disdain. 'I think that's a bit of an exaggeration, don't you? I just don't want to see you get hurt, that's all.'

'I don't care!' She is shouting, she realises. Her voice must have been rising all this time. She makes herself breathe.

'I'm a grown-up.' Her voice is lower, but still it shakes out of her like coins. 'I can make my own decisions. I don't ask you not to go sailing, do I? I don't tell you you can't play golf.'

'But that's during the day!'

'What? So there's a time to leave your spouse on their own for hours on end and a time not to? And the time you pick is OK and the time I pick isn't? Why? Because you picked it? God, you're ridiculous! All I ever do is wait for you to show up, and I just want...' She feels her eyes fill, blinks fast. 'I just want to go out and have a conversation with someone who isn't checking their work emails, OK? Who doesn't look bored by what I say, if they even listen at all. For God's sake, why is this such a big deal? I just want to go out with her for a couple of sodding drinks!'

He sighs, won't look at her. 'It's up to you.'

'Yes,' she says quietly, biting her bottom lip, calming herself by inflicting this small point of pain. 'It is.'

A horrid silence falls. The lizard on the tiles is not sunbathing; it is dead. Kate kicks at it, watches it spin and skitter under Jeff's sunlounger. Good, she thinks. Good.

'Actually, I might go out tomorrow evening then,' he says.

'Oh, that's mature. What's that, like a tit for tat? Who with?'

'It's just that last night Coco mentioned Troy was interested in some fitness training. I said I could take him out for a run.'

'When did she say that?'

'Erm, it was... it was when you were getting the drinks.'

'OK.' Kate tries not to roll her eyes, but it's difficult, it really is. 'And this is in the evening?'

He shrugs. 'Why not?'

Jeff never, ever runs in the evening. Hate fills her.

'You're pathetic,' she says, then turns on her heel and leaves him before she wraps her hands around his neck and throttles him.

Upstairs, she digs her journal from her dressing-table drawer and takes it down a floor to the spare room. Her heart is pounding. Half of her doesn't believe the argument she's just had, the argument last night, herself in those arguments, the way she stood her ground. It was horrible, absolutely horrible, but at the same time she feels exhilarated, fired up, alive. She never sticks up for herself like that! The way she feels now, if Jeff tried to come into this room, if he said one more word, she would push him backwards across the landing, back, back, and down those slatted stairs – just one decent shove, that's all it would take. An accident. She could call the police in tears. What would be the right Spanish? *Ayuda, ayuda* – she's pretty sure that's help, help – *mi hombre* – no, that's my man, bit primitive – *mi marido* – yes – *mi marido esta muerto*: my husband is dead.

She opens her journal.

I'm not sure why, she writes, *but seeing Coco after all these years has made me look at my life in a way I haven't dared to in a long, long time.*

She is aware that this act, this act of writing, feels like winding a ribbon around her hand to stop her thoughts from unspooling and flying away. She is securing her feelings, her rage, herself. She is wrapping her knuckles in silk.

It's true what Coco says: I have let Jeff off with too damn much over the years. These arguments are only happening now because I'm sticking up for myself for once. Usually, I would have cancelled this evening. But I didn't! It felt so good to fight back! Horrible too, of course, and sad. And perhaps he's right, perhaps I've asserted myself in the wrong way, at the wrong moment, and perhaps it is wrong to leave him alone when I know evenings are for us. But last year he went out with Felix and didn't get back until after ten, saying that Felix had invited him back to his place, and his wife had cooked the squid they'd caught, and his phone had died and he'd lost all track of time. I didn't argue. I can't believe that now. I was probably beyond tears, worry, anger. Now I'm looking back in the light of what Coco said and I'm thinking: what a mug. Have I minimised his selfishness over the years, the lack of consideration – manners, even? Why? Maybe it's about Lou. I won't have wanted to make a scene in front of her.

Well, Lou's not here now, is she?

She lays the journal to one side. Her stomach rumbles. Damn. It would be so much easier to conduct a decent strop if she weren't so hungry. A huff doesn't work if five minutes later you need to return to the kitchen for a sandwich.

It is after one. Two o'clock in Britain. Surely Lizzie has finished feeding her brood. Worth a try.

Thankfully she picks up. 'Kate!'

'Hi!'

'Sorry, I was going to ring, but Daisy got a dried pea stuck up her nose. Milly was out with her boyfriend, so I had to take three of them to A and E. Nightmare.'

Kate laughs. 'Oh my God.'

Lizzie laughs too. 'Exactly. Who said girls were easier? So yeah, sorry. They've just had their lunch, so hopefully they can do without me for five minutes. God, it's so hot here – is it hot with you?'

'No, it's freezing.'

'No way!'

'No, it's scorchio obviously. I feel like a melted candle. Anyway, I just wanted to ask, you know, about that party? The Halloween party?'

'Yeah, right. I mean, nothing to tell really. We went, me, Jeff and Ben. It was the night that student died. Do you remember that?'

Kate is nodding. 'That rings a vague bell.'

'Shocking. But anyway, Coco was defo there, and Drew and Mia and those guys. I seem to remember I got horribly drunk. But, not being funny, why don't you just ask him?'

'I can. I could. It's just... honestly, last night was so weird. If you'd been there, you'd know what I mean.'

Kate reiterates what she said on WhatsApp, in a little more detail, the way Coco and Jeff stared at one another in silent horror, the ensuing scene between her and Jeff once Coco had left, this morning's encounter with Coco.

'So, unbelievably, we ended up having coffee. Me and Coco Moss, can you imagine? All very nice but a bit... weird. I mean, if she and Jeff did meet at that party, if they did have, like, a snog – God, I feel too old to use that word, do you know what I mean?'

Lizzie laughs. 'French kiss?'

Kate snorts. 'That's even worse. No, but, whatever, if anything did happen with Coco, there's no way Jeff would've forgotten it, but she might have done. She even suggested going out for a drink later, and I don't think she'd do that if she had a guilty conscience, do you? But when I mentioned it to Jeff, he got all weird. Like he disapproved, saying I had to keep away from people like her.' She sighs. 'I mean, he's never keen on me doing things without him, but—'

'What do you mean, never keen?'

'I just... He just likes me to be around, you know? I think he sees me like a... like a backdrop. Like a chair or something. Like if I wasn't there and he sat down, he'd be shocked to find himself on the floor, do you know what I mean?'

Lizzie is giggling, but Kate presses on; she wasn't actually joking. 'I think I've managed to become someone who's there for him to drop and pick up when it suits him. He works *so much* of the time. Honestly. It's every evening, weekends, sometimes all weekend, and then if he's not at work, he's at the gym, and then on holiday he leaves the villa before I'm awake to do these long runs, and half the time I have no idea where he is and then he just rocks up and asks what's for lunch. I mean, I probably deserve it—'

'Don't say that.'

'But I've colluded in it, haven't I? I mean, I *am* always here. There *is* always lunch, dinner, clean underwear, et cetera. I've done that.'

'He can't help working long hours, doll.'

'I know. I know he works hard, but...'

But what does she know? Nothing. Nothing is clear. Jeff works hard, but so does she. The fact that he takes himself off fishing or jet-skiing is just part of what their holidays have become over the years. Kate wakes up later because she likes a drink in the evenings on holiday – a little drink to wind down, take the edge off. For the last sixteen years, Lou has been with them, and Kate has always been happy to hang back and build sandcastles with her, take her for ice cream, mooch round the boutiques, read under an umbrella while Lou sunbathed.

'I do remember a bit about that night though,' Lizzie is saying, possibly an attempt to change the subject. 'I've been thinking about it all morning. Jeff was dressed as Dracula. I painted his nails and put eyeliner on him.'

'Wait, what?' Kate reels. 'Jeff wore eyeliner?'

Lizzie laughs. 'Yep! He looked amazing.'

'And nail varnish?'

'Yep. Dark burgundy, if I remember rightly.'

'What the hell? Why has he never mentioned this? My Jeff? Super-straight, serious, teetotaller Jeff?'

Surely he would have mentioned it during one of their weekly phone calls if he'd gone out wearing make-up? There's no way he wouldn't have told her about it, no way.

So why didn't he?

'Kate? Kate, are you still there?'

'Sorry, yeah,' Kate says, resurfacing. 'I'm just shocked, you know? And did you guys come back together?'

'I think that was the time I puked on Ben's shoes and he had to take me home. So no, I don't think so. It's such a long time ago, hon. So many parties. My memory's shot.'

In the background, a child's voice is calling *Mum* over and over again, like someone pressing repeatedly on an intercom.

'I'll let you go,' Kate says. 'But if you remember anything else, can you tell me?'

'Just ask him. There'll be a perfectly good reason, I guarantee it. Maybe he isn't even being weird. Maybe he's just a bit put out that you're doing something without him for a change. Sounds like you need to take some power back, my love. But he's just square old Jeff, you know? Ask him.'

Downstairs, the front door bangs. Kate listens out, breath held in her chest.

'Kate?' Lizzie says. 'You still there?'

'Sorry. Just heard the door slam. I think he's stormed off, probably gone for a big sulk somewhere. Probably to get some lunch!' She giggles.

'Oh dear.' Lizzie giggles too.

'I think I'll keep it to myself for the moment,' Kate says into the pause that follows. 'It feels like too big a thing to ask; like, if I ask, I'm basically accusing him of lying, aren't I? Because he said it was nothing.'

Her mouth fills with saliva, a sick feeling in her stomach. Just the thought of Jeff flirting with Coco all those years ago is enough, the thought of asking him even worse: another no-win predicament.

'If that's what your gut's telling you...'

'I'll see what Coco says later. Ply her with drink, try and find a way of mentioning the Halloween party and see how she reacts.'

'OK. If that's what you think.'

Kate closes the call. Lizzie has been as supportive as ever. If she's telling Kate to be honest with Jeff, it's probably the right advice. But what Kate couldn't say even to Lizzie is that she's not sure she trusts Jeff at all right now, and it feels new and shocking and just... awful. For all the loneliness over the years, she has never felt a lack of trust. Plus, she told Lizzie she's going out with Coco to find out about that night, but that's not the whole truth either. There's another, darker, almost humiliating reason she can only barely admit to herself.

Fascination.

CHAPTER 23

COCO

She really had rattled your cage, hadn't she, old KateKatieKitty-KatKatherine? As had I, I admit. I knew when I saw your text that my new friend had got home and announced our little tête-à-tête plan for this evening, and I knew how freaked you'd be. You really don't know how to have fun, do you? You're so dependent on your moral compass, you get the heebie-jeebies when your ship veers even a little into uncharted territory. But nothing is ever discovered by sticking to the course, and it's not like we're doing anyone any harm, is it? Not yet at least.

That text!

Where are you? I need to see you NOW.

Those capital letters! Very masterful, I must say. Quite exciting, if I'm honest, although I'm very glad I hadn't yet given you the address of Drew's villa; you might have come stomping up the hill and battered on the door like Heathcliff or some such. As it was, when my phone dinged, I grabbed it and quickly switched it to silent, not that anyone took any notice. The boys were on their Xboxes as usual and Troy was in head-phones, busy recording something in the bedroom, so I just left them to it and texted you on the way out.

Bar Boia in 15 mins?

When I entered the bar, you stood up like a perfect gent. But it wasn't manners, was it? You were beside yourself, darling. Spoiling for a fight you couldn't have because we were in full view. As we sat down, you leant towards me so that no one would hear and hissed through your lovely, slightly too-white teeth: 'What the hell do you think you're playing at, taking Kate out for a drink?'

'Gosh,' I replied. 'Can I at least order my coffee?'

Your jaw flexed. Your eyes boiled. Such rage, Jeff! Such. Rage.

Your espresso cup was empty. You didn't want anything else. I ordered a mint cordial, almost questioned the wisdom of you having had even one coffee. You were *jangling*.

'What the hell, Coco?' A fleck of your spit landed on my cheek.

My feigned mild shock became affectionate bemusement. I wiped my cheek clean with my fingertips. 'I thought you'd like the idea.'

'*What?*' How narrow your eyes go when you're cross – they're like little slits! 'What are you even saying?'

My cordial arrived, lurid green like something from a cartoon lab. We both sat back in our chairs. Your chest went up and down, up and down. The waiter left us to it, probably glad to escape the thin air.

'Look,' I said, 'it's no good me going all cool on Kate, is it? She'll immediately wonder why, and under the circumstances, that's not good. The friendlier I am towards her, the more chance we have of... being together. You and me, I mean. If she trusts me, she'll trust you, no? And if she gets a pass to go out, you can ask for the same. Sounds like you're out a lot of the day anyway. I think she's used to being abandoned.'

'I don't abandon her! I just like to be active, that's all. Kate likes to read. She's happy.'

'Do you actually think that or is it what you tell yourself?'

Your nostrils flared like a dragon's. I half expected fire to come out.

'There's really no need to be so angry,' I said calmly. 'I'll go out with Kate tonight. I'll get her drunk so she'll sleep late tomorrow morning. By the end of the evening, we'll be besties. If she has any residual suspicions, I'll put them to bed, tuck them in and kiss their fevered little brows goodnight. And tomorrow, I'll send the boys to Sa Conca or somewhere and you can come over, OK? Leave a little note to tell Kate you're going snorkelling or whatever it is you normally do. No note if you don't usually, yes? OK, darling?'

You pressed a scratchy bar napkin with all the absorbency of acetate to your forehead. When you looked at me, your eyes had mellowed a little.

'I just think it's risky,' you said, still simmering. 'What if you admit to... something?'

I had to laugh. 'Oh my God, shush now. I never admit to *anything.*'

CHAPTER 24

KATE

At 7 p.m., Kate waits on the bustling street outside Bar Casino. The blue day is falling pink over the sea; the water winks with artificial light from the countless restaurants and bars. On the air floats the aroma of cigarettes, garlic, fried fish, citrus cologne. Squeaky-clean tourists stroll along the seafront in their bright evening wear, stop beachside for a leisurely *caña*, the dinky glasses of lager you can drink even at ten in the morning without anyone batting an eyelid. They link arms, point at things, no more on their minds than where and what to eat.

Kate wonders if Coco will be late, what she'll be wearing, if she'll arrive scruffy like she did last night. Will she be as affectionate as she was earlier today or will the whole idea of this nascent friendship be boring her already? Perhaps she'll have forgotten the arrangement entirely, whereas Kate has thought about nothing but this evening since their triumphant toast this morning – *Sod lousy men!* Now, waiting and alone, she's not at all sure she has it in her to ask Coco about the Halloween party after all. It was so long ago; she risks looking paranoid, needy, insecure. Besides, if there's nothing in it, she'll kill off the friendship before it has begun.

And she's waited for it for over thirty years.

At 7.10, there's still no sign of her. After the phone call with Lizzie, Kate had steeled herself to ask Jeff directly about the Halloween party. But by 6.30, he still hadn't returned from his strop, and her determination gave way to dismay, then to a rather unpleasant draining-away of respect. What a baby, she thought. What a pathetic, point-scoring child. It didn't escape her that forty-eight hours ago, she would've been crushed. She would have ended up texting him an apology, asked him to please reply, to not leave it like this. Instead, she scribbled a quick note to say that there was some lasagne in the fridge, that she'd see him later.

Sounds like you need to take some power back, Lizzie said.

You've got to stick up for yourself with that husband of yours, Coco said.

If Coco is on the same page as Lizzie, she must be a good egg.

Kate pulls at her simple Max Mara maxi dress – a bright fuchsia she wouldn't dream of wearing back home but which feels perfectly acceptable on holiday and on this new, braver version of herself. Her new wedge sandals have already started to rub; she wanted to be as tall as Coco but realises now she should have worn her old Havaianas flip-flops, which is what Coco would have worn with this dress. She once read in a fashion column in *Grazia* that getting fashion right is like making a good sandwich. For a sandwich you need a combination of fat and acid – cheese and tomato, ham and pickle, brie and cranberry. With clothes, it's the same apparently: formal combines best with casual – dress and trainers, boiler suit and heels, maxi and flip-flops.

Why didn't she remember this? There's always something she gets wrong.

Keen to spot Coco before Coco spots her, she glances about her. No sign. It's 7.16. Coco's not coming. She has forgotten.

Kate promises herself that if Coco doesn't arrive by twenty past, she will go.

At 7.19, the familiar shag of bleached hair bobs towards her along the main street. Coco is wearing a midnight-blue strapless dress that is, to Kate's wild joy, a maxi like her own. Over one bony shoulder a faded denim jacket hangs from her forefinger. Of course. Coco will never even have read that article; she will have just known.

'Hi!' Kate waves from the elbow so as not to dislodge her pashmina.

'Hey!' Coco looks not just pleased but *delighted* to see her, bounding over and pulling her into an unexpected hug, which she holds for a little too long.

It is Kate who breaks the embrace, fearing the menopausal heat she can feel rising inside her like lava.

'Hot pink,' Coco says approvingly. 'I *love* hot pink.'

'Thanks.' Hot pink, Kate thinks. Not fuchsia. Hot pink is cool. Fuchsia is not.

'Shall we grab a drink here first?' Coco casts about for a possible seat.

'Sure. I'll get them What do you want?'

'Just, like, a San Miguel or Peroni or something. Cheers. I'll bag us a table – there's one over there.'

She disappears off across the road towards the round silvery tables that crowd the bulge of the land's edge. The road itself is choked with bodies – waiters battle through, trays high above the heads, their faces stern with concentration. A dusty green Fiat Panda tries to pass – a fool's errand.

When Kate looks back to where Coco is, she sees an elderly lady walking slowly through the tables. On the roadside, her husband hovers with two small glasses of what might be fino. He is possibly unsteady on his feet, Kate thinks, not wanting to make a trip in vain. Meanwhile, Coco and the old woman are both heading for the same table, the only one free.

As Kate watches, Coco glances up at the old woman. A split second later, she throws her jacket over several heads towards the free table. It lands on one of the empty chairs. The lady startles, stops. Coco smiles widely at her, shrugging cutely, her expression a kind of *whoops, sorry*. By now she is sitting down, already arranging her jacket over the back of the chair. The elderly lady is rooted to the spot; mild bewilderment crosses her face before she frowns, turns and walks back towards her husband, shaking her head.

Unsure what to make of what she's just seen but fighting off an appalled feeling, Kate approaches a waiter, who tells her gruffly to order from the table. A little embarrassed, she makes her way towards Coco, eyes averted from the elderly couple, who are now strolling to the next bar with painstaking pin-steps, arm in arm for support.

As Kate approaches, she notices two guys appraising Coco, quite openly, before exchanging an approving glance. Already rolling a cigarette, Coco pretends not to notice but looks about her constantly with a kind of continual twitching motion. There is power in being so attractive, Kate thinks. And Coco knows she has it. That move with the denim jacket, the killer instinct disguised as a *silly me* routine, is a result of a lifetime learning to use it.

'Hey,' Coco says brightly, carefully placing one rolled cigarette on the table.

'Hey.' Kate sits at the table, the last before the drop to the sea. One chair leg astray is all it would take and you'd be over the side, snagged on the rocks that point like jagged jaws from beneath the shallows. For a split second, the image of Coco falling to her death flashes.

A waiter arrives. '*Sí?*'

Coco asks for *dos cervezas* without checking what Kate wants, but Kate is too swept along to change the order, can't think how to do that without coming across as uptight. She would have preferred a glass of rosé, but *wheat plays havoc with my flatulence* isn't exactly a cool thing to say, is it?

'I half expected you not to come,' Coco says. 'Thought maybe Jeff would play the *poor me* card.'

Kate almost startles. The remark is astonishingly accurate, as if Coco has installed CCTV in their villa.

'Not at all,' she says quickly. 'He's... I think he'll wander out and score some tapas, then take himself back to finish his book.' She has just said 'score'. Good grief, what is she, eighteen?

'Cool.'

The waiter returns. The beers slide onto the table, followed by the little metal disc, the bill under a clip. The waiter disappears to take orders, clear tables, before circling back. Kate brings out her credit card. Coco has made no move for her purse. A second later, Kate has pressed her card to the reader and both waiter and bill have vanished.

'So, are things OK with you guys?' Coco asks. 'You seemed pretty low earlier.'

'I'm fine. Everything's fine.' Kate can feel her face warming.

When Coco says nothing more, she rushes in to fill the space. 'I mean, we've been married a long time, you know?' She laughs, despite herself. 'We have our ups and downs, but there's something lovely about knowing we were each other's first choice. We'll always have that.' She laughs again, worried she came across as smug. 'That probably sounds really lame,' she adds.

But Coco is smiling. 'Not at all. It sounds lovely. So Jeff didn't have anyone else before? What about while you were together? He never... cheated?'

Kate feels her cheeks burn. Is this about the Halloween party? Is Coco calling her bluff?

And why is she, Kate, smiling like a fool?

Kate, no. Don't be so paranoid. She'd hardly ask if your

husband had ever cheated if he'd cheated with her*, would she?*
Get a grip.

'We'd both had relationships in sixth form,' Kate answers as calmly as she can. 'Teenage things, you know? I went out with a guy from Cedar House for about two minutes when I first got to uni, and I think Jeff might have got off with a girl at a Law Soc drinks in, like, the first week. But that was before we got together.'

'Sweet.' Coco takes a drink. 'I wish I'd met someone at uni. Think I would've saved myself a lot of heartache.'

'But you're happy now?'

She rolls her hand. 'I have no trouble *attracting* men; it's the keeping them that eludes me. But I'm too busy with the boys to worry about whether I'm happy or not, so it's all good.'

'And Troy?'

'Troy's great. But he's *always* practising. Especially at the moment. And that does leave me dangling sometimes.' She leans forward, pats Kate on the arm before handing her a cigarette. 'That's why I'm so glad I ran into you. Now. Tell me *everything* about yourself.'

CHAPTER 25

Four hours later, they have secured two low straw pouffes on the cobbles outside a backstreet bar called Brown Sugar. Kate is waiting for Coco to come back with the drinks, wondering vaguely how many they've had. Somewhere between a lot and too many. Around her, a mix of Castilian and Catalan bubbles up into the night, the odd smattering of pidgin English, an occasional burst of German. Smoke hangs. The night is still so warm, infused with tobacco, perfume, incense. Inside the bar, balanced on top of a tall cupboard, a guitarist with long grey hair tied in a ponytail plays jazz-infused flamenco. In all the years she's been coming to Cadaqués, Kate has never been to this place. It is Coco, of course, who discovered it, discovered it three years ago, the very first time she came.

'One margarida for ma ladeee.' Coco slurs a little as she bends to hand it to Kate, salt glittering at the glass's edge. 'Courtesy of Troy's credit card, which I may or may not have lifted from the pocket of his shorts.' She chuckles.

'Cheers.' Kate raises her glass.

'Cheers.' Coco mirrors her, sitting down but missing the

pouffe and landing on the cobbles. Her drink splashes over the front of her dress. She bursts into a fit of helpless giggles, which sets Kate off. Through tears of hilarity, Kate watches as Coco makes great work of sliding her bottom up onto the cushion. Her eyelids are half closed. Kate has the impression she herself is not as drunk as Coco. She feels clear-headed in fact, clearer than an hour ago, has possibly drunk herself sober.

'Glorious temperature,' she says, once Coco has achieved sitting position, pushing her hand into her hair. 'The nights here make the purgatory of the days worthwhile, don't you think?'

'You look good,' Coco replies apropos of nothing. 'You look good with your hair mussed up a bit like that.' She reaches over and pushes her own hand into Kate's hair, her fingernails scratching softly against her scalp, before leaning back, a lazy smile wide on her perfect mouth. 'Yeah. Looks better like that.'

'Thanks.' Kate can still feel the sensation of Coco's fingertips on her scalp.

Coco is rolling yet another cigarette from the packet of tobacco she claims to have bought only for this evening. She doesn't smoke, she has said, several times. Not any more. They haven't eaten anything beyond crisps and a few olives. They have talked a little about the old days, a lot about Kate's life. Coco has been surprisingly curious. It has been flattering having someone ask her so many questions. When she goes out with Jeff to one of his tedious client events, she often finds herself almost interrogating his colleagues, business associates, their spouses. In the absence of anyone enquiring what she does, asking question after question is the only way to keep the conversation afloat. On the last drink before this one – or maybe it was the one before – she told Coco all about how she and Jeff got together, how they got married, how eventually they managed to have their beloved Lou.

'I'm glad Jeff and I were friends for so long,' she says now, returning to her theme with the earnestness of the truly sozzled. 'Before, you know? It's important to be good friends so that when the passion dies, you've still got something. We were best friends really before we became... you know, boyfriend and girl-friend or whatever.'

'Lovers, you mean,' Coco corrects, and Kate feels herself blush. Why does she find this stuff so embarrassing? She's not a child. 'But he's not home much, you said?'

'Long hours,' she says, nodding. 'Then there's his fitness, his golf. He missed Lou's birth actually. Had an important meeting.'

The last two words she has said in a silly bloke voice. God, her head weighs a ton. She's amazed it hasn't dropped into her lap, which would be terrible, although, she supposes, at least then she could carry it home like a bowling ball, which, frankly, would be easier than trying to hold it upright on her neck. She imagines her neck thin as a golf tee, her head the white golf ball smiling inanely as the club swings towards it. A private titter escapes her.

'I'll tell you a secret.' She pushes her finger to her lips and leans so far forward her nose almost touches Coco's. 'His friends are soooo boring, shh. I'm not really a corporate kind of person, you see. I do run my own business, but... not... not like that.' Her forefinger is up in the air; she studies it a moment.

'That was the cakes, right?' Coco is rolling another cigarette, the first a neat white line next to her drink. 'Sounds pretty impressive to me. I mean, you literally make profit from kind-ness and sugar, as far as I can tell.'

Their eyes meet. Coco is smiling at her warmly, her expres-sion intense, direct. *What is it about this woman*, Kate thinks, *that makes me want to cry?*

'Kindness and sugar,' she says, breaking Coco's gaze before it breaks her. 'That's lovely. That's the loveliest thing anyone's ever said about my business. Or me.'

She presses the flat of her hand to her mouth a moment. She is talking too much. She has been talking too much all evening. She's like a tap that's been stuck fast for years; now that it's been wrenched open, the water is just pouring out, and no one can shut the damn thing off.

Coco's eyelids are closing. No wonder. Probably bored to death.

'What is it you do?' Kate asks. 'You never said. I did ask, didn't I? Before. But I can't remember if you—'

'I'm a painter,' Coco says. 'An artist.' She giggles. 'I don't paint houses.'

'An artist? That's so cool. Have you got any photos of your work?'

Coco picks up her phone and, with much grunting and swearing, shuffles across the cobbles until she is sitting next to Kate. She flicks through some images of bright, tasteful abstracts, her forearm resting on Kate's thigh.

'I sell them to rich women who don't know their own taste,' she says.

Despite the fug of alcohol, Kate cringes inwardly.

'Ah,' she says. 'That would be me.'

'Don't be silly,' Coco says. A moment later, her head is in Kate's lap.

'We are so drunk,' Kate whispers, lifting up a lock of Coco's hair with her forefinger and letting it fall. 'We are so goddam deerrrrunk.'

Coco has closed her eyes. 'Think I need a little sleep.'

Kate stares down at her, the thick sweep of her eyelashes, the tiny diamond stud in her perfect nose. Her breath has deepened; she might even be properly asleep. What must it be like, to be so relaxed that you can fall asleep anywhere, like a cat?

Kate ponders their evening, tries to summarise their rambling conversation. All in all, Coco hasn't said much about her life. She broke up with her first husband, who was rich but boring. Troy is a musician. The boys drive her mental and, like Kate, she spends a lot of time alone. Did she say something about being able to attract men but not keep them? There was a real sadness to that, but it's not true; it can't be. She's married to a complete hottie.

Coco opens her eyes, appears to startle.

'Fuck,' she says, pulling herself up. 'Sorry.'

'It's OK.'

'You've gone all quiet.' She sits up, reaches for Kate's hand. Holds it. 'You sure you're OK, darling?'

Kate slides her hand free. 'Can I ask you something?'

'Sure. Shoot.'

Coco shuffles back to her pouffe, grabs the two roll-ups, lights one and passes it to Kate, lights the second for herself. Kate decides to let this one burn out between her fingers. She still feels sick from the last four.

'When you came to the villa,' she says, 'I know you said you thought Jeff was an old boyfriend, and I totally get that, but earlier today I was chatting to my best friend, Lizzie. She remembered you actually.'

'Did she? Cool.' Apparently Coco Moss has no idea that literally everyone would remember her.

'Yeah. Anyway, we were chatting about the old days, and she mentioned a Halloween party in final year?' Kate studies Coco closely, sees, or thinks she sees, an almost imperceptible tightening in Coco's jaw, a flicker of something in her eyes. Coco takes a drag on her cigarette and looks away.

'It was in Woodhouse,' Kate presses on. 'Apparently you and Drew and those guys were there that night.' She raises her eyebrows, keeps her voice light, as if what she is saying is mere flotsam on a breeze. 'You won't believe this, but Jeff was there too.'

Coco doesn't smile or laugh or show any kind of surprise.

She sips her drink, appears to study it, replaces it with excessive care on the low table.

Despite Kate's resolve to stay calm, to not say too much, she finds herself unable to leave the silence to extend. 'Lizzie said he was dressed as a vampire. Apparently he was wearing a tux, black eyeliner and dark burgundy nail varnish.' A pause, a tinkling laugh. 'Jeff wearing nail varnish! I have to say, I was pretty shocked.'

Coco, who has dominated the conversation all evening with her forensic questioning, has now fallen silent. Her lips part slightly. She is no longer looking into Kate's eyes as she has been all evening with an intention that has felt at times almost predatory.

'Don't suppose you remember seeing him there, do you?' Kate asks quietly. 'A vampire with burgundy fingernails?'

Coco's eyes flare almost imperceptibly. After a moment, her bottom lip pushes hard against the top and she shakes her head. 'Sorry, no. I mean, I *barely* remember that party.' Her eyes narrow; her head cocks, as if she is searching through her memories. Even through her haze, Kate can see the gesture is performative. 'It was fancy dress,' she says then. 'I remember that. That would explain your husband's cross-dressing Dracula.'

'I know it was fancy dress. Lizzie said that. It's just not like Jeff to go for it in that way, that's all. But it's weird, because he's never mentioned that party in all the years we've been together. I would've remembered. Even at the time, he never mentioned a fancy dress party, let alone his costume or the fact that he let Lizzie put nail varnish and eyeliner on him. I just can't believe he wouldn't have told me that, you know? So when I found out you had been at the same party, I guess I... But if you say you can't remember him, then...' She trails off, scarcely able to believe she's said as much as she has – too much, that is. As usual.

'Oh my God, darling, stop.' Coco's laughter is a puffing cloud of smoke. She takes another drag, the cigarette at its end. She stubs it out on the cobbles and flicks the butt away onto the street. 'I can't even remember seeing a vampire at that party, let alone Jeff. I mean, it's perfectly possible I saw him, even spoke to him, but you're talking thirty fucking years ago, darling, and I didn't know him. Not to mention the fact I'll have been wasted.' She squeezes Kate's hand. 'Honestly. I'd totally tell you if we'd snogged or—'

'I didn't say snogged.'

Coco waves her hand. 'Or spoken or whatever. I mean, I don't think you'd be mad at me if I'd had some sort of drunken fumble with him at a party, would you?'

'Well, no,' Kate says, meaning *yes, a bit.*

'I mean, A, I didn't know him, and B, I certainly didn't know he was with someone.'

'Maybe I'd be a bit put out he hadn't told me, or—'

'Not that I did. Get off with him, I mean. I wasn't so out of it I wouldn't have remembered something like that. But no. He's not my type at all. More's the pity. I tend to go for bad boys unfortunately. All very exciting but a disaster on the husband front. No, last night I thought he was this guy I used to have a thing with who was a bit, y'know, jealous and controlling. Nothing more exciting than that, I'm afraid.'

'What was his name?'

'Who?'

'Your ex? The guy who was controlling.'

'What? Erm, James. James something. It was a long time ago.'

Kate wants to believe her, just as she wants to believe Jeff. But she doesn't, not quite, not one hundred per cent, for reasons she can't see or hear, only feel.

'Just out of interest,' she says, 'what were you dressed as that night? Can you remember?'

'God, no.' Coco's eye bulge, her head rears back, the shadow that moved across her face a moment ago gone.

But as in the villa last night, it was there. And Kate saw it. Something. She might not be able to describe or pinpoint what was hidden in that shadow, but she saw it.

CHAPTER 26

JEFF

Jeff waits. It is lonely, frankly, here in the villa without Kate. He tries to think of a time when he's been here or at their home in Surrey without her and finds he cannot. She is always there. Always.

He heats up the portion of deli lasagne that she left for him in the fridge and pours himself a San Pellegrino, cuts a wedge of lemon, squeezes it a little before popping it in the glass. The temptation to drink gnaws at him. This antsy feeling, he knows, would subside immediately if he were to submit to the cool slide of Kate's wine down his throat or the ice burn of the vodka she keeps in the freezer for her vodka tonics. But no. No. Because it won't be one glass; it'll be a bottle. It will be every drop in the house. And he cannot trust himself to keep his secret sober let alone drunk, not faced with his wife, whom he has already betrayed a thousand times before Coco Moss ever rocked up to upend his hard-won, bolted-down life.

On the high Philippe Starck stool he sits and eats. The pasta, meat and bechamel is heavy. It feels like it's settling at the bottom of his stomach, half digested but still in its layers. He eats a little more, the silence pressing in now. Scrolls through

Spotify, chooses a playlist to stream through the Bluetooth ceiling speakers: *Nineties Alternative Mix*. A mistake. The first track almost winds him: Orange Juice's 'Rip It Up'. It takes him a moment to compose himself, but memory is a stubborn assailant and within seconds has overpowered him: him and Kate dancing to this song at some first-year bop, her in his jeans, a brown leather belt, a white shirt, also his, falling off one shoulder. Her hair is tied up and messy and still brown. In the sepia tint of this long-ago image she looks... she looks lovely.

He loved her then. He did, didn't he? Before Coco, he did love Kate.

He groans, pushes his face into his hands. He can't think about that. He can't help what happened that night. He can't turn back the years. He has tried so hard to do everything right ever since. It is his life's work. Since that night he has not put one foot wrong. When Kate said they should marry, he said yes, let her organise it, do it all her way. When she questioned his lack of involvement, he blamed work, work he was doing for them so that they would one day have a nice house, a decent car, a future with designer clothes, foreign travel, luxuries. He gave Kate the child she begged him for, and OK, OK, maybe he wasn't there for the long nights of colic when Lou finally came, or the cold, rainy weekends, the school holidays she complained were endless. But all this money didn't earn itself, did it, and he was busy, goddammit. And OK, when she lost the first baby – a son – he could have missed that sailing weekend, but when he asked, she said it was OK, that he should go. And the second time it happened – a girl that time – she said it was fine, that she was going to stay in bed anyway, that he should go into the office if he needed to.

But he has given her a wonderful home, hasn't he? Not to mention countless holidays – a safari once in Kenya when Lou was twelve, the skiing in Switzerland, the turtles in Cuba –

along with the restaurants, the hotels, the gym memberships, the private fitness coaches, the anniversary gifts...

His secretary, Joan, has wonderful taste.

No, no, he can't think about what lies beneath, he cannot. He will not. And yet here it comes, rising to the surface despite him, the one thing he has not been able to give her all these years: his love.

That night. Coco is pulling him into the living room to dance. He has no choice but to obey – no choice! It would be *rude* not to follow her; he would have to reject her outright, and that is simply not possible. Besides, his conversational skills are terrible. He knows it. Better to lose himself in the music than try to talk to a girl like Coco Moss. How do people like her know what to say all the time anyway? What is it about them? Is it in their DNA? He doesn't know and by now he doesn't care, because Coco Moss is leaning against him. He rests his head on her shoulder, smells soap, cigarettes and fresh perspiration. The mix is intoxicating. Nervously he casts about for Lizzie. She has her camera with her, could easily take an incriminating shot. But he can't see her or Ben, can't see anyone he knows.

Anyway, it's just a dance. Just a little smoochy dance. Nothing to get in a tizz about. He's young. He can make one little mistake. One, that's all he's asking.

The slow song ends. Someone shouts *get that crap off*, a beat too late; straggly laughter follows. It surprises him to see the party has thinned out; there are barely twenty people left. He has no idea when the exodus happened. A second later, loud thumps pump out of the speakers: 'Liberator' by Spear of Destiny.

Coco whoops and throws herself from him, her arms flying wildly, her Doc Martens stamping, her ripped fishnets doing little to hide her long, slim, muscular legs.

Shaking himself from his stupor, he reminds himself to move, to dance as best he can. He's in danger of grinding to a halt just to watch her move – or worse, becoming too aware of himself and forgetting how to coordinate his own limbs. Now and then she grabs his hands and makes a puppet of him, pulling his arms up and down. He laughs it off, though his cheeks burn. What does she see when she looks at him? She does not see him at all, not really. She sees only the disguise that has drawn her to him. It is a con. He is a con man.

He swigs his beer, finds the can empty – again. He doesn't care. He doesn't care about anything at all.

The record ends. In the pause, Coco lifts her face to his and kisses him, fully and deeply on his black-stained vampire's mouth. She draws back, looks at him slyly and whispers: 'Hey, Dracula. Let's get out of here.'

CHAPTER 27

KATE

A little after 2 a.m., Kate almost falls through the door. Oops. *But still*, she thinks, holding up one finger for emphasis, *I am not as drunk as Coco, who was sick in a planter on the way up the hill.*

One hand flat against her belly, she stops. The uneasy feeling she has had since last night has faded. There's nothing between Coco and Jeff; there never was. A coincidence, that's all.

Jeff was embarrassed that Kate had invited a stranger for drinks. Coco thought she'd seen her horrid ex. Thassall. Thassit.

She hiccups. Thinks: comedy. Giggles. One shoulder hits the wall. She titters, wheezes like Muttley from *Wacky Races*. Thinks: this is very, very funny.

Walking now to the kitchen. Slowly, easy does it, one foot at a time. All is well. A fraught start to the holiday, that's all. Nerve endings a bit raw now that Lou has flown the nest. She and Jeff need to learn to be together again. They need to get back to the way they were. Jeff doesn't even *like* Coco very much. He never did. If Kate were to be honest with Coco, she'd have to admit that back then, she and Jeff spent a lot of time bitching about her and her friends with their endless privilege, their maroon cardigans and their big shouty voices. Jeff accuses Kate of not evolving; well, it is *he* who is still wearing his chip on his shoulder like a military medal, thank you very much. Coco is actually really down to earth when you get to know her, if you don't count the fact she doesn't appear to have to work for a living. Painting abstracts for rich women unsure of their taste cannot possibly pay a mortgage, can it?

Hic. Oops. Coco doesn't have a mortgage, Kate. Doh. Funny, for someone who has never had to pay for anything, she certainly had a lively interest in Kate and Jeff's finances. After they'd cleared the air about the Halloween party, Coco asked whether they had any more houses, what their house was like in Surrey, which private school Lou went to. They might even have got into Lou's horse riding and, come to think of it, Coco might even have asked how much Jeff earned, though the conversation is a little fuzzy.

Kate sits on the bottom step to take off her wedges, which are killing her. Her right foot is bleeding at the heel, the left not far behind.

'That's going to look classy in your flip-flops for the rest of the fortnight,' she mutters. 'Not.'

Gingerly she stands up, wobbles, focuses hard on walking barefoot into the open-plan area without falling over. On the bar, half lit by a pallid moon, is a half-eaten portion of lasagne. She has no idea how long it has been there, but it is not completely cold.

At the bar she stands and eats the lasagne. It tastes better than anything she has ever eaten, ever, oh man, it is bloody *delicious* – creamy, salty, tomatoey, meaty and, oh God, it is *yum*. She opens the fridge, finds some apricot yoghurts and a bar of Milka chocolate.

'That'll do, pig,' she whispers, giggles until she's crying a bit.

With dedication, she sits and eats two yoghurts, breaking

the chocolate into squares and dropping them into the creamy goo one by one before fishing them out with her teaspoon and delivering them into her mouth. Next she discovers half a baguette, which she slathers in the butter Jeff has left out. It is so good, so, *so* good. She can smell toast actually – faintly. Jeff must have made some before going to bed.

One hand pressed to the gritty counter, she finishes the baguette and belches like a builder.

'Bloody gluten,' she mutters and pours herself some of Jeff's San Pellegrino to aid digestion. 'High in bicarnabate of soda. Bicarnabate!' She cackles softly to herself.

The paracetamol is upstairs. Taking the stairs carefully now: two feet on one step before moving to the next. Her soles stick to the wooden slats, unpeel themselves with a soft lapping sound.

In the first-floor bathroom she finds some backup painkillers. She takes two, pre-emptively, and downs the water. She feels a bit sick. Too little to eat, then too much to eat, too much to drink for sure – a mess. She is a mess. She is frumpy and unfashionable, and her conversation is boring. Coco's an artist. She's rich and married to a *babe*. She lives in London. Her sexy young husband is a musician. She didn't talk much about him. Kate wonders whether, when Coco says she and Kate are in the same boat, they actually are, or if she's just saying that to make Kate feel better, create a meaningful bond. Or is all of this Kate's own little black dog, the insecurity that has hounded her her whole life? Lizzie told her not to overthink, but it's hard to believe that Coco Moss could go from such coldness at uni to an almost... For God's sake, she was practically *flirting* tonight – all that stroking, the intense eye contact, the soft scratch of nails on scalp. Surely a night out with Kate Barrett is a comedown for the likes of Coco Moss?

But... *but*: life has a way of humbling us all – even people like her.

In the spare room, she begins to unbutton her dress, but it is a monumental effort of coordination. Christ, it's so *hard*. Her fingers ache; the buttons slip away, pesky buttons. She lies back, half undone. The button she was focusing on pops out of her grasp. Oh, but the bedding is soft and clean and fresh. It is the softest, cleanest, freshest bedding she has ever lain down on.

She brings her legs up onto the bed and closes her eyes. She'll rest. She'll just have a little rest and then she'll undo the buttons. She's not that drunk, not plastered or anything. She's just tired, really tired. It's late. And it's a long, long time since she's had a boozy night with a girlfriend. Does she have any girl-friends really? Acquaintances, yes. Dinner parties in couples, yes. Women she can talk to about interior decor and clothes and listen in confusion to stories about filler and Botox and hear about how it's just the same as dying your hair really, how it's just like putting on make-up at the end of the day. Everyone does it. Just give it a try. I know this great place in Kensington...

But as for friends, real friends who you can share your life with over a drink, safe in the knowledge that they won't blab your business to everyone or silently judge you? Friends who don't give a toss what you're wearing or whether you've put on ten pounds, gone a bit jowly, a bit slack, need your roots doing, whether your living room is painted the right shade of the right brand of paint?

That kind of friend?

Tears slide into her hair.

'I am so lonely,' she whispers – to no one.

CHAPTER 28

COCO

To think I thought I'd be bored on this holiday! The boys screaming at me while I'm trying to read: *Watch me dive in! Watch me do a handstand! Look at me kicking a ball!* Troy: *Listen to this, do you think I should end on this cadence or this one?* The endless demands for attention, or the alternative at the other extreme: Troy mute, in headphones, mouthing notes, tapping rhythms; twins locked in virtual reality, and who can blame them? I thought it would be Tedium Central, but I'm not bored, not at all, and that's thanks to you, Jeff, and your lovely wife.

I think last night went very well. Kitty Kat was waiting for me, as I knew she would be. I bet she got there at 6.59 p.m. I can honestly say she would've looked more relaxed if she'd had a spike up her arse, but after a few *cervezas*, her shoulders finally lowered, and she began to open up. It was such a wonderful idea to take her out. Several drinks in, I could ask her the kind of questions I could never ask you. What you're like to live with, for example, your tastes and foibles, your habits, your financial situation. You're a teetotaller apparently. You gave up alcohol to focus on your career, she said. I remember that about you: that chip-of-ice ambition. There was never going to be anything allowed to stand in the way of the law, was there?

Or should I say *anyone*?

Don't worry, I heard that loud and clear.

As for your position, wealth-wise, well, it's so easy to get information about money out of working-class people, especially ones who have been successful. There's that endless need to draw attention to it, whether to flaunt or to justify or somehow pretend it's not there. Honestly, I've yet to meet a person of humble beginnings who can cope with the surprise of their own wealth; they're either hoarding it like a miser, spending it like water or bragging about it to anyone who'll listen. Or making excuses, telling you they only got their Lamborghini because Carol's mum died or Keith's Premium Bonds came in. It's either look at me, didn't I do well, or please don't look at me, I have no idea how to handle this and it makes me ashamed.

For people like you, it's as if you can't believe you don't have to scrimp or even save any more; you don't know what to do with yourselves because this scrimping and saving has been drilled into you since birth. Part of you still can't understand how you can stretch out your hand and see money blossom there like a bunch of flowers from a magician's sleeve – so *available*, so endless – and the guilt is palpable. And it's the guilt that makes you blab. You have this need to over-explain where the money came from for the huge house, the elite school, the pony in the stables, stables that *aren't as expensive as people think*. Really? I'm quoting Kate directly, by the way, about the stables. I don't think she believes that for a second. She was trying to frame it as some bargain she got from a guy down the pub – *two stables for a pound, love; tell you what, I'll throw in some free hay*. I imagine the pony was going cheap too, was it? Neigh!

Poor Lou, on her cheap pony in its cut-price stables.

I sound harsh, I know, but honestly, I do understand that

women like your wife are all about making others feel comfortable. It's in their DNA. Why do they do that? Apologise, I mean. Play down, even fib. Do you know, Kate told the waiter we were old friends, reunited after thirty years? Did she tell you that? What the hell does the waiter care? Why do women like her do that out of some uncontrollable fixation with assuring a fellow human being that you see them as such? *Don't worry, I know you've brought me this beer, that you've served me, but I don't see you as a servant in any way because I am nice, I see you, I value you, I care...* I mean, please, it's exhausting, *so* unnecessary and, I suspect, less kindness than a desire to control perceptions, to be *liked*.

That old chestnut.

I've thought about this oversharing a lot. Ironically, my mother used to do it, but the less said about her the better. Perhaps it's because people like Kate simply don't want anyone to feel as they feel, even for a moment – tight inside, inadequate and somehow *not right*, like they're dressing up in someone else's clothes, clothes that don't fit very well. You could argue that those born into privilege have the advantage. They are accustomed to not having to think about the desperately tedious practical issue of how much things cost and who's going to pay. Their rent? Paid. Heating? Fear not, they will be warm as toast! Food? On the table. Clothes? They fit, are appropriate, every last thread, always, from a shooting weekend in the Highlands to a holiday on so-and-so's ranch in Ibiza.

But actually, privilege aside, absolutely *everyone* has to work out how to be comfortable in their skin. That's what I think, and I think about these things all the time. You could say thinking about these things is my life's work. Because that's what I had to do – I had to *work it out*. People tell me I'm entitled, but I'm the exact opposite. I don't expect others to provide me with happiness; I take it for myself.

Personally, over the years I've found this whole class thing rather pathetic, the barriers people put up, the idea that it's only in America that anyone can *be what they wanna be*. It's the same here! It's the same anywhere! Everyone thinks it's all right for me because I come from the right class or whatever, but they don't know what it was like for me – no one does. You don't know me, Jeff. You think you don't love Kate because you love me, but you don't love me because you don't know me. You can't, ever, know me because I won't let you. You don't even know what you did to me. I'm simply a conduit for your frustrations and desires, your midlife crisis. You think we're bonded because of one night a long time ago, but that's the stuff of romance; it's meaningless. I am a screen onto which you have played the film of all your fantasies. You think you were unhappy before, but lean in, Jeff, while I tell you a secret: if you believe you were unhappy without me, it is because you were unhappy with yourself.

Shock horror, gasps all round, eh?

And what about when I told you I never stopped thinking of you? You believed it the way I wanted you to, because you believe you never stopped thinking about me. I have been unable to get you out of my head, though not in the way you think, but it's not the truth for you. You *did* stop thinking about me. Of course you did, you idiot. You thought of your work, your wife, your daughter. You've ploughed everything you have into providing for them. If you remained distant, that's not their fault; it's *yours*. Happiness was there waiting for you, but you chose not to help yourself. Why? If you could only get past yourself!

And now you're romanticising your own feelings because I've stirred them up again. You're reinventing the past. You were happy enough, happy as anyone, it's just that I've presented you with a time capsule at a point in your life where you can feel yourself fading. I'm not blind. I can see how much you work out, how you met me with your vest slapped over your shoulder so that I could take in the glory of that ripped torso while you smiled at me with your whitened, straightened teeth. You are fighting against time itself, my love. You think you can take back what has been lost, return to that mysterious vampire with the bloodied nails.

You can't, my darling. No one can control time.

But I won't be telling you that – why should I after the state you left me in?

You've been a fool, is what I think. You've made a clown of your wife, a stranger of your daughter and now you're alone. I've had to manage with what I have. You, Jeffrey Barrett, have made the classic error of turning your attention to what you don't have.

I am what you don't have, Jeff. And I will be claiming all your attention.

CHAPTER 29

KATE

Found some photos. Check these out. We were CHILDREN.

Kate is bent over her phone. Lizzie has sent a photograph of her, Jeff and Ben, in fancy dress, standing in the grotty living room of their house in final year. Kate remembers helping them find this house in the summer of '88, before she flew to Madrid. It was a dump, she can see that now, even in the photo. They didn't think it was a dump then; they thought they'd struck gold!

She zooms in. The brown velvet sofa looks like something from the fifties; she can practically smell it through the screen. The wallpaper is woodchip, painted that omnipresent shade of the time: magnolia.

'Standard,' she mutters to herself and smiles.

Lizzie must have set the timer on the camera. The three of them are grinning. Ben is on the left in a Siouxsie and the Banshees T-shirt, holding a white cloth in his hands; Lizzie on the right, hands paw-like at her chest... What is she, a cat? Jeff is in the middle, an arm around both Ben and Kate. His fingers are not visible.

Kate scrolls to the next picture. This time Ben is wearing

the white sheet. A ghost then. She giggles. His eyes hint at his hangdog expression. Ben always hated anything he feared would make him look foolish, especially in front of Jeff. Ah yes, his not-so-well-hidden feelings for Jeff. Kate was in the way; she can see that now in a way she couldn't then.

For a fleeting moment, she imagines Jeff and Ben together. That night. Coco saw them. That's the secret.

No. For Jeff, maybe, but what would Coco care?

But here they are before whatever happened, if anything did: young, a little drunk perhaps, ready to go to a Halloween party Coco Moss might have attended. In this photograph, the fingers of Jeff's left hand are visible on Lizzie's shoulder, and sure enough, they are dark, almost black. He looks... he looks unbelievable actually. Never, *never* has she seen him look anything like he does in this picture. His stare holds a conviction she imagines he must have at work, a real ice-cold killer gaze, and she is aware of herself stirring with feelings that have been dormant for a long, long time. Along with those feelings, the doubts she thought she had quelled begin to resurface.

'Jeffrey Barrett,' she whispers to his blurry image. 'What happened between you and Coco Moss?'

One thing she knows for sure is that any woman who met him that night would have been hard pushed not to find him attractive. He looks like a movie star.

Why has she never seen this photograph? Why has she never heard about this party, not even anecdotally, from her husband of over three decades?

She sends Lizzie a message.

These are amazing! Do you have any of the actual party? X

I think so, but I can't find them. I'm rootling through the box now, but there are loads of photos and I'm getting sidetracked! Will send if I find anything. X

OK. Thanks xxx

No sign of Jeff. Kate wonders if he's sulking or if he's just

AWOL for the usual selfish reasons. That he has seen no need to try and reconcile with her after yesterday's argument stings, that he can go so long without even testing the water, making some effort to communicate, repair.

Morning, she texts him. *Where are you?*

She adds a kiss, in the hope of thawing the ice – they really need to start getting along better.

After a quick plunge in the pool, she fixes herself coffee and toast. Her eyes are sticky, her head aches, but as hangovers go, she has got off lightly. She cannot get the vision of her vampire husband out of her mind. The direct way he met her eye, his penetrating stare cutting through the decades, afraid of nothing – nothing at all.

When Kate got home from Spain, Jeff had definitely changed. She has never phrased it like that, not even to herself, but now, alone, she does: he was *different*.

It wasn't just giving up drinking; it was his whole demeanour, his personality almost. She put it down to how hard he was working, how desperate he was to succeed. She was back in Leeds, lost in French feminism, twentieth-century Spanish theatre, singing in the Spanish choir, playing hockey for the third team, going out with her mates. She saw Jeff a couple of times a term, then at weekends in the holidays. Once she graduated, he began working at a large firm in Manchester, was already earning good money, living with his parents while he saved up enough for a deposit on the flat that was to become their first home.

'I'm so busy,' he used to say. 'The hours are insane, but they'll get better, I promise. I just have to get through the next couple of years.'

Was there more to it? Was he not busy but distant, already retreating from her?

Was there something wrong even then?

On her laptop, she pulls up Facebook. Jeff has lost touch

with so many friends over the years, Lizzie and Ben included. All she knows is that Ben stayed north, became a physics teacher at Leeds Grammar, joking that that was what all failed astronauts did.

Ben Shaw. There he is. Head of department now, head of Year 10. She wonders if he's happy, if he found someone, what his life is like. Into Messenger she types:

Ben! Long time no see! How's things with you? Realise this is a bolt from the blue but I was wondering if you'd have a couple of minutes to talk? It's to do with Jeff. Don't worry, it really is nothing serious, just be quicker to chat. Love, Kate xxx

She presses send. The message is deliberately vague; what she has to say cannot be committed to the written word. He probably won't pick it up, even if it is the school holidays; he might not even go on Facebook any more.

She packs her *Hola!* magazine, her Kindle and her beach stuff and is about to head out when her phone buzzes.

Ben. Oh my God, he's actually calling. On Messenger. Oh Christ, a video call!

Kate runs to the loo and checks her appearance. Oh, dear Jesus. She splashes her face. The phone stops buzzing. She can call him back in a second; she just needs to not look quite so terrible. There are black slashes under her eyes; her cheeks are hanging with exhaustion like baggy underwear. Oh God.

She rubs on some tinted moisturiser, but it dilutes with the sweat and smears. Oh, this is hopeless. It's too hot for make-up. Shades, that's all that will work. She's on holiday, yes, that's fine. If she goes onto the terrace to call, she can wear shades without looking weird.

She half runs to the patio, remembers Coco calling it a sun deck. Sun deck, check. The recliner is folded out, hallelujah. She'll say she was just fixing a drink, that she's sorry she missed his call.

She fixes a drink, for authenticity. She can hold it up and

say, *I was just fixing a drink,* and he will see the drink and think, yes, that makes sense, that drink looks freshly fixed.

Kate, she thinks. *Kate, you are mad.*

Shades on, she returns the call. Ben picks up immediately; his blonde eyebrows and blue eyes almost steal the breath from her. That face, that face is from so long ago. How can she have lived enough years to see a face from this long ago? Back then, she didn't like him because she could tell he didn't like her. Now, what she feels at the sight of him is close to love.

'Oh my God, Ben! You haven't changed!' It is the truth; he hasn't – a little thinner in the face, a few lines, his hair close-cropped these days rather than the wavy mane of his youth. Middle age suits him better actually. He looks like he's grown into himself.

'Oh, I don't know about that,' he says, laughing easily. 'You don't look so bad yourself.'

'Give over. I'm fat and old, Ben, fat and old.'

'Now, now,' he says, grinning, and shakes his head. 'Looks like you're somewhere nice.'

'Spain. Cadaqués. Just on holiday actually. It's very hot. So, how's things with you? Have you got time to chat?'

They catch up. There is none of the awkwardness she was expecting. He is happily married, he tells her, to a great guy called Michael, and she finds she is moved to hear it. When everything is stripped away, she thinks, the posturing and the jealousies, the drama-seeking and the insecurities of youth, all that remains is this: the hope that life has treated your old friend well, that they found love along the way, that they have been happy or at least not unhappy.

She tells him Jeff is a workaholic and a fitness freak, to which he replies *no change there.* She tells him they're muddling along, you know, that their daughter is seventeen now. She apologises on Jeff's behalf for his neglect of their friendship, but Ben tells her not to worry, that it's just the way of things, but that it would be great to get together sometime.

'Let's do that,' she says, meaning it.

He smiles. A short silence falls. The moment has come to ask about that night without sounding suspicious or mad.

'Listen,' she says. 'Nothing big or anything, but...'

She gives him a version of events, lies that Coco said something about a Halloween party in final year.

'Do you remember it at all? Apparently you, Lizzie and Jeff went. It's just that when I mentioned it to Jeff, he kind of closed up. I mean, I know he doesn't like talking, but it was really weird, like something bad had happened there or something...'

'I remember that party,' Ben says. 'Jeff went as a vampire; he looked amazing.'

'I know, yeah, but... *did* anything happen?' She's horribly aware of sounding mad, obsessive. The pretext for this call is uncomfortably thin. 'It's just, I got the impression it did, and Jeff won't tell me what it is. I'm not sure why it's got to me so much, but it has.'

He frowns. 'There was some argument, I think. Some aggro with Coco and that lot.'

'So Coco was there?'

'Yep. Definitely. I thought you said she brought it up?'

Kate feels herself blush. 'Yes, sorry. Of course. I mean, did she... did she have any contact with Jeff that night? Did she speak to him at all, do you know?'

And now the real pretext is all but exposed. She is practically asking if Jeff got off with Coco. Thirty years ago. And just like that, what had felt so urgent now seems unbearably pathetic. She hates this, hates herself.

Ben's eyebrows rise but his mouth presses tight. She studies him. The expression says, *God knows. He might have.* The expression says, *I really don't want to be in this spot.*

'Can't remember much about it, to be honest,' he says after a moment. 'He might have danced with her. Or danced near her. I mean, everyone was dancing. Everyone was drunk.'

'I don't suppose you have any photos, do you?'

He frowns, shakes his head. 'Lizzie might. She took her camera everywhere, didn't she, in those days?'

Kate nods. Lizzie used her camera the way Kate used cigarettes: a prop, something to hold up and talk about. Hide behind.

The call ends with promises to not leave it so long, to get something in the diary, to see each other soon. *Take care, yeah, take care, see you soon, OK, OK, yeah, bye, bye, bye then.*

In the empty villa, Kate sits listening to the pool pump, the hum of the fridge, the silence beneath.

There is nothing here, she tells herself. If there is, it is in the past.

What, really, is the point of dragging it into the present?

CHAPTER 30

JEFF

Walking down the lane, Jeff is smiling like an idiot. Coco is still on his skin, on his lips, in his hair. The last thing he wants to do is wash her off. Really, he wants to find a quiet spot so he can breathe her in from his own hands, play it all back second by second. He wants to run back up to the Carretera de Cadaqués and shout at the top of his lungs: *I have just slept with Coco Moss!*

She texted just after nine.

Boys have gone. Come up.

There was a rudimentary address, directions in case the satnav didn't work, and the colour of the door: blue.

Kate was still asleep in the spare room, alcohol thick in the air. She was still half in her dress, one leg over the side as if she'd crashed out midway through an intention to go to the bathroom or something. He didn't leave water or painkillers, didn't want her to know he'd checked on her.

He took a long shower, dressed with care – a brand-new plain white T from the pack of five, and the pale blue linen twill shorts he picked last time he collected his suits from Ede & Ravenscroft. He got to Coco's place half an hour later, almost

trembling at the door of the three-storey maisonette. He
knocked, waited, thought about knocking again. But then he
sensed movement. His chest swelled. A moment later she was
there, a loose sky-blue kaftan sheer over her quite obviously
naked body.

'We're wearing the same colour,' he said, like a moron.

But she only smiled and held out her hand. 'I've waited a
long time for this.'

Too choked to speak, he felt his thoughts tumble through
him: *If only you knew how much you have meant to me these
lonely thirty years. I have built this life with my bare hands, every
brick laid so as to block you out, forget you. It was what I had to
do to survive. All I ask for is this. If we can be together again, just
once, I can return to my life and know that I at least had this.*

But he did not say those things, was too afraid of spoiling
the moment, had a sixth sense that last time this was what he
did: frightened her away with his intensity, too young to know
he should have kept his feelings hidden. Now, choosing to trust
she felt the same, he took the hand she was offering him and let
her pull him inside.

He closes his eyes, opens them. Breathes. The aroma of the
town drifts towards him: sugar, heat, petrol. Best thing to do
now is go for a swim. If he returns to the villa smelling of the
sea, he won't smell of the wondrous sex he's spent the last two
hours having. He can tell Kate that he thought she'd need time
to sleep off her night out. He will make it up to her, as Coco
suggested. He needs to keep his wife on side.

'Tell Kate you've decided not to go training with Troy,'
Coco said. They were still in bed, skin still shining, legs still
entwined on the white whip of the sheets. He had recounted
his argument with Kate from the day before. 'I mean, for a start
it was a terrible lie, so the sooner it's abandoned the better. Tell
her your evenings are for her. This can be your olive branch
after your churlishness yesterday, OK?'

'OK,' he said, though he was unsure.

'You don't get it, do you?' Coco laughed then, propping her head on her hand, returning his gaze so hard he felt himself stir all over again. She threaded her fingers through his. 'The secret here is to make Kate feel seen, OK? You and I can be together in the mornings, can't we? I can message you once the boys are gone. Kate will be snoozing off her latest hangover and you can come on up. Troy often takes the twins out because they love to do all the boysy stuff, whereas I'm happy reading, shopping and sunbathing, so there'll be nothing unusual in it. From what Kate told me, you're always off on some long run or some diving escapade, so...'

'Yes,' he said, beginning to see.

'Yes? You get it? There's no need to change any arrangements, is there? If you change anything at all, it will make her suspicious, especially after the way we looked at each other. And now she's got wind of that fucking party. We have to be careful. What she doesn't know can't hurt her.'

He could feel his own slow smile spreading. 'Yes. Yes, you're right.'

How he loves to hear her talk, he thinks now. Especially like that, in bed. Loves the slow, elegant roll of her voice with its hint of Home Counties, silver tableware, crumbling old houses in a shire somewhere. He did ask her where she was from, but she only answered, *oh, all over, you know*, which was exotic in itself, and by then she was biting his ear lobe, one hand on his cock, asking if there was any more gas in the tank.

He has reached the beach. It is packed. He has one foot on the black sand when his phone vibrates in the pocket of his shorts. Vibrates again. And again.

He pulls it out and stares at it. Facebook Messenger, an audio call. He'd forgotten he was even on Facebook, but now his phone is ringing and the call is coming from Ben Shaw's profile. Ben? What the...

'Ben? Mate! Bloody hell!'

'Long time no speak.'

For a moment, Jeff is unable to reply. First Coco appearing, now Ben. If the past is another country, it has boarded a plane and landed here on the Costa Brava.

'In Spain on your hols then?' Ben asks. 'Cadaqués. Very nice.'

'What? Yes. I mean, how d'you...'

Instinctively Jeff looks around, expecting to see Ben in the shade of the café, phone clamped to his ear, mischievous grin on his face.

Ben is chuckling. 'I just spoke to your missus.'

'Kate?'

'Er, yeah. Unless you have another one?'

Jeff's stomach flips. 'Er, no. No, of course not. How come? How come you spoke to her?'

'Mate, she called me. Literally just now. She was asking about that Halloween party in final year. In Woodhouse, do you remember? Apparently you're sharing your holiday with Coco Moss?'

'I'd hardly call it sharing. We just bumped into her, that's all. She came to our place for a drink, but I don't think I'd call that—'

'Whatever. Listen, just to give you the heads-up, Kate's convinced you and Coco got together back in the day. She didn't put it like that exactly, but she almost did. I didn't say anything obviously.'

Faint nausea rises in Jeff's gut. 'What do you mean? Anything about what?'

'Y'know! You and Coco getting it on. I mean, you barely came up for air, mate.'

Jeff's heart quickens. 'I didn't... You saw that? I thought you'd left.'

'I left at that point, I think. Lizzie had puked, so I had to take her home. I was going to tap you on the shoulder and say goodbye, but you were... busy. So we split. What happened that night anyway? I've always been curious. Did you and her, y'know...'

'No! God, no. It was just a kiss. But I... I never told Kate, that's all. And it's too late to tell her now without her thinking it was a big deal.'

'So you didn't go back to Coco's? I seem to remember you coming home late morning.'

'What? No! I... I went to get my car the next day. I left it over in Woodhouse. I'm pretty sure I told you at the time.'

There's a horrible pause. 'Yeah. You did. You looked rough as hell though. You looked like you'd been up all night, so I guess I thought maybe... I mean, not that it matters, I just always thought you and Coco had...'

'So, what, all these years you thought I'd slept with Coco Moss?' Jeff laughs. He's pretty sure it's convincing, this laugh, hollow and chesty, as if what Ben's suggesting is utterly preposterous.

Now Ben is laughing too. 'Well, it was none of my business!' Another pause, just as terrifying. 'It was a long time ago. And that girl... the girl who died. It was that night, wasn't it?'

'Which girl?'

'I can't remember her name. Wasn't she that twat Drew's girlfriend?'

'Oh yeah,' Jeff says, as if thinking, as if, really, he has to rack his brain. 'Was that the same night?'

'Yeah. I'm pretty sure. God, my memory's terrible.' Ben gives a brief sigh.

'Yeah,' Jeff agrees. 'Mine too.'

'Terrible, though, wasn't it?'

'Yeah. Terrible.'

Jeff makes small talk for a further twenty painful minutes before closing the call. Shaken, he strips down to his underwear – tight black cotton boxers that can easily pass for trunks – and plunges into the sea, swims down to the seabed, fights to stay submerged there, where all sound is muted, where no one can see him.

Fifteen minutes later, he finishes his swim and emerges onto the sand, wiping the salt water from his eyes. On the shoreline, he sits and stares out at the boats bobbing in the harbour, families splashing about, the coloured balloon-like floats of swimmers further out. He finds his sunglasses, lies back on the cradle of his hands, closes his eyes. Despite the calming power of the ocean, his heart is still racing.

Ben saw him and Coco kissing. All these years and he never let on. Not that Jeff's seen him much. Not at all in the last ten, fifteen years.

Chill out, Jeff. Stay rational. There is no reason to panic, none whatsoever. Think it through. It was just a kiss. It was just a drunken kiss.

But Kate called Ben. And if Kate called Ben, she must've already called Lizzie, since there's no way she'd call Ben before Lizzie. Which means she is really suspicious. But which also means Lizzie couldn't tell her anything.

So Lizzie saw nothing.

All Ben saw was the kiss.

If Jeff has to come clean on that, it's not the end of the world. It's not a deal-breaker. In fact, it could be a good diversion.

God, he hates this. All he's done is this one tiny thing, years ago. All he wanted was to finish what was started that night, and already the wheels are coming off. He never gets away with anything! All he and Coco did was lose their shit for a second, less than a second, and Kate is on their scent like a gun dog. If only he'd been able to get a grip on himself when he saw Coco standing there in his living room like a bloody ghost. But he couldn't, not quickly enough anyway, and now his wife knows he's hiding something, something he has managed to hide for decades. It's not fair. No, really, it's not. He has not put one single foot wrong in thirty years, has stuck to the rules like a total champ, and now, in his fifties, all he wants is some goddam relief, a reward even, for all he has done, how he's kept it all together for so, so long.

Life owes him that much, doesn't it?

Calm down, Jeff.

Ben called him to warn him. Ben has been a mate and covered for him, and he doesn't even know what he was covering for.

Which leaves Kate. She knows about the Halloween party. She knows Coco Moss was there. But that's it, that is it.

What would Coco do in this situation? Keep everything normal, she said. Hide in plain sight. Above all, don't do anything differently.

He will go back up to the villa and apologise to Kate for yesterday's argument, and at some point, when it feels natural, he will suddenly remember where he might have spoken to Coco Moss back in the day.

Oh my God, he will say, slapping his forehead. *I remember now... She was at this Halloween party I went to. She was in fancy dress, that's why I couldn't place her at first!*

Something like that.

Two days. Two days is all it has taken to turn him into a lying cheat. But he needs a plan, and the plan is this: be nice, and above all else, say nothing about the girl.

No one, *no one* can know about her.

CHAPTER 31

KATE

The moment Jeff returns to the villa, Kate can sense that whatever foul mood he was in has evaporated. Jeff brings moods with him, she thinks, like electricity. Over the years, she has grown receptors that can pick up his currents at a distance. He has forgiven her, it would seem, judging by the lack of static in the air. He has absolved her of the sin of going out independently of him. Of nothing at all, in fact. And sure enough...

'Hey,' he says, throwing his keys on the bar and hovering at the patio door, his shadow falling on the ground beside her sunlounger. He is wearing not his sports kit but one of his pristine white T-shirts and his pale blue linen shorts. 'Listen, I'm sorry about yesterday. I was out of order.'

'Oh. OK. Thanks.' She sounds stilted, even to herself, but the fulsome apology with no attempt to frame it as a response to her poor behaviour is, frankly, a shock.

He heads back into the kitchen. She gets up, follows him inside, but to her further astonishment, he stops abruptly, turns towards her and takes her in his arms. He pulls her close and holds her tight. The moment for the hug to end comes and goes, but he is still holding her, almost as if he needs her. She tries to think when he last did this. Cannot. Her eyes fill with tears. The physical contact is almost more than she can bear, but she leans into the painful tenderness of it.

'I'm a shit,' he mutters into her shoulder. He smells of the sea; his hair is still wet.

'You're not,' she says.

'I basically do what I want, don't I? And you... you look after me.'

She hesitates. It is hard to contradict him.

'You work hard,' is all she can think of to say. It is easier with his head on her shoulder, his eyes where she does not have to look into them. 'You look after us too.'

'I know, but... You're alone a lot. I abandon you, don't I?'

'I...' She cannot think how to reply, whether he means the constant work, the evenings spent at the gym, the Sundays lost to golf, the holidays to snorkelling, running, swimming out to sea, or all of it, all the not being with her.

He loosens his hold and steps back, but his fingers are wrapped tight around her upper arms. He is looking at her, right at her. This is... it is too much. She cannot hold his gaze.

'I'm not going training with Troy tonight,' he says. 'I was being petulant. It's great that we're independent, but evenings we should be together. That's our routine, isn't it? Unless you're not happy with that? I mean, we can go out in the afternoons if you like. Or you could go out with Coco again. I mean, it'd be fine if you did.'

'I know that,' she says, bristling despite sensing the sincerity of his intentions. Usually she would melt into an overture like this. She thinks she would. It is hard to know, since there has never been one before. 'I'm a grown woman,' she adds, for strength. 'I can go out with whoever I want.'

'You know what I mean.'

She nods – a concession. 'I thought you didn't like her? I thought you said she only wanted me for my villa?'

'I was being a dick. I really am sorry. I was just trying to warn you, that's all. I mean, I don't trust her, but I might be wrong. Do *you* like her?'

'Yes. I do actually.'

'Well, that's the main thing.' He lets go of her and wanders over to the fridge. 'Did you guys have a good time last night?'

'Yeah,' she says, still a little unnerved. 'We talked a lot.'

She falters. Jeff has started to get things out of the fridge and is placing them on the bar: ham, olives, some salad leaves. He is not reaching in and lowering the nearest thing to hand into his waiting mouth. It's as if... it's almost as if he's putting this stuff out for both of them. And if he's been for a swim, why is he wearing one of the multipack of brand-new white M&S T-shirts he likes her to buy for him before every holiday? And his best shorts from Savile Row, for that matter?

'Kate?' he says. He is studying her. 'Did you hear me? I was asking if you're hungry?'

She watches in disbelief as he fetches two white plates from the rack. 'Sorry. Miles away. Lunch. Yeah. Sure.'

'She's probably lonely,' he says, placing two glasses on the bar, and for a moment she can't think who he's talking about. Coco, of course. *Focus, Kate.*

'Probably married to some dick who takes no notice of her.' He grins, to show her he's joking, that he's self-aware, that *he's* the dick. It is all very confusing.

'Actually, she *is* lonely,' Kate replies. 'Her husband spends every evening composing, and the twins aren't exactly scintillating company.'

'There you go. Maybe you should ask her to go out again next week.'

'Er... sure.'

'I mean, I can share you if it means you make a new friend.'

He smiles like charm itself. He is putting the Manchego onto a wooden board. Next to it he puts the quince paste, a cheese knife. An oozing piece of Cabrales follows, followed by a flourish of walnut halves. Her husband is preparing lunch. He is not asking her if she fancies some lunch while remaining steadfastly reclined on a sunlounger. He is actively, purposefully preparing lunch. There really is no doubt left.

And like that, the tension returns in a wave. She finds she is staring at him as if at a stranger. Something weird is happening here. She wonders whether to challenge him, call him out right now, but what would she say? *Why are you making me lunch, you psychopath?*

And now he's slicing up the baguette he must have brought from town and telling her to sit down. He must have stopped at a bakery and bought a baguette. He must have thought: *I know, I'll pick up some nice fresh bread while I'm out. For lunch.*

Kate's head spins.

'Do you want a glass of wine?' he asks. 'Or a beer?'

Oh my God, make it stop.

'No,' she says, her hand flat against her forehead. 'I've got a bit of a headache actually. Just a second. Need to wash my hands.'

In the downstairs loo, panting with confusion and anxiety, she messages Lizzie.

Jeff is making lunch. I didn't even ask him to. That's four weirds. BTW, I spoke to Ben re Halloween party, but he was no help. Have you found out anything else about that night?

For once, Lizzie replies quickly.

Found this, was just about to send. It's blurry and I didn't think anything of it, but once it was in my phone, I zoomed in. Don't freak. I don't think it's anything serious and everyone was super drunk, OK? It's a long time ago. PS Jeff is nice, you nutter. He loves you.

What was *a long time ago? Jeff is nice?* Kate's scalp shrinks to her head. *Don't freak.*

A moment later, a grainy image lands on her WhatsApp. It

is a crowded room in a house, young couples – kids really – with their arms around one another. A slow dance, possibly, the end of the night. On the left, a tall, skinny woman with a half-white, half-black skinhead is locked in an embrace with a dark-haired man. Kate zooms in. The woman is wearing fishnets; the man is resting his head on her shoulder, just as Jeff did on Kate's moments ago. The man's face is not visible. The woman's back is to the camera. Kate zooms in as far as she can. The man's hands are resting on the girl's waist.

His fingernails are painted a dark blood red.

The phone shakes.

'No,' she whispers, but even as she says the word, she knows this is Jeff. This is her husband. It has to be. There can't have been more than one man wearing nail varnish, can there? With Jeff's exact hair colour, his exact way of putting his head on a woman's shoulder? But who is the girl? She is a punk, by the looks of it. From the back pockets of her denim miniskirt hang five white tails spotted black. There is something familiar about her legs, the shape of her calves, her slim thighs. More than familiar. There is some part of Kate, deep within her, that knows.

She messages Lizzie.

That's not Jeff, is it?

That's Jeff, yes.

Who's the girl?

Lizzie is typing. Kate holds her breath. She knows. She knows she knows she knows who the girl is. And yet still, silently, she tells herself it won't be her. It doesn't mean anything anyway. It's just a dance, a drunken dance at the end of a party. It won't be Coco Moss, of course it won't be, because Coco Moss would never have dyed her hair like that. Coco Moss would never, not in a million years, have danced with a boy like Jeff.

The next message lands.

That's Coco Moss.

A burning sensation spreads over Kate's skin. Breath a solid ball in her chest, she rings Lizzie. There is no way Lizzie will have had time to put down the phone, no matter what manner of vegetable one of her girls has put into one of their orifices. Sure enough, she picks up after one ring.

'What the hell?' Kate whispers, conscious of Jeff only a few metres away, of herself, sitting crouched and sweating and agonised on a bloody toilet seat.

'Don't freak.' For some reason, Lizzie is also keeping her voice low. 'She came as a kind of goth Cruella de Vil. It was quite cool actually.'

'Lizzie!'

'Soz. Look, it was just a dance. I can't even remember it. I don't even think I took this photo. Ben must've taken it; you know how possessive he was about Jeff. I think I'd been sick by then.'

'But Ben said nothing happened.'

'Well, he's probably forgotten. He might even have been covering for Jeff. God knows he won't have wanted to split on his mate, would he? Look, just ask him. Get it out in the open. It was decades ago, and it's just a drunk slowy.'

Kate's heart hammers. 'If it was just that, why hasn't he told me? If it's no big deal, why in all these years hasn't he told me?' Her voice is thick with tears. She pushes at her eyes, sniffs, blows the air from her lungs in a shaking blast.

'I don't know,' Lizzie almost whines. 'How would I know?'

'Did anything happen afterwards? Did he act strangely or did he, I don't know, stay out all night or anything?'

There is a pause. Kate waits, bites her lip. The pause is too long; it is a void into which her as yet unarticulated fears empty like sewage from a pipe.

'I think,' Lizzie says eventually, 'if I remember rightly, I *think* Jeff was ill around then. I know he left before term ended, some flu bug or other. His mum came to get him. But look, he's a super-straight stand-up guy. If Coco turned up at yours by surprise and he did have a bit of a snog or something with her back in the day, he probably started panicking. I mean, it's totally the sort of thing he'd get in a tizz about – you know Jeff.'

Does she?

'Kate? Are you coming?' Jeff is calling her from the kitchen area. Since when does he ever call her for lunch? A lunch that he's prepared?

'I have to go,' she whispers. 'But you're sure he didn't bring her home that night? Did he go back to hers?'

'No! I saw him the next morning. He'd come home, but he went back to Woodhouse to get the car. You see? That's Jeff. Would pick his car up promptly the next day and park it where he could see it, complete with that crook lock he used to have – do you remember that? Who had a crook lock, for God's sake? Jeff, that's who. Chill, will you? Coco's got both of you spooked, that's all. Don't make it into more than it is.'

'I'm not! It's just horrible feeling like I'm the one in the dark while they... I mean, they both obviously remember. That's why they both looked like they'd seen a ghost. And even if Coco's forgotten, Jeff won't have. There's no way he would've forgotten that; it's Coco Moss, for God's sake!'

'So ask him.'

Kate hears the trace of exasperation in her friend's voice.

'Look,' Lizzie says, clearly hearing it herself. 'I'll call you if I find anything else, OK? But I really don't think it's a big deal. It's not like he's had some *affair* with her, for God's sake. There's no way I wouldn't have known about that, and no offence, but that would be some serious punching.'

'Thanks a lot.'

She laughs. 'You know what I mean.'

Kate rings off. In the silence of the small white room, she sits for a second and tries to compose herself. Things are fitting together, but the picture is refusing to build into something that matches what she has seen, what she knows in her guts.

'Kate?' Jeff taps gently on the door. 'Are you OK? You're not ill, are you?'

'I'm fine. Just a second.'

Hands cradled in her lap, she waits for his footsteps to recede. Why is he suddenly so attentive? Doesn't notice her for hours on end, days, often weeks, and now he can't cope with her going to the loo. Why has he made *lunch*, for God's sake? And why, if he's been for a swim, is he dressed in his smart-casual attire?

Kate suppresses a roar of frustration. Jeff's behaviour would all look perfectly innocuous to anyone else, but not to her. It's not *normal*. And some slow dance that never came to anything thirty years ago does not tally with her husband's sharp change in behaviour, nor with the way he and Coco looked at one another two nights ago. Lizzie said it was just the sort of thing he'd get into a tizz about, but that wasn't a tizz; it was horror. It was utter, turn-you-to-stone shock. She has been told it was not, but she saw it, she bloody well saw it.

The trouble is... the trouble *is* that no matter how she tries to sand the cracks, blur the edges, the picture does not fit with that horror, that shock, not to mention the decades-long vow of silence. A deep blush – that would have fitted. Palpable embarrassment, a nervous laugh, an 'oh, dear, this is a bit awkward'.

She splashes her face and washes her hands for the second time, smooths her hair, eyeballs herself. She looks so tired; her face is etched with tension. This thing is weighing her down, spoiling her holiday. Is Lizzie right? Should she just come out and ask him?

She should. Absolutely. Marriage is about honesty, transparency. One taboo is enough to estrange even the closest couple, and they are not, she admits, the closest couple. The moment there's something important you can't talk about, communication begins its sluggish march towards silence, towards death.

Just ask him.

But she *has* already asked him. He has already told her there was nothing. She can't ask him again, not until she has evidence beyond some blurry photo of him and Coco Moss thirty years ago, which he can dismiss, claim it isn't even her. And then where will she be? She will look paranoid. He will tell her this is all Coco's doing, that he told her so, didn't he tell her that people like Coco Moss make people like Kate Barrett nervous? She is not confident enough for such a friendship. She is not up to the task. Coco is, quite simply, out of her league. Friendship-wise, she is, as Lizzie would say, punching.

No. There is no way she'll hand Jeff that ammunition. She needs more information.

Think, Kate. Think.

CHAPTER 32

JEFF

Kate has locked herself in the loo.

He has done exactly as Coco advised and made some conciliatory effort, but now his wife is hiding from him.

She knows something.

The horrific possibility of a love bite dawns on him.

'Shit.' He runs to the hallway, examines his neck in the hall mirror.

No, no. A sigh leaves him, small and high.

'Kate?' He raps softly on the door. 'Are you OK? You're not ill, are you?'

In the mirror, he checks himself once again, pulls up his T-shirt, tries to see his back, the back of his neck. They were all over each other; it's possible Coco's left a mark where he can't see it.

The chain flushes. That's the second time. He can hear the tap running. Has she been sick? Is it the hangover? Or can she see through him, sense Coco Moss on him through some basic animal instinct?

No. That's impossible. What has happened between him and Coco has only just happened. Well, if you don't count thirty-odd years ago. No one gets busted that quickly, and in terms of his and Kate's routine, as Coco said, he has not done *anything* out of the ordinary!

Unless... unless Kate followed him out of the villa this morning? He eyeballs himself, looking for clues. Mad, he is going mad. No. She can't have followed him. She was still asleep when he left.

Nerves jangling, he returns to the kitchen, puts an olive into his mouth, pours himself a San Pellegrino. He chews the meaty flesh, spits the stone into his hand, throws it into the bin. He's being insane. Paranoid. It's not even an affair, this thing with Coco, not as such. A morning of passion, that's all. Unfinished business from long decades ago. He's getting het up over nothing; it's what comes of having lived a blameless life. He could still tell Coco he can't go through with it, that it's not fair on Kate, that what they did this morning they were helpless to resist. Because they *were* helpless, both of them. And so there is no blame, not really. If they don't do it again, it will have been a one-off, a misdemeanour at worst, a force over which neither of them had any control.

They lost their heads, that's all.

He sips the fizzy water, worries it will rot his teeth, resolves to change to Evian.

Knuckles pressed to the breakfast bar, he breathes deeply. Chill, Jeff. He's getting worked up over nothing. Even if he did spend one more morning with Coco, that wouldn't make any difference, not really. Even if he saw her every day, it would only be for this fortnight, nothing more. It's all he asks. It's all he will ever ask. It's not much, not really, not considering all he has done. He's not about to ruin Kate's life, is he? He's not a pig! Coco might have defined his life, but Kate has given him every-thing. She pretty much brought Lou up on her own, he can see that now.

Lou. The thought of his daughter knocks the breath from

him; the marble worktop is hard against his knuckles. Lou cannot know. If she ever finds out, she will hate him forever. They both will.

Ignorance is key: this thing with Coco must remain a secret. If Kate never finds out, then neither will Lou. He cannot afford to let anything come to light – from the present or the past.

And in that moment, it occurs to him: both now have the power to destroy him.

'Hey.' Kate has entered the kitchen looking pale, a little drawn.

'Hey,' he says, too brightly. 'Not feeling great?'

She stares at him, as if confused. 'I'm... I'm just a bit tired from last night.'

Hung-over. She is hung-over. She would never admit it.

'You need some food,' he says mildly, avoids the words alcohol and poisoning. 'Your blood sugar's probably low.'

Unnerved by her staring eyes, he averts his gaze. Peels off a slice of jamón and drops it onto a plate before handing it to her. 'This ham is salty. It'll pick you up. I'll find some crisps.'

She takes it, looks at it as if she's never seen a plate before.

'Oh, by the way,' he says, heart quickening. 'When I was running, I remembered I *did* meet Coco once when we were at uni. It just dawned on me, you know?'

'Oh yeah?' Her eyebrows rise. She is still looking at him with an intensity that makes him want to scratch himself. He glances away, affects an intense focus on choosing his lunch.

'Yeah,' he goes on, super-conversationally. 'There was this Halloween party in Woodhouse in final year. I went with Lizzie and Ben. I must've told you about it?' He makes himself look at her.

She shakes her head. 'No.'

'I will've done. You've probably forgotten. *I'd* forgotten actually. But I've been trying to think where I might have spoken to her before, and I *think* it was at that party.'

Kate's eyes are hard, blue. And in that moment, he knows. Lizzie has told her about the dance, possibly about the kiss. He can see it in her face. She is waiting for him to tell her the truth. Shit. He clears his throat.

'Sorry,' he says. 'Swallowed an olive stone.' He grabs his drink, downs it. His eyes water. He smiles, to show he is simply recovering from this minor obstruction in his throat.

'Are you OK?' Kate asks.

He nods, holds up one hand while he racks his brain. What would Coco do? She would come clean about the one aspect that has been discovered, he's pretty sure. If you tell the truth about something relatively big, the rest can remain hidden.

'Sorry about that,' he says, then frowns, an expression of contrition. 'So listen. The thing is, I was very drunk at that party. I mean really drunk. If I never told you about it, it's probably because I did actually end up dancing with Coco Moss that night, weirdly enough.' He grimaces. 'I'm sorry. I felt really bad at the time, but I didn't want to tell you while you were in Spain. I suppose I didn't want you to think... I didn't want you to worry and, I mean, it was just a dance.'

Her brow furrows. 'But surely you remembered that the moment you saw her? Here, I mean.'

He exhales heavily. Nods. Would throwing up his hands be too much? He does it anyway, two clean palms – *arrest me, officer, it's a fair cop.* 'Sorry. I should've told you.'

'And that's why you looked so shocked?'

Again he nods. 'I guess I panicked.'

Her eyes are screwed up, raisin-like. 'But it was just a dance, wasn't it? Unless it was more?'

He closes his eyes, as if what he has to confess is huge. 'I... I kissed her. Just once! It was only once and I really was completely bladdered, you know? I can't even remember it; it was Ben who told me I'd done it, the next day. It was more... embarrassing than anything else. We were both wasted. I should have told you, but I just didn't want you to get upset or think that it meant anything, because it didn't, it absolutely didn't. And then by the time you came back it was just so... so in the past, and mentioning it would only have upset you, and there seemed no point in that when nothing really happened. Just a drunken snog at a party.'

Kate's eyes have filled with tears. But she is smiling at him with what looks like relief. He has played it right, he thinks. He has made sense of his reaction to Coco Moss – at least in Kate's eyes – without landing himself in it.

But her next question bruises him.

'Is that why you're being so kind to me?' She gestures to the food. 'I mean, it was thirty years ago. Are you sure it was just a kiss?'

He feels heat creep up his neck, his face. 'Of course it was. It was just a drunk thing. But when I saw her again, I was mortified because I'd never told you and I thought you'd be so... I mean, *rightly*, pissed off because I didn't tell you at the time. And then when you said you were going out for a drink with her, I panicked because I thought she might tell you and obviously I didn't want her to. I mean, only because I wanted to tell you myself. I'm sorry. I'm making a mess of this. I should've told you when you asked, but I... I couldn't find the words.'

'It's OK. I know you.' She laughs, actually laughs, and he feels the tension drain from him, down, down, into his feet. 'That's how I knew you were hiding something.'

He meets her eye, not daring, nowhere near daring to laugh with her. 'So you're not furious?'

She shakes her head. 'I'm relieved actually.'

'Did Coco tell you?'

She shakes her head again, serious now. 'I just knew there was something. We've been together a long time, remember.'

She does not mention speaking to Lizzie or Ben, but he

guesses it would be a bit rich to accuse her of going behind his back.

'I just wish you'd told me earlier,' she says, her voice calm, rational. 'It was pretty horrible knowing you were lying to me. It makes me seem like a monster, like you're scared of me or something.'

'I'm so sorry, darling.'

'Does *she* remember?'

'I don't know. I mean, how *would* I know? Probably not, I imagine. Probably best not to go there.'

'But she looked pretty shocked to see you too.' Kate is still watching him, as if to gauge his reaction. He feels hot, despite the air-conditioning.

'Maybe she did remember. Probably best not to mention it. No point dragging up the past. Sleeping dogs and all that.'

Her mouth flattens. 'If you say so.'

'Are you pissed off?'

Her eyes film with tears. 'A bit actually. But I'll get over it. I... I don't think I want to see Coco though, not for a few days. It feels a bit icky.'

'If you're sure.' He attempts an expression that is both understanding and perhaps a little sad, and which, most importantly, disguises an almost overwhelming urge to punch the air for joy. He throws out his arms, pulls her into a hug, kisses her hair. 'People like us need to stay away from people like her.'

After lunch, he tells Kate he has to quickly sign something off for work, but that once he's finished, they'll go for ice cream.

'Ice cream?' She looks at him strangely, as if bewildered or afraid. 'Um, OK.'

Upstairs on the bed, he opens his laptop so that should she come in, she will assume he's emailing the office. She'll be annoyed at him for working on holiday, but she is always annoyed about that; her annoyance is like a fly buzzing in a room: it's irritating but you know if you ignore it, it will eventually stop. Besides, it is a little galling, frankly. Quite how he affords their amazing lifestyle seems to escape her in these moments, the fact that he is always the one with the biggest bonus, that he'll make partner in a year, that his shares alone are enough for them to retire very comfortably indeed – now, if they wanted to.

Money doesn't grow on trees after all.

He messages Coco.

K knows about us at the Halloween party. Bit of a shock but I kept my cool, told her it was just a dance and a kiss. Thought it was best to give her something that explains things. Can't wait to be with you again. LOML, J x

He presses send. A moment later, he sends a second message.

PS I didn't tell her about Joanne.

CHAPTER 33

COCO

I could be wrong, but I *think* I have bound you to me, Jeff Barrett. I hope so. For a pair of relative strangers, we have so much history. And you haven't changed one bit!

Seeing you earlier took me back, actually, to the morning after that night, when I realised I'd gone to bed with Bram Stoker and woken up with Mr Bean. I'm teasing, of course, but I can vividly remember taking one look, one sober look, at your bedroom and thinking, get me out of here.

Can you believe, I thought the only reason I hadn't seen you around was because you were one of those mysterious guys who never showed up to lectures, who was tied to the university only by a gossamer-fine thread, a dude for whom the Student Union, the socials, the club nights were all one big fat yawn. That whole silent handsome thing, the guyliner, the nails, the slicked-back hair. And of course, when I first saw you, I'd just had that terrible fight with Joanne after she walked in on me giving Drew... my attention in the upstairs bathroom. But that's just what Drew and I were like. We were friends with benefits before that was even a thing. If he'd told Jo-Jo they were exclusive, that wasn't my fault.

So anyway, back to you and your lovesick puppy-dog routine. My God, Jeff, you need to learn to play it cool. Really. It's too much, although I confess, I do love it – it's so, so wonderful to be adored. Plus, I've had three decades to work out how to use it to my advantage. But back then, when I started putting on my clothes, convinced you were still asleep, I almost had a heart attack when your tremulous little voice came whining out from behind me.

'You're not leaving, are you?'

'I need to go,' I said, trying not to notice the increasingly pervasive smell of dirty socks, the furry half-mug of tea, the black mould creeping down from the corner of the ceiling.

'Don't go,' you said. 'Please.' And then – I don't know if you remember this – you kind of threw your legs around my waist like some kind of creepy lasso. Do you remember that?

'Don't go. Can't you just stay a bit longer? I love you. I love you, Coco. I've loved you since the moment I saw you. Please, *please*.'

Good Lord. I had the impression you might even be crying.

'I know you feel the same,' you went on, words to that effect. 'Please tell me you feel the same. Come on. Please!'

In what world – in what *universe* – would that kind of talk work on a woman you'd only just met? You frightened the living bejesus out of me! After that, I couldn't get out of there fast enough. I actually worried you might murder me rather than let me leave, like some kind of Stephen King novel, a gender-reversed *Misery* or some such.

'Take your legs from around my waist,' I said, my voice a simmering calm.

To be fair, you did, immediately. But then you were kissing my neck, begging me not to leave, cupping my breasts while I was trying to put my top on. It was so embarrassing.

'You loved me last night,' you said. I was correct – you *were* almost crying. 'I don't understand. Last night you told me I was amazing. What's changed?'

'I have to go.' I pulled on my Docs and made myself face you. You were sitting up on the bed, shrouded in that absolutely gross black-and-grey striped duvet cover that had *virgin* written all over it.

'We need to talk about what happened,' you said.

'No, we don't. We absolutely do not. Last night was last night. Today is today. We don't need to talk about it, now or ever. Forget about it. Seriously, OK? OK, Jeff?'

Your face crumpled.

I turned away. 'I really need to go.'

I was out of there a few seconds later. It was all I could do not to run home, praying to God you wouldn't tell your flat-mates you'd slept with Coco Moss, that I wasn't some sort of trophy you wouldn't be able to stop yourself holding up for all to see. That word wouldn't get out. I had a reputation to maintain after all.

But then I got home and Drew told me the news.

Turned out my reputation was the least of my worries.

CHAPTER 34

JEFF

Coco is typing.

Jeff waits, sweat pricking his brow. From downstairs comes the clank of plates going into the dishwasher. If Kate comes up, he will hear her footsteps.

Coco's reply chimes softly. Swearing silently, he switches his phone to mute.

That was the right call. You've given her an explanation that makes sense, so she'll be fine now. She'll have to act a little bit cross for her own pride, but she'll recover, trust me. She's hardly going to jettison the cash cow, is she?

Jeff blinks in disbelief. That's hardly how Kate views him, is it? If anything, rather irritatingly, she's always saying she could walk away from all of it tomorrow and go back to a simple life. By which she means – and it pains him to admit it – go back to the way they were before Coco, before that night, when they were happy – in love even. Maybe that's why it annoys him so much. All these years, Kate has attributed the change in him to his career: the promotions, the status, the money. But it happened long before that.

He texts Coco back.

She was quite odd at lunch. She looked spooked. Maybe she's hung-over or spaced out, but I'm not sure it worked.

The message nutshells what he thinks. Yes, it is that simple. He's not sure Kate bought it.

Spooked? Did you do anything different? Behave differently?

I apologised for yesterday like you said, told her I thought we should have evenings together, and then I told her I'd remembered where I'd seen you. I just had a feeling she knew more than she was letting on, the way she was looking at me.

He waits, watches the rolling dots. Did he behave differently? He came in, threw down his keys, gave her a long, affectionate hug. Fixed lunch.

Shit, he thinks then. It must be months since he's held her in his arms like that, since they've shared much more than a peck on the lips. Longer even. And as for lunch... He wonders if he's ever prepared a meal in all the years they've been married. It's possible he hasn't. Oh God, he thinks then. His wife was looking at him strangely because he was doing something nice for her. He was being too kind. It was the *kindness* that freaked her out.

Kindness is the thing he did differently.

What the hell does that say about him?

His phone buzzes.

You could have said less but it's OK. She'll be OK. You're feeling paranoid, that's all, trust me. I can't wait to see you tomorrow, my darling. I'll text you once I've got rid of the boys. Remember, be charming this evening, just don't overdo it. She'll think you're making up for your little faux pas. Women love it when men are in the wrong. Xx

Jeff throws his phone onto the bed, confusion filling him. Coco's words are laced with a kind of knowing cruelty that plants a seed of discomfort deep within him. But the thought of her tomorrow, of them together, makes his heart race. He should end it, immediately, really he should, but he can't. He is too far gone, the image of Coco this morning, the smell of her, the taste of her – he cannot get any of it out of his mind. He wants to go back there right now, no matter the risks, bury his head in her neck and inhale her.

A click from downstairs.

Was that the door?

'Kate?' He jogs to the top of the staircase and stops, listens. Nothing. 'Kate? Are you there?'

No reply. He runs down the stairs, into the living area. She's not there. She's not outside by the pool, not in the loo.

She's gone. Without him. They were supposed to be going for ice cream and she's just taken off without saying goodbye. She never passes up an offer of him spending time with her. Normally, if he'd promised her something like that, she'd be moaning at him by now, asking him if he was ready yet. Last year she practically burst into tears when he made her wait two hours before coming with her to buy a gift for Lou. He had to make up for it by hanging around, bored to death, while she tried on the cheap beachy clothes she always wastes her money on even though she knows she'll never wear them back home. She always makes him do something like that while they're on holiday, like some sort of proof of devotion – it's so tedious.

No. He can't afford to have these thoughts. They will show in his face. He must keep it together, keep up the pretence, now more than ever. She looked so wary at lunch; he will have to work extra hard to soothe her nerves, quash her doubts, but without being so kind as to make her suspicious. Oh God, it's a tightrope! He's no good at this! Be normal. Just be normal. Being normal is key, Coco said.

But what is his normal? He thinks back to this morning with Coco, how he regaled her with his best funny stories, how when she spoke, he listened as if every word from her lips was profound. He is not like that with Kate. At least, he hasn't been for as long as he can remember. With Kate he has become lacklustre – he can see that in a way he couldn't before Coco came back into his life and reintroduced him to this better, funnier version of himself. Yes, with Kate he is inattentive, dismissive. God, how depressing. How did they become this couple? No wonder Coco spotted straight away that they weren't happy. No wonder Kate drinks too much sometimes. The bottle can help gloss over things that should never be glossed over; isn't that part of why he denies himself even a sip? He doesn't deserve to have anything glossed over; dares not loosen his tongue.

Focus, Jeff. Stick to the point. Kate cannot find out any more about that night.

That night, when Coco drags him out of the party, it is like being in some sort of dream. He wishes he could remember every detail, but it is hazy. He has fantasised so many times about how they would meet, how they would get talking, how they would somehow find themselves alone. In these dreams he is easy, confident, witty. Outside that dank house, the clamour of what remains of the party muted behind them, Coco is holding his hand in the dark. Her grip is clammy. They are both staggering drunk. The air is freezing, icy down the back of his damp neck. The famous Leeds wind that would come howling down the hill into town, a wind you had to push against as you walked home from a night out. That wind blew through your bones. It seeped into your marrow.

'Oh my God, it's freezing. Do you have a car?' Through her leather jacket, she is chafing her arms against the cold.

'Yes, but I'm over the limit.'

'Ooh,' she mocks. 'We are a good boy, aren't we?' She leans in; her nose almost touches his, her breath tinged with cigarettes. 'Didn't have you pegged for a goody two-shoes.' She traces her forefinger down his chest. 'Where do you live? It can't be *that* far away.'

'I'm in Leeds 6.' Near you, he wants to say, but is afraid it will creep her out if he lets on he knows where she lives. Through the alcoholic fug, he's still processing that if she's asked him where he lives, it means, or might mean, that she's prepared to come home with him. Wants to even. Into his bedroom, into his fantasy, oh God.

'That's, like, five minutes away.' She makes a show of looking at her watch. 'It's after midnight. There's no one even on the roads. Come on. We'll go slow, I promise. Come *on.*'

She is pressed against his chest, the soft stubble of her hair the most delicious graze against his chin. She seems to be suggesting they go home together. But Lizzie and Ben will be there. They might see. Or hear.

Fuck it.

So what? This is Coco Moss. This is the jackpot! This is his only chance.

He pulls back her head, kisses her deeply and, he hopes, expertly on the mouth. He is, in that moment, how he has been in his dreams. He can be that. Dressed like this, he can be that.

'Let's go back to mine,' he says.

CHAPTER 35

KATE

Finding herself finally alone, Kate digs out her journal and writes:

Jeff has finally confessed. It's such a relief, I almost forgot to be cross. Lizzie was right – I should have asked him sooner. Not only does it explain why he and Coco looked so shocked but also why I haven't felt able to trust Coco a hundred per cent either, despite her being so friendly. She categorically said she didn't get together with Jeff that night, which really puts the cow in coward, doesn't it?

Above all else, it's just nice to know I was right – I felt like I was going mad there for a second!! Jeff said he didn't sleep with her. I want to believe him, but frankly, at this stage, there is no way I'll ever know for sure, so maybe I should make my peace with it and move on. It was a long time ago, and it's not like it's cast a shadow over our marriage or anything.

One thing it has done is give me some perspective. I spent years idolising Coco, decades idealising her memory, almost went to pieces when I saw her – for what? She's just some rich kid who's never had to do a day's work in her life, some girl

*who got drunk and copped off with boys at parties the same as
any other. Guess she didn't know Jeff and I were together back
then, so I can forgive her. And she probably didn't think it was
her place to say – which I get. No, I've got no beef with Coco. I
just don't trust her, that's all.*

*I'm glad Jeff's left me in peace, even if the mere mention of
work while we're on holiday really pisses me off. But for once I
didn't feel aggrieved. It's a surprise, this feeling. I suppose I've
had a lot of space, all my married life. I've resented it, but now
I'm thinking I should make more of it. I actually wish I'd
spent a lot less time waiting for him over the years and more
time getting on with what I wanted to do.*

*Well, no more waiting! I'm going to seize life by the
cojones! Lou won't be home for much longer and I was
dreading her leaving, but now part of me is almost looking
forward to the new possibilities that lie ahead for me. Another
business? An MA? Whatever I want!*

I feel strong. Stronger. I feel OK.

She sits back and rereads her latest entry. In her belly, a hot
ball of unease is growing. She started today's entry by saying she
feels relieved, but now the creep of anxiety has returned. Jeff's
doting behaviour at lunch was not only different; it was a total
personality transplant. While they were eating, he even asked
how her business was going, which almost made her choke. And
when he suggested they go for ice cream, she could have
laughed in his face.

Perhaps it is seeing the words in black and white, who
knows, but the sense that she has been told *a* truth but not *the*
truth now lodges in her chest like a brick. How briefly she felt
that glorious calm when he confessed. Really, she could have
wept. But while it was quite lovely to be attended to like that,
now, thinking about it, it strikes her that her husband has not
been himself since Coco Moss arrived in this house. Coco Moss,

who found him attractive once, who therefore could again. And just as his explanation for his previous weirdness makes sense, so today's Stepford Husband routine can easily be attributed to his intense feelings of guilt – but the thing is, it felt false.

Yes, now that she has taken the time to write, to process, it is a little like watching a TV drama only to reflect on it in the moments afterwards and see nothing but plot holes. Jeff's solicitousness, his offer of ice cream felt like flattery, a kind of wooing. He has never done this, ever. They were best friends who got together. No courtship, no roses, no can-I-take-you-out-to-dinner, just a drunk bout of wrestling that turned into a drunk bout of taking off each other's clothes. Today's Jeff was a man whose behaviour suggested he has a lot more to make up for than a minor infidelity from thirty years ago. Surely he would know that something like that wouldn't put his marriage of decades in actual danger? Because here's another thing dawning: for Jeff to behave like that, he'd have to be almost *frightened*.

Once again the picture has built and there is something that doesn't square up.

Kate doesn't trust Coco Moss, fine. After this week, she won't see her again.

But the trouble is, now she doesn't trust the one person who is at the absolute *centre* of her life, the person with whom she was planning to spend the rest of that life: her husband.

Kate heads out of the villa. She doesn't call upstairs to Jeff to see if he wants to come, doesn't ask if he remembers they were supposed to be going for ice cream. She'll text him in half an hour, she thinks, and ask him to join her. But for now, she needs to be alone.

At Bar Melitón, she orders a decaf iced coffee and sits in the shade. She has brought her Kindle with her but is too antsy to read. Something is edging in, but it needs time and space to arrive. Lizzie mentioned something – what was it? She takes out her phone, scrolls through the messages. Nothing. Whatever it was, she must have said it over the phone.

Hi again, Kate writes. *Sorry about this. Not overthinking, honest! You mentioned something over the phone – happened the same night as party but I can't remember what it was...*

She leaves her phone on the table in case Lizzie texts back. The fidgety feeling has not gone away. She should have brought her journal with her. Damn.

Seeing no sign of the waiter, she pops across to Quiosco Morana next door, buys a small notebook and a biro, and dashes back to her table to find her coffee and the bill waiting for her. She sits down, opens her notebook, feels the muted thrill of fresh stationery. And writes:

What else did Lizzie say?

She circles it three times, nib hard against the paper. Sits back, sips her iced coffee. She has asked for it without sugar, a decision she now regrets. She empties two sachets of white sugar into the glass and stirs it thoroughly.

She is still staring at those five words, racking her brain, when some sixth sense makes her look up. On the far side of the terrace, DH – Troy – is sitting down with the twins. She feels herself blush. He really is very attractive. Coco has subverted the whole older-rich-man-with-glamorous-young-wife cliché and got herself... almost a toyboy. He isn't yet forty, she thinks. Though at forty, Jeff looked thirty, so it's hard to tell. What he isn't is fifty. Definitely not. Kate could pretty much bet her life on that.

She watches. The boys obviously adore him, judging by their animated chatter, their laughter. A nice dad then, taking them to the beach, for ice cream; a kind, present husband, one who makes time to give Coco a break. It must be great to divorce someone stratospherically rich only to meet a new handsome, interesting man to make a family with. Talk about landing on your feet!

What would it be like to leave Jeff?

The thought hits her before she has time to stop it.

What would it be like to just... walk away?

Her pulse races. It is a terrible thought, terrible, and she shouldn't be thinking it. But like a forbidden fantasy, it comes at her over and over. What would it be like to meet someone who would find you new and shiny, someone who would laugh at all your old stories, pay you compliments, tell you you're amazing, take you to bed and kiss every inch of your skin, unpeel you layer by layer, listen to even your most mundane chatter as if it were gold, who would woo you, fix lunch for you, carefully, without being asked, without it being in compensation for bad behaviour?

Really, though, what would that be like?

Exhilarating.

Wonderful.

Terrifying.

Taking care not to slurp the last drops through the straw, she finishes her iced coffee, picks up her notepad and slides it into her bag. As she stands, Troy looks up briefly. Before she's thought it through, she waves.

He smiles, though it is obvious he has no idea who she is. She crosses the terrace, trying her best not to look crazy.

'Hi, sorry,' she says. 'I'm Coco's friend from uni. Kate. Kate Barrett. She might have mentioned me?'

'Ah, Kate! She did, yes. You've got a place here, right? She came to you for drinks the other evening? Nice to meet you.' Almost flustered then, as if he has forgotten his manners, he stands up, offers his hand, which she shakes. It is warm, dry, the grip firm. 'I'm Troy.'

'Hi,' she says again. 'Sorry,' she adds, again, realises she hasn't let go of his hand, pulls hers away. 'Nice to meet you too.

And these are...' She realises she has no idea what the boys are called. Is it possible Coco hasn't told her the names of her sons? 'The twins?'

'Yes, that one's Alfie,' Troy replies. 'And this one's Rory.'

The twins laugh.

'I'm Rory,' says Alfie, rolling his eyes.

'I'm Alfie,' says Rory, grinning.

They laugh again, although this is obviously an old routine.

Troy is still smiling at her. He has a lovely way about him, nothing like the terse man she observed a few days ago. He places his hands on his hips and looks over her shoulder momentarily. 'Has Coco gone back up?'

Kate hesitates. 'Coco? No, I'm... It's just me.'

'But you saw her earlier?'

'No. I haven't seen her all day.'

His face closes a little. 'I thought she was hanging out with you today.' His eyebrows rise. 'Must have changed her mind.'

Kate shakes her head. 'We didn't have an arrangement, I don't think. Unless I've missed a text or something.'

She pulls out her phone.

'No,' she says, looking up. 'There's no message.'

'She said she was meeting you,' Troy says matter-of-factly. 'That's why I took the boys. Hangover brunch, she said, then you were going to hang out at... You have a pool, she said? She said she was meeting you here, in fact.'

'Oh.' It is all Kate can think of to say. Inside her, a pressure is building.

'Don't worry about it,' Troy says. 'It's very Coco. Trust me.' He gives a flat smile before sitting down. It is Kate's cue to leave, she knows, but she can't move.

'Maybe she just wanted a lie-in,' she says.

'Maybe.' The word repeated sounds cynical. Troy's eyebrows twitch; his smile tightens. Whatever lightness filled him a moment ago is gone.

'It was nice to meet you anyway,' Kate says, turning to go.

'Kate?'

She turns back. Troy's hands are raised, palms out, as if to calm a horse. He looks pained.

'Are you OK?' she asks.

He puffs out his cheeks, lets out a long exhalation. 'Look. I shouldn't say this, but you seem... you seem nice. Just... keep your distance, OK? You and your husband. Coco is... she's a law unto herself.'

CHAPTER 36

Kate walks up the hill, conscious of her own deep breathing. Something like a panic attack is threatening; there is a pain in her chest and her eyes are stinging.

Why would Coco tell Troy she was meeting up with her today if she wasn't? She didn't suggest it last night; there was never any arrangement, even in pencil. Why would Coco lie to her husband? Is it as Kate has just suggested, to get a lie-in? Some peace? And why did Troy warn her off Coco? Despite his gentle manners, his lovely way, is he actually quite controlling? So selfish that Coco has to concoct a lie just to get a break from the kids? Or is he acting in good faith – telling her to stay away from Coco because she is in some way dangerous, toxic?

Appearances can be deceptive. Kate knows that better than anyone. Anyone looking at her and Jeff having dinner in a restaurant would see a successful middle-aged couple enjoying one another's company, him pouring wine for her, picking up the bill. They would not know that this couple spend most of their time apart, that it is years, perhaps decades, since they have had anything in common, and that without their daughter as buffer, time spent together now feels strange, unnatural – even unpleasant.

Kate laughs softly to herself – it is the hollow, mirthless laugh you give when someone makes a pointed joke that jags its tip under your skin. Even she didn't know these things until a day or two ago. For years she has been watching that couple from across the street, seeing the same picture, believing the same picture because she wanted to. She has not wanted to cross the street, go into that restaurant and look at them more closely. She stops, panting now with distress. *My God*, she thinks, *if I only now have the courage to look in the eye the uncomfortable truth of my own relationship, how the hell would I know anything about Coco and Troy?*

When she first saw them, she saw only the abrupt way Troy spoke to her, the way he threw down his credit card and walked away. Perhaps that picture is more honest. Perhaps they too are... the word lands hard in her chest... *estranged.*

Is that what she and Jeff are? Is that even what Coco and Troy are? Is Coco not lonely but in fact no longer inclined to spend time with her husband?

Unless...

No. No way. That's too paranoid, even for her.

But just as she failed to shut down the whispered fantasies of leaving Jeff, so now she fails to stop another voice, close enough in her mind's ear that she can feel its hot breath on her cheek.

Jeff and Coco knew one another before. Long ago, they shared a kiss, perhaps more. Jeff never told Kate. Today he downplayed it, but the glance they exchanged two days ago sent shock waves as if from a blast, warping the air, making everything stop dead still.

She has told herself she doesn't care if it was more than just a kiss all those years ago. She has told herself that was in the past, that it has no bearing on her marriage.

But what if that old attraction has rekindled between them?

What if Coco lied to her husband because she was meeting up not with Kate but with Jeff?

She stops, gasps, hand flying to her mouth.

Is that why he was wearing casual wear, not sports gear? And now she thinks of it, earlier he said that it was while he was running that he remembered where he knew Coco from. How can he have remembered while running if he wasn't wearing his running kit? And why was he in such a good mood? He didn't say where he'd been, but he smelt of, was damp from, the sea. Running aside, which he does every single morning, he would never go for a swim in his smart casual clothes, certainly not his best linen shorts, a brand-new white T-shirt. She noticed his clothes because the fact of them was odd, off. She read his changed behaviour as a guilty conscience. He confessed – guilty conscience explained. She forgot about the clothes. Yet here it is again, that niggling thing: *a* truth, not the truth. Guilt for sins past... or sins present?

The urge to be sick comes to her. Rage follows, her body filling with its heat, hands curling into fists. How dare he? How bloody dare he?

She lets herself into the villa, falls back against the door as it closes behind her.

'Kate? That you?'

'Who else would it be?'

A chuckle. Even that – that chuckle – is wrong. He hasn't *chuckled* in ten years.

'I thought we were going for ice cream?' he calls down, his voice cheery. *Chucklesome.*

'Oh,' she says, playing for time. 'I know, but I thought you'd got caught up with work.' Like you do, like you always, always do.

'Not at all. It was just a couple of emails.'

Since when is it ever just a couple of emails?

He appears at the top of the stairs. He is wearing the same linen shorts and no top, his hairless gym-honed body already tanned. Almost hairless – there is the telltale spike of regrowth at his chest. It was three years ago that he started removing his chest hair, an attempt to look younger that he denied without ever giving her an alternative reason. Had he started sleeping with someone else back then, someone from the office perhaps, when he began his excessive grooming, the painfully controlled calorie intake to add to his exercise addiction, the bloody teeth-whitening? Who is all this effort for?

Because it's not for Kate.

She looks up at him. He is leaning over the stairwell, one hand on the banister, his biceps flexed.

I don't know who this person is, she thinks. *I have no idea.*

'Are you OK?' he asks, still at the top of the stairs. 'You seem a bit... out of sorts.'

'I just needed a bit of time to process things, that's all. It's hit me a bit.' If he can pin it all on that one kiss, then so can she. She knows there is more, she absolutely knows it. Where was he this morning, and why did he come back as if he'd had a personality transplant?

She knows where. She knows why. She knows.

He frowns, looks at his watch. 'We could go out now?'

She shakes her head. 'Let's just... let's go out later for dinner. I'm really tired. I might have a nap actually.' She begins the slow climb of the stairs. At the top, he steps back to let her past.

'Where are you going?' he says when she doesn't take the second stairwell up to their room, heading instead into the spare bedroom. What is he expecting? That they climb those stairs, go to bed together? After he's so obviously been to bed with...

Really? Can it really have gone so far so quickly?

'I need to sleep.' How calm she sounds, how tired. But it is not a lie. She is almost preternaturally calm and incredibly, overwhelmingly exhausted.

She closes the door behind her and crawls onto the spare bed. Her eyelids are heavy, so heavy, her heart a rock. Sleep is coming at her like a drug.

Her phone buzzes. She scrabbles for it on the bedside table, peers at it. Lizzie.

Do you mean about the girl dying?

'Oh my God,' Kate whispers. She had forgotten she was waiting for Lizzie to reply. The girl dying. That's the other thing Lizzie mentioned; how could she have forgotten?

That's it. Did you know her? What was her name, do you know?

Joanne Dickson. I didn't know her. She hung out with Coco and those guys. She might have been seeing Drew.

Kate's stomach flips. The picture builds, clarifies. A girl died. But it wasn't just a girl; it was someone in Coco's close circle. This, something like this, finally, would be big enough to explain the look of horror that passed between her husband and Coco Moss.

Is her mind playing tricks? A full-blown affair would, let's face it, also be enough. Is she overthinking, becoming a conspiracy theorist, conflating two things that are completely separate? The look of horror – could it simply have been that Jeff slept with Coco, perhaps more than once, a secret he's kept their entire marriage? Did that encounter, an encounter that Kate organised for reasons that seem ridiculous to her now, cause them to resume their affair?

Or is there something more?

She's had enough. Enough! A fresh wave of utter fury heats her skin. She is beyond sadness, beyond resentment. Quite simply, she could kill them both – slowly – and enjoy watching them die. She hates them with a hot feeling in her belly, a tension in her entire body that feels muscular. This cannot go on any longer. If it's the end of her marriage, so be it. It isn't like there's much left of it anyway; she suspects it was over before they came here. Jeff is welcome to his life. It was always on his terms, and she'd be perfectly happy – God knows, she'd be relieved – without it. Whatever is going on needs dragging into the light, no matter what.

And the only person who's got the balls to do that is her.

CHAPTER 37

JEFF

From the corner sofa, he hears the slow, careful tread on the wooden stairs and feels his jaw clench. It is a little after seven. Kate has been hiding away in the spare room since she got back. She appears at the doorway and they exchange a quiet 'hey' before he pretends to go back to his book. He is acutely aware of her, her hovering hesitation before coming into the open-plan living area, as if she is crossing some invisible boundary.

She is wearing a red sundress, a pale pink scarf thing over her shoulders. She has washed her hair, put on make-up. She looks good, better than usual, and he feels a pervading sense of nostalgia. In her face, even at a glance, he can see the girl she was at eighteen; the young woman holding their baby girl in her arms the morning after she was born; a slightly older Kate looking up from her laptop at the dining-room table to tell him she'd made her first profit. Kate. His Kate. He is probably the only person in the world who can see beneath the lines at her eyes, the grooves on her forehead, the softening shape of her face, and the thought moves him.

They were kids, he thinks then. Lizzie, Ben, Coco too – all of them were just kids. He and Kate were best friends before anything happened between them. When it happened, he didn't love her more, just differently. He loves her still, of course he does, but it is very different to how he feels about Coco. Coco pushes him outside of himself, causes a kind of kamikaze madness. She makes him want to set light to everything he knows and walk away from the blaze with her hand in his. He loves Kate as he loves his daughter, with that deep feeling of family, of longevity, of a life if not completely shared then at least lived side by side. That life is not terrible. It is a life many would envy. There is something in that, isn't there? Something worthwhile?

'I've been thinking,' Kate says eventually.

Despite the ominous feeling in his guts, he arranges his features into a pleasant smile and looks up from his novel. 'Oh yes?'

'I'm going to invite Coco, Troy and the boys for dinner tomorrow night.'

He studies her, to see if she is toying with him. But she isn't. She wouldn't be. Kate does not play games. She is just... Kate.

'Right.' The word almost chokes him.

'I just think it'd be nice if we try and clear the air. All this subterfuge is silly, isn't it? After so much time.'

Heat fills him, a rising panic. 'You want to *talk* about what happened? I'm not sure—'

'Of course not!' She laughs. It is a light, almost merry sound. 'I just mean to show Coco it's all cool, that's all. I think everyone's getting het up over nothing, and if we're not careful, it's going to spoil our summer holiday.'

It is his turn to laugh, though he is unnerved. 'So, what? You *wouldn't* mention it?'

'I'll go for coffee with Coco tomorrow morning – or call her or something first. I'll tell her I know but I'll keep it light, tell her I don't blame her, that it's all water under the bridge.'

She is looking at him intently. Is she watching him for

clues? But if she asks Coco for coffee tomorrow, Coco will have to tell her she's with Troy, and if Kate sees Troy without Coco, she'll wonder where Coco is and that could...

'Sure,' he manages. 'But... won't she be with her kids in the morning?'

She smiles; her eyes crinkle at the edges, as if he is her son and has answered his mother's question correctly. He realises his breath is caught, releases it in an audible rush.

'Good point,' she says, sending the breath back into his lungs, trapping it there. 'But I think Troy does the lion's share with the kids during the day. I saw him when I went out before. He was taking the twins for ice cream. They'd been out all day.'

He tries to keep his expression neutral, but his voice is thin. 'You seem to know a lot about their set-up. Did you speak to him or something?'

'I did. He's really nice.' She frowns, the merest shake of her head. 'He asked where Coco was. Apparently she'd told him she was meeting *me* today. Isn't that weird? Don't you think that's weird?'

His blood pulses at his temples. Kate is sliding her feet into her flip-flops, telling him her new shoes have bloodied the backs of her ankles. Her tone is light, conversational, but he is not fooled. She knows something. Suspects anyway.

'Was it a misunderstanding?' he asks. 'With Coco? Have you checked with her?'

Kate shakes her head. She picks up a plate from the break-fast bar and moves towards the dishwasher. 'Not yet.' Her voice thins as she bends to load the plate, thickens again as she straightens up. 'She probably planned to text me but fell back asleep, I should imagine. She was pretty wasted last night. She was sick in a plant pot on the way up the hill.'

'Was she?'

Kate nods. 'We were both quite well oiled, to be honest.'

His chest deflates, breath hissing out of him. Kate knows nothing. Nothing.

'There's your answer then,' he says confidently. 'She'll have dropped back to sleep. Definitely. Hey, shall we go and grab some dinner?'

'Sure.'

'Great. Where do you want to go?'

'Wherever.'

'Tapas?'

'*Por qué no?*' She giggles.

They are both so calm, he thinks as he closes the vault-thick Danish front door they had installed a few months after buying the place. There are two security cameras, front and back, which he can check from home in the UK, three motion-sensor lights, and a sophisticated alarm system they only use when they're leaving the place empty. The security on the villa makes Fort Knox look like an open tent, but tonight, turning the key anticlockwise in its reassuringly stiff lock, he feels anything but safe.

CHAPTER 38

COCO

I've just sent you a text, my darling. You're not going to like it, but I had to cancel our morning tryst tomorrow. Troy came in all guns blazing, accusing me of being up to my old tricks. He actually used those words. For someone so young, he sounds like such a fogey sometimes, and I told him so.

'Is it him?' he said. 'The husband? Really? What the fuck!'

'It's none of your business,' I said calmly. Troy hates it when I stay calm – it really winds him up. 'I'm allowed to have friends. You're not my keeper.'

He glared at me with something akin to hate – hate and love being so close and all that – and said, 'You'll never stop using me, will you? It's like...' He cast about the room for inspiration. 'It's like you set these traps, and just when I think you've changed or calmed down, the trap springs and I'm... I'm caught. You're out of control, do you know that? What about the boys?'

'What about the boys? What trap?' I laughed in his face, which was no more than he deserved. 'I seem to remember it's *me* who got us a fabulous villa for a whole month so you could practise your compositions, *me* who spends the entire evening playing Scrabble with the twins, and me who has to sit here alone at night like a fucking handmaiden.'

'Oh yes,' he sneered. 'Saint Coco. Don't pretend to care about the boys; they're just an inconvenience to you – always have been.'

I was still laughing. The piety. Honestly, it was hilarious.

'I needed a lie-in,' I said. 'I never texted Kate because I slept until one. Meanwhile, you see Kate having coffee on her own and that automatically means I'm sleeping with her husband? Oh my God! I wouldn't touch him if he were the last man on earth, so just... Do you know what? Just leave me alone.'

Honestly, darling. Such bad luck he bumped into Kate. Bad, bad timing, but nothing cast iron in terms of incrimination, so no need to panic, I just need to play nice for twenty-four hours.

Anyway, there it is. Tryst postponed, how very *triste*. That's French for sad, by the way – it's your wife who's the linguist, isn't it? Not you. I forget who I'm seducing sometimes, I really do. But I am disappointed not to see you, my love. I'd been looking forward to it, imagining your hands on my skin and... oh, all sorts of other things. I've been thinking about everything you said to me this morning, and the more I think about it, the more I think you're right: leaving Kate *is* what makes the most sense. Your marriage is over, best admitted to sooner rather than later. You were so sure, and I do like a man who knows his own mind.

What could I do but agree?

'We've already lost decades,' I concurred, running my hands over those funny little spikes of hair on your chest – really, though, what's that about? 'I suppose it's not fair to live a lie, is it? On her, I mean, as well as us. One must try to be authentic.'

'Thing is,' you said, 'you fit in so much better with my lifestyle.'

Charming, I must say, like choosing new furniture to better match the sitting room – but I ignored it.

'Kate has never really adapted,' you went on. 'She's a down-to-earth lass at heart. She gets so nervous at the kind of social occasions I'm expected to attend. And when she gets nervous, she drinks. It's embarrassing. You're... you're at home in that world. You'd know what to do, how to be.'

I love that you think I'd fit in. You're right, I would. I could anyway. I am if nothing else a great adaptor. And no matter how close people think they get, they never get to know the real me. Sometimes I don't even think *I* know the real me.

Because here's the thing, the thing I'll never tell you or anyone else, Jeff Barrett. I'm not who or what you think at all. You have me pegged as to the manner born, but my parents didn't have a pot to piss in. And while I've never actually told anyone where I'm from, when I say I'm from 'around and about', I'm not actually lying. I think I must have moved ten or eleven times as a kid, traipsing round the UK with my mum in an attempt to shake off my psycho father, said father duly finding us, hammering on the door: *Maggie! Maggie, I know you're in there. Open this fucking door before I break it open.*

Terrifying, I think you'll agree. At least you would if I were saying any of this to you. I did tell someone once. My ex. What a mistake that was. I mean, when I say I told him, it was more of an unwilling confession. I'd passed off my birth certificate with some bluster about my college nickname, choosing my grand-mother's maiden name because I liked it, et cetera, but it didn't take much for him to trace my origins not to deepest Hamp-shire, as I had told him, but to somewhere near Wolverhampton. I suppose I should be thankful the private investigator didn't contact my parents, that all I got from my self-righteous ex was a raisin-eyed rebuke about the immorality of pretending they were deceased. How could I? How could I do such a thing?

It must all have been quite a shock for him. He was only trying to find out if I was sleeping with his colleague, which I have to confess, I was. But only because people like me can't afford to not have options. We need a parachute, and we need to keep that parachute strapped to our backs at all times. There is no way, *no way*, I would do what Kate has done – put all my eggs in one basket, even a good, solid basket like you. Seriously, I want to shake your wife by the shoulders and say, darling, you had time, you had so much fucking *time* to find something and someone else just in case, but all you did was feel sorry for yourself and – and this is the worst – wait. All this *waiting*. And for *what*? For your husband to want to spend time with you? To change? To love you? And now, you're so miserable and lonely, probably desperate to leave, but you have no one to jump ship with and no life raft in the water. But I have – someone to jump ship with, I mean.

You, Jeff Barrett, are my emergency dinghy.

CHAPTER 39

KATE

While Jeff studies the menu, Kate wonders about asking for a divorce. She could lean over the table and say in a low voice, *Hey. I was thinking we should probably split up. Call it, you know? Like they do with dead bodies on ER. What do you think?*

Watching Jeff contain his panic has not been as much fun as she thought it would be. She is not hard enough for games. It is actually really stressful, and she is so, so sad – for Lou, for the fact that her husband is so incredibly inept at keeping his midlife-crisis affair secret. It isn't the affair that has finished them, she thinks. It is the affair on top of all the rest.

Idly she picks up her knife, her own reflection flashing small and blurry in the blade. Moments before they came out to dinner, when Jeff popped to the loo, she checked his phone and found the thread she knew would be there. A shock even so, a real kick in the solar plexus.

Her jaw flexes, her hand tightens around the handle of the knife. The most recent message read:

LOML, alas, we can't be together tomorrow now. Troy suspects and I need to play nice for a day. Am devastated. Can still feel your hands on my skin, am longing for you to come back so we can do it all again. Will text as soon as the coast is clear, but it might be the day after. Hold on, my love. Soon we will tell K and then we can be together always and forever. Yours, LOYL, C xx

Listening to Jeff pee behind the door, she scrolled to the top, found her husband's message sent at 10.30 that first evening: hours after the drinks, after he'd denied all knowledge of Coco Moss, after he'd gaslighted Kate into believing she was a gauche wannabe who had created a deeply awkward situation for everyone concerned. But there it was, in black and white:

We need to talk. J x

Her husband started it then. Restarted it rather. His unfriendliness towards Coco at the beginning of the evening was a cover. Kate had assumed Coco must have seduced him, but no. He had made the first move. The thought winded her. She had to lean against the wall to stop herself from stumbling. He must have gone into her phone that same evening and retrieved Coco's number, saved it under C. There was such purpose to that, such intention. A registered call, six seconds long, was made by Coco the following morning. Did they meet after that – to 'talk'? Did they go back to her place? When she saw Coco later that morning, looking a little out of breath and pink of cheek, had she been with Jeff?

It was possible, more than possible.

With impeccable timing, the toilet flushed. She closed the screen and placed the phone back on the occasional table. Breathing hard, she ran out onto the street, across to the geraniums on the far side, red and waxy in the dusk, wondered whether she could raise the planter above her head and hurl it at him. It was heavy, heavy enough to kill him, but too heavy for her to lift, alas. She thought about dashing inside, grabbing the carving knife from the magnetic strip, waiting for him to emerge from the cloakroom. The element of surprise: she would drive the shining tip into his pathetic, disloyal heart before he'd had time to shake his hands dry.

You've fallen for your own youth, she would spit into his face while the blood pumped from him. *You've thrown us and everything we've built under the bus for a stupid infatuation, you absolute bloody cliché.*

What did LOML mean? She wondered this only later, as they walked to the restaurant together, Jeff holding her hand, something he hadn't done for a decade at least. And LOYL? Was it some reference to pet names past?

She had known it would get worse, that finding out more would cause only pain. She was killing herself slowly in order to live, she told herself. The pain would set her free – eventually. Ending a marriage was an enormous decision, a feeling of failure no one wanted, and there was Lou to think of.

But it wasn't Kate who had ended it, was it? That blame fell squarely on Jeff.

Earlier still, after her text exchange with Lizzie, Kate had googled the words *Joanne Dickson Leeds University death 1988* in various orders but found nothing. Increasingly she is beginning to think it is a red herring, though the lack of fuller information still niggles her.

Now, in the restaurant, she glances up at her husband. Objectively, he is attractive, more so than when they were young. Confidence has done this; confidence, professional success and wealth – and of course hours in the gym, the teeth he had straightened in his forties for a small fortune. Does he think he loves Coco Moss? How can he? Whatever happened in the past, he barely knows her. And yet he is prepared to throw away his life for *her*, some girl he once kissed. Because that really is all she is: some girl, a person, only a person. Kate had thought her so unreachable, so other-worldly, so amazing, but she is not. It has taken this horrific betrayal for her to realise that

Coco is just a fellow human being, and not a particularly nice one.

Under the table, she texts Coco.

Hey, babe. Just chatting with Jeff and we're wondering if you, Troy and boys want to come over for dinner tomorrow? 7-ish – what do you think? Xx

Jeff looks up. His chic new Armani reading glasses glint in the candlelight. Kate wonders if he thinks she can't see that he has his phone hidden behind the menu, the way his softening under-chin glows slightly when he receives a message.

'What're you having?' he asks.

A middle-aged, middle-class couple out for a romantic supper, she thinks, almost laughs.

She glances at the starters. The tapas place was full, so they are here at Eduarda's again, possibly for the last time. Kate will not ask for a share of the villa, will probably never return to Cadaqués. She hates the heat.

'I think,' she says, 'I'm going to go for the boquerones. The anchovies. Do you know why?'

His eyes meet hers. In his she sees a flicker of fear. 'No, why? Should I?'

'Because all these years, I've pretended to like oysters out of some stupid idea that they're more sophisticated or something. But I don't like them, never have.' She emits a giddy, slightly mad giggle. 'So,' she says, tears pricking, 'I'm having the anchovies. Because I prefer them and because they're my favourite. In fact, I might never have oysters ever again.'

His face shifts into a closed little smile, as if he's ashamed of his teeth. But he is not ashamed of his teeth. He spent four thousand pounds on his teeth. What he is is totally freaked out.

'OK,' he says slowly.

Under the table, her phone lights up on her lap. She glances down. Coco.

Sounds marvellous. Count me in. Will try and persuade the others. Xx

Kate suppresses a grin of satisfaction. It is exactly as she predicted. Coco has no intention of persuading anyone. She never asked anyone the first time. Apparently she doesn't like spending time with her boys. She is lonely and bored, far more than Kate ever has been, but for different reasons. She will come alone tomorrow to keep up appearances, perhaps even to toy with Jeff, who knows, maybe play footsie under the table, sneak a kiss whenever Kate leaves the room. It's a game to her, all a game. Who cares? Kate is the puppeteer now. Coco and Jeff are going to be dancing at the end of her strings.

Jeff is studying the menu as if it contains the secret of eternal youth. Momentarily his chin glows. A text, then, from his shiny new mistress, with whom all his old stories will be new, his faults hidden, his best self proudly on show. But those stories are only new once; his faults will emerge, just like anyone else's, and his best self will eventually, Kate guesses, stay at work, where it always was.

Coco is welcome to him frankly.

Kate fights a smile. It occurs to her that she's beginning to enjoy herself after all.

While her husband tries to pretend he isn't reading Coco's text, which presumably says something like *OMG your wife's invited me to dinner*, Kate thumbs a reply to Coco.

Great! Don't worry if T busy and boys don't fancy it. We can make it just us three – Leeds alumni! Xxx

Perfect, she thinks. She will host a lovers' dinner. She will do roast sea bream, Jeff's favourite, then she will ask them both what the hell is going on. And in that moment, quite bizarrely, it occurs to her what LOML stands for.

'Love of my life,' she says, out loud.

'What?'

'You, darling,' she says smoothly. 'You're the love of my life.'

CHAPTER 40

JEFF

After some bizarre speech about anchovies versus oysters, Kate informs him that Coco is coming for dinner the following night, but not to worry, she won't mention the Halloween party.

'Great,' he says, near to spaced out now with stress, itching to reach his phone and text Coco.

Don't come for dinner. Please. K's behaving weirdly. I have a feeling she knows.

As it is, he only texts her an hour later, after they've eaten an incredibly good mixed sea platter for two with rosemary roasted potatoes and a crisp green salad. Unusually, his wife has only had one glass of rosé.

'Just popping to the toilet,' she says, and despite everything, he winces. He keeps telling her that toilet is vulgar, that she should say loo, but she was corrected too many times to the contrary as a child, her parents insisting that the shortening to loo was, in fact, common.

Coco replies: *You're being completely paranoid. We've literally only slept together once – how can she possibly know unless she's Sherlock fucking Holmes? Calm down. Seriously, Jeff. You'll give the game away if you freak now, OK? I love you. All will be well. See you tomorrow night. Maybe you could walk me home?*

The message ends with a winking emoji and a heart. The promise of risky sex, of love, in two miniature images. He texts a heart back and slides the phone into the inside pocket of his linen sports jacket.

When he looks up, Kate is crossing the restaurant towards him. She is smiling. Her hair has been blown into soft, scruffy waves by the salt breeze from the sea. In her flip-flops and red dress, she looks like a hippy type who might have a tattoo hidden somewhere and sell fat silver rings on the quay. Their eyes meet. It is almost unbearable. Half of him wants to shift gear to reverse, to forget Coco and live the life he actually has with this woman, his wife, who is now sitting opposite him and asking if he's going to have dessert. Her cheeks are flushed, as if she's been exercising; her eyes sparkle.

'I think I'll just have an espresso,' he says. 'Decaf.'

'Me too,' she says, reaching for his hand, squeezing his fingers.

He feels his shoulders fall, his breath settle. Coco is right. Kate knows nothing. All will be well.

CHAPTER 41

KATE

Kate wakes early, showers and throws on an old sundress, the fabric soft against her skin. Downstairs, the kitchen is empty. From Jeff, there is no sound. It is strange to be up before him. By the time she rises, he is usually out or back from his morning run, still in his Lycra, but today the silence is different, loaded somehow with his presence two floors up.

She makes tea and steps out onto the terrace, where the air is still cool, the water bright. Everything is in a kind of hyper-focus, outlines precision-drawn. It reminds her of when Jeff bought their first high-definition TV – a monstrous cinematic affair that made her feel a bit sick, overwhelmed as she was by the near-3D clarity of the images on the screen. That's how it feels now – this villa, this part of her life. It is the last time she will see this place; she knows it somewhere inside herself. It's possible she will leave late tonight. Once this evening has come and gone, she won't stay. Jeff and Coco are welcome to it, all of it.

Settled on the sunlounger, she opens her laptop and googles Joanne Dickson once again. The niggling feeling has not left her. She adds more variations on her search – but nothing. She checks the WhatsApp, then, wondering if Lizzie has the spelling right, tries her search again with Dixon.

This time there's a link to the *Leeds Post* archives. She clicks, enters *Joanne Dixon* into the bar. Waits. After a moment, a story loads:

Girl Dies in Halloween Tragedy
Students warned of dangers of alcohol after student death

The hairs on Kate's arms rise. She reads on.

A young woman, who has been named as Joanne Dixon, was found unconscious in Leeds 6 in the early hours of Tuesday, 1 November. An ambulance was called, but paramedics pronounced Miss Dixon dead at the scene. The precise time of her death is not known.

In a brief press conference, Rudra Singh, a spokesperson for Leeds Infirmary, said that Ms Dixon died of hypothermia following a collapse due to having consumed an excessive amount of alcohol.

Friends close to Miss Dixon confirmed that she attended a student fancy dress party in Woodhouse the previous evening and was seen leaving around 11 p.m. following an argument with her boyfriend, Andrew Richman. She was wearing only a flimsy white dress and sandals and did not have a coat.

'We're all devastated,' said close friend Bunny Walters. 'We can't believe it. She was such a special person. Everyone loved her.'

Andrew Richman was unavailable for comment. Leeds University has appealed to its students to drink responsibly and to avoid letting anyone walk home alone.

'Too much alcohol impairs judgement,' Deputy Chancellor Kevin Reed commented. 'This is a tragedy that could

have been avoided, and our deepest sympathies go out to Joanne's parents.'

Kate's entire body has filled with heat. The human element of the tragedy laid out like this brings tears to her eyes. Poor kid. Poor, poor kid. Her poor parents. My God, if anything like that happened to Lou, she would never get over it, never.

'You're up early.' Jeff's voice reaches her from inside the villa.

She closes the laptop, swings her legs over the side of the sunlounger towards him. 'I am. I slept really well actually. The bed in the spare room is more comfortable than ours.'

That Jeff didn't ask why she wasn't coming up to their room with him last night cannot have escaped either of them. It was a tacit acknowledgement that, despite her positivity, Kate is still not over the Coco thing. Only Kate, however, knows how far from not over it she is.

'Is that because you only had one glass of wine, do you think?' Jeff is pulling his heel up to his backside, stretching.

'What?' She feels herself bristle.

'Why you feel refreshed,' he says. 'You only had one glass last night.'

'Didn't realise you were counting.' She hears the tremor of anger in her voice, more anger than the comment strictly deserves, but there is a bulging reservoir of rage inside her – the rage of years left unacknowledged, she suspects – and the dam is struggling to hold.

Jeff looks pained. 'I wasn't. I just... No, not at all. You can get pissed every night for all I care.'

'Nice. Tender. Thank you so much. Is that what you think I do?'

He throws up his hands. 'I didn't mean it like that.'

'I think you probably did. The subtext was deafening.'

He shakes his head. 'That's not fair.'

'Sometimes I wish you'd just come out and say it. It'd be so much better than sitting there judging while I slowly destroy myself.'

'If that's how you see it, maybe you should stop.'

'It's not how I see it. It's how you see it.' Her face burns.

'You don't know how I see it,' he says, sounding like a child at primary school. 'Only I can know how I see it.'

Unable to bear him a second longer, she stands up, shoulders her straw bag.

'Tell you what,' she says, heading past him for the door, 'I'll go into town and shop for the meals I'm going to be preparing for you over the next twenty-four hours while you take some leisure time, OK? I'd hate for you to miss out on your leisure time.'

'What's that supposed—'

The door slams behind her. She doesn't hear the rest.

At Bar Boia on the beach, Kate treats herself to a wonderful breakfast of jamón, eggs, freshly squeezed orange juice and a perfect cortado. As she eats, she stares out across the wide, winking bay. It is still early, relatively few people about, the temperature a decent twenty-six degrees.

She has already managed to have a good laugh about her magnificent parting flourish of passive aggression, her dramatic flouncing out of the villa. Really, it is so much easier to be articulately furious when actually you are not; there's real power in it.

But now her thoughts have returned to Joanne Dixon. Close friend of Bunny Walters, girlfriend of Drew Richman. Bunny was definitely part of Coco's crowd, and Drew and Coco are still close. Bunny was loud and annoying, brash and flirtatious. She wore dungarees, her hair in high blonde plaits, and sang loudly as she walked through the corridors that connected the lecture halls with the self-consciousness battiness of someone who thinks that actually they have a pretty great voice.

The article confirmed that Joanne Dixon was at that party. She left before midnight, alone, after some sort of argument. She had consumed a lot of alcohol, enough to collapse and not get up. Alone, she died where she fell. Dear God, how utterly awful.

But is there a link to Jeff and Coco? If Jeff did sleep with Coco that night, they would have left together. Kate wonders how late that was. If sex was on the cards, it might not have been so much later. They must have walked, since Jeff went to fetch his car the next morning. Did they go back to Coco's place? If so, where did she live? Neither Ben nor Lizzie saw Jeff come home, but it's possible they'd gone to bed before Jeff and Coco got back – if Jeff dared to bring Coco back to his digs. If Ben and Lizzie were as drunk as Lizzie said, they would probably have slept heavily. Joanne was found in Leeds 6. That was the area where Jeff, Lizzie and Ben were living. Coco could have left with Jeff in the morning when he went back for the car, before Lizzie and Ben woke up. It's equally possible that Jeff picked up the car on his way home from Coco's, if he stayed at hers, and lied to Ben and Lizzie, using the car as his alibi.

He will not have wanted them to know he'd cheated on Kate.

But what of Joanne? Is there a link? Did they meet her on the way home? Was there some sort of fight, an argument that ended badly? Or was the look of horror in the villa simply the shock of their past affair hitting them both in the face at the same moment, a shock they had to pretend not to feel in front of Jeff's now wife?

She settles the bill before heading to the Spar.

As she crosses the Carretera, Jeff emerges from the alleyway by the bakery in his Oakley wraparounds, Nike vest and matching Lycra shorts, and proceeds to run through the town.

Like clockwork – he always runs before his swim. He always has his kit on. Never his smart-casual attire, not in the morning. Perhaps Coco is unavailable. Perhaps Jeff is scared, too scared to risk a liaison today. Whatever, he doesn't see Kate watching him weave between the tourists, cross in front of Bar Casino, head towards Platja des Llane Gran.

Her chest heaves. It occurs to her that it is a relief to see him doing what he told her he was going to do. One truth, one solid truth to hold on to. Only yesterday morning, he slept with Coco Moss, of this Kate is certain. Yesterday morning, while Kate was still in bed, he must have gone straight to her villa the moment her family left and made love to her without delay, without qualms – lovers reunited.

He came home later, smelling of the sea. He must have calculated that to come home smelling of Coco's perfume or whatever brand of shower gel she uses would give him away. So he went for a swim, thinking this would fool his wife, but it did not. Over three decades they have been together: his habits are not only set but as familiar to her as her own. One break, one false note, and she knew. And there have been several false notes.

Besides which, since the look, she has been on high alert.

She checks her watch: 10 a.m. Was he in bed with Coco by this time yesterday? Did they do away with words and simply fall on each other, tear at each other's clothes like they do in films?

There is a strange masochistic pleasure in torturing herself with these thoughts. It is over ten years since Jeff has even removed her clothes, let alone torn them off. At 10 a.m. yesterday, she was still asleep, lost to the after-effects of God knows how many margaritas.

Certain that Coco will come alone, Kate buys three shiny silver bream and adds twelve large king prawns for a starter, along with fresh salads, some cold cuts and cheeses for lunch.

Next, she calls at the bakery and buys a baguette, some seeded rolls and a raspberry tart she doubts anyone will eat. Finally she stops at the deli and picks up some roasted vegetable couscous and some bright shredded beetroot. There are bottles of beer still at the villa and half a case of rosé Rioja, but Kate won't be drinking much. She needs to keep her wits about her. Coco and Jeff are clever, cleverer than her probably, but they are not as clever as they think.

CHAPTER 42

Once back at the villa, Kate announces she won't be eating lunch and heads to the pool to read. Jeff goes upstairs to work. In the late afternoon, he appears at the patio door and tells her he's going for a walk.

'I think I'll stay here and do the prep for tonight,' she says, though he has not asked her to come. Apparently there are no offers of ice cream today.

The moment the front door closes, she grabs her sunglasses and bag. After a few seconds, she edges the door open and spies him heading up the lane. She closes the door carefully, silently, and follows. He is heading away from town, is about eight metres away. If he turns around, he will see her and know she is following him. This is a fool's errand, she knows, but she cannot help herself.

He takes a right, another left. They are on the Carretera de Cadaqués now, at the edge of town. After another hundred metres or so, he stops. Kate shrinks into the shadows, then, panicking, scuttles across the street to where three hulking municipal recycling bins stand on a square of tarmac. Hiding behind one of them, she can see her husband waiting outside an old blue door, the paint peeling in curls. He looks about him, smooths his hair with the flat of his hand before breathing into that same hand and sniffing his palm.

'For God's sake,' Kate mutters, her jaw clenching in fury.

A moment later, the door opens, and Coco Moss emerges, dressed in the same white kaftan as that first day. She smiles and throws out her arms. Jeff steps into those arms, plunges his face into her long neck.

The door closes.

Kate's heart hammers.

You knew this, she tells herself, but it does not stop her blood from racing through her, her skin hot and alive with rage and dismay. Good riddance, she thinks, but the words don't fool her nearly enough to stop the tears from streaming down her face. She lets them fall, lets herself cry, cries some more after she reaches the villa and closes the door behind her. She does not open the freezer, does not grab the bottle and tip it to her lips. She lets herself feel it, every nuance of it, until finally she stops, sniffs hugely and announces to no one: 'Right. Let's do this.'

An hour later, Coco texts.

It's just me for dinner later, sorry. Hope that's OK. X

Kate wonders if she and Jeff are still in bed, whether Jeff helped her to compose this message, the two of them sharing an illicit giggle at her expense. Probably.

She hates them.

Upstairs, she takes a shower, to cool off and to wash the tears from her face. They are the last tears she will shed. Tonight will be the last time she will wait for her husband to come home.

No more. No bloody more.

Back downstairs, she begins to prep the three fish she

bought before Coco even told her there would only be three for dinner.

Jeff returns just as she's drizzling the lot with extra-virgin olive oil.

'Hi,' she says from behind the breakfast bar. 'Good walk?'

'Yes,' he says. He does not approach her. 'Hot though. I think I'll grab a quick shower.'

'Sure.'

Of course you will. Wash her off.

He turns one-eighty. His feet slap on the wooden stairs. She drinks half a glass of wine for courage; the rest of the glass because the first half was not enough. It's the last of the bottle, so she opens another and pours a glass from it so that her husband will think that's all she's had.

A few minutes later, he emerges in fresh shorts, another white T-shirt, the folds from the packet still in evidence, the way he likes.

'Do you need help?' he asks. 'Shall I set the table?'

'Sure. Yeah. Actually, let's just set the bar, shall we? As there's only three of us.'

Weirdness, she thinks. Total weirdness. There's a name for it, this weirdness. Inauthenticity, that's what it is. All her married life she has clung to this smiling brand of inauthenticity, and where has it got her, really? It was inauthenticity that brought Coco back into their lives – Kate pretending to be someone she was not – but those lives were fake well before Coco ever stepped into this villa. Here is where inauthenticity has got her, right here, this ridiculous game of pretend.

Well, tonight will be her last inauthentic night. No more oysters, no more stifling heat, no more bullshit.

Jeff tells her it's after 6.30 – should they have some music? Yes, she says. Why not? It is all so civilised.

She sips her first/third glass of wine and hiccups, slides a chorizo and Manchego amuse-bouche into her... well, into her *bouche*, wonders if there's an equivalent term in Spanish – *divierta-boca*, perhaps. Amuse-mouth. Idioms are so comical when translated. Mad as a goat, they say in Spain. That's how she feels: mad as a goat.

Jeff puts on some music she doesn't recognise. He tells her it's Max Richter, that he really likes this album. She knows without any doubt whatsoever that this is music Coco has introduced him to, that it's possible they made love to it only hours ago.

'Kate? Kate?' Jeff is staring at her. 'I was asking if you'd like an aperitif,' he says, his expression neutral.

She holds up her wine and tells him she's just poured one, thanks, that there's San Pellegrino in the fridge.

'OK,' he says, but he doesn't look at her.

'I'm just going up to change,' she says, letting him top up her glass.

'You look nice like that,' he says.

She glances at him to see if he is joking. Apparently not. She's still in her favourite ten-year-old sundress, but that's not quite the point. Since when does he ever tell her she looks nice?

Ah yes, since he started sleeping with Coco Moss.

'Thanks,' she says. 'But I'm not wearing my old sundress.'

Upstairs, she finds the white Dolce & Gabbana number she always brings but never wears. It is far too elegant for a casual supper, but life is for living and clothes are for wearing, and tonight she's wearing this sucker. She giggles. Her glass is empty again. She can't remember bringing it upstairs with her. When did she drink it?

The dress goes on more easily than it has in a while; the last few days she seems to have deflated a little from all the walking up and down the hill, the stress, the constant grind of her thoughts. She admires her reflection in the mirror. The dress is cut away at the shoulders, fitted at the waist and hips. It is that longed-for thing: flattering. A miracle dress.

She puts on a little make-up and slips on her high-heeled sandals with the long straps that wrap around her legs, avoiding her rather scabby ankles. She shakes her head, decides to leave her hair to dry naturally, to leave its natural wave. It's far too hot for hairdryers.

'Wow,' Jeff says when she enters the living space.

She feels herself blush. Worse, the swelling urge to burst into tears. They could have been like this with one another, she thinks. She could have been like this, if only she'd thought he would notice.

Kindness, that's all it would have taken.

No, not kindness; attention.

He is moving towards her, as if to take her in his arms.

'Thanks,' she manages and averts her eyes from him, finds herself staring at the row of knives shining on the metallic strip. She steps away under the pretence of topping up her glass. If he holds her in his arms, she has no idea what she'll do.

In the fridge, salad leaves are arranged on three individual plates. She pretends to study them while she gets herself under control, face as far into the cold interior as she can. When Coco gets here, they can take their places at the bar. After some polite chit-chat over the snacks, she will slide elegantly towards the stove and flip the prawns in the skillet, spin like a chef to serve them hot onto their cold green beds. A spritz of lemon juice, a handful of finely chopped parsley, *Olé!* On the bar, three slices of lemon float in three finger bowls.

'Just popping to the loo,' Jeff says.

'OK.'

The moment he's gone, she opens the freezer and lifts the bottle from its bed of frozen peas. The neat vodka burns her with its heat, the icy bottle almost sticking to the skin of her fingertips.

Jeff is on his way back. She stashes the bottle back in the freezer and closes the door just in time.

'Do you need me to do anything else?' he asks, checking his watch, a trickle of sweat running down his brow. 'It's almost seven. I can fix the drinks when she gets here. Are you sticking with wine or do you want a G and T? She drinks beer, doesn't she? Do we have beer in the fridge?'

'Why did you stop drinking?' She makes herself look into his eyes.

He frowns. As in the restaurant last night, that flicker of doubt, worry, possibly fear.

'What do you mean, why did I stop drinking?'

Please do not prefix my question with what do you mean.

'I mean just that,' she replies steadily. 'Why did you stop? Why *then*? *When* did you stop exactly?'

His eyes round, his chin recedes into his neck.

Unattractive, she thinks. Coward, she thinks. Fuck you, she thinks.

'I can't remember the exact day,' he says, the last two words laced with irony.

'Can't you?' She takes a large swig of her wine. It tastes acidic; her tongue feels numb. She has drunk more than she meant to. She meant to keep her powder dry, but she has blown it, of course she has. She always does.

'No actually. No, I can't,' Jeff is saying. He takes a breath, as if he is about to add something.

The doorbell chimes.

'You'd better get that,' she says; only just stops herself from adding: *That'll be your girlfriend.*

CHAPTER 43

She waits, listening to her husband at the door pretending not to know their new friend, who in turn is pretending to be on warm but formal terms with her husband. It's a game, she thinks for the umpteenth time. It's all a game. Her wine glass is almost empty again. She has lost count of how many she's had. She should ask Jeff. He'll know. He will have counted. She suppresses a hiccup just as Coco bursts into the room.

'Hello, darling,' she says, throwing out her arms. Her eyes are glossy – a little glassy actually. Is she... is she *drunk*?

Behind her, Jeff is carrying a bottle of champagne in both hands like a chalice.

'Hi.' Kate allows herself to be hugged, kissed on both cheeks. Coco smells of alcohol, of cigarettes.

'Are you OK?' Coco asks, still holding her by the arms. 'You're shaking.'

'Am I?' Kate breaks away, steps back. 'No, I don't think so.'

'I brought champagne.' Coco looks about her, as if she is familiar with the contents of the kitchen units. 'Do you have flutes or – even better – coupes? I kept it in the fridge till the last sec, so it should still be lovely and cold.'

Kate nods. Knows she cannot handle champagne on top of however many glasses of rosé she's had, plus the vodka; that it will send her over the edge. But the edge is close, so close; she is floating towards it. In fact, she can hear it calling her name: *Kate, Kate, come on, come on over and let yourself fall. There is such freedom here in the abyss.*

Jeff is already placing two flutes on the breakfast bar, his face expressionless.

'Won't you join us?' Coco is looking directly at him, her eyes twinkling with mischief.

'I don't drink.' Jeff pops the cork, pours the foaming yellow fizz into the two flutes. The glasses frost.

I don't drink. As if Coco doesn't know this. As if Coco is his wife's friend, someone to explain things to.

'We were just talking about that actually,' Kate says as Jeff hands her a glass.

They say cheers, Jeff holding up his tumbler of water. They drink, slide their glasses back onto the bar.

'About what? What were you talking about?' With some effort, Coco climbs onto a stool and reaches for a chorizo and Manchego roll, which she drops into her mouth. She is wearing dark brownish-mauve lipstick. The colour of figs, Kate thinks.

'About Jeff not drinking. He stopped the year he graduated, didn't you, darling?' Kate wraps her smirk around a jamón-wrapped prune.

'It was for my career really,' Jeff says. 'And then it just stuck, I guess. I felt better.'

Kate stares him down. 'Lizzie said you left Christmas term early, about a week after Halloween. She said you were ill. Flu, she said.'

He pushes his mouth into a moue of ignorance and shakes his head – a wordless lie that Kate has no difficulty spotting. That's what decades together does to two people.

'I didn't even do final term,' Coco announces. 'I never finished my degree.'

Jeff stares at her, confusion writing itself across his brow – a genuine reaction this time, Kate thinks. 'Didn't you? How come?'

She shrugs. 'I'd had enough, you know? Not as if I ever went to any lectures.'

'I didn't know that,' Jeff says quietly, apparently forgetting his claim not to know her beyond a quick grope at a party, before he remembers himself with an almost imperceptible shudder. 'I mean, no reason why I would, I suppose.' He sits at the end of the bar, his face pale beneath his tan. Kate knows she should sit too but cannot quite remember how to coordinate her limbs.

'So,' she says, 'you didn't graduate?'

Another shrug. 'I dropped out. Went to art school. I'm not really an academic as such.'

How the privileged roll, Kate thinks. If one avenue fails, there is always another: funded, safety-netted, guaranteed. It is all she can think, all she can hold on to, the chip on her own shoulder.

Her champagne flute is full, though she knows she drank from it a moment ago. The room sways. She holds on to the bar with her free hand.

'Well, this is nice,' Coco says.

Kate puts her glass down heavily on the cool marble surface, holds on to the edge with both hands. 'So, did you drop out after that girl died?'

Coco takes a breath. It is only that, only an inhalation followed by an exhalation, but Kate knows it is a play for time, that Coco is about to lie.

'What girl?' she asks.

'Joanne Dixon.' Kate tries to hide her satisfaction at the flare in Coco's eyes. 'She died the night of the Halloween party. You remember, the party I asked you about?'

'Did you?'

'I did, yes.' She doesn't move a muscle.

'When we had drinks?' Coco says slowly after a moment. 'I mean, I don't know what her name was, but yes, a girl got tragically pissed or something. Was it the same night?'

'You know it was.' Kate is not one hundred per cent sure that the words sound as she has them in her head, but she ploughs on regardless. 'And she was your friend, so you do know her name. I'm not really sure why you're pretending you don't, although claiming not to know people is your speciality, I suppose. But she was your friend, wasn't she? She was Drew's girlfriend, and she was at that party. Why would you lie? But then I suppose you lied about not getting off with my husband, so—'

'Kate!' It is Jeff. She catches him glancing at Coco. 'I think my wife might have had a bit too much to drink.'

'Your wife is in the room.' Kate hears her words sliding together. 'Hi. It's me. I'm your wife. Helloooo.' She giggles. 'Or are we going to refer to me in the third person? I mean, I suppose I am the third person in this little triangle, aren't I? The third wheel.'

'Kate!' Jeff grabs for her glass, but she swings it away from him. 'What are you... Look, if Coco says she didn't know her, she didn't—'

'She didn't what?' Kate's voice is much louder than she intended. 'Don't be stupid, darling. You both knew her, didn't you? Funny that you're *both* pretending you didn't.'

Jeff's face is red; the veins in his neck are bluish and bulging. 'Kate, will you stop? Honestly, you're making a complete—'

'Jeff. Jeff!' Coco is holding up a hand. She is looking at him, holding his gaze. 'Jeff. It's OK. What can she do about it anyway?'

Jeff's face crumples. 'Coco, please...'

'Babe. Relax.' Coco turns her gaze to Kate. Despite their warm tones, her eyes are cold, hard. 'Kate,' she says quietly. 'Why don't you have a seat? This could take a while.'

Kate tilts her chin. She will not be outmanoeuvred by this woman, she will not.

'OK then.' She slides inelegantly onto a stool. 'Maybe we should start with why you're fucking my husband.'

CHAPTER 44

JEFF

The air stills. A triangle, Kate said, moments ago. She knew. She knew and let him carry on while she watched at a distance. How humiliating.

'Oh, darling Kate,' Coco is saying, not without kindness. 'You're right, Jeff and I are involved.'

Jeff lowers his head into his hands. Coco's voice is a slow rolling drawl.

'The thing is, you said it yourself. Jeff is an absent husband. You were lonely anyway, so I thought you wouldn't be too bothered if I... you know, took him off your hands.'

Jeff cannot look at his wife, he cannot. He does. A glance, no more. Her face is set in a kind of peaceful expression, tears she makes no move to swipe away trickling silently down her cheeks.

'I don't care,' she says. She is sitting bolt upright, as if her spine has been secured with steel. Despite the tears, she looks dignified; aloof even. 'You can have him,' she says plainly. 'I've wanted a divorce since I found out you were carrying on like a couple of desperate rabbits. Actually, what am I saying? I've wanted a divorce since before we came away – I just wasn't ready to admit it to myself. So really, I should be thanking you. I know that sounds sarcastic, but it isn't. There actually is a small part of me that's grateful to you, Coco. I mean, I was furious at first, but I'm not furious now. I was curious, actually, to see how you were both going to play it, what little subterfuges you would have going. Last night, Jeff tried to hide his phone behind the menu.' She giggles. 'It was funny, because I was hiding mine too.'

Her face falls; something like sadness or resignation crosses it now. 'I didn't like being lonely. I hated it, all the endless waiting. But marriage is about putting up with things we can't change, isn't it? And I could put up with it. I had my business, a few friends and I loved Jeff. Always have. I was OK. Compromise is key. I hate the heat, but...' She looks around her. 'Here we are in the peak of the summer in Spain.' She laughs, a horrible scornful sound, and pours herself another glass of champagne. It fizzes, rises, overflows. Undaunted, she pours the rest into Coco's glass. 'There you go, drinking buddy. Sorry, I'm interrupting. Do go on. I'm mainly interested in what happened that night. So can you, y'know, cut to the chase?'

Even Coco looks disconcerted. But after another sip of her champagne, she goes on.

'OK, so Jeff and I got together at the party. I know you know that. I'd had a row with Jo-Jo – that's what we called Joanne. She found Drew and me in the upstairs bathroom... together or whatever.' She rolls her eyes, makes a dismissive gesture with her hand.

Jeff feels his mouth drop open. 'You and Drew?' he whispers. 'You were...'

'Oh for God's sake, Jeff, that's not the point at all.' She holds up her hand in a stop sign, as if he is irritating her.

'Where was I?' she asks, fingers pinched at her brow. 'Oh yes, that's right, fight with Jo-Jo, yes, so I ran after her and tried to explain that Drew and I just had that kind of arrangement.

Still do sometimes. But she just freaked. I mean, she was totally wasted. We all were. We'd smoked a bit back at the house...'

Coco's voice trails off. He can still see her gesticulating, her mouth moving. She was with Drew that night. In the bathroom. In... that way. They couldn't even have locked the door. And then, barely an hour later, she came on to him as if nothing had happened, as if she fancied him, liked him even. He has loved her all his life, but to her he was just another... What *was* he?

'So I see Jeff in the kitchen,' Coco is saying, 'and he's wearing this really cool suit and he has this amazing eyeliner on and he looks kind of hot, you know?' She throws up her hands. 'I mean, I didn't know he had a girlfriend or anything like that.'

'Drew had a girlfriend.' Kate's jaw clenches.

Coco shrugs. 'I mean, yeah, but they weren't *exclusive* or anything. That's what he said anyway.'

The room tips. Jeff closes his eyes. A memory flashes. Coco, seconds after they first spoke to one another. *Drew's girlfriend just had some fucking hissy fit on me and stormed out. She's such a drama queen.* He thinks that's what she said. Her friend was being a drama queen, nothing more. No mention of her running off alone, inebriated and mortified into the dark. No worry that she might be vulnerable. She wasn't shaken or mortified or... He had felt sorry for *Coco* – how upsetting to argue with a friend, he had thought, but had not wanted to pry, oh God.

Coco is relaying their slow dance, how he kissed her, her words coming and going as he tries to stay in the room, caught between then and now. She is telling his wife how they staggered outside and how he suggested driving them home. The way she tells it is different from how he remembers it. *She* kissed *him. She* persuaded *him* to drive them home. Coerced him. Yes. She coerced him. It was her fault.

'Wait.' Kate looks from Coco to him, back to Coco, back again to him. 'Lizzie said you went to get your car the next morning.'

Jeff shakes his head – fully, horribly back in the now. 'I... I must've told her that.'

'You told Ben that too.'

'I suppose I must have. I can't honestly remember.'

'So we drive back to his,' Coco says, with the air of someone bored of interruptions, 'and at this point I still think he's like this really cool dude, a bit dangerous even, and then we turn into Chestnut Avenue and, OK, I mean, Jeff *was* probably going a little too fast.'

Jeff's stomach flips; he feels nauseous.

'And at first I thought it was a fucking ghost, you know? The woman in white!' Coco makes an O with her mouth, raises her hands and shakes them, fingers spread – a grotesque pantomime of fear. Her hands fall to her sides and she continues. 'Miss Havisham actually – that's who she'd gone as I think. It was Jo, of course, you've probably guessed, and she's halfway across the road and we're literally speeding towards her and she kind of just looks up at the last second and—'

'I braked,' Jeff says. 'I did brake.'

'Jeff totally braked, and we kind of screeched to a halt and it all happened so fast, but Jo-Jo was, like, on the pavement, just flat out. I mean, we didn't hit her; she'd hit her head... I mean, I think she must've hit it against the wall of one of the front gardens and she was just, you know, laid out, kind of sprawled, and she was kind of crying. I mean, don't get me wrong, it was really horrible.'

Kate's mouth is contorted with what looks like disgust. 'You got out of the car? Please tell me you got out of the car.'

'Of course! We checked she was OK – of course we did.' Coco's eyes on his are a jolt. It is almost a shock to find himself there in his beautiful villa, his trainers white on the cool red tiles.

'I didn't hit her,' he says. 'I didn't hit her. She fell.' He cannot look at Kate. He cannot.

'He didn't hit her,' Coco repeats, though her voice is quieter than it was. 'He braked.'

Jeff closes his eyes. When he hears Kate's voice, she sounds far away.

'She didn't collapse at all,' she says, the words thick and rising. 'She didn't *pass out*. She *dived*. She dived out of the way because she was in fear for her *life*. She hit her head, she... What... what did you do then? Jeff? Look at me.' He makes himself look up, finds his wife's eyes blue and burning into his. 'Jeff! What did you do then?'

CHAPTER 45

That night. That terrible night. The girl is just... there, she's just fucking *there* – white, like she's been lit up from the inside. Lit up from the outside of course, illuminated by his headlamps, but she looks like some heavenly apparition or something.

She still comes to him in flashes sometimes – sometimes when he's at work, when his mind wanders, or tonight, when Kate first appeared in the doorway in that long white dress. He saw her and his breath caught. He told her she looked nice, and she did, but it was a cover, as it has all been all his life. He only said it because it was better than saying, Oh my God, I thought for a second you were *her*.

Her.

He's coming round that corner on two wheels. He can remember the tilt of the car, the vague drunken sense that he is not in control of the vehicle. His arms are rod straight, hands pushed to the steering wheel, his back pressed hard against the driving seat. He's trying to accelerate out of the bend, afraid they're going to go skidding into a wall, a house. Barely has he got the car round the corner when he sees her. He's doing forty, fifty maybe – he has no idea. Her face is so pale. She is, all of her, so pale. It's as Coco said, she looks like a ghost. That black open mouth, that look of terror. In his memory she stares right into his eyes, but it can't have been like that. There was no time for it to have been like that.

He pushes his feet down – emergency stop – feels the car slide. Closes his eyes. The car screeches, slows. Stops. Then nothing. He opens his eyes, not understanding. There has been no impact, no body thrown across the windscreen, no horrific bump under the tyres. For a moment he thinks, yes, it *was* a ghost. It was an actual ghost, a phantom made from the sharp prick of his conscience penetrating his drunken state. But Coco is saying *oh my God oh my God* over and over, her voice somehow clearer, as if she's been jolted sober.

'Where did she go?' he says. 'Where is she?'

'She's on the pavement.' The clunk of the door handle, the groan of rusty hinges. Coco is getting out of the car. 'Oh my God, it's Jo-Jo. Fuck.'

He gets out, runs around the front of the car, sees the girl's feet beyond: white sandals on the pavement, the strange position of them. 'Is she dead?'

He creeps towards Coco, heart thumping. The girl is flat on her front. She isn't wearing a coat. Her legs are bare, her naked feet in strappy sandals. Coco is kneeling over her. 'She's breathing. She's fine. She's hit her head, I think, but she'll be fine. You need to ring someone's doorbell, ask if we can use their phone to call an ambulance.'

And here it is. Here is his life's defining moment.

'No,' he says. 'We can't do that.'

Coco looks up at him, her eyes narrow with something he can't read. 'Jeff. Listen to me. We need to call an ambulance.'

He shakes his head, points to the car. 'Get in. We need to go.'

'*What?*'

'She's not dead. She's not dead, OK? I didn't hit her. She can... she can get up and walk home.'

'I'm not sure she can.'

'That's not my fault. I didn't hit her. We didn't hit her.'

'I know that, but she's out cold and it's my fault she's even out here on her own!' Coco stands, sighs, begins to march towards the nearest house. He catches her, grips her wrists in his hands. She tries to fight him, but he is stronger.

'What the hell are you doing? Let go.'

'We have to leave.' His voice is so calm it's as if someone else is speaking on his behalf. 'If the police come, they'll breathalyse me and that'll be it. I can't do that. I can't do it. I can't lose my life, OK? I don't have another one. Now get in the fucking car.'

'But... we can call, then make a run for it.'

'No one must see us! They could get the car registration. We'll be arrested for fleeing the scene. Coco, please. I'm a law student – don't you get it? If I get a conviction, I will never be able to practise.' He is pulling her towards the car, sensing first the dig of her heels, then the slow relenting.

'She'll be OK,' he says. 'Trust me. She's just pissed. But we need to get out of here. I can't get done for drunk-driving, I just can't. I'll never work – it'll be over, completely over. I'll be finished.'

He is pushing Coco into the car now, shoving the top of her spiky head down like he's a cop and she's the offender.

'All right,' she complains. 'All right, all right.'

'OK? OK.' He slams the door, runs back to the driver's side, starts the engine. A moment later, they are turning out of Chestnut Avenue into Brudenell Road, turning again, into Elizabeth Street. He parks up, kills the engine, sits back, closes his eyes.

And then Coco is kissing him full on the mouth, her fingernails scratching his scalp. He opens his eyes, sees hers glinting in the dim light of a street lamp.

'What the hell did we just do?' she whispers.

He grabs her by the hair, kisses her so hard he can feel her teeth against his. 'Let's go inside.'

Is this, in fact, the moment that damns him forever, damns them both? The moment they go inside, him pulling her by the hand – *her*, his miracle, his one beautiful mistake? *Her*, the woman he's been in love with since the moment she walked into Cedar House, pink hair glowing in the strip light of the common room, defiant black eyes staring at everyone and no one all at once. Himself playing pool with Ben, barely able to stop the cue sliding from his grasp in wonder.

No, it is after that, when she pushes him against the wall, pulls up his shirt, kisses him, runs her hands over his back. Behind her, the telephone on the little stand. Green Bakelite, green plastic, whatever, the green phone that plugs into the wall with the old-fashioned number wheel. Three numbers, 999, that's all he has to dial. He could make the call anonymously, could say he was walking home and thought he saw a girl collapsed on Chestnut Avenue. He thought it was a bundle of clothes or bedding or something, but now he's home, he thinks it might have been a person. Could they send an officer to check?

But Coco is nibbling at his ear lobe and the sense is leaving him. They are both fired up with a terrible exhilaration he has tried ever since to comprehend. The relief that they hadn't hit her? Perhaps. The hot, riotous thrill of having got away with it, the thrill he has no idea is the precursor to the terrible, terrible guilt that has followed him ever since?

Who knows? Coco is pulling his jacket from him, asking which is his room.

'Upstairs,' he whispers. 'Come on.'

That. That is the moment. That is his last chance.

CHAPTER 46

KATE

Kate can feel the hang of her open mouth, saliva gathering on her tongue. 'You... you left your friend to die? In the freezing cold, with no coat?'

'We didn't know she was going to *die*,' Coco says and laughs – with indignation or flippancy, it's hard to tell.

Kate's legs are trembling; her knees feel like they're about to give way. 'That's not the point. How can you not see that that's not the point?'

Jeff throws up his hands. 'Trust me, I know how bad it looks. I know, OK? But it would have ruined me! I'm a lawyer, Kate! Think about it. And... and I've spent the rest of my life trying to make up for it.'

She stares at her husband, who has the grace to look like he's going to be sick. Kate thinks she might be sick herself. How can anyone not be sick? 'What do you mean?'

'I just mean... I get it, OK? From the moment we heard, I—'

'When did you hear?'

'The next day,' Coco says, her expression sheepish.

Sheepish, Kate thinks. Is that all?

'It was later the next day,' she goes on. 'It was on the news. I didn't see it, but Drew came into my room and told me, and I went straight round to Jeff's.'

How intimately she says his name, as if they've known each other years.

Jeff nods miserably. 'Coco came over and told me what had happened. I think we went for a walk.'

'We did,' Coco says. 'We walked over to Hyde Park and talked, and we agreed never to see one another again, never to speak of it to anyone. It was the only way. I mean, it's not like we could've helped her, is it?'

'Not then,' Kate cries. 'It was too late by then, but you could've helped her that night!'·

'I mean, we'd agreed not to see each other before that,' Coco says, as if Kate hasn't spoken, as if that is in any way relevant. 'When I left that morning, I told Jeff it was a one-off, a moment-of-madness-type deal. I think we were both high afterwards, you know?'

Kate's eyes crinkle in disbelief. 'You're telling me you had sex because you were getting off on the excitement of *leaving a girl to die*?'

'No!' Jeff's eyes film with tears. 'It wasn't like that!'

'Wasn't it?' Kate cannot take her gaze from her husband, who is snivelling. Who is he? Who the hell is he?

'Actually, darling, it was a bit,' Coco mutters.

It takes Kate a moment to realise she is talking to Jeff.

'We *were* kind of hot afterwards. I mean, full disclosure.'

'Oh my God.' Kate hears the tears in her voice, feels the ache of them in her throat. 'Oh my God, this is... it's—'

'Kate, don't,' Jeff says. 'Please. Honestly, I've tried so hard to, you know, atone. Ever since. My whole life. I stopped drinking straight away. I literally haven't drunk a drop since. I worked hard, really hard... I mean, once I'd got over it. I was really cut up about it. That's why I went home that term. I had... I had a sort of breakdown. Told my parents it was stress.

Then when you came back from Spain, I was faithful. I never cheated on you while I was in Manchester, I've never—'

'What? I'm supposed to be grateful?'

'No! Not like that. I just mean... I don't know. I've tried not to put a foot wrong ever since. When you wanted to get married, I said yes, didn't I? And we got married and we've been OK, haven't we? We've been OK?'

Something is falling. Sense... sense is falling around her. Her husband left someone to die. He chose sleeping with a woman over another woman's life. How could he have done that? He must have been crazy in love with her, mustn't he, for him to do that? He is telling Kate that he married her because she wanted it. Because *she* wanted it.

'What do you mean?' she asks. 'What do you mean, *I* wanted to get married? Didn't *you* want to get married?'

He gasps, wipes his hand across his mouth. 'I...'

But it is too late. She knows what has happened, knows all of it at once.

'Oh my God,' she says. 'I'm your good deed, aren't I? I'm your good fucking deed.'

His face crumples. 'But we'd been together so long. We always said we'd—'

'I'm your atonement.' Her voice is quiet, shaking. She is trembling from head to toe. 'I'm not your number one at all, am I? I never was.' She glances at Coco, whose mouth is turned down. 'She is.' Kate points at the woman she admired from afar, the woman she was, she knows, a little bit in love with. 'She's your first choice, isn't she? Her. Not me. I'm not even someone you settled for after the one that got away, am I? I mean, I am, but mainly I'm all about you doing the right thing to make *you* feel better. I'm the fat cheque you hand over in front of the cameras so everyone knows what a great guy you are, oh my God!'

She can't breathe. She can't... She has to get out of here. She has to get out.

Behind her, she can hear her husband calling her name, telling her he's sorry, to calm down, to come back. She flings the door open to the warm breath of the night.

'Kate,' he wails. 'We can work through this.'

What does that mean? What does anything he says mean?

She steps out, weeping uncontrollably now, and runs, runs up the lane, her shoulder glancing against a guy out for a late walk. The smell of cigarettes. She runs, the metallic taste of blood in her throat. She runs, up towards the winding road, the Carretera de Cadaqués. Staggering, weeping, swearing, she runs. When at last she hits the dark, silent road that heads out of the town, she stops, takes off her high-heeled sandals and carries them by the straps. Up and out of the town she runs, towards the looping turns, the sheer drops, the dense spiky brush of the Cap de Creus.

She is a woman in white, booze-thinned blood racing through loose marionette limbs. She is raging. Black eye make-up streams down her face as she runs – away, away, away.

CHAPTER 47

JEFF

In the silence, he and Coco stand staring at one another. He has the sense of himself in a dream, floating, before he shakes himself awake, grabs her by the shoulders.

'What the hell were you thinking? Why the hell would you tell her?' Flecks of his spit land on her cheeks. She does nothing, only stares back at him, impassive.

'She knew,' she says with a shrug. 'She already knew, for God's sake.'

'No she didn't! She only knew her name, that's all. She had nothing, nothing on us whatsoever, but you had to blab it all out like you had verbal diarrhoea or something. Why the hell would you do that?'

'Because it was ages ago. It doesn't matter any more. She can't do anything!'

'*What?*'

'Look. I told her because if she hates you, it's better for us, yes? You'll be free. She'll grant you a divorce and we can get on with our lives. She can't prove a thing.'

In her face, no trace of irony, no guilt, no terror. Nothing. Kate is stale bread, to be thrown away without a care. Coco is conducting a hostile takeover. His head is pounding. In the candlelight, Coco's features lengthen. The lines at the side of her mouth make her look like a cruel puppet. Where before she was edgy, beautiful, now she is hard – hard-faced, grasping.

'What have you done to me?' he asks her. 'Who the hell even are you?'

'Oh, don't be such a drama queen.'

He runs into the hall, grabs his car keys from the phone table. The door to the villa is open.

'Where are you going?' Coco shouts after him.

'I'm going to find her obviously.'

'Why? She won't get far; she's not exactly fit, is she? Jeff. Leave her. For God's sake.' Coco appears in the hallway, draped against the door jamb. 'Jeff.'

'We have to find her.' The sight of her infuriates him – her heavy eyelids, the sour, mocking tilt of her straggly blonde head. What is she hoping to do, seduce him? 'Don't you get it?'

'Oh my God.' She laughs – a loud, open-mouthed laugh, full of disdain. 'Idiot. What the hell would she say? Oh, *por favor,* Señor Policia, my husband... er... didn't kill someone three decades ago? Come on!'

'But we did kill someone. You know we did!' He stares at her, tries to see if there is any understanding, any humanity in her eyes, but finds none. How the hell can he have spent his life in love with this person? She is a shell.

'Look,' he says, trying to reason with her, 'we have to find her before she... I don't know.'

'Before she what? What are you going to do, *silence* her? *Kill* her?'

'Oh for God's sake, are you going to come with me or not?'

He turns away, cannot bear to look at her a moment longer. Behind him, he can hear her complaining that she hasn't even got her shoes on; to chill out, for God's sake, this is ridiculous.

Outside, the smell of cigarette smoke drifts in the air. He

aims the remote control and opens the garage door. Inside the garage, the light goes on slowly, smoothly, automatically. When you're rich, so much of what you do is at a distance. You can turn on a light without flicking a switch, open your garage door without touching it, have someone killed without bloodying your hands.

A noise comes from the shadows, a kind of dull scuffling.

'Hello?' he calls out. '*Hola?* Is there someone there?'

No reply. Unnerved, he clicks the key fob. The Merc flashes into life. He gets in and backs onto the lane, pulls forward, lowers the windows just as the door to the villa flies open. Coco steps out and calls to him.

'Have you got the keys to the house, darling?' It is as if she has already moved in, as if they are heading out for dinner or something.

'Yes. Hurry up.'

Muttering, she closes the front door behind her. The shadow thins. There is no one there, no one at all.

'Hurry up,' he shouts. 'We need to stop her.'

'If we see her,' Coco says, pausing at the passenger door, 'you need to put your fucking foot down, OK?' She gets in.

'What, run her over?' he replies. 'Of course. We could say it was an accident.'

She doesn't pick up on his sarcasm, adding as she dips her head to fasten her seat belt, 'Exactly. Just finish it already.'

'Finish it? You'd love that, wouldn't you?' He is almost laughing.

She slams the door shut. He guns the engine, drives as fast as he dares down the black lane.

Before they even reach the seafront, he can see that it's packed; there is no way through.

'If she's come this way, we'll never find her.' He stops, reverses up a side street, edges forward to pull out.

'It's one-way,' Coco says.

'Only till the next junction. If I can get there, I can hang a left and get back up the hill. There's nothing coming – I can make it.'

A jeep appears on the rise. Jeff floors the accelerator, speeds directly towards the jeep, makes the left just in time.

'Nice!'

Coco slaps the dashboard with what looks horribly like glee. A wave of queasiness rolls over him.

He speeds up the steep, narrow lane towards the Carretera de Cadaqués. He has no idea where his wife is, where she might think to go, knows only that she's beside herself with distress and that she's had a lot to drink. Perhaps she's going nowhere. Perhaps she needs simply to run until exhaustion numbs her enough to cope with what she has just found out. The look on her face is one he will never forget – her expression caught in the grip of a slow, agonising download. Nothing she cares about remains apart from their daughter. Who knows if she even had space to think about Lou in that moment. He hopes she can think of her, that it will stop her from doing anything stupid now she is alone.

She has always been alone, he thinks. Tonight she will have understood it at the deepest possible level. He is no longer someone she could even consider being with, not now. Their life together was built on a lie only he ever knew – that is how she will see it. Anything else he has given her, or could give her, she will not want. She never could peer through the rose-tinted spectacles of wealth, never could see how money made everything so much more palatable. Everything she put up with – his absence, his dark moods, his selfish habits – she did not because of material goods but because she believed they loved one another, that they were each other's first and only. He found it quaint, childlike, but at the same time, he has always known it was neither to her. To her, it was deadly serious.

And friends – any friends they had were his colleagues and associates, hers fading into the background with each passing year. He was too busy for them, it was never a good time, he had a deadline, a deal, a triathlon, an important dinner, an important networking event. He has forced his life on her. The end result was that she was never happy, never fitted in. For him, she went along with it, desperate to get it right, mortified whenever she got it wrong, which was often. And the drink, the drink that softened it all for her, helped her cope with the nerves until it didn't any more, only made her more clumsy, embarrassing to be with, too tired to do anything beyond walk or read.

Did he do that to her? It feels like he did now, driving along this dark, winding road, his lover leaning over the dashboard, face set in a kind of scary grimace, telling him to go faster, faster.

Kate. Waiting all these years for a future she will no longer want. She has clung on for decades, for what? To find out that her husband was only ever going through the motions, that he sacrificed a living, breathing young woman for his career. He even sacrificed the love of his life: not Kate, as she has always believed, but Coco Moss.

But it is Coco Moss who is sitting beside him now, and he is no longer sure about anything. Between the sheets, lost in a mist of infatuation, he has plotted to spend the rest of his life with this stranger, whose callousness tonight has shaken him so hard he feels uprooted, unsteady. He agreed to leave his wife for this woman, telling her in confident tones that Kate would be fine, well looked after, provided for. He was able to say these words because in that moment, wrapped in Coco's warm limbs, all logical thought had left him. But now he is no longer sure that Coco is who he wants, this woman squinting through the windscreen, searching for his wife, still ranting about making it look like an accident.

'We are not going to kill her,' he says now through gritted teeth.

'But you said we were.'

'I was being sarcastic, for Christ's sake.'

'But it's the only thing that makes sense.' She does not look at him. 'We could say... we could say we were worried about her, that we had an argument because she was really drunk, and she went running out. She was hysterical, so we took the car and were driving round trying to find her, worried sick, and she... yes, this'll work... she was waiting behind a bend and just jumped out! There was no time. It was just – bang.'

'Shut up,' he says, fingers clamped around the steering wheel. 'Stop saying that, just stop.'

'We have to,' she says, louder now. 'The more I think about it, the more I think the police might still have photographs of tyre marks on the road, you know, in their files? They could probably match them with the car you were driving at the time. They have cases like that, don't they? Cold cases.'

'No, they won't. Don't be ridiculous. She died of hypothermia. It's a closed case, for God's sake. It was never open.'

'OK, but it was you who said we should stop Kate. You know what you meant. At least own it, you bloody coward.'

'*What?*' He glances at her. She is sitting back, arms crossed, scowling. A moment ago, she called him an idiot; now he is a coward. But she's wrong about the girl. There's no proof of anything. Joanne Dixon died of hypothermia. She was drunk. It was cold. She had no coat on. She fell over. Even if he hadn't been drink-driving, she could easily have stumbled on the kerb. Was it even his fault actually? Did she even see the car? She could easily have...

The road bends sharply. He tries to accelerate through the curve, but he's going too fast. There are no lights this far out, only the distant glimmer of the bay far below. There is no way Kate could have got this far. The drop is sheer. It is so dark.

'There she is,' Coco shouts.

A flash of white. A ghost.

Coco's hands are over his own. The wheel turns. In panic, confusion, he tries to brake, but she's thrown him off centre and his foot hits the accelerator. The engine revs. A loud smack. A pale creature rolls over the bonnet. He finds the brake. The car screeches, stops. Over the black road, a terrible silence falls. Into it rises the high cheep of cicadas. Coco has opened the door.

'Call an ambulance,' he hears her say. 'I think we might have killed her.'

CHAPTER 48

Coco is the first reach to Kate's body. He watches her from the driver's seat, immobilised by shock, watches her take Kate's pulse, then stand, look around, before jogging back to the car.

'Get out,' she says. 'She's alive.'

'You pushed my hands. You—'

'Get out of the car. Jeff? Jeff. Get out.'

Kate is lying in a tuft of dry grass. One more roll and she would've gone over the edge. She would have surely died. She may still die. As it is, she is unconscious, bleeding down one side of her face. Her other arm lies limp and odd, her legs splayed and flat. Her feet are bare, bloody, the soles black. Tied to her wrist is one sandal. There is blood on her white dress.

This wasn't an accident, he thinks. It was something else. Coco took the wheel. Coco forced the wheel. Coco tried to... She... If Kate doesn't make it, it will be Coco who has killed her, not him.

'We need to call an ambulance,' he says. 'We need to call an ambulance now.'

'I couldn't help it.' Coco is biting her thumbnail, her eyes slick with tears. 'I love you. I only wanted us to be together.'

'We could have been together,' he whispers. 'I told you I was going to leave her. For Christ's sake, what have you done?'

'I couldn't help it. It... it was a crime of passion.'

'It was *not* a crime of passion,' he almost yells, hot tears pricking. 'You planned to do it and you did it. You're a murderer, a fucking murderer. I hate you.'

She laughs. 'I'm a murderer? Oh, that is priceless. It was you who left a girl to die in the cold, who told me we couldn't call 999 because it would ruin your career. It was you who said we had to stop your hysterical wife from going to the police. All I did was give you the push because I knew you didn't have the balls.'

'Shut up.' His face is in hers, the urge to wrap his hands around her neck almost overwhelming. 'Just shut up.'

Crying, panting with fear, he googles how to call the police. His hands shake. He can hardly see. Is it possible that they have argued here at the roadside, his bleeding wife at their feet? That they have stood here throwing blame at each other instead of calling for help? They are monsters, absolute monsters.

'Oh, for God's sake.' Coco snatches the phone from him. A few moments later, she presses it to his ear.

'*Accidente*,' he says when it connects. '*Accidente.* Car. *Coche.* Carretera de Cadaqués. Near Cadaqués. Going towards Calella. *Uno, dos kilómetros.* Please. *Por favor.* Help, help. My wife.'

Sirens sounds in the distance almost immediately after he rings off.

'Kate,' he whispers, crouching down to her, squeezing her hand. 'Stay with me, darling. The ambulance is on its way. You're going to be OK.'

On the road, Coco paces. She has rolled a cigarette and is smoking it. The smell drifts to him, disgusts him. Since when did she smoke?

'Jeff,' she says, at his shoulder now. 'Remember what we said in the car, OK?'

He stands up, feels his fingers flutter to his forehead, the tips soft against his hairline. 'What have we done? Oh my God, what have we done?'

'Look at me.' Coco is in front of him. She has taken his hands in hers. The sirens are louder. 'Jeff. Look at me.'

He looks. Her eyes are blazing coals.

'Listen, darling. We don't have much time. If we keep our stories straight, we'll be fine, OK? Just like we said in the car. Kate was drunk. She left the house in a state. We were worried about her. We were trying to find her and she just jumped out in front of us. You're stone-cold sober. You're a model citizen. Are you listening to me? Jeff? Jeff?'

He nods, feels the familiar heaviness of his head.

Coco squeezes his hands. 'Just stick to the story, OK? If you stick to the script, you'll be OK.'

'OK. OK.'

The sirens are upon them now. They sound so different, almost trumpet-like: *babadab, babadab*, not the atonal wail of home. A moment later, a yellow van rounds the bend, three pairs of orange lights flashing. The word *Ambulancia* is written backwards above the windscreen. The ambulance stops. Two paramedics jump out, a man and a woman in orange-and-yellow high-vis. They address him immediately in rapid-fire Spanish.

'*No hablo español*,' he says, helpless. Thinks: *my wife does*. Oh God. Begins to cry.

'Is OK. OK,' the woman says as the man gestures for him to move aside. He kneels beside Kate, pushes up her eyelids, shines a thin torch into her eyes. He takes her pulse.

'She's my wife,' Jeff says, his voice hoarse. 'Is she alive? I mean, will she live?'

'She's alive.' The woman's accent is strong, the 's' sibilant.

'Please,' she says, gesturing for him to step further back, to get out of the way. 'Sir.'

The male paramedic straps an oxygen mask to Kate's face. Jeff can't look at Coco, but he can sense her pacing up and down the edge of the road, smell another cigarette burning in her fingers.

The paramedics work quickly and calmly. They fetch a stretcher from the back of the ambulance. With the briefest of nods and one swift coordinated move, they load Kate's body onto the stretcher. She doesn't stir. Her white dress is streaked with red blood. More sirens sound. A moment later, a dark blue police car comes to an abrupt halt at the side of the road. The click of doors opening; the cough of static.

He makes himself look at Coco, who shoots him a loaded glance before flicking her cigarette onto the tarmac and grinding it out with her foot. She looks, more than anything, annoyed.

The female paramedic is closing the ambulance doors. *My wife is in that ambulance*, Jeff thinks. He loves her. Had forgotten, that's all.

'I need to go with her,' he says. Gestures, mimes.

'You give estaymen.' The male paramedic nods brusquely at the police officers striding towards them. A second police car is pulling up at the opposite side of the road. Statement. That was what he said. Estaymen. Statement.

'OK,' Jeff says, holds the paramedic's gaze a second to show that he too is an honest, serious man. 'Of course.'

The second pair of cops appear to be closing the road with hazard signs. The first pair have driven a little further and are doing the same the other side. The female cop has taken Coco near to where Kate's body lay only moments ago. She has a notepad. She is talking. Coco is nodding, her face grave.

In strongly accented English, an impossibly young police officer with large brown eyes is asking Jeff what happened.

'Can you tell me please? Slow.' He is holding a pen, a notepad.

From the bushes, the crickets shriek. Jeff's breath comes shallow and shaky. He has to fight not to cry. What has he done? What the hell has he done?

'We were trying to find her,' he says, has the impression he's said this several times already, that he's been standing here for hours. 'She ran. My wife, she ran. She was hysterical, you know? *Histérica*? Upset. Very, very upset. She had a lot to drink. A lot. *Vino.*' He mimes drinking with his thumb, tips back his head. 'We have... we had an argument. She ran away. Out of the villa.' His hand flutters to convey his wife fleeing up to the only road out of town.

He glances over at Coco, who is weeping. The switch in her is chilling. He returns his attention to the cop.

'I drive.' He mimes himself twisting the steering wheel to convey the curves in the road, these blind curves, these dangerous blind curves that would give you no chance, no chance whatsoever of avoiding an accident in the dark. 'My wife jumped. I tried to... avoid.' Another twist of his imaginary steering wheel. His wife is a hand now, his own, leaping out of the dark; his opposite fist is his car. The fist hits the hand: smack. 'I hit her. I tried to... no hit her, but...' He shakes his head as fresh tears prick his eyes. 'Too late.'

The cop frowns, seems to have understood the mix of pidgin English and performance.

'OK,' he says, slips his notepad into his breast pocket before walking slowly back to the car.

Jeff cannot look at Coco, he cannot. Instead, he looks down at his pristine white trainers. There is a dark mark on the side of the left one. Is that... is that Kate's blood?

The cop has returned, is standing in front of him holding what must be a breathalyser. Jeff feels himself strengthen. He is stone-cold sober. He is not a scared, plastered student who has done something stupid. He is a grown man, a model citizen. He has got his story straight. It will be OK.

His chest empties. He even manages a shaky smile. He breathes into the short tube, catching the eye of the cop intermittently, trying to think how a man who has knocked over his wife by accident would look: a combination of shock and contrition. He *is* shocked. He *is* contrite. There is no need to fake anything.

The breathalyser beeps. The cop removes it from his mouth. Jeff glances towards Coco, who is still talking to the female cop, wiping her eyes with a tissue.

The cop studies the breathalyser. Jeff watches, waits, caught in hovering terror, the irrational fear that he might somehow be over the limit. Another beep. The cop nods gravely at the result, a moment of glancing eye contact, gruff approval, a grim nod.

'We go,' he says, his English a lot better than Jeff's Spanish. 'Your wife has been taken here.' He holds up his phone. 'Hospital de la Santa Creu i Sant Pau. But we go to the *estación* of police.'

'What about the car?'

'The car stays here.'

'OK. *Gracias. Muchas gracias.*'

'I take your phone.'

'My phone? Why?'

The cop's hand comes out, his palm flat. 'Please.'

Jeff hands over the phone, nerves gathering in his gut. It's just procedure, he thinks. Just procedure.

In his peripheral vision, Coco is getting into the back of the other police car. She doesn't look at him. The door shuts. A moment later, the car pulls out. The police station, the guy said. That's where they're going. A formal statement of course. Procedure. They haven't cuffed him. He is not under arrest.

'Thank God you were sober.' Her voice comes to him in the

dark back seat of the patrol car. When she said this, he can no longer remember.

'You tried to kill her,' he hissed back at her, hot with white rage. 'You tried to kill my Kate.'

But Coco only laughed. 'If she was yours, why didn't you take better care of her?'

CHAPTER 49

On the wall outside the cell, the clock reads 11 p.m. He has been in this place for over forty-eight hours. His eyes sting. A pervading feeling of staleness, stickiness, a bad taste in his mouth. He needs to clean his teeth. He needs a long, cool shower. This is outrageous. He has already given a statement. When they got here, he was led to an interview room where he spoke to a plain-clothes detective alongside the uniformed policeman who had taken notes at the roadside. The detective's English was more fluent, less heavily accented. She told him her name was Carmen Falo-Sant. He gave her the same story he had given the cop. Word for word, he's pretty sure.

The clink of keys. The door to the cell opens. Detective Falo-Sant stands at the open doorway.

'Mr Barrett,' she says, her face inscrutable. 'Please. Come with me.'

Fighting an encroaching sense of doom, he follows her down a long white corridor, into another interview room. Falo-Sant tells him to take a seat, asks him to give his statement again. He tries to keep the irritation out of his voice as he repeats himself, unnecessarily, to this woman who he suspects is enjoying her power just a tad too much. As he speaks, she makes notes against the ones she already has – what is she trying to do, psych him out? Let her try. He is word-perfect. And indeed, when he has finished, she sits back in her chair and looks at him through heavy-lidded eyes.

There, he thinks, as he too sits back in his chair and folds his arms. *You can take that supercilious expression off your face and let me go.*

'Mr Barrett,' she says. 'Can you tell me what you were arguing about in the moments before your wife left the villa?'

His heart quickens. 'What do you mean, what were we arguing about? What has that got to do with—'

'Before your wife became upset and left the villa, what were you arguing about?'

He takes a deep breath, tries in his confusion to figure out why she is asking him this now, what relevance it has. Desperately, he wishes Coco were here. She would tell him what to say, exactly what to say.

'We were arguing because... because she found out that I'd been having a relationship with Coco. Ms Moss.'

Carmen pauses. 'Do you mean Caroline Barton?'

'Who's Caroline Barton?'

The detective's eyebrows rise. 'You don't know her name? Your friend? Your... lover?'

'No... no, her name's Coco Moss. I've known her since I was eighteen. We were at university together. It's not some sordid affair. We love each other. We always have.'

Another uncomfortable pause. He feels scrutinised, unclothed. Caroline? Maybe Coco is a nickname, a shortening. Maybe Moss is her mother's maiden name or something. People often have different names on their birth certificate, doesn't mean to say—

'Mr Barrett,' Carmen says, adjusting herself on the hard plastic seat.

'Are you going to tell me what's going on?'

She gives a cold smile. 'So your wife discovers that you and Caroline Barton, who you know as Coco Moss, are having an affair, and you have an argument. Is that all?'

'What else would there be?' Sweat prickles under his arms.

'And your wife, she ran out of the house, yes?'

'I told you that. We were worried. I was worried she might do something stupid. We went after her.'

'Can you tell me what you spoke about with Caroline Barton – Coco Moss – after your wife left?'

'I... We were upset. We were worried. We were figuring out what to do... what to do for the best. We agreed it was best to go and find her. I don't drink, so I went out to start the car.'

'So you didn't argue because Ms Barton had told your wife about a girl who had died in 1988, a... Joanne Dixon?'

'*What?*' His scalp tingles.

'You didn't shout at Ms Barton for telling your wife about you leaving this girl to die on the road in' – she checks her notes, refocuses on him – 'Leeds.'

'What? No! Who told you that?'

'And when you were getting into the car, what did you talk about then?'

'What? What do you mean? We just said we had to find her. I might have told Coco to hurry up. As I said, I was worried – worried sick.'

'So you didn't say "we need to stop her"?'

Sweat runs down his torso. 'No. I mean, yes. I mean, yes, I might have said that, but only because I was worried. I meant stop her from doing anything stupid. She was... she was very drunk. Hysterical.'

'*Histérica,*' Carmen says, her eyes scathing slits. 'You're telling me that you didn't mean you wanted to stop your wife telling the police about Joanne Dixon's death? Stop her by killing her?'

'No! God, no!'

'You didn't say "let's make it look like an accident"?'

Hot confusion flushes through the length of him. 'What? No! I mean, I was joking, it was a *joke*.'

'Did you say "let's get this finished" or "finish it", or words to that effect?'

'What? Of course not! Coco said that. I mean... No, wait. No, she... I didn't mean that. You're twisting—'

'Mr Barrett, does the name Joanne Dixon mean anything to you?'

'Joanne... wait.' He folds his arms, heat prickling all over his scalp, head throbbing, vision blurring. 'I... I need a lawyer.'

Carmen Falo-Sant gives a gracious nod. 'Mr Barrett, I am arresting you on suspicion of the attempted murder of Katherine Barrett. You have the right to remain silent...'

He does not hear the rest.

CHAPTER 50

KATE

A soft pulsing beep. Pain... somewhere. Her leg. Her throat is dry. Where's Jeff? Something weird in her arm. No drugs, no drugs, no thank you. Pint of lager, yeah, great. Cheers. Shot, yeah, sure. Down in one, oopla! Jeff, black hair fluffy, bad haircut, bad, bad haircut. Zits too, red on his cheek, a Dire Straits T-shirt. He's so square, God, he's square, but she doesn't care, she doesn't care because he kisses really well, and somehow they just work together. He makes her laugh. They're bezzie mates. She can relax with him. Comfortable, without being bored. He doesn't have all the smooth chat-up lines she hates. He's awkward. She loves that. He can't dance. She doesn't care. She loves him. She wants to be with him forever, have kids with him, the whole deal.

The light is bright, too bright. She blinks. A white ceiling. Lights. The lights have come up. Kicking-out time, don't you lot have homes to go to?

Where is Jeff? Where is he?

White covers on a white bed. A foot in plaster. Her foot. Is it her foot? Her foot is in plaster. Why is her foot in plaster?

'Hello?' Her voice is a croak. Her throat is made of sand. She's crying. She is so, so sad, oh God.

'Hey, hey.' A man's voice. 'It's OK. It's OK.'

'Jeff?' She can't move her head. It is attached to the bed. Is it?

A movement. A handsome man appears above her. He smiles kindly. She knows his face.

'Kate,' he says. 'It's me, Troy.'

'Troy? Where's... where's Jeff?'

She feels his hand dry and warm around her own.

'You've been in an accident,' he says. 'But it's OK. You're going to be OK. You're in hospital and you've got a broken arm and a smashed ankle. You lost a bit of blood, but they've topped you up, OK? They're taking very good care of you. You're going to be all right.'

'Lou?'

'She's fine. Don't worry about anything. It's all fine. Just rest up now.'

She closes her eyes.

Kate wakes. It is light, bright. She tries to move her head but can't. She's in hospital. Yes, that's right. Troy was here. She's been in an accident, and she's broken her ankle and her arm. But she's going to be OK.

A nurse appears, smiles. '*Como está, señora, eh? Como está? Bien, bien, bien. Muy bien.*'

The nurse is tanned, with dark blonde hair and blue eyes. A moment later, the bed rises. Kate finds herself semi-supine, a hospital ward laid out before her. Troy is sitting on a chair next to her with his hands in his lap. He smiles at her, gives her two thumbs-up. There is something brave about the way he is smiling. Her stomach flips with fear. Where is Jeff? Where is Coco?

There was a terrible argument. Jeff told her... She... It's all over. She ran out of the villa. Oh God.

What has happened?

The nurse removes something from her neck, replaces it with a surgical collar. She is talking constantly. Kate picks up words here and there, the general sense. A doctor will be here presently. She is doing well. Breakfast is coming. Would she like coffee or tea?

'Coffee,' she says. The coffee will be better than the tea; they always serve those terrible bags on the cotton threads, lukewarm water.

The nurse walks away.

'Troy,' Kate says, trying to read his face but finding nothing. Tears fill her eyes. 'What's happened?'

Troy leans forward. 'How are you feeling?'

'I'm fine. Please.' Her breath quickens. Panic rises. 'Please. Tell me what the hell is going on.'

He nods. 'You've been in an accident. Jeff and Coco...' He looks deeply into her eyes with a terrifying expression of sympathy. Why is he sorry for her?

'Are they alive? Is Jeff alive?'

He takes her hand in both of his, closes his eyes and bends forward until his forehead touches the back of her hand. When he raises his head, his eyes are still closed.

'Troy! For God's sake, tell me what's going on! Is my husband alive or isn't he?'

He opens his eyes. 'You were on the main road out of Cadaqués,' he says. 'Jeff and Coco were driving... There was an accident. They... God, this is hard. It looks like they... ran you over.'

'*What?*' Tears spill; her heart beats hard. The memory comes: running along the road in the dark, raging, drunk. Taking off her sandals. The rough road on the soles of her feet.

The whitening of the grassy bank, turning, seeing the headlights.

Then nothing, nothing at all.

'That was *them*? What... Did they... It was an accident. It must've been an accident. Jeff would never...'

Troy shakes his head. 'I don't know. They're at the police station. Formal statement, you know? I guess they'll update us when they can. I'm so sorry.' He squeezes her hand. 'I've sent the twins to get snacks so we can talk.'

'It will have been an accident. There's no way... Jeff wouldn't... There's no way he...'

Jeff left a girl to die, cold and helpless and alone in the depths of a Yorkshire winter. He and Coco left a young girl to die. Coco knew her. She was her friend, whose boyfriend she had been...

'Perhaps.' Troy's expression is hard to read: a smile full of sorrow.

'What do you mean, perhaps?'

He sighs. When he opens his mouth to speak, Kate has the sense he is about to say something heavy, difficult.

'Troy?'

The look he gives her makes her stomach turn over.

'I'm so sorry,' he says.

She squeezes his hand but can feel herself filling with anger.

'Troy.' She says his name firmly. 'You need to tell me. For God's sake, you have to tell me what's going on. Now.'

'OK,' he says, his breath shaky. 'Sorry. I was coming to your place. Coco had told me not to come, said she needed me to look after the twins, but the twins are fifteen, you know? And we'd spoken, hadn't we, you and I, and I was... I was worried about what she was up to. After I spoke to you. The thing is, Coco is... she's out of control.'

'She was sleeping with my husband.'

He nods. Doesn't seem at all surprised, or even pissed off for that matter. His expression is, if anything, one of weary resignation.

'Where are they?' she asks.

'They're being questioned,' he says.

'*What?*'

'They've not been charged, so far as I know. But they're being held, I think on suspicion of attempted murder.'

Kate gasps. 'No. No, that can't be true.' Her heart hammers. She feels hot, too hot. Tears clog her throat; her throat aches. 'Oh my God.'

'Señora Barrett.'

A different nurse has arrived. She is arranging a bed table over Kate's lap, onto which she places a rectangular plastic plate with a croissant wrapped in cellophane, a yoghurt, a bunch of grapes and a cup of black coffee. There is sugar in sachets and two miniature pots of UHT milk.

'*Muchas gracias*,' Kate manages as the nurse bustles off, then turns back to Troy, who looks miserable and small. 'Tell me. Please.'

'OK,' he says. 'I was on my way to your villa, and you came running out. You bumped into me. You were distraught. I didn't have a chance to take in what was going on, and by the time I realised it was you, you'd run away up the lane.'

'I remember,' she says. 'The man out for a walk. Our shoulders clashed. Were you smoking?'

He nods. 'Yes. I should have gone after you, but I could hear shouting coming from inside the villa. I didn't know what to do, so I... Well, I guess I was eavesdropping.' He looks down into his lap momentarily, as if ashamed.

'What did you hear?' Kate asks, another wave of heat filling her. 'Troy. What did you hear?'

'Your husband... Jeff... he was really angry. He was asking Coco why she told you something, something to do with a girl?'

Kate closes her eyes. 'Joanne.'

'Coco was shouting back, saying you knew already. She was being... I mean, I know what she's like when she's like that. She has this way of turning everything around. Jeff seemed furious. My guess is that Coco had said something he wanted to keep secret.'

'She did.' Kate presses her hand to her forehead, opens her eyes to the food she knows she will not eat. 'Years ago, 1988, they were driving home from a party together. I mean, they didn't actively kill her, but they were responsible for her dying, if that makes sense. Jeff was drunk-driving, which was so unlike him, so incredibly unlike him, I can't help thinking Coco must have persuaded him, not that that excuses him or anything, but it's the only thing that makes sense. He was in love with her back then, you see. Well, he still is. Back then we both were, a bit – a crush, I suppose you'd say. She was so... luminous, you know? There was no one like her. I didn't realise Jeff was just as under her spell as I was until this week. The girl's name was Joanne Dixon. He didn't hit her, but...' She falters. 'Oh my God. Oh my God.'

'Are you all right?'

She glances at Troy. His brown eyes are shining with sympathy, with compassion.

'I'm... sorry, it's just that now I'm thinking – is that what really happened? Or did Jeff try and mow the girl down? Did they actually just miss? He was so in love with Coco, and love makes us crazy, and this girl, Joanne, had caught Coco with her boyfriend and made a scene. Did she tell Jeff to drive into her for some sort of drunk revenge? He would have been so high on the fact that he was taking her home, you know? He would have been seeing stars. And he's still besotted with her, so now I'm thinking... did Coco egg him on to... to...?' She bursts into tears.

'Hey.' She feels the bed shift, senses Troy beside her. A

moment later, he is pressing a tissue into her hand. 'Don't upset yourself.'

He does not say she's wrong. Or mad. She is so glad of him there beside her and that he is not trying to tell her that what she's saying is not true. How can Coco have married this tender man? How can she, Kate, have married such a coward?

'You're thinking history's repeating itself,' he says softly. 'That's... that's a lot to take in.'

She sniffs, wipes her eyes, blows her nose. Her heart hurts. It hurts like it's being crushed. 'They said the girl fell. She dived out of the way and hit her head. They knew she was out cold and they just... left her there. They didn't call the police. They just left her to die.'

Through her tears she sees Troy pale, his features dropping in shock. 'Jesus.'

'She wasn't even wearing a coat. This is Leeds, in winter.'

'God, that's awful. And she died?'

'Hypothermia. They didn't find her until the morning. Jeff... he could've called an ambulance, but he was worried he'd be breathalysed. He was way over the limit, so he fled the scene essentially.'

Troy closes his eyes. 'That makes sense. It sounded like he was still cut up about it, but Coco... well, Coco's a very different kind of person. She said something about it being ages ago and that it didn't matter any more, which is just what she would say. Hard for me to say that about her, but it's true. It was Jeff who said they'd killed her.'

'He said that?'

Troy nods.

'It's just that when we fought,' Kate says, 'before I left the house, he was going on about the fact that he didn't hit her, that he braked, as if that made a difference, as if it wasn't his fault, and I guess that's when something in me kind of died. I just looked at him and thought, *you're a void*, you know? A void.'

She glances at Troy, who looks so sorry even though he hasn't done anything wrong. 'Go on,' she says. 'Please... please tell me the rest. What else did you hear?'

He sighs deeply. 'So. Jeff came out. I was hiding by this point, in the shadows behind the porch. He must've heard me, because he shouted out, "Is there someone there?" I just hid. I was holding my breath, still trying to make sense of what I'd heard. I wish... I wish I'd shouted out, but I didn't. I didn't.' He sighs, shakes his head sadly.

'Jeff reversed onto the lane. The engine was running, so I thought they must be going to find you. Then Coco came out and asked if he had the keys to the villa and Jeff told her to hurry up... he said something like, "We need to stop her." And then Coco was getting in the car, and she said that if they saw you, he had to put his foot down.'

Kate's hand flies to her mouth. 'Oh dear God.'

Troy looks pained. 'I'm sorry,' he says. 'I couldn't take it in. I couldn't take in what I was hearing. I mean, I know Coco's bad, but... I'm so sorry.'

'Don't be. It's not your fault. Just... go on.'

'Jeff said' – his eyes are brimming now – 'Jeff said... he said, "We could say it was an accident."'

Kate's eyes fill; hot tears spill over onto her cheeks. 'He said that? He definitely said that?'

'Yes. Then Coco said something I didn't hear. She was in the car by this point, but she was facing him, and I didn't catch what she said over the engine. And then Jeff started laughing and he said... well, what I heard was "finish it". Or "Let's finish it. You'd love that, wouldn't you?" And at that point I ran out of the shadows. I was going to stop them, but Jeff just drove off. I ran after them. I was waving and shouting at them to stop, but he was too fast. I just wish I'd moved sooner, but I was so shocked, I couldn't process... and by the time I realised what they were saying, what it meant, I...'

Kate squeezes his hand – for her own comfort as well as his. A sob escapes her. She feels like she's about to be sick.

'Listen to me,' she says. 'Troy? Listen to me. You couldn't have stopped them.'

But even as the words leave her, all she can think of is her husband saying: *Let's finish it.*

Her. He meant *her*.

CHAPTER 51

That afternoon, Kate gives a statement to a nice policewoman called Estrella. She tells the truth, exactly as she remembers it, though she tries to keep what Troy has told her out of it, for reasons she can't explain even to herself.

Estrella informs her that her husband and Caroline Barton are still being questioned but that she will let Kate know as soon as she has any more information.

'Who's Caroline Barton?' Kate asks.

Estrella checks her notes. 'Caroline Barton,' she says. 'Your friend?'

'My friend?'

'We take your husband Jeffrey Barrett and your friend Caroline Barton for questioning.'

'Coco? You mean Coco Moss?'

Estrella shrugs. 'The name on her passport is Caroline Barton.'

Later the same evening, Troy comes to see her again, tells her he's left the twins at a hotel.

'How're you doing?' he asks with genuine concern, sitting on the seat next to the bed.

She shrugs. 'Physically, I'm OK. Spoke to Lou about an hour ago. That was hard. Told her I'd been in an accident, but I was OK. I haven't told her about Jeff and Coco yet. Although according to a police officer I spoke to, that's not her name.'

'I know. I can't believe it; can't believe I didn't know. I've always called her Coco. Always.' He shakes his head. 'It's very like her to help herself to a name she wanted rather than living with her own. I just... didn't think anything of it. The twins call her Coco too. Never Mum or Mummy.'

'Have you heard anything more?'

He shakes his head, no. He looks heavy, pained, almost repentant, and she feels something in her shift, some unease harden in her gut.

'They have seventy-two hours to charge them,' he says. 'Presumably they'll be able to analyse the tyre marks, all that stuff.' He sighs.

There is something else, Kate thinks. There is more.

'Troy? What is it? Whatever it is, you need to tell me. I know it's hard, but you can't withhold information. It's not fair.'

He nods, over and over, his eyes filling. 'I need to tell you... I need to... After they drove off, I called the police. I wanted to tell you earlier, but you were already too upset. I called them, and my phone call was pretty damning. I gave a formal statement. I told them Jeff and Coco had been having an affair, and what I overheard, well, everything I told you. I suppose I want you to know that I did try and stop them. I'm so sorry.'

His breath comes shallow and quick; Kate reaches for his hand, but he snatches it away.

'No,' he says. 'I need to...' His face darkens, his brow furrowing. 'I should have called them sooner. Maybe I could have stopped it. But I was so shocked, and it was so hard to call, to make the call... The twins, you know? And Coco—'

'Hey,' she says. 'She's their mother, I get that. Of course. But you did everything you could. There's no guarantee you could have stopped them even if you'd called immediately.'

He meets her eye. A shaky smile. 'I hope so. I really hope so. I didn't mean to make things worse. It just took me a couple of minutes to gather my wits, you know? It was a big thing to do, a really big thing.'

A silence falls.

'It must have been tough finding out she was having an affair,' Kate offers after a moment. It is less than she means, but there is so much to say, so much they don't yet know. 'It can't have been great finding out that she and Jeff—'

'Coco has had dozens of affairs,' he says. 'She's a user. Not a nice thing to say, I realise, but there it is. She uses people. Uses me, always has. I'm the bank. I'm the nanny, the cook. Free childcare.' His words are upbeat, but they are laced with bitterness.

'I did notice you're with the twins a lot.' *While your wife is busy finding herself a boyfriend,* she does not add.

'I've always done a lot with them. I actually love hanging out with them, but really, I only come on these holidays because I know Coco will ignore them the whole time and I don't want that for them. It was worse when they were little. I practically brought them up. Coco can't... she can't *commit*, if that's the right word. She's always searching for something else, something better. Something new and sparkly.'

They sit with this a moment. Jeff, Kate thinks. Jeff was new and sparkly. And herself. Yes, perhaps even she, Kate Barrett, was new and sparkly for a brief moment. But she loved Jeff when he was old and dusty, when he was someone Coco did not want.

'When you called the police,' she says, 'did you really think Jeff and Coco were going to kill me? Or was it about the affair? A revenge sort of thing?'

He frowns. 'I don't care who Coco sleeps with. I just want the boys to be OK. They were out to kill you, no doubt about it. I know Coco. She's capable of a great deal. She's done some shocking things over the years, things you wouldn't believe. She's very good at getting people to fall for her, to do things for her. She's very good at spotting weaknesses, often weaknesses people don't even know they have, and exploiting them. But even so... calling the cops on her, that was hard. It was hard. So yes, I truly believed they were out to kill you.' His breath staggers. He looks like he might cry. 'I would have to have believed it one hundred per cent.'

'Hey,' she says. 'Don't upset yourself.'

'Thing is, I'm thinking about her parents now. I mean, she always said they'd died in a fire, but what's to say they aren't still alive and well? She never showed me any photographs, never really said where they were from, what they were like. If I ever asked her, she'd just... close up.' He pauses for a moment, appears to be gathering his thoughts. 'They might be out there wondering what the hell ever happened to their daughter. They won't even know they have grandchildren.' He looks up, his gaze resolute. 'I'm going to find out if they're alive and try and trace them. Whatever happens, if they're alive, I'd like to meet them.'

'Wow,' Kate says helplessly. 'That's a lot to take in. But yeah, I mean, try not to get your hopes up too much, but if they do turn out to be alive, I guess they would want to meet the twins, wouldn't they?'

'And me too, I hope.' There is something vulnerable in the way his brown eyes sink at the edges when he says this. His panama and shades have hidden much of his face, but he is, she thinks, extraordinarily good-looking in a way that is about more than his features alone.

'If they...' she begins. 'If Coco... you know, goes to prison... will you be OK?'

'I don't know. Just the thought of seeing her makes me feel sick. I want to... I want to cut her out of my life, but I'm not sure I'll be able to, you know, not with the twins.' He looks up, lays a hand on her arm. 'But I'm the only one who cares about them, and I'm going to apply for custody. And I'd like to keep in touch with you, if it's not too difficult. I mean, if you don't want to, I'd understand.'

Kate feels herself melt. How can this sensitive, lovely man ever have been attracted to someone as hard, as cruel as Coco? It doesn't make sense.

'Of course,' she says, smiling despite everything. 'We can support one another, can't we? It's not just me who's been through the mill here. And for the record, I totally understand why you hesitated before making that phone call. It must've been tough calling the cops on your own wife.'

Troy frowns. Their eyes meet.

'Wife?' he says.

'Coco. Caroline. Whatever.'

His eyes widen. 'Coco's not my wife. Why would you think that?'

'Partner then. I mean, she—'

'Coco's not my wife,' Troy says, leaning forward. 'She's my mother.'

CHAPTER 52

COCO

Jeff, Jeff, Jeff. Dear, dumb, duplicitous Jeff. You fell for me the moment you saw me. That's what you told me. You fell for me all over again less than a week ago. A week! Except you didn't fall for me at all. You, Jeff, fell for some objectified idea of a sexy mistress, put on this earth to service your fantasies, just as your wife was put on this earth to provide a stable home while servicing your big atonement project. Oh Jeff. Your misogyny is quite terrifying. Really, I'm hoping Kate will see a way to be grateful to me eventually, for saving her from you. Women are *people*, Jeff. I don't think you realise that, do you, even now? Kate is not another thing you can buy with all that money you're so proud of. I mean, I can't talk, not really. I adore money and I was determined to get yours from the moment I peeked through the windows of your lovely villa and saw into your not-so-lovely marriage. I was happy to be bought, trust me.

But honestly, you and Kate really should have learnt to cover the cracks. There is such danger in sniping at one another, complaining about one another – especially in front of someone you barely know. As it was, you held up those fault lines for all to see.

I meant for it to go slower, I'll admit. Your wife is to blame for that. Although perhaps you're to blame actually. If you hadn't gone blurting out all sorts of information no one asked you for, we probably wouldn't be in this mess now, would we? We could have made a controlled exit. But you blew it, just as you blew it back then. Kate knew you were cheating on her almost before you did. What did you tell yourself, Jeff? That you could keep two women dangling, have your week in the sun? That you could use me to satisfy your long-frustrated crush and then throw me away at the end of the holiday, go back to the life you don't have the grace or the gratitude to see is perfect? Don't you think I didn't realise that? I don't know which I despise more, your misogyny or your stupidity frankly.

And so Kate, bless her, brought things to a head. Not going to lie, the whole showdown thing was pretty impressive. I almost wanted to high-five her and say, *Respect, sister*. But I can see she might not have been in the mood. And of course, you went to pieces, as you were always going to. The moment we got to the kill, quite literally, you started backing out. I knew I'd lost you. Lost my opportunity. Which is a shame. You are so very wealthy; I would have been set up for life. And even though you hate me now, I could've been everything you needed me to be. As I've said, I am nothing if not the queen of adaptation. For you, for all that you had, I could have faked it for as long as you needed me to – forever, if it kept me in furs.

So, back to you. Once you'd quite clearly got cold feet, what was left for me to do if not *adapt*? That's what we survivors do. I could see, feel, hear, smell, *taste* how much you hated me, how the lust you believed was love had shrivelled away like... well, like a cock in a freezing-cold sea. I knew you'd never leave Kate, that this life we'd spent all of a few stolen hours planning would never come to pass. I knew too that my own mask had slipped. I had made the mistake of baring my teeth and from then on there was no way back. You saw through me; I could see it in your face. And so yes, I realised I'd have to be the one to kill her, but only because you couldn't. Another failure on my part, I'll admit. A broken arm and leg, that is literally all she sustained.

The only option left was to make sure you stuck to the story. And you did, my love, you did. I rehearsed you, directed you, and you spoke your lines to perfection.

Well done you.

But as soon as the lovely policewoman took me to the side of the bloodstained tarmac, I told her a slightly different story – sorry!

I told her how you were raging, how you started to talk about killing Kate, how you said we should make it look like an accident, how you said we had to stop her.

Later, in the interview, I gave my formal statement. Oh, Jeff, if only you could have been a fly on the wall. You would have been buzzing with rage. The lovely Carmen asked me what we'd argued about. I told her *all* about Joanne Dixon. Again, a slightly different version. How you'd told me you'd only had one drink that night, that you were fine to drive, that after you almost hit her, you coerced me into leaving her there, how you'd threatened to kill me if I ever told anyone. I didn't mention our little post-trauma tryst.

She asked me, 'Did you know Mr Barrett was intending to kill his wife?'

And I sort of blinked for a bit, like I was trying to keep it together.

'He told me to hurry up,' I said. 'He said, "We need to stop her." And I said something like, "You need to put your foot down, OK? If you're so worried about her."'

And on and on. My version. How scared I was, how I didn't want to get in the car with you, but how could I let you drive off and kill Kate? I know I betrayed her, but I did like her, and there's no way I wanted her or anyone dead, you know? I mean, you were going to leave her, there was no motive for me, and besides, I'm not some cold-hearted murderer, for crying out loud!

I told her how you started laughing, this mad, manic laugh, how you said "let's finish it" or "let's finish her" or something like that, I can't remember exactly, it all happened so fast. I told her that you had a lot at stake, that you knew that, as a lawyer. And at this point, I wept. Jeff, I wept!

'I thought he'd changed,' I wailed. 'I really did. He said he was sorry about Jo. He said he'd crucified himself with guilt every day since that night. And I believed him.'

Carmen was scribbling it down, lapping it all up.

I stopped for a second, as if to regain my composure, as if my internal struggle was playing out on my lovely features.

'He was really worried about what happened back then,' I said. 'I tried to talk him down, humour him, you know? Told him it was years ago, not to worry about it. I don't believe that obviously. What he did was terrible, and I blame myself too for being so scared of him. But then in the car he went back to saying we could make it look like an accident, that he was going to mow Kate down. His own wife! "Mow the bitch down," he said. He was wild. I was trying to keep him talking, because it was the only way... the only way I could save her.'

I paused, looked up. The recording device was still going, so I added, unprompted: 'And then Kate just appeared from nowhere. Jeff shouted out, "There she is!" and accelerated hard. I tried to grab the steering wheel from him, but he was too strong, oh God, he was too strong, and he... he just drove into her as if she were a... I don't know, a doll. It was terrible, just terrible.'

And then I let rip – floods of tears, magic realism tears, the sort that cascade down the street, form rivers, flow into the sea.

I am good, I thought. *I am so good at this shit.*

The rest of the interview was calmer. I told them you'd said you'd kill me if I didn't give the police your version, which was of course my version, but let's not split hairs.

Hours later, they told me they'd charged you with the attempted murder of Kate and that you were under suspicion of murdering Joanne Dixon! What a turn-up. That's when they told me Troy had called the police on us. Would you believe it? I couldn't, not at first. How could he do that to me, my own son? But then it transpired he'd done me the biggest favour without meaning to. He'd heard us arguing, you see, and his version pretty much matched mine – in all but interpretation! Thank God I'd given a plausible spin on what we said instead of changing the words themselves. What did I tell you? Stick as close to the truth as you can.

The truth is surprisingly flexible.

After all the paperwork was done, Carmen showed me back to the reception area. She asked if there was anyone who could pick me up, but I told her it was OK, I'd take a cab.

I didn't tell her that I probably wouldn't be contacting Troy and the boys again. To be honest, I think that's best for everyone. I never was much of a mother, and Troy is much better with the twins than I am. As for me, I need my freedom. Always have. I think I realise that in a way I never have before, and I suppose I need to thank you for that, darling. From now on, I'm going to be a lone wolf.

Anyway, as we reached the exit, I turned to my new best friend Carmen.

'Can I ask you to pass a message on to Jeff?' I asked her.

She was polite, all respect and smiles, as if to apologise for her rudeness now she realised I was entirely innocent, that I had been used by the cold-hearted bastard handcuffed and locked up back in the police station cells.

'Sure.'

'Do you have a piece of paper?'

CHAPTER 53

JEFF

Jeff closes his eyes as Carmen reads him his rights. He knows what's happened, understands exactly. Coco, Caroline, whoever she is, has betrayed him in the most comprehensive way. A simple dodge: feint to the left and go right – crimes past and present land on him and him alone. Of course. Of course she has done this. He has been a fool to think she would do anything else.

As Carmen accompanies him back to the cell, he thinks of Coco rehearsing him at the roadside, her eyes full of hate and rage and something like ill-veiled disgust.

He should have known. How did he not?

And now she will walk free and here he is: shining cuffs, a long white corridor, a fetid cell. His wife lies in a hospital bed believing he tried to kill her, and nothing he can say will ever repair what he has broken, what he broke a long, long time ago. The daughter who adored him will believe her father tried to murder her mother when the truth is, he didn't, he never would have. It's so unfair. It's so fucking unfair! He has been a model citizen for over thirty years – thirty years! How was he to know that the woman he thought he loved all this time was an illusion? How could any man not love Coco Moss? It's not his fault she hid her real self from him in the cruellest way.

As soon as he saw the reality, he no longer wanted it, did he? He'd learnt his lesson, goddammit; he could have gone back to Kate, and everything would have been all right. He would have made more effort. Spent more time with her. Because it occurs to him now that the one woman he wants is the one he believed he didn't want at all. He wants her desperately, with an overwhelming pit of sadness in his guts, wants to curl up with her in bed at home and listen to her retell him the story of his life. The way they were before *her*, the way they could have been if that night had never happened. He could have made it right if Coco Moss hadn't shown up and tricked him. Kate would have understood. He's given her everything a woman could ever want over the years, everything! She owes him a second chance, owes him that at least.

Night falls. The heat is stifling. He can smell his own stink, his own animal nature. In the dark cell, Kate comes to him.

'I was your best friend,' she whispers.

Yes, he thinks. *You were.*

After that night, he let himself drift, convinced he didn't want Kate because he didn't want himself. He didn't want her to see him, see into the dark heart of him. In her eyes, all he could ever see reflected was a lost boy, a coward, a fool. A murderer.

How could he spend time looking at that? How could anyone?

And so the work. And so the golf. And so the gym. And so the... anything, anything at all that kept him moving, kept him from his thoughts, from Kate, himself.

And now he has been arrested for a crime he didn't commit, when he has already done his time for Joanne, for God's sake. He has already suffered!

The cell door unlocks. Falo-Sant steps inside.

'You have a message. It is from Ms Barton.' She hands him a handwritten note. 'She said you would understand.'

She leaves him to his confusion. The key clunks through its rotations.

He unfolds the note, and reads:

Dear Jeff,

I'm sorry you've ended up in this mess. I hope they don't put you away for too long. Who knows, you might even get away with a suspended sentence. I imagine you can afford the best lawyer.

It had to be this way. I hope you understand. I have to be here for my boys. From the way you spoke about Troy, I guessed you'd assumed, as most people do, that he was my husband or partner or whatever. But he's not. I was going to tell you, but things got crazy and now we are where we are. So I'm telling you now.

Troy is my son. But the thing is, he's not just my son. He's your son too.

Jeff pushes the note to his chest and closes his eyes.

'No,' he whispers. 'No, no, no.'

He opens his eyes, forces himself to look down at the paper shaking in his hands.

There. You'll be shocked, I do appreciate that. But not as shocked as I was all those years ago. Our son is the reason I didn't finish my degree, you see. He is the reason I never came back. I know you'll be upset, even angry that I didn't tell you, but trust me, it was much worse for me. I was barely twenty, and I think it's safe to say you ruined my life. If you hadn't been so careless, I wouldn't have been forced into some of the decisions I've had to make. You owed me, you just didn't know it. When I saw you and your villa, heard about your life of luxury, it made me seethe frankly. To know I could have had a share in all of that. But I didn't know you'd make it quite so spectacularly, did I? You didn't seem like the type, no offence.

Troy doesn't know he's yours by the way. It's up to you to tell him if you want to, and then maybe he'll come and see you, wherever you end up. Maybe he won't want to know either of us now. Who knows?

Anyway, there's little to add except I'm sorry it worked out this way and I genuinely do wish you well. We had some fun, didn't we?

Yours,

C xxx

He folds the note, tries to tune into the silence below the coughs and the shouts, the footsteps and the bangs. Coco left university in the final term because she was pregnant with their son. She never told him, never thought she'd have to. What had passed between them concerned a dead girl and it was best that they never saw one another again. It was, after all, the agreement they had made.

His son is a successful musician. His son called the cops on his own mother, fearing for Kate's life. His son is a good person, braver than him. His son is a grown man he has never met. If they do by some miracle meet one day, his son will know him for the coward he is. That bitch, that con artist, has poisoned his son against him before he can even try to get to know him.

His breath staggers. He thought his punishment was complete, but here is the final turn of the screw. Coco walks away free while he has nothing, nothing at all. It's so unfair. He has led a blameless life. Everyone makes mistakes. His hands close into fists.

He never gets away with anything.

CHAPTER 54

KATE

'You like a café con leche,' Troy says. 'That's right, isn't it? One sugar?' He is preparing coffee in the Bialetti while Kate reclines on the sunlounger in the shade, her arm in plaster across her waist, her ankle cast raised on two cushions. It is surreal to think that this kind man is Jeff's son, let alone Coco's. When they took her in to see Jeff, he was still in shock about it, but now that she knows, she wonders why on earth she didn't recognise his features in Troy's, his colouring, the way he wrinkles his nose sometimes when he's thinking – those things are all Jeff.

In the pool, Coco's boys laugh and shriek and frolic. Frolic is such a good word, she thinks. There should be more laughing and shrieking and frolicking in this pool. In this life.

Troy appears, proffering a perfectly made cup of coffee. It is a gift. Troy is a gift. He is a wonderful, wonderful human being. She could not have made it this far without him. He says the same of her. It was hard, telling him that Jeff was his father. But she was glad it was her who broke the news. The last few days have forged a bond between them as deep as family. They are technically family – they say this to one another periodically as they pick over and over the aftermath, compare notes. It's all so unbelievable – they say that too.

'Have you spoken to Lou?' he asks.

'Yes.'

'Have you told her?'

'A watered-down version. She's upset, but I've told her we're OK, to stay there with her friends. Natasha's mum is with them and she's keeping an eye out. Even if Lou jumps on the first plane home, there's no one there for her. If she looks at the news, which she never does, I'll tell her it's the usual lies and hysteria. I don't know what else to do. I'll take her somewhere safe and tell her everything calmly. I imagine there'll be press all over it. All over us.'

His mouth presses into a sad smile.

'And you? How are you feeling?' He is looking at her, so directly and kindly, his head on one side.

'Do you mean health-wise? Or the rest of it?'

'Everything, I guess. What's ahead.'

'I'm nervous,' she says. 'There's a lot to face. Future unknown, I guess. But mostly I'm... I dunno – surprised?'

'How so?'

'Just... what's happened is horrible; it's beyond horrible. But at the same time, there are all these things I expected to feel, things I think I should be feeling, you know? Like the loss of my husband. The father of my daughter. My family. Not to mention Jeff trying to...' She blinks away the tears that come, composes herself. When she went to visit Jeff, he pleaded with her: he didn't run her down on purpose, he would never do that, she had to believe him. It was Coco, all Coco – Caroline, whatever her name is.

I don't believe anything you say. Those were the last words she said to him as she left him weeping. Why would she believe him? He is not, has never been, honest. He is an inauthentic human being. But in that visiting room, her thoughts were not so clear. All she saw was a coward – an angry, wrong-headed coward.

'Best not to think about all of it at once,' Troy says gently. 'It's too big.'

'Part of me is relieved. Isn't that terrible?' She glances at him but sees no judgement in his eyes. 'At least I *know* he's out of the picture instead of hoping all the time that he might enter the frame. He was never there. When he was, he made me tense, made Lou tense too, always on at her, you know? Always correcting us. And yet I waited and waited, day after day, year after year, for him to come home. Now I think that deep down I was waiting for the Jeff I met all those years ago to come through the door, but I don't think that Jeff ever existed. We were young. We clung on to a relationship started when we were kids, for different reasons. So yeah, maybe I'm in denial, but... Sorry, I'm not explaining it very well...' She meets his eyes, finds that familiar steadfast kindness she has grown to love in a matter of days.

'I once tried to boil an egg,' she says into the silence, smiles when he glances at her, his expression mystified. 'Bear with me. I put it on to boil, forgot about it and left the kitchen. I was probably folding laundry or attending to a client or something, and anyway, a while later, I heard this great pop. I ran into the kitchen. The air smelt of burning. I thought something had blown, the microwave or the toaster or something. But it was the egg. The water had all evaporated and the egg had just exploded. Literally – boom! I found bits of exploded white and shell all over the place. I cleared it up obviously.'

He nods, but his expressions says: *where the hell is this going?*

'Anyway, much later, I was clearing the breakfast bar to lay it for dinner and I saw this perfect yellow ball, the size of a golf ball. I mean, that's what I thought it was at first – one of Jeff's golf balls. But it wasn't. It was the yolk! The rest of it had exploded, the pan had burnt black, but here was this perfect round yellow egg yolk, born of disaster.'

Troy raises his eyebrows, smirks at her. 'I'm picking up a strong metaphor. You're the egg yolk, am I right?'

She smiles. 'I suppose. Something like that. That's how I feel. A lot has happened, there's a lot to clear up, but... I am whole.'

'I get it.'

'I knew you would. That's why I told you.'

Her eyes fill. She squeezes his hand. Holds on while together they watch the twins laughing and shrieking and frolicking in the cool blue water.

CHAPTER 55

COCO

One last thing, one last tiny little thing, darling. A postscript, if you will.

I'm at Barcelona Airport. Got chatting to the most charming man called Nigel – we'll gloss over that – who is really very, well, *dashing* for an older guy, I suppose you'd say, as you would say if you were posh old Coco Moss. And I have spent much more of my life as Coco than I ever did as Caroline, so I'll be damned if I'm going back to Caroline now.

You see, I became Coco Moss pretty much the day I got to uni. It was a twenty-four-hour transformation. I had the chops. I was always bolshie at school, always acting out to prove my new-girl credentials, but seeing my mother go back to that bastard, I cranked it up a gear. Yes, I think that's what really finished Caroline Barton off once and for all. My mother, turning round and telling me we were going to be a family again in that stupid, simpering Midlands twang, looking at me with a trembling smile and doe eyes as if we'd somehow made it, me and her, because we were going to live with Dad again back in Wolverhampton.

God, the betrayal.

No, I thought. *No fucking way. When I leave for uni, I leave for good.*

And that's what I did. Which sounds heartless, but it couldn't be any other way. If my mum knew where I was, then so would he, and I wasn't about to spend my life cowering in a corner. Which is why when I saw Kate failing so spectacularly to leave her roots behind, I thought, wow, how pathetic frankly. I mean, I feel for her, I do, but come *on*. If I can shake off my lowly beginnings, surely anyone can? It's like betting on the horses: you just have to study the form.

After I'd dumped my bags at Cedar House and caught the bus to the campus, I headed for the Union. I climbed the steps past bobble-hatted students selling *Socialist Worker* with their half-swallowed mockney cries, rolled-up drainpipe jeans and eighteen-hole Doc Martens. I continued inside to the clamour of overconfident teenagers selling social clubs – Drama Soc, Hiking Soc, Jazz Soc, Circus Soc... Uninterested, I ventured further in and bought a Coke from the Old Bar to clear my head. It was dark, dingy, a little damp-smelling, thick with cigarette smoke. I recognised a girl from Cedar. I'd seen her getting dropped off in a sleek navy-blue Mercedes Benz. She was talking to another girl who turned out to be Mia and a tall, pop-idol-good-looking guy with Brylcreem-slicked hair: Drew. Drew and Mia were asking the girl what her name was.

'Everyone calls me Bunny,' she said simply.

Note 1, I thought: never explain, even if your name is a small furry animal.

'Cool,' they said.

Note 2: never react, even if someone else's name is a small furry animal.

I listened and I watched. They didn't see me, didn't notice me at all. I studied the way they dressed, moved, spoke.

Note 3: affect tramp-like scruffiness even though you have

lots of perfectly smart clothes bought for you from Selfridges by Mummy and Daddy.

They nodded a lot, said 'cool' a lot, smoked like absolute chimneys.

Note 4: ditch the Silk Cut, learn to roll.

Drew had been to India for the summer. Oh my God, so had Bunny, oh my God, Mia went there last year, that's amazing, where were you? No way, I was there too, oh my God, such a coincidence.

Such a coincidence, I thought. Dial down the sarcasm, Caroline, I thought.

Note 5 (a little more specific, this one): research India, mention in passing that you went there over the summer.

How hard can it be? I thought. To be like that.

I found a second-hand clothes shop on the Otley Road and kitted myself out with a fringed suede jacket, some eccentric pinstriped trousers, a few men's shirts and a cool leather miniskirt. I cut holes in my jumpers, ripped my jeans, laddered my tights. Went into town, spent a huge portion of my grant on a new pair of Doc Martens, which I scuffed against a wall. Stole some bleach for my hair, some pink dye. I had to be like them – but more so.

I found out later, much later, once I'd established myself as not only part of but *queen* of the group, that Bunny's name was actually Pauline. Pauline! Bunny was the cuddly little rabbit she had as a child, the one she'd brought with her to uni. Drew was, for me, an exotic shortening. Any Andrews I'd known went by the more prosaic Andy.

'Mummy always wore Coco,' I said, when my turn came. (Note 6 was: posh people refer to their parents as if they are themselves still five years old.) 'It was her favourite perfume,' I added. Seemed a shame not to use my prepared backstory. 'Daddy always bought it for her when he went away on business.' And here I looked into my lap briefly before raising my head, eyes shining. 'My surname is actually Barton, but since Mummy died, I go by her name: Moss.'

Mia's eyes popped. 'Oh my God, like Kate?'

They never did figure out I was one hundred per cent not who I claimed to be. And it was in those first few weeks that I realised, actually, you can say anything you want to people. People believe you. Why wouldn't they? They believed me so hard that even when my accent slipped, they'd say, *Oh my God, do it again, you're so amazing at accents, you sound exactly like Noddy Holder*. And then we'd laugh and laugh at how funny I sounded with my non-RP accent; funny, funny, *funny* old Coco.

Of course, after a while, it was no longer an act. I became her, she became me, and I had no idea where the divide was. I *was* Coco Moss, cool girl, toff, pink-haired rebel, fashionista, star.

And as with any stage persona, Coco Moss was a good deal more daring than Caroline Barton. Coco Moss was the sort of girl who would take the piss out of mousy Kate Hanson, who actually, now I think about it, looked rather similar to poor old Caroline Barton when she first arrived in Leeds.

Anyway, enough of all that. Nigel has just invited me into the British Airways lounge for a cheeky glass of champagne. What a sweetie you are, Nigel, I said, feeling beyond glad that I'd picked up a little Zara number before Troy could cancel his credit card.

Anyway, Nigel's really rather funny and he's *so* well travelled. I'm a fine artist on a recce, looking for galleries in and around Barcelona to show my work. I've never been married. No, no kids. The life of an artist is a calling, Nigel.

And here's the best thing, the absolute cherry on top of the icing on top of the cupcake. Call it my parting shot, my so-long, my *adieu*.

Nigel's wife doesn't understand him.

Isn't that just peachy?

I can't *wait* to meet her.

Wish me luck. I really do think that this time things will work out.

No hard feelings, eh?

Life's too short, darling.

Toodle-pip.

A LETTER FROM S.E. LYNES

Dear Reader,

Firstly, thanks so much for reading this book. If it's your first by me, I hope you liked it enough to want to read some of my others. If it's your twelfth, congratulations, you deserve a medal, a drink *and* a packet of crisps. If you'd like to be the first to hear about my new releases, you can sign up to my newsletter using the link below. Your email address will never be shared, and you can unsubscribe at any time.

www.bookouture.com/se-lynes

Often, inspiration for a book comes in the form of an offhand comment, an interesting article or a news story that ignites a spark of outrage or interest, which in turn mutates into something else entirely – *The Housewarming*, for example, was inspired by the looting of supermarkets during lockdown but became the story of a missing child and an exploration of why individual responsibility within a community matters.

For *The Summer Holiday*, the inspiration was much more on the nose. Many of the circumstances in this book were pulled from my own life. I met my husband in my first year at Leeds Uni back in the eighties, as Kate did. I was a language student who went to Spain in my third year, as Kate did. When I got back to uni, my friends outside my course as well as my then boyfriend had all left. And yes, in the immortal words of

Charlotte Brontë via Jane Eyre: *Reader, I married him.* As Kate did.

In 2021, whilst on holiday in Dorset, I spotted a woman I recognised. She'd been my housemate back at uni, but I hadn't seen her for over thirty years. By the time I'd realised who it was, she had continued on her way. The next day, my other half bumped into her outside our holiday cottage and reintroduced himself. I saw them out of the window and came out to say hello. My former friend looked shocked and a little bewildered as she visibly tried to piece together what my husband and I had by then had twenty-four hours to process. Slowly we joined the dots and made a rudimentary line drawing of the previous three decades. At the end of this conversation, I asked her where she was staying. She pointed to the cottage next to ours and said, 'There.'

'Oh my God,' I said. 'That's my next psych thriller!'

A couple of days later, we hung out on the beach and really caught up, listing off all the names of our mutual friends and acquaintances. A moment later, she was calling another friend who had lived with us back in the day, and before I knew it was passing me the phone. I then spoke to another pal I hadn't seen or heard from in over thirty years. When I learnt that she too was happy and, like me, had married her uni sweetheart, I had tears in my eyes and could barely speak.

So often we fall out of touch with people we care about because life is busy. And back then, there was no Facebook, no Instagram, no mobile phones. All I had by way of contact details was one home phone number for my friend's parents, which, as the months became years, I felt too shy to use. For their part, they thought I'd disappeared off the face of the earth, dropped them like stones.

Peggy and Gay, I am so glad we are now back in touch. I have fulfilled my promise to write a psych thriller based on this event. There are dark jokes to make here in the light of this novel, but I will refrain. As you will see, it is wildly different from the reality. At least I hope it is – joke...

Because this is where inspiration meets the art of psychological suspense. The above is a lovely story, but whilst I do try to write about what matters and always, I think, make a strong case for love, I don't write lovely stories. For this spark to work, the circumstances had to be different, and for every writer, that means the big old baseline question:

What if?

What if the woman from the past had stalked the main character and ended up booking the cottage next door? No, no good – can't think of what happens next. What if... let's see... what if the woman from the past was not a friend at all? Maybe, but where's the connection? OK, so what if the woman from the past was someone not from the main character's social circle but someone who had a kind of star status back then? Better. What if the husband had had a bit of a crush on her? What if they both had? What if they admitted to their fascination but hid parts of it from one another? Interesting. What if the woman from the past was not all she seemed? Natch. What if the happy marriage was not a happy marriage at all? What if, actually, one of them couldn't bear spending time with the other? Ouch, now I'm uncomfortable. From these and other questions, *The Summer Holiday* was born. And the rest... well, you've just read it.

The Summer Holiday is about whatever you think it's about. For me, it is ultimately an exploration of authenticity versus inauthenticity, the pretences we adopt in order to be attractive to people we believe to be in some way better or higher up the social pecking order. I am fascinated by this because I always wonder why anyone would want to be attractive to another person on the basis of a false representation of themselves, thus dooming themselves to feeling forever uncomfortable or fake in that relationship.

Jeff is inauthentic because he is ashamed of what he did and has put all his chips on status, success, physical excellence. Coco is inauthentic because she is a con artist and a sociopath – or a frightened, hardened young girl, depending on how you read her – who has learnt to exploit the weaknesses of others. Kate believes she has changed since those inauthentic, insecure days of her youth, but she has not. After all these years, she still has little idea who she is or what she wants; she is still pretending. A lack of love has kept her locked in this almost clownish insecurity. Her catharsis is extreme, but she does at least end up with the start of a genuine friendship with Troy, who has seen her at rock bottom, to add to her good relationships with her daughter and Lizzie, her old friend. My hope is that, going forward, she will dispense with all the fakery and get on with her life, forever armed against the red flags she will hopefully now recognise in both others and herself.

That's it for now from me. If you have any questions about this or any of my other books, I would love to hear from you.

Don't hesitate! I always try to reply.

Until next time, take care.

Best wishes,

Susie

facebook.com/Lynesauthor

twitter.com/selynesauthor

instagram.com/selynesauthor

ACKNOWLEDGMENTS

First thanks as ever go to my publisher, Ruth Tross, whose continuing kindness makes my job a happy, safe place, whose razor-sharp insight improves my work beyond measure and whose intelligence often saves me from looking like the fool I actually am. Thank you to my agent, Veronique Baxter, who called this novel 'a feminist tour de force' – that will go with me to my grave.

Thanks to Catherine Ball, who is the exception that proves the rule that one shouldn't let one's mum be the first reader.

Thank you to the continually amazing team at Bookouture, particularly Noelle Holten and Kim Nash, Sarah Hardy, Jess Readett and Alexandra Holmes, plus all the Bookouture authors, who are the best virtual colleagues a girl could wish for.

Thanks to my copy-editor, Jane Selley, and my proofreader, Laura Kincaid.

Thanks to Teresa Nikolic and everyone at Facebook's Socially Distanced Book Club. Thanks as ever and always to Tracy Fenton and all the team at Facebook's The Book Club. Thanks to Anne Cater at Book Connectors, to Wendy Clarke and the team at Facebook's The Fiction Café, and Mark Fearn at Bookmark! Thank you, in fact, to all the online book clubs and the people who gather there to share their love of reading. I'm sorry I don't go on there much due to writing deadlines, but if I'm tagged, I always respond – I think! Also, and I always say this: if I've missed you or your club out, I'm sorry – message me and I'll make sure to give you a shout-out in the next book, which I'll already be writing by the time you read this.

Huge thanks to flag-waving readers like Claire Mawdesley, Helen Boyce, Lorraine Tippene, Gail Shaw, Gail Atkins, Sharon Bairden, Teresa Nikolic, Eduarda Abreu (restaurant owner in Cadaqués!), Nicky Dyer, Fi Kelly, Laura Budd, Tara Munday, Philippa McKenna, Karen Royle-Cross, Ellen Devonport, Frances Pearson, Maddy Cordell, Jodi Rilot, CeeCee, Bridget McCann, Karen Aristocleus, Kirsty Whitlock, Audrey Cowie, Donna Young, Mary Petit, Donna Moran (I gave you your own little newsagent's in this one), Ophelia Sings, Lizzie Patience, Fiona McCormick, Alison Lysons – say hello to your lovely book club – Dee Groocock, Sam Johnson and many more not named here. Thank you. I read every single review, good or bad. If you don't see your name here, please let me know and I'll acknowledge you in my next book.

Huge thanks as ever to the amazing bloggers, who are unpaid and who work very hard spreading the word about the books and authors they love. I would like to thank the following bloggers, using their blogging names in case you wish to check out their reviews:

Bookworm86, Once Upon a Time Book Reviews, Coffee Break Book Reviews, Pages and Pups, Little Miss Book Lover 87, B for BookReview, Blue Moon Blogger, Robin Loves Reading, Jan's Book Buzz, Melanie's Reads, TippyTupps, Spooky's Maze of Books, MeWriter, Curling Up with a Coffee and a Kindle, LianaReads, Cal Turner Reviews, Author Sharon Bairden at Chapter in my Life, The StaffyMum's Book Nook, StaceyWH17, Anne Cater at Random Things Through my Letterbox, Leona OMahoney, BooksReadByPrairieGirl, Read, Write & Drink Coffee, By The Letter Book Reviews, Ginger Book Geek, Shalini's Books and Reviews, Fictionophile, Book Mark!, Bibliophile Book Club, B for Book Review, Nicki's Book Blog, Fireflies and Free Kicks, Bookinggoodread, My Chestnut

Reading Tree, Donna's Book Blog, Emma's Biblio Treasures, Suidi's Book Reviews, Books from Dusk till Dawn, Audio Killed the Bookmark, Compulsive Readers, LoopyLouLaura, Once Upon a Time Book Blog, Literature Chick, Jan's Book Buzz, and Giascribes... Again, if I have missed anyone, please let me know.

Thank you to the tremendously supportive writing community – you know who you are and are now too many to count. Special thanks to my Harrogate harridans Louise Beech, Kate Simants, Nicola Rayner and Emma Curtis; my half-woman, half-cheese #luckybitches writing retreat buddies Emma Robinson, Kim Nash (again!) and Sue Watson; and my other spooky haunts writing retreat buddies Callie Langridge, Claire McGlasson, Bev Thomas, Kate Riordan, Emilie Olsson, Lisa Timoney and Clarissa Angus. You ridiculously talented women were responsible for a large percentage of laughs in 2022, and if I ever find myself in prison, I hope it's with at least a few of you.

Thanks to my dad, Stephen Ball, who once said, 'I haven't read it yet; I'm waiting for the poor weather' – an introduction to northern parenting for beginners if ever there was one.

Penultimately, thanks to Peggy Rawes and Gay Flashman for not running away at the sight of me thirty years on. Neither of you has changed a bit.

Finally, and as always, thanks to the love of my life for realz, Paul Lynes – if you actually did go to a Halloween party back in 1988, I'd keep shtum if I were you.

Just kidding.

Printed in Great Britain
by Amazon